Mills & Boon is proud to present
a wonderful selection of some of the
best novels from Australian
bestselling author

Emma DARCY

Each volume has three terrific, powerful
stories written by one of the queens of the
genre. We think you'll love them…

March 2014

April 2014

May 2014

June 2014

July 2014

August 2014

Emma DARCY

AUSTRALIA

IN BED WITH THE PLAYBOY

Published in Great Britain 2014
by Mills & Boon, an imprint of Harlequin (UK) Limited,
Eton House, 18-24 Paradise Road, Richmond, Surrey, TW9 1SR

ISBN: 978 0 263 24604 9

010-0514

Harlequin (UK) Limited's policy is to use papers that are natural, renewable and recyclable products and made from wood grown in sustainable forests The logging and manufacturing processes conform to the legalenvironmental regulations of the country of origin.

Printed and bound in Spain
by Blackprint CPI, Barcelona

Emma Darcy's life journey has taken as many twists and turns as the characters in her stories, whose international popularity has resulted in over sixty million book sales. Born in Australia and currently living in a beachside property on the central coast of New South Wales, she travels extensively to research settings and increase her experience of places and people.

Initially a French/English teacher, she changed careers to computer programming before marriage and motherhood settled her into a community life. A voracious reader, the step to writing her own books seemed a natural progression and the challenge of creating exciting stories was soon highly addictive.

Over the past twenty-five years she has written ninety-five books for Mills & Boon, appearing regularly on the Waldenbooks bestseller lists in the USA and in the Nielsen BookScan Top 100 chart in the UK.

HIDDEN MISTRESS, PUBLIC WIFE

Emma
DARCY

CHAPTER ONE

'THE Valentino king of rose-giving is on the loose again,' Heather Gale remarked, swinging around from her computer chair to grin at Ivy. 'He's just ordered the sticky date and ginger fudge with the three dozen red roses to go to his current woman. That's his goodbye signature. Take it from me. She's just been crossed out of his little black book.'

Ivy Thornton rolled her eyes over her sales manager's salacious interest in Jordan Powell's playboy activities. Ivy had met him once, very briefly at her mother's last gallery exhibition of her paintings. That had been two years ago, soon after her father had died and she'd been coming to grips with running the rose farm without his guidance.

Much to her mother's disgust, she'd worn jeans to the showing, completely disinterested in competing with the socialites who attended such events. For some perverse reason Jordan Powell had asked to be introduced to her, which had displeased her mother, having to own up to a daughter who had made no effort to look stunningly presentable.

There'd been curious interest in his eyes, probably because she didn't fit in with the fashionable crowd. The encounter was very minimal. The gorgeous model hugging his arm quickly drew him away, jealous of his attention being directed even momentarily to any other woman.

Understandably.

Keeping him to herself would have been a top-priority aim.

The man was not only a billionaire but oozed sex appeal—twinkling, bedroom blue eyes, perfect male physique in the tall-dark-and-handsome mould, charming voice and manner with a strikingly sensual mouth that had worn a teasing quirk of amusement as he'd spoken to Ivy. No doubt, with his wealth and looks, the world and everyone in it existed for his amusement.

'How long did this love interest last?' she asked, knowing Heather enjoyed keeping tabs on his affairs. Jordan Powell was the rose farm's biggest spender on the private-client list.

Heather turned eagerly back to the computer to check the records. 'Let's see…a month ago he ordered jelly beans with the roses so that meant he wanted her to lighten up and just have fun. She probably didn't get the message, hence the parting of the ways. A month before that it was the rum and raisin fudge, which indicates the heavy-sex stage.'

'You can't really know that, Heather,' Ivy dryly protested.

'Stands to reason. He always starts off with the double chocolate fudge when he first sends roses to a new woman. Clearly into seduction at that point.'

'I don't think he needs to seduce anyone,' Ivy muttered, thinking most women would willingly fall at his feet, given one ounce of encouragement.

Heather was not to be moved from her deductions. 'Probably not, but I think some play hard to get for a little while,' she explained. 'Which is when he sends the roses with the macadamia fudge, meaning she's driving him nuts so please come to the party. This last one didn't get the macadamia gift.'

'Therefore an easy conquest,' Ivy concluded.

'Straight into it I'd say,' Heather agreed. 'And that was…almost three months ago. He didn't stick with her very long.'

'Has he ever stuck with any woman very long?'

'According to my records, six months has been the top limit so far, and that was only once. The usual is two to four months.'

She twirled the chair back to face Ivy, who was seated at her office desk, trying to get her mind into work mode but hopelessly distracted by the conversation which touched on sore points from her mother's most recent telephone call. Another gallery exhibition. Another shot of advice to sell the rose farm and get a life in Sydney amongst interesting people. Insistence on a shopping trip so she could feel proud of her daughter's appearance.

The problem was she and her mother occupied different worlds, had done so for as long as Ivy could remember. Her parents had never divorced but had lived separate lives, with Ivy being brought up by her father on the farm, while her mother indulged her need for cultural activities in the city. Horticulture was of no interest to her and she was constantly urging Ivy to leave it behind and experience the full art of living, which seemed to be endless parties with endless empty chatter.

Ivy loved the farm. It was what she knew, what she was comfortable with. And she had loved her father, loved him sharing the farm with her, teaching her everything about it. It was a good life, giving a sense of satisfaction and achievement. The only thing missing from it was a man she could love, and more importantly, one who loved her back. She had thought, believed… but no, Ben hadn't supported her when she'd needed support.

'Hey, maybe you'll get to meet our rose Valentino again at your mother's exhibition! And he'll be free this time!' Heather said with a waggish play of her eyebrows.

'I very much doubt a man like him would turn up on his own,' Ivy shot back at her, instantly pouring cold water over ridiculous speculation.

It didn't dampen Heather's cheerful outlook on possibilities. 'You never know. I bet you could turn his head if you hung out your hair and dolled yourself up. How often do your see that glorious shade of red-gold hair? If you didn't wear it in a plait, the sheer mass of it would catch his eye.'

'So what if it did?' Ivy loaded her voice with scepticism. 'Do you think for one moment Jordan Powell would be interested in a country farm girl? Or for that matter, I'd be interested in being the next woman on his Valentino list?'

Undeterred, Heather cocked her head on one side consideringly, her hazel eyes sparkling with mischief in the making. Her brown hair was cut in an asymmetrical bob and she tucked the longer side of it behind her ear as she invariably did before getting down to business. She was brilliant at her job, a warm friendly person by nature, and although she was two years older than Ivy—almost at the thirty mark, which was when she planned to have a baby—they'd become close friends since Heather had married Barry Gale, who was in charge of the greenhouses.

She had wanted to work at the rose farm, too, and with her computer skills was a great asset to the business. Ivy thanked her lucky stars that Heather seemed to have dropped out of the heavens when someone to help manage the office work was most needed. It had been a very stressful time after her father had been diagnosed with inoperable cancer. Even knowing his illness was terminal she had not been prepared for his death. The grief, the sudden huge hole in her life…without Heather, she might not have been able to keep everything flowing to maintain the company's reliable reputation.

'Seems to me Jordan Powell could well be up for a new experience and it could be good for you, too, Ivy,' she drawled now, having fun with being provocative.

Ivy laughed. '*Up* is undoubtedly the operative word for him. Even if I did catch his eye, I don't think I'd like the downer that inevitably follows the up. I know his track record, remember?'

'Exactly! Forewarned, forearmed. He won't break your heart since you're well aware he'll move on. You haven't had a vacation for three years, nor had a relationship with a man for over two. Here you are, wasting your prime in work, and if you vegetate too long, you'll forget how to kick up your heels. I bet Jordan Powell could give you a marvellous time—great fun, great sex, an absolutely lovely trip to wallow in for a while. Definitely worth having, if only to give you a different perspective on life.'

'Pie in the sky, Heather. I can't see Jordan Powell making a beeline for me, even if he does turn up alone at the gallery.' She shrugged. 'As for the rest, I have been thinking of taking a trip somewhere now that everything on the farm is running smoothly. I was looking through the travel section of the Sunday newspaper yesterday and…'

'That's it!' Heather cried triumphantly, leaping to her feet. 'Have you still got yesterday's newspapers?'

'In the paper bin.'

'I saw just the thing for you. Wait! I'll find it.'

A few minutes later she was slapping the *Life* magazine from the Sunday *Sun-Herald* down on Ivy's desk. It was already opened at a fashion page emblazoned with the words— *The* it *factor.*

'I was talking about a taking a vacation, not clothes,' Ivy reminded her.

Heather tapped her finger on a picture featuring a model wearing a black sequinned jacket with a wide leather belt cinching in her waist, a pink sequinned mini-skirt, and high-heeled black platform shoes with pink and yellow and green bits attached to straps that ended up around her ankles. 'If you wore this to your mother's exhibition, you'd knock everyone's eyes out.'

'Oh, sure! That pink skirt with my carrot hair? You're nuts, Heather.'

'No, I'm not. The retailer will have other colours. You could buy green instead of pink. That would go with your eyes and still match in with the shoes. It would be brilliant on you, Ivy. You're tall enough and slim enough to carry it off.' She pointed again. 'And look at these long jet earrings. They'd be fabulous swinging in front of your hair which you'll have to wear down like the model. Yours will look a lot more striking against the jacket. The black handbag with the studs is a must, as well.'

'Probably costs a fortune,' Ivy muttered, tempted by the image of herself in such a *wow* outfit, but unable to see herself wearing it anywhere else in the future.

Such clothes simply weren't worn around here. The farm was a hundred kilometres south of Sydney, situated in a valley which had once been a pastoral estate but had become a settlement for hobby farms. Very casual dress was the norm at any social occasion.

'You can afford it,' Heather insisted. 'The farm raked in heaps with the St Valentine's Day sales. Even if it's only a one-off occasion for this gear, why not? Didn't you say your mother wanted you to appear more fashionable at her exhibition this time?'

Ivy grimaced at the reminder. 'So I'd fit in, not stand out.'

Heather grinned. 'Well, I say, sock it to her. And sock it to Jordan Powell if he turns up, too.'

Ivy laughed. On both counts it was terribly tempting.

Sacha Thornton's jaw would probably drop at seeing her daughter look like a trendy siren. It might even silence the barrage of critical advice that Ivy was usually subjected to every time she was with her mother.

As for Jordan Powell—well, there was certainly no guarantee that he'd be there, but…it would be fun to see if she could attract the sexiest man in Australia. It would do her female ego good, if nothing else.

'Okay! Get on your computer and find out from the listed retailers where I can buy all this stuff,' she tossed at Heather, feeling a bubbly sense of throwing her cap over a windmill. And why not? Just for once! She *could* afford it.

'Yes!' Heather punched the air with her fist, grabbed the magazine and danced back to her chair, singing an old Abba tune—'Take a chance on me…'

Ivy couldn't help smiling. If she was going to be mad enough to wear that outfit, she needed to acquire it as fast as possible so she had enough time to practise walking in those crazy shoes. The exhibition opening was this Friday evening, cocktails at six in the gallery. She only had four and a half days to get ready for it.

CHAPTER TWO

JORDAN Powell sat at the breakfast table, perusing the property sales reported in the morning newspaper as he waited for Margaret to serve him the perfect crispy bacon with the perfect eggs hollandaise that not even the best restaurants had ever equalled. Not to his taste, anyway. Margaret Partridge was a jewel—a meticulous housekeeper and a great cook. He enjoyed her blunt honesty, too. It was a rarity in his life and he wasn't about to lose it. All in all, Margaret was far more worth keeping than Corinne Alder.

The delicious scent of freshly cooked bacon had him looking up and smiling at Margaret as she entered the sunroom where he always ate breakfast and lunch when he was home. There was no smile back. The expression on her face disdained any pleasantries between them this morning. Jordan quickly folded his newspaper and set it aside, aware that Margaret's feathers were seriously ruffled.

She dumped the plate of bacon and eggs in front of him, planted her hands on her hips and brusquely warned, 'If you invite that Corinne Alder back to this house, Jordan, I'm out of here. I will not be talked down to by a good-for-nothing chit like that, thinking she's got it over me just because she was born with enough good looks for you to want her in your bed.'

Jordan raised an open palm for peace. 'The deed is done, Margaret. I finished with Corinne this morning. And I apologise profusely for her behaviour towards you. I can only say in my defence she was as sweet as pie to me and…'

'Well, she would be, wouldn't she?' Margaret cut in with a sniff of disgust at his obvious gullibility. 'I don't mind you having a string of affairs. At least that's more honest than marrying and cheating. You can parade as many women as you like through this house, but I won't be treated with disrespect.'

'I shall make that very clear to anyone I invite in future,' Jordan solemnly promised. 'I'm sorry my judgement of character was somewhat blurred in this instance.'

Margaret sniffed again. 'You could try practising looking beyond the surface.'

'I shall attempt to plumb the depths next time.'

'Out of bed as well as in it,' she whipped back at him.

He heaved a sigh. 'Now is that nice, Margaret? Am I ever anything but nice to you? Haven't I just shown how much I care about your feelings by breaking it off with Corinne?'

'Good riddance!' she declared with satisfaction. 'And it's on account of the fact that you're always nice to me that I didn't burn your breakfast.' A smile was finally bestowed on him. 'Enjoy it!'

On her way out of the sunroom a triumphant mutter floated back to him. 'She had a big bum anyhow.'

Clearly a flaw to true physical beauty in Margaret's mind. It left Jordan's mouth twitching with amusement.

Margaret was virtually bumless, a short, skinny woman in her fifties, totally disinterested in enhancing her femininity. She never wore make-up, was hardly ever out of the white shirtmaker dresses which she considered a suitable uniform for her position, along with flat white lace-up shoes. Her unashamedly grey hair was invariably screwed up into a neat bun on top of her head. However, she did exude quite extraordinary energy and there was a lot of sharp intelligence in her bright, brown eyes, along with the sharp wit that occasionally flew off her tongue.

Jordan had liked her immediately.

When he had interviewed her for the job she had told him she was divorced, didn't intend ever to marry again, and if she had to keep a house and cook for a man, she'd rather be paid for it. Her two children were doing fine for themselves and she liked the idea of doing fine for herself, being employed by a billionaire in a house full of luxuries. If he would give her a month's trial, she would prove he'd be lucky to find anyone better.

Jordan considered himself very lucky to have found Margaret. He especially appreciated how fortunate he was as he tucked into his superbly cooked breakfast. There were always beautiful women vying for his attention and he enjoyed having a taste of them, but none of them stayed as constantly delectable as Margaret's meals.

Corinne could be easily replaced. As for looking for more than a bed partner…no, he wasn't going down that road again, having almost been drawn into proposing marriage by the extremely artful Biancha who had presented herself as the perfect wife for him, so perfectly obliging to his every need and desire it had struck a slightly uneasy chord in him, though not enough to pull him back from the brink until the deception unravelled.

She'd known all along that her father's supposed wealth was a house of cards about to fall…totally dishonest about her family situation…and when the collapse could no longer be held off, it had become sickeningly obvious that she had targeted him to be her rescue package. No way would she have put herself out so much for the man…without the billions to keep her life sweet.

Margaret might have spotted Biancha's true colours if she'd been working for him then. Not much got past his shrewd housekeeper. In fact, having such a jewel running his house, he saw no reason whatsoever to take a wife, especially when he was never short of bed partners.

Too few marriages worked for long, especially in his social set, and there was nothing more sour than the financial fallout that came with divorce. He'd witnessed enough of those problems with his sister's marriages. Three times now Olivia had blindly hooked up with fortune-hunters, not even learning from experience, which annoyed the hell out of him. As the old saying went, once bitten should have made her twice shy. A million times shy in his book!

At least his parents had had the sense to keep their marriage together, although that had been a different generation. His father had been very discreet about his string of mistresses, allowing his mother to maintain her pride in being the wife of one of the most prominent property tycoons in Australia and enjoy the pleasure of the brilliant lifestyle he provided. Besides, she had had her 'walkers' whenever his father hadn't been available to accompany her to the opera or the theatre—gay men who loved the arts as much as she did, and who were delighted to have the privilege of escorting her, thereby getting free tickets.

His parents had kept the bond going for thirty years, and there'd still been some affection between them at the end, his mother genuinely grieving over his father's death. It was a lot of shared years, regardless of the ups and downs. Jordan doubted there was a woman alive who could interest him enough to want to share more than even a few months with her. They invariably turned out to be too damned full of themselves.

I want…I need…look at me…talk to me. If I'm not the centre of your universe, I'm going to sulk or throw a tantrum.

He'd just finished breakfast when his mobile rang. He took it out of his shirt pocket, hoping it wasn't Corinne calling to appeal for some reconsideration. That would be extremely tedious. She'd been nastily dismissive of Margaret's feelings, and he wasn't about to accept any excuse for her rudeness to a highly valued employee.

It was a relief to find it was his mother wanting contact with him.

'Good morning,' he said cheerfully. 'What can I do for you?'

'You can be free this Friday evening to escort me to an art gallery,' she replied with her usual queenly aplomb. It was amazing how many people bowed to her will when she employed that tone. Of course, the wealth backing it had a big influence. Nonie Powell was known to be enormously charitable, and she was not above using that as a power tool.

Jordan, however, did not have to be a courtier. 'What's wrong with Murray?' he demanded, wondering if the 'walker' she most relied upon had somehow lost her favour.

'The poor boy slipped on wet tiles and broke his ankle.'

The poor boy was a very dapper sixty year old.

'I'm sorry to hear that. What's on at what gallery?'

'It's dear Henry's gallery at Paddington. He's showing Sacha Thornton's latest work. You bought two of her paintings at her last exhibition so you should be interested in seeing what she's done more recently.'

He remembered. Lots of vivid colour. A field of poppies in Italy and a vase of marigolds. The paintings had brightened up the walls at the sales office for one of his retirement villages. He also remembered the vivid red-gold hair of Sacha Thornton's daughter. She'd worn jeans. Margaret would have approved of *her* bum. Very neat. But it was the hair that had drawn him into asking for an introduction.

Wrong time, wrong place, with Melanie Tindell hanging on his arm, but Jordan felt a strong spark of interest in meeting the artist's daughter again. Wonderful pale skin—amazingly without freckles—and eyes so green he wouldn't mind plumbing *their* depths. She could have looked spectacular with a bit of effort. He'd wondered why she hadn't bothered. Most women would have played up such natural assets.

The name came back to him…Ivy.

Poison Ivy?

There'd definitely been some tension between her and her mother.

All very curious.

'The doors open at six o'clock,' his own mother informed him. 'Henry will serve us decent champagne and there'll be the usual hors d'oeuvres. If you'll be at home at five-thirty I'll direct my chauffeur to pick you up along the way.'

His current domain at Balmoral was only a slight diversion on his mother's route from Palm Beach. 'Fine!' he replied, deciding he could improvise with alternative transport should Ivy prove interesting enough to pursue.

'Thank you, Jordan.'

'My pleasure.'

He smiled as he closed his mobile and tucked it back in his pocket.

He didn't mind pleasing his mother, especially when there was the possibility of pleasure for himself.

CHAPTER THREE

IVY was late. The Friday-evening peak-hour traffic had been horrific, and finding a parking place had been equally frustrating. She had to walk three blocks virtually on her toes in the trendy shoes, silently cursing the designers who dictated foot fashion. They deserved a seat in hell. No, not a seat. They should have to walk forever in their own torturous creations.

As she turned the last corner to the street where the gallery was situated, she saw a chauffeur popping back into a Rolls-Royce which was double-parked outside her destination. *Easy for some,* she thought, her mind instantly zinging to Jordan Powell. Everything would be easy for a billionaire, especially women. Certainly in his case. A fact she was unlikely to forget.

In Heather's lingo, she was a red-hot tamale tonight.

If Jordan Powell was here by himself…if he bit… what should she do?

Have a taste of him or run?

Wait and see, she told himself. There was no point in crossing bridges until she came to them.

She switched her thoughts to her mother. It was a big night for her. At least this outfit should not take any of the shine off it. It was sequin city all the way.

Henry Boyce, the gallery owner, was obsequiously chatting up one of his super-wealthy clients when Ivy walked in, but his eagle eye was open for newcomers. When he caught sight of her, his jaw dropped. The gorgeously gowned woman with the perfectly styled blond hair who had lost his attention turned to see who was the distraction, a miffed look on her arrogant face. The man who stood on the other side of her shifted enough to view the intrusive object.

It was Jordan Powell.

And *his* face broke into a delighted grin.

Ivy's heart instantly leapt into a jig that would have rivalled the fastest dance performers in Ireland.

'Good heavens! Ivy?' Henry uttered incredulously, his usual aplomb momentarily deserting him.

'Who?' the woman demanded.

She was considerably older than Jordan, Ivy realised, though beautifully preserved and very full of her own importance.

'Forgive me, Nonie,' Henry rattled out. 'I wasn't expecting…it's Sacha's daughter, Ivy Thornton. Come on in, Ivy. Your mother will be so pleased to see you.'

Not looking like a farm girl this time.

He didn't say it but he was thinking it.

He'd wanted to turn her away from the last exhibition until she'd identified herself.

Ivy recovered enough from the thumping impact of Jordan Powell's presence to smile. 'I'll go through and find her.'

'A pleasure to see you here again, Ivy,' the rose Valentino said, stunning her anew that he actually remembered meeting her before. 'I don't think you met my mother last time,' he continued, stepping around the woman and holding out a beckoning hand to invite

Ivy into the little group. 'Let me introduce you. Nonie Powell.'

His mother. Who looked her up and down as though measuring whether she was worth knowing. She had blue eyes, too, but they had a touch of frost in them, probably caused by the sheer number of women who streamed through her playboy son's life, none of whom stayed long enough to merit her attention.

Ivy's smile tilted ironically as she stepped forward and offered her hand. 'A pleasure to meet you, Mrs Powell.'

'Are you an artist, too, my dear?' she asked, deigning to acknowledge Ivy with a brief limp touch.

'No. I don't have my mother's talent.'

'Oh? What do you do?'

Ivy couldn't stop a grin from breaking out. She might look like a high-fashion model tonight, but... 'I work on a farm.'

Which, of course, meant she was of no account whatsoever, so she gave a nod of dismissal before she received one. 'If you'll excuse me, I've arrived a little late and my mother might be feeling anxious about it.'

'A farm?' Nonie Powell repeated incredulously.

'Let me help you find her,' Jordan said, moving swiftly and smoothly to hook his arm around Ivy's, pouring charm into a wicked smile. 'I'm very good at cutting a swathe through crowds.'

Ivy gaped at him in amazement while her heart started another wild jig. Did he pick up women as fast as that?

'Take care of my mother, will you, Henry?' he tossed at the gallery owner and they were off, Ivy's feet blindly moving in step with his as she tried to regather her wits.

'Kind of you,' she muttered, her senses bombarded

by the spicy cologne he was wearing, the hard muscular arm claiming her company, the confident purr of his sexy voice, the mischievous dance in his bedroom-blue eyes.

'Pure self-interest. We didn't get to talk much last time, and I'm bursting with curiosity about you.'

'Why?' she demanded, frowning over how directly he was coming on to her, even after she'd said straight-out she was a farm girl. Did that make her a novelty?

'The transformation for a start,' he answered teasingly.

She shrugged. 'My mother was not pleased with my appearance at that showing so I'm trying not to be a blot on her limelight again.'

'You could never be a blot with your shade of hair,' he declared. 'It's a beacon of glorious colour.'

He rolled the words out so glibly, Ivy couldn't really feel complimented. The playboy was playing and some deep-down sense of self-worth resented his game. She should be feeling happily flattered that Jordan Powell was attracted to her, delighted that her dress-up effort had paid off. Yet, despite the charismatic sexiness of the man, she was inwardly bridling against the ease with which he thought he could claim her company. Everything was too easy for him and she didn't like the idea of him finding her easy, too.

She halted in the midst of the gallery crowd, unhooked her arm and turned to face him, her eyes focussed on burning a hole through his to the facile mind behind them. 'Are you chatting me up?'

He looked surprised at the direct confrontation. Then amused. 'Yes and no,' he replied with a grin. 'I speak the absolute truth about your fabulous hair but I am…'

'I'm more than red hair,' she cut in, refusing to

respond to the heart-kicking grin. 'And since I've had it all my life, it's quite meaningless to me.'

Which should have dampened his ardour but didn't.

He laughed, and the lovely deep chuckle caressed all of Ivy's female hormones into vibrant life. Her thighs tensed, her stomach fluttered, her breasts tingled, and while her eyes still warred with the seductive twinkle in his, she was acutely aware of wanting to experience this man, regardless of knowing how short-term it would be. Nevertheless, resentment at his superficiality still simmered.

'Would you like me to rave on about your hair or how handsome you are?' she asked with lofty contempt. 'Is that the measure of you as a man?'

His mouth did its sensual little quirk. 'I stand corrected on how to chat you up. May I begin again?'

'Begin what?'

'Acquainting myself with the person you are.'

That was good. Really good. It hit the spot of prickling discontent. Nevertheless, Ivy couldn't bring herself to surrender to his charm without a further stand.

'Don't be deceived by this trendy get-up. It's for my mother. And Henry, who's a snob of the first order, not welcoming the common herd into his gallery. I'm simply not your type.'

He raised a wickedly arched eyebrow. 'Care to expound on what my type is?'

Careful, Ivy.

It was best for business not to reveal how she knew what she knew about him.

She cocked her head to the side consideringly and said, 'From what I observed last time we met, I'd say you specialise in beautiful trophy women.'

His brow creased thoughtfully. 'Perhaps they're the ones who throw themselves at me. Wealth is a drawcard so it's difficult to know if anyone actually likes you. It's more about what you can give them. I tend to sift through what's offered and…'

'May I point out it was *you* who grabbed me. *I* didn't throw myself at you.'

He smiled. 'Wonderfully refreshing, Ivy. Please allow me to learn more about you.'

It was impossible to muster up any more defences against that smile. Ivy sighed and gave in to the desire to have him at her side, at least for a little while. 'Well, my mother will be impressed if I have you in tow,' she muttered and curled her arm around his again. 'Lead on. Can you see her anywhere?'

He glanced around from his greater height, not that Ivy was short in these high-heeled platform shoes, but the top of her head was only level with his nose.

'To our right,' he directed. 'She's talking to a couple who appear interested in one of her paintings.'

'Then we mustn't interrupt, just hover nearby until she finishes with them and is free to notice me.'

'I think she'll notice you whether she's free or not,' Jordan said dryly.

Ivy didn't see anyone else in sequins. 'I hope I'm not too over the top in this outfit,' she said worriedly. 'The aim was to pleasantly surprise her with an up-to-date city version of me.'

'She didn't like the country version?'

Ivy rolled her eyes at him. 'When someone makes an art form of glamour, anything less offends their sensibilities, so no, she didn't care for my lack of care.'

'No problem tonight. You look as though you stepped right off the page of a fashion magazine.'

'I did.'

'Pardon?'

Ivy couldn't help laughing, her eyes twinkling at him as she explained. 'Saw a photo of these clothes, bought them, and hey presto! Even you're impressed!'

'You wear them well,' he said, amused by her amusement at her magic trick.

'Thank you. Then you don't think I'm over the top?'

'Not at all.'

She hugged his arm. 'Good! I've got you to protect me if my mother attacks.'

'I'm glad to be of use.'

He was a charmer. No doubt about that. Ivy was suddenly bubbling over with high spirits, despite knowing his track record with women. It wouldn't hurt to enjoy his company at the gallery, she decided. Much more fun than being on her own.

Her mother was dressed in a long flowing gown that fell from a beaded yoke in deepening shades of pink. Unlike Ivy, she wore pink beautifully, but then she wasn't like Ivy at all except for the curly hair. No one would pick them as mother and daughter. Sacha Thornton had grey eyes. Her hair was dark brown—almost black—and cascaded over her shoulders in a wild mane of ringlets, defying the fact she was nearing fifty. Though she didn't look it. Artful make-up gave her face the colour and vivacity of a much younger woman.

Bangles and rings flashed as her hands talked up the painting she was intent on selling to the couple. The expressive gesticulation halted in midair as Ivy—linked with Jordan Powell—moved into her line of vision. A startled look froze the animation of her face.

Ivy barely clamped down on the hysterical giggle

that threatened to erupt from her throat. She wished Heather was here to see the outcome of her pushing—first Henry, then Jordan Powell and now her mother totally agog. Heather would be dancing around and clapping her hands in wild triumph. And Ivy had to admit that even her tortured feet did not take the gleeful gloss off this moment.

It was ridiculous, of course.

All to do with image.

An image that didn't reflect who she was at all.

Nevertheless, she would happily wear it tonight for the sheer fun it was bringing her.

Her mother swiftly recovered, flashing an ingratiating smile at the prospective buyers. 'You must excuse me now.' She nodded towards Ivy. 'My daughter has just arrived.'

No hesitation whatsoever in acknowledging their relationship, nor in directing attention to her. The couple looked, their eyes widening at what they obviously saw as a power pair waiting in the wings. Jordan Powell was a splendid ornament on Ivy's arm.

'But please speak to Henry about the painting,' her mother went on. 'He's handling all the sales.'

She pressed their hands in a quick parting gesture and swept over to plant extravagant kisses on her daughter's cheeks in between extravagant cries of approval.

'Darling! How lovely you look! I'm so thrilled that you're here for me! And with Jordan!'

She stepped back to eye him coquettishly. 'I do hope this means you've come to buy more of my work.'

'Ivy and I came to greet you first, Sacha,' he answered, oozing his charm again. 'We haven't had a chance to see what's on show yet.'

'Well, if there's anything that takes your eye…'

They chatted for a few minutes, Ivy wryly reflecting that Jordan Powell was more important to her mother than she was. The man with the money. And the connections. She understood that this was what tonight was about for Sacha Thornton, not catching up with a daughter who didn't share the same interests anyway. At least she had succeeded in not being a drag on proceedings. The next telephone call from her mother should be quite pleasant.

'Ivy, dear, make sure Jordan sees everything,' her mother pleaded prettily when he was about to draw away.

'I'll do my best,' she answered obligingly. 'Good luck with the show, Sacha.'

'Sacha?' Jordan queried, eyeing her curiously as he steered her into the adjoining room which wasn't so crowded with people. 'You don't call her Mum?'

'No.' Ivy shrugged. 'Her choice. And I don't mind. Sacha never felt like a real mother to me. I was brought up by my father. That was her choice, too.'

'But you came for her tonight.'

'She always made the effort to come to events that were important to me.'

'Like what?'

'School concerts, graduation. Whenever I wanted both parents there for me.'

'Will you be staying the weekend with her?'

'No.'

'Why not?'

'Because I'd rather go home.'

'Which is where?'

'About a hundred kilometres from here.'

She wasn't about to identify her location to him. The

farm's website gave it away and he might have read it when he decided to use their service for his rose gifts.

'That's quite a drive late at night.'

'It won't be late. People drift out of here after a couple of hours.' She gave him an ironic grimace. 'You whisked me off before I could get a brochure detailing the paintings from Henry. Did he give you one?'

'Yes.' He took it out of his jacket pocket and handed it to her.

Ivy withdrew her arm from his and checked the numbers of the nearby paintings against the list in the brochure, determined on deflecting his physical effect on her. 'Right!' she said briskly, pointing to number fifteen. 'This is *Courtyard in Sunshine*. Do you like it?'

He folded his arms and considered it, obligingly falling in with her direction. 'Very pleasant but a bit too chocolate-boxy for me.'

Privately Ivy agreed, but the painting already had a red sticker on it indicating a sale, so somebody had liked it. 'Okay. Let's move on. Find something that does appeal to you.'

'Oh, I've already found that,' he drawled in a seductive tone, compelling Ivy to shoot a glance at him.

The bedroom-blue eyes had her targeted. It was like being hit by an explosion of sexual promise that fired up a host of primitive desires. She had lusted mildly over some movie stars, but in real life...this was a totally new and highly unsettling experience. She didn't even like this man...did she?

'You're wasting your time flirting with me,' she bluntly told him.

'There's nothing else I'd rather do,' he declared, grinning as though her rebuff delighted him.

Ivy huffed at his persistence. 'Well, if you must tag

along in my wake, you'll have to look properly at every painting or I'll lose patience with you.'

'If I buy one or two of them, will you have dinner with me?'

Had Ivy not been wearing such dangerous shoes, she would have stamped her foot. As it was, she glared at him in high dudgeon. 'That is the most incredibly offensive thing anyone has ever said to me!'

He actually looked taken aback by her attack. The dent in his confidence gave Ivy a wild rush of satisfaction. Jordan Powell wasn't going to find *her* easy.

He frowned. 'I thought it would please you to have your mother pleased tonight.'

'My mother has enough talent to draw buyers to her work or Henry wouldn't have it hanging in his gallery,' she retorted fiercely. 'She doesn't need me to sell myself to have a successful exhibition.' Her chin lifted in proud defiance of his obvious belief that anyone could be bought. 'I wouldn't do it anyway.'

He grimaced an apology. 'I didn't mean…'

'Oh, yes you did,' she cut in. 'I bet you think that all you have to do is offer your little goodies and any woman will fall in your lap.'

The grimace took on an ironic twist. 'I wouldn't call them *little* goodies.'

He might not have meant to put a sexual twist on those words, but Ivy felt her cheeks flame as an image of his naked body bloomed in her mind. 'I don't care how big they are,' she insisted vehemently. 'Why don't you go on back to *your* mother? I don't fit into your scene and never will.'

And having cut his feet out from under him, Ivy fully expected him to go. It would be the most sensible solution to the warring urge inside her to take what he was offering. Just to see, to know, to feel…

Which would inevitably end badly with her being discarded as he discarded all the rest.

CHAPTER FOUR

JORDAN was faced with a decision he wasn't used to facing. No woman had ever told him to leave her alone. No woman had ever thrown so many negatives at him, either. Maybe Ivy Thornton wouldn't fit into his scene and he should walk away, stop wasting his time with her.

But he didn't *want* to walk away.

He liked her thorns.

They made her more intriguing, more challenging than the women in 'his scene'. And the fire-power coming from her incited visions of passion, lifting her desirability to virtually a must-have level. Just the sight of her had excited him. His fingertips itched to graze over every hidden part of her pale, almost translucent skin, not to mention stroking through the red-gold hair guarding her most intimate places.

Missing out on that…no.

He had to win her over.

'Never say never, Ivy. Things can change,' he said mildly, hoping to undermine her hard stance.

'I can't see that happening.' The fascinating green eyes flashed scepticism, but the tone of her voice was not so fierce.

'It was crass of me to link buying your mother's

paintings to my invitation to dinner and I apologise for the offence given,' he went on, projecting absolute sincerity. 'Please take it as a measure of how much I wanted you to accept, how much I wanted to spend more time with you.'

She frowned. After a few moments of cogitation, she gave him a narrow look that telegraphed he was on shaky ground, but her words granted him a second chance. 'Well, if you still want to accompany me around the gallery, I'll go that far with you.'

Triumph zinged through his mind. He only just managed to keep his smile appealingly rueful. 'I shall monitor my conversation with rigid regard to your sensibilities.'

It drew a laugh. 'I don't think you can hide your true colours, Jordan. Getting your own way must be habitual. You have all the tools to do it. Wealth, looks and charm to boot.'

He affected a helpless expression. 'None of which appear to carry any weight with you.'

She laughed again, shaking her head at him. 'I can't deny you're entertaining.'

He grinned. 'So are you, Ivy. I've just found a masochistic streak in myself. You can put me down as much as you like and I'll pop up for more.'

The green eyes sparkled. 'I might test that.'

He suddenly saw her in a black leather corselet, high-heeled boots laced up to her thighs, a whip in her hand. With her white skin and red hair, it made a fantastic vision. 'Are you a dominatrix?' he asked, seized by an irrepressible curiosity. He wasn't into that kind of kinky sex, but with Ivy he might give it a try.

'A what?' She looked aghast.

'I thought you could have been suggesting it with

your "test" remark. Sorry. Had to ask. I do like to get my bearings with people, and you've completely knocked me off them.'

Her cheeks flamed again, the heat glow making her green eyes even greener. Her colouring was so entrancing, Jordan felt a considerable flow of heat himself though it was concentrated below the belt, not above it.

'I'm certainly not a dominatrix,' she stated emphatically.

'Good! Because I'm not really a masochist.' And he much preferred the idea of controlling the sexual games he played with Ivy, not the other way around.

She planted her hands on her hips. 'And just how did this conversation get to the bedroom? Do you have sex on your mind all the time?'

'Most men have sex on their minds most of the time,' he informed her with an ironic grimace.

'Do you think you can lift yours off it while we look at paintings?'

'Difficult with you dressed as you are, but I'll do my best.'

'Try hard.'

'I shall.' He whipped the brochure out of her hand, checked the number of the next painting and directed her attention to it. 'This one is called *Waterlilies.* Much more to my liking. Reminds me of Monet's great works. Have you ever been to Monet's garden at Giverny, Ivy?'

'No.'

'It's marvellous. Inspirational. After seeing what he created there, I was determined to bring something like it to every one of the retirement villages I've had constructed. There's nothing like a wonderful garden in bloom to make people feel good. Best environment you can have.'

The leap from sex to gardens was diverting but for Ivy the damage was done. She couldn't lift her own mind from thoughts of how he might be in the bedroom. He had wonderful hands, long and elegant, and she couldn't help imagining that their touch would be sensitive. Ben's had never really been gentle enough. With him she had often wished…though their relationship had been very companionable and she might have married him if he'd been more understanding during her father's last months.

No chance of marriage with Jordan Powell.

Only bed and roses.

But the bed part might be an experience worth having.

Maybe she would never meet a man who would be happy to share their lives. Ben had been the only possibility and she was already twenty-seven. For the past two years there had been no one of any real interest on her horizon. Jordan Powell was interesting, though not, of course, in any lasting sense. But for a while…

It was tempting and becoming more tempting by the minute.

He bought *Waterlilies.*

Henry put the red dot on the frame of the painting, congratulated Jordan on a fine buy, smiled at Ivy as though to say she had done well by her mother, and moved off, probably hoping she would do more on the sales front with a billionaire in tow.

'This was not a bribe, Ivy,' Jordan assured her. 'If you weren't at my side, I would still have acquired it.'

'What will you do with it?' she demanded, wanting proof that his liking for it was genuine.

'Hang it in one of the nursing homes. It gives a sense of serenity. I'm sure the residents will enjoy it.'

Her curiosity was piqued. 'You seem to care about the people who buy into your properties.'

'I like them. They've reached an age where impressing a person like me is irrelevant. They say it how it is for them and I respect that.' There was a glint of cynicism in his eyes as he added, 'Honesty is a fairly rare commodity in my world.'

Yes, it probably was, Ivy thought, and wondered if the high turnover of women in his life was related to some form of deception on their part. Although that was putting them in the wrong and she shouldn't assume he was not. Undoubtedly Jordan Powell had his shortcomings when it came to relationships. She suspected he had a wandering eye, for a start. The last time she'd been in this gallery he'd sought an introduction to her when he was with another woman.

Sliding him a searching look, she asked, 'Are you honest yourself, Jordan?'

'I try to be,' he answered. The wicked twinkle reappeared. 'On the whole, I think I deliver whatever I promise.'

He was definitely thinking sinful pleasures.

Ivy's stomach fluttered in sinful excitement.

He cocked a challenging eyebrow. 'What about you?'

'Oh, I always deliver what I promise,' she said. The reputation of her business depended upon it.

'Ah! A woman of integrity.' He rolled the words out as though tasting them and his smile said he liked them.

Ivy was beginning to like him. She had managed to

keep her father at home where he'd wanted to be during the last months of his life, but if he had gone into a nursing home, one of Jordan Powell's would definitely have been the best choice. Sacha had done a painting of roses to hang in his bedroom, but her father would have liked *Waterlilies,* too.

A sudden welling up of sadness brought tears to her eyes. 'Let's move on. There might be something else that appeals to you,' she said huskily, turning aside to draw Jordan with her as she blinked rapidly and took a deep breath to restore her composure.

Gentle fingers stroked the hand resting on his arm. 'What is it, Ivy?' he asked caringly.

She shook her head, not wanting to explain.

'Something upset you,' he persisted. 'Was it my comment on integrity? Did you think I was being flippant? I assure you…'

'No.' She summoned up a wry little smile. 'Nothing to do with you, Jordan. I was thinking of my father.'

'What about him?' There was concern in the eyes that searched hers.

Ivy was touched by it. Her heart swelled with the sense of caring coming from him. Maybe he simply wanted to dispose of the distraction from him, get it out of the way so he could pull her back to what he wanted, but it tripped her into spilling the truth.

'Sacha's last show…when we first met here… It was soon after my father had died. Your mention of nursing homes reminded me of how hard it was for him at the end.'

'What did he die of, Ivy?'

'Cancer. Melanoma. He had red hair and fair skin like me and he was always having to get sun cancers removed. It made him fanatical about protecting my skin.'

Jordan nodded. 'So that's why you have no freckles.'

The comment made her laugh again. 'I'm a slave to block-out cream, hats and long sleeves. And you look like a slave to the sun—' with his gleaming olive skin, '—which should make you realise I definitely don't fit into your scene.'

He grinned. 'I have no objection to hats, long sleeves and particularly not to block-out cream. In fact, I think it would give me a lot of pleasure to spread it all over your beautiful skin. It would be criminal to have it marred in any way.'

Desire leapt between them—his to touch, hers to be touched. It simmered in his eyes and shot a bolt of heat through her bloodstream. Her pulse started to gallop. Ivy wrenched her gaze from his in sheer panic, riven with an acute awareness of feeling terribly vulnerable to what this man could do to her, for her, with her.

It would probably be a big mistake to let it happen.

She might end up wanting more of him than was sensible or practical, given his track record and her circumstances.

'What about a painting for yourself?' she rattled out, waving at the next section of the exhibition.

'Actually, I'm happy with the selection I have in my house,' he said, apparently content to follow her lead. For the moment.

Ivy was extremely conscious of him waiting, patient in his pursuit of a more intimate togetherness. It didn't need to be spoken. His intent was already under her skin, boring away at needs she had been dismissing for years. He'd brought the woman in her alive, kicking and screaming to be used, enjoyed, pleasured.

'I guess you have a collection of European masters,' she said lightly, thinking he could well afford it. She remembered Van Gogh's *Irises* had been bought by an Australian billionaire.

'No. I'm a proud Australian. I like my country and our culture. We have some great artists who've captured its uniqueness—Drysdale, Sydney Nolan, Pro Hart. I think I've bought the best of them.'

Sacha Thornton was not in that echelon of fame, although her work was popular and sold well. Ivy was impressed by the names he'd rolled out, impressed with his patriotism, as well. She'd never liked the snobbery of believing something bought overseas had a cachet that made it better than anything Australian.

'You're very lucky to have them to enjoy,' she remarked as they strolled on.

'It would be my pleasure to show them to you.'

She shot a teasing grin at him. 'I'd have to say that's one up on etchings.'

He grinned back. 'It's not a bribe.'

Her eyes merrily mocked him. 'Just holding out a persuasive titbit.'

'The choice is yours.'

'I might think about it,' she tossed at him airily, turning back to her mother's art.

He leaned close to her ear and murmured, 'You could think about it over dinner.'

The waft of his warm breath was like a tingling caress.

Temptation roared through her.

Fortunately two waiters descended on them, one offering a tray of hors d'oeuvres, the other presenting two glasses of fizzing champagne. 'Veuve Clicquot,' the drinks waiter informed them. 'Especially for you, Mr Powell. Compliments of…'

'Henry, of course. Thank him for me.' Jordan picked up the two glasses and held one out to Ivy who was busy choosing a crab tartlet and a pikelet loaded with smoked salmon and shallots.

'Hang on to it while I eat first,' she pleaded. 'I'm starving.'

'Then you need a proper meal,' he argued. 'If you like seafood, I know a place that does superb lobster.'

'Mmmh…' Superb lobster, superb works of art, superb Casanova?

The temptations were piling up, making Ivy think she really should throw her cap over the windmill for one mad night with this man.

She finished eating and took the glass of champagne he was holding for her. 'It's Friday night,' she reminded him. 'Wouldn't all the restaurants that serve superb meals be fully booked? How are you going to deliver on what you're promising?'

'There's not a maître d' in Sydney who wouldn't find a table for me,' he answered with supreme arrogance.

It niggled Ivy into a biting remark. 'And not a woman who would refuse you?'

The blue eyes warred with the daggers of distancing pride in hers. 'Please don't, Ivy,' he said with seductive softness. 'I haven't met anyone like you before.'

Her heart turned over. She'd never met anyone like him, either. 'The spice of novelty,' she muttered, mocking both of them—the strong desire to taste a different experience.

'Why not pursue it, at least for this evening?' he pressed persuasively.

She sipped the champagne, felt the fizz go to her head, promoting the urge to be reckless. 'All right,' she said slowly. 'You've sold me on the lobster. I will have dinner with you. If you can deliver what you promise,' she added in deliberate challenge, making the seafood the attraction.

It didn't dent his grin of confidence. 'Consider it done,' he said, whipping out his mobile telephone from a coat pocket.

A treacherous tingle of anticipation invaded Ivy's entire body. She didn't wait to hear him make arrangements, moving on to look at the few paintings they hadn't already seen, pretending it was irrelevant to her whether or not he secured a table for the promised dinner. Undoubtedly he would. Jordan Powell could probably buy his way into anything, any time at all.

But he couldn't buy her.

She would only go as far as *she* wanted to go with him.

One evening...maybe one night...

One step at a time, she told herself. He might turn her off him over dinner. The temptation could fizzle out. She couldn't remember the last time she had indulged her tastebuds with lobster. That, at least, was one pleasure she could allow herself without any concern over what was right or wrong.

CHAPTER FIVE

THEY rode away from the gallery in Nonie Powell's chauffeured Rolls-Royce—borrowed briefly for the trip to the restaurant. Jordan's mother had rolled her eyes over the request, chided him for deserting her and given a long-suffering sigh as her gaze flicked over Ivy before waving them off, obviously resigned to her playboy son's weakness for a new attraction.

Ivy didn't care what his mother thought. Her own mother had been quite happy for her to leave with the billionaire, probably seeing him as the ultimate *city* man who might very well seduce her from country life. Ivy didn't care what Sacha thought, either. As far as she was concerned, this was simply an experience she wanted to dabble with while it was desirable.

When it stopped being desirable, she would take a taxi to her car and drive home. In the meantime, she was enjoying the experience of riding in a Rolls-Royce. She'd never done it before and it was most unlikely she would ever do it again. It felt luxurious. It smelled luxurious. She focussed her mind on memorising everything about it to tell Heather because it helped distract her from an acute awareness of the man sitting beside her.

He totally wrecked that mental exercise by reaching across, plucking her hand from her lap and stroking it with his long, elegant and highly sensual fingers. Her pulse bolted into overdrive. She found herself staring at their linked hands, fascinated by the juxtaposition of his olive skin and the extreme fairness of hers. She visualised them in bed together…naked…intertwined…black hair, red hair. The image was wickedly entrancing.

Ben's skin had been fair, though not as fair as hers. Jordan Powell was very different, in every sense. Was it the sheer contrast that made him so appealing? Why did being with him excite her so much? Was it the idea of living dangerously, which was not her usual style at all?

'What are you thinking?' he asked.

No way was she about to reveal those thoughts! 'Where are we going?' she countered, giving him a bright look of anticipation.

'Wherever you want to go,' he purred back at her, the sexy blue eyes inviting her to indulge any desire she had on her mind.

'I meant the restaurant,' she stated pointedly. 'My car is parked near the gallery. If I decide to walk out on you, which I might want to do, I'd prefer not to have a long journey back to it.'

He laughed, squeezing her hand as though asserting his possession of her even as he replied, 'Your escape route won't be a hardship. The restaurant is at Rose Bay. In fact, we're almost there.'

'Good! What's it called?'

'Pier. It specialises in seafood—spanner crab, lobster, tuna. I can recommend the trout carpaccio as a starter.'

'Then I hope you don't say anything offensive before we dine.'

'I'll watch my tongue,' he assured her, smiling as though he found her absolutely delicious.

Ivy immediately started wondering about how sexy his tongue was, in kissing as well as other intimate things. She had to wrench her gaze away from his mouth before he started guessing what she was thinking.

The idea of new experiences could be terribly beguiling.

It was another new experience to be welcomed so effusively into a classy restaurant, led to a table with a lovely view of Sydney Harbour, and given immediate smiling service. Obviously Jordan Powell was known to be a very generous tipper. Who could blame the average working person for bending over backwards to please him? Besides, he really was charming. To everyone! The maître d', the wine waiter, the food waiter, to her especially. Being in his company *was* an undeniable pleasure.

And the seafood was superb.

Especially the lobster, done simply in a lemon butter sauce.

Ivy sighed in satisfaction.

'Up to your expectations?' Jordan asked, his eyes twinkling pleasure in her pleasure.

'Best I've ever had,' she answered truthfully. 'Thank you.'

He gave her a slow, very sensual smile. 'I think the best is yet to come.'

Her stomach muscles contracted. Her mind jammed over what to do next—have a one-night fling with him or scoot for home. 'I couldn't fit in sweets, Jordan,' she said. 'Though coffee would be good.'

A glass of champagne at the gallery and a glass of chardonnay over dinner should not be affecting her judgement, yet she couldn't seem to manage any clear thinking with his eyes tempting her to stay with him and find out if he would deliver 'the best'. Maybe the coffee would sober her up enough to make the break, which, of course, was the most sensible thing to do. This whole thing with Jordan Powell was fantasy stuff. It wouldn't—couldn't—develop into a real relationship.

He ordered the coffee and handed his credit card to the waiter, indicating they would be leaving soon.

'I'll need to call a taxi to get back to my car,' Ivy quickly said. 'I can't walk that far in these killer shoes.'

'A taxi in twenty minutes,' Jordan instructed the waiter, apparently unperturbed about going along with her plan.

Twenty minutes later they left the restaurant.

A taxi was waiting for them.

It was only a short drive to where she had parked her car, but every minute of the trip shredded Ivy's nerves. Jordan had taken possession of her hand again and somehow she couldn't bring herself to snatch it free. Her heart was pounding. Her whole body felt on edge, fighting against the restrictions her mind was trying to impose on it. The pulse in her temples seemed to be thumping, *Go with it. Go with it. Go with it.*

The taxi stopped right beside her car.

Jordan released her hand, paid the driver, and was out, reaching back to help her alight on the kerb side of the street. Ivy finally teetered upright in the vertically challengingly high high heels and was fumbling in her handbag for her car keys when the taxi took off, leaving Jordan with her. Alone together. In the shadows of the night.

She scooped in a quick breath, desperate to relieve

the tightness in her chest. 'You should have kept it,' she said with an agitated wave at the departing taxi.

'A gentleman always sees a lady safely on her way,' he replied with mock gravity.

With roses, her mind snapped.

'I have to change my shoes,' she muttered, dropping her gaze from his, fighting the physical tug of the man. 'I can't drive in these.'

She pressed the Unlock button on her key fob and forced her legs to move, needing to open the trunk and get out her flat-heeled sandals.

'Let me help you take them off,' he said.

Those seductively sensual hands on her legs, her ankles, her feet… Ivy's mind reeled at how vulnerable she might be to his touch. 'I can manage,' she rattled out, reaching down to lift the lid of the trunk.

He intercepted the move, taking her hand, turning her towards him. She darted an anguished look of protest at him, caught burning purpose in his eyes, and suddenly her defences caved in, totally undermined by a chaotic craving to know what it would be like at least to be kissed by him.

'Ivy,' he murmured, stepping closer, sliding an arm around her waist. He lifted her hand to his shoulder, left it there and stroked her cheek, featherlight fingertips grazing slowly down to trace the line of her lips, his thumb hooking gently under her chin, tilting it up.

She was aware of weird little tremors running down her thighs, aware of her stomach fluttering with excitement, aware of her breasts yearning for contact with the hard wall of his chest, aware of the wanton desire to experience this man running completely out of control. He lowered his head. She stared at his mouth coming closer and closer to hers. She did nothing to stop him. It was as though all her common-sense mechanisms were paralysed.

His lips brushed hers, stirring a host of electric tingles. His tongue swept over them, soothing the acute sensitivity and teasing her mouth open. He began with a soft exploratory kiss, a tasting, not demanding a response but inevitably drawing it with tantalising little manoeuvres. Ivy couldn't resist tasting him right back, revelling in the sensual escalation that sent heat whooshing through her body.

The urge to feel him was equally irresistible. Her hand slid up around his neck, her fingers thrusting into his hair, loving its lush thickness. Perhaps it signalled her complete acquiescence to what was happening. Ivy was no longer thinking. Her mind was consumed with registering sensation, pleasure, excitement, the rampant desire to have her curiosity about Jordan Powell satisfied blotting out any other consideration.

His thumb glided along her jawline, caressed the lobe of her ear—an exquisite touch, moving slowly, sensually, under her hair to the nape of her neck. The arm around her waist scooped her into full body contact with him as his kissing became more demanding, less of an invitation, more an incitement to passion.

Ivy barely knew what she was doing. She loved being held so close to him, feeling the hard, male strength of his physique—the perfect complement to her highly aroused femininity. Excitement was flooding through her. Her mouth hungered for more and more passion from him, exulting in the deeply intimate aggression of his kisses. Never had she been so caught up in the moment. Never had she been driven to respond so wildly, so uninhibitedly.

She felt his hand clutch her bottom, pressing her more

tightly into contact with his sexuality. Her stomach contracted at the hard furrowing of his arousal. It should have been a warning to break away from him. Her body didn't want to. Her body wantonly rubbed itself against the blatant evidence of his excitement, exhilarated by it, madly bent on fanning this desire for her. It was wonderful to feel wanted again. She had been too long alone, and the woman inside her was craving connection—connection with this man, regardless of time and place and circumstances.

He swung her back against the trunk of the car, lifting her onto it, his mouth still ravishing hers as his hand burrowed under her mini-skirt, moved her silk panties aside, found the soft moist furrows of her sex and stroked her to a fever pitch of need, her whole being screaming for it to be fulfilled. Nothing else mattered. Nothing else existed for her.

It all happened so fast, the jolt when he plunged into her, the savage joy of it, the relief, the release of all nerve-tearing tension as her inner muscles convulsed and creamed around the marvellously deep penetration. And he repeated it, storming her with waves of ecstatic pleasure, pumping hard to the rhythm of his own need until he, too, reached the sweet chaos of climax.

She lay limply spreadeagled on the trunk of the car with him bent over her, the heat of his harsh breathing pulsing against her throat. If traffic had passed by them on the street, she hadn't heard or seen it. The night seemed to have wrapped them in a private cocoon, intensifying the feelings that still held her in thrall.

His arms burrowed underneath her, gathering her up. Amazingly her legs were wound around his hips and he supported them in place as he lifted her from the car and carried her to the passenger side, only relinquishing their intimate connection when he opened the door and lowered her to the seat. He kissed her while he fastened the safety belt, fetched the handbag she had dropped somewhere and laid it on her lap, kissed her again before closing the door and rounding the car to the driver's side.

She watched him in a daze—this virtual stranger with whom she'd shared such an erotically intimate experience. Languor was seeping into her bones. Somehow any action was beyond her. She barely grasped the fact that he had seized control of the situation, putting her in the car, retrieving her handbag and the car keys which he was now inserting in the ignition, having usurped her driver's seat. Her mind was stuck in one groove, endlessly repeating…

I can't believe I did that.

CHAPTER SIX

JORDAN drove on automatic pilot, his mind still grappling with a loss of control which was totally uncharacteristic, especially in his relationships with women. He'd just acted like a randy teenage boy who couldn't wait to get his rocks off—a rampant bull, incapable of stopping. No sophistication. No finesse.

And worse! No thought of protection!

Shock billowed again.

He never took the risk of getting a woman pregnant. The possibility hadn't even entered his head. He'd wanted Ivy Thornton from the moment he'd seen her tonight, wanted her more and more with every minute they spent together, wanted her so much it was impossible to tolerate her driving away from him, but he'd meant to persuade, to seduce, to promise pleasure, not to…

'I can't believe I did that,' he muttered, shock tumbling into words he didn't mean to speak aloud.

He was still out of control.

'I can't, either.'

The shaky reply startled him into darting a glance at her. She wasn't looking at him. Her head was bent, the rippling fall of her glorious hair hiding most of her face. Her hands lay limply in her lap, palms upward, and she seemed to be staring down at them as though they didn't belong to her—hands that had gripped him in a fever of passion, inciting the wild act of intimacy they had both engaged in.

She was in shock, too.

Instinctively he reached across, took one of her hands, squeezed it. 'I'll make it better,' he said.

Do it right, he thought, which was why he'd put her in the car and was driving her to Balmoral—take her to bed with him and do all the things he'd imagined doing with her instead of succumbing to a mad rush of lust. It was too late to be worrying about protection now, not too late to enjoy all he wanted to enjoy with Ivy Thornton. Though he should check if she was using some form of contraception, know if there was a possibility of unwelcome consequences.

He frowned. It seemed crass to ask at this point. Besides, the damage was done if it was done. Using condoms for the rest of the night would be ridiculous. He might as well have the pleasure of totally unrestricted sex with her. It would be good. Great. Fantastic. He could bring up the issue later. She could take a morning-after pill if it was needed. Right now he wanted her riding with him, still caught up in what had happened between them.

It had been such an incredible rush—the excitement of her response, the mounting sense of urgency to seize the moment, take it as far as he could, her uninhibited complicity driving him to the edge, past it into plunging chaos. He couldn't remember ever feeling so exultantly *primitive*. Sex with Ivy had to be explored further. Much further.

'Where are you taking me?' she asked, her voice still slightly tremulous.

They were crossing the harbour bridge to the northern side of the city. He threw a reassuring smile at her, but her gaze was now fixed on the road ahead of them.

'I have a house at Balmoral. I'm taking you home with me,' he answered, hoping she was not about to protest the move.

She didn't.

She sat in motionless silence as he drove on over the bridge and took the turn to Military Road. Maybe she was having trouble putting thoughts together. Whatever...there were no stop signs coming from her and Jordan felt the buzz of anticipation shooting through his body again. He knew the desire was mutual. No doubt about it. It was only a matter of rekindling it, stoking the fire, making it a slow build-up of heat so the intensity didn't burn them out too fast.

He wanted the whole experience of Ivy Thornton.

A wham-bam on the trunk of a car was almost an insult to the fascinating woman she was.

He'd make it better for her.

A lot better.

Ivy's mind still felt as though it had been hit by a brick. Thoughts came slowly, as though emerging from a sea of molasses. She'd had sex with Jordan Powell. On the trunk of her car! He was driving her to his house at Balmoral. These were definite facts. She found it impossible to decide how she should be reacting to them.

Sex had never been like that for her...so compellingly reckless, so explosive, so erotically euphoric. Whether it was the man he was, the unusual set of circumstances, the long lack of any physical excitement in her life... Ivy couldn't quite put it together. He was a tempting devil and she had been tempted into going along with him, at the gallery, to the restaurant, and now to his home.

Why not?

Luck had blessed her in what could have been disastrous carelessness. She was in a safe week—no chance of falling pregnant. And it was too late to worry about sexual-health issues. Hopefully Jordan Powell was too fastidious a man to run those risks. Though he had done so tonight. Probably part of his shock at his behaviour.

Anyhow, she was problem-free and she hoped he was, too, because it was done now. She'd gone past the point of no return and finishing the night with him had a lot of appeal. How good a lover was he in bed? Could he give her an even more amazing experience? She'd never been inside a billionaire's house. It would be interesting to see how Jordan Powell lived, the paintings he had talked about, whether his bedroom had *playboy* stamped on all its furnishings.

Her car would be parked outside. She could leave whenever she chose to. This was an experience that was unlikely to ever come her way again and she wanted it. Yes, she did. Of course, it had to be limited. One night would satisfy her curiosity. She could allow herself that much. Any further involvement with Jordan would definitely not be sensible. Tomorrow she could leave with a smile on her face…knowing all she wanted to know.

Decision made.

Her mind moved on to working out how she should handle this new situation. It was hard to be cool and objective in these circumstances, having just shared such incredible intimacy with the man. Her nervous system was still buzzing. It seemed best simply to follow his lead. Unless his lead struck wrong chords, which wasn't likely with his well-practised charm. He'd done this with umpteen women. Though on the trunk of a car might have been a first, given his comment of disbelief. It was certainly a first for her.

All her inner muscles contracted with the memory of such intense pleasure. If Jordan could give it to her again…was she wicked to be wanting it? So what if she was! Did it matter just for once? Heather would undoubtedly say *go for it*. It wasn't as if she'd be hurting anyone. She was free to do as she liked.

Her gaze dropped to the hand still firmly linked to hers—a hand that knew how to touch, how to arouse overwhelming sensations, a tempting hand, a winning hand. But she was winning, too, wasn't she, being the object of its expert attention? She might never get to feel like this with any other man.

His fingers caressed her palm, making her skin tingle. 'Are you okay with this, Ivy?' he asked caringly, his deep rich voice washing over her thoughts.

'Yes, thank you,' she answered, wincing at sounding like a prim schoolgirl. The plain truth was she was not a *player*, not like him, and she didn't have any experience of acting like one. 'You can show me your paintings,' she quickly added, flashing him a smile to show she could be sophisticated about spending the night with him.

He laughed and squeezed her hand again. 'Your pleasure will be my pleasure.'

Which surely meant she should have a marvellous time with him. *Just relax and let it happen,* Ivy told herself.

He drove into a large paved courtyard fronting a very large white house with a double garage on the left and another double garage below an extended wing on the right. 'You have four cars?' Ivy asked as he parked hers adjacent to the very elegant portico framing the double front doors.

'Three,' he answered. 'The fourth space is taken up by Margaret's.'

'Who is Margaret?'

'My housekeeper. She lives in the apartment above the garage on the right, and Ray, my handyman and chauffeur, lives in the apartment above the garage on the left.'

Naturally he would need people to maintain such a luxurious property, as well as cater to his needs. 'How long have you had this place?' she asked, wondering if he really considered it his home or whether it was simply one of a string of residences.

'About five years. I like it here.' He flashed her a smile before alighting from the driver's side. 'I hope you'll like it, too.'

It didn't matter if she liked it or not, Ivy told herself, watching him round the bonnet to the passenger side, his mouth still curved in pleasure at having achieved his aim with her. She had her own aim, which was simply to satisfy her curiosity. And then leave. It would be really stupid to be seduced into staying more than one night with him, by what he had in his house or anything else. But when he opened her door and she stood up beside him she found her body still shaken to the core by his physical impact on her. It took gritty determination to keep her wits.

'My car keys,' she said, holding out her hand.

He gave them to her as he closed the door. She locked the car with the remote-control button and put the keys in her handbag. 'Lead on,' she invited, trying to adopt a nonchalant air, desperately hoping her jelly-like legs would firm up enough to allow her to walk with dignity in the perilous high-fashion shoes.

They didn't. She took one wobbly try and sat down on the steps leading up to the portico. 'I'm taking off these killer shoes right now,' she declared, bending over to unbuckle the straps.

'Let me help.'

In an instant he was crouching down in front of her, his strong fingers brushing her fumbling ones aside. He propped her foot on his bent knee for easier access and Ivy leaned back and let him do the job—much easier than doing it herself. And she let herself enjoy the way he caressed her ankles and massaged her toes when he'd freed them from all constriction.

'Better?' he asked, the blue eyes twinkling satisfaction in his handiwork.

'Yes. Thank you. Sorry about discarding the model image, but barefoot is more me,' she said flippantly, not wanting him to know she was craving a lot more of his touch.

'I'm happy for you to be comfortable with me,' he purred, kicking her heart into pounding at the thought of how comfortable they might get together.

She picked up her shoes, placed her feet firmly on the wide stone step and stood up. Which brought her virtually face to face with him because he stood on a lower step. Their eyes met. Raw desire in his. Ivy had no idea what he saw in hers, probably the naked truth of what she was feeling because she'd had no time to disguise it.

Instinctively she scooped in a quick breath. Then he was kissing her again and she couldn't help kissing him back. Her arms flung themselves around his neck, shoes and bag dangling from her hands. His arms crushed her into a fiercely possessive embrace. Excitement surged. She felt his erection furrowing her stomach, felt the moist rush of her own wild anticipation to experience him again. Her lower body automatically squirmed against his.

One hard muscular thigh pushed past hers, stepping up. He started arching her back, stopped, wrenched his mouth from hers. 'Must be out of my mind!' he muttered, shaking his head as though to clear it. His eyes blazed fierce determination. 'Come on, Ivy. We're going to do this in bed. In comfort!'

She'd completely lost it! Twice in one night! Passion-crazed!

Without his arm around her in support, she doubted her legs would have carried her to the front door. He swept her into the house with him. She didn't have the presence of mind to notice any decor details of the foyer. She saw nothing but the staircase in front of them. When they reached it her foot didn't lift high enough at the first step and she stumbled. He caught her before she fell, hoisted her up against his heaving chest and charged up the flight of stairs so fast he had to be taking them two at a time. It was like being rocked in a speeding train.

Ivy didn't notice anything else.

They landed on a bed.

'And we're not going to do this in the dark!' Jordan said, still in that tone of fierce determination. He reached across her and switched on a bedside light, but all she saw was his face hovering above hers, the strong masculine lines of it, the incredibly sensual mouth, the vivid blue eyes burning with wicked purpose, the black hair she had mussed with her fingers, the spiky look giving him a devilish aura.

I'm a fallen woman, she thought dizzily, but couldn't

bring herself to care, only too acutely aware that her body was willing her to fall all the way with Jordan Powell tonight.

'Let's get rid of these clothes,' he said, taking her shoes and handbag and tossing them on the floor, then straddling her thighs as he worked on removing her sequinned jacket, cami, bra, half-lifting her up from the pillow, laying her back down.

It was easy to be passive, let him do it, silently revelling in the glide of his hands on her naked skin. She didn't want to talk, only to feel. The bed linens were not linen. They were satin. Black satin. As befitted a playboy, she thought, but enjoyed the decadent sensuality of it for this time out of time.

He moved aside to strip off her skirt and panties—quick, deft actions—then paused to softly rake his fingers through her pubic hair, staring down at it as though fascinated, making Ivy wonder if the women he was usually with all had Brazilian waxes. She'd never had it done, only a bikini wax, and that only for indoor swimming. The sun was her enemy.

If her natural state turned him off…

'Amazing,' he murmured, and bent over to brush his mouth over the tight red-gold curls.

Definitely not a turn-off.

And the hot kisses he planted there were a nerve-jumping turn-on for Ivy. His tongue slid into the crevice between her thighs and teased her clitoris with mind-blowing delicacy—a tantalising tasting that generated an exquisite level of pleasure. It was all she could do to hold still. She wanted to focus on it, remember it forever. She forgot to breathc. Her whole being was concentrated on what he was doing to her. When he lifted his head, the trapped air in her lungs gushed out in a long, tremulous sigh.

'Don't move!' he commanded, placing a staying hand on her stomach. 'I want to feast my eyes on you while I undress.'

Feast…

He'd made her desperately hungry for him.

'You look incredible!' he said, his eyes glittering with awed excitement as they roved over her. 'Your skin… the pale creamy sheen of it…like the sheen of perfect pearls. And the red-gold blaze of your hair…what a brilliant contrast! The black pillow underneath it makes it even more vivid. You're a living work of art, Ivy. More fantastic than anything I've seen in a gallery.'

His admiration completely wiped out any build-up of angst about being viewed naked. Not that she had been fretting over it. They'd gone too far too fast for it to be a factor. And her attention was now totally fixed on him, watching the emergence of his naked physique as he stripped off his clothes.

He truly was a magnificent male—his body in perfect proportion to his height, muscular enough to be beautifully masculine without looking like a gym junkie obsessed with weight-lifting. The darker tone of his olive skin gleamed with good health. The sprinkle of black hair across his chest arrowed down in a narrow line, provocatively pointing to the impressive evidence of his sexual arousal.

He certainly didn't disappoint on the physical front. Ivy's inner muscles quivered at the sight of him. Her hands itched to touch, her breasts yearned to feel his weight on her, her arms and legs buzzed in anticipation of curling around him, holding all that male power, feeling it. She had never known such compelling, urgent lust for a man.

But when he came to her, he caught her reaching hands and held them above her head. He lay beside her with one strong thigh slung across both of hers, locking them down. 'I want to taste all of you, Ivy,' he said, his hotly simmering gaze dropping to her breasts.

Her breath caught in her throat as he dipped his head and circled one aureole with his tongue, causing her nipple to harden further into a taut bullet. She closed her eyes and concentrated on the wild flow of sensations as he licked and sucked. He was so good at it, soft and slow, flicking, lashing, drawing her flesh into his mouth at just the right strength. It was so blissful, her back instinctively arched, inviting him to do more, take more.

She slithered her hands out of his grasp, wanting, needing to touch him, to stroke his hair, to glide her fingers over his back, to press him closer, imprint all of him on her memory. She felt his flesh flinch under her caresses and smiled, knowing he found it erotic, glad she excited him as much as he excited her.

'Can't wait,' he muttered, jerking up to change position, swiftly inserting his leg between hers.

At last, she thought exultantly, moving just as swiftly to accommodate him, to give him achingly ready access for the intimacy she craved. A wave of ecstatic satisfaction swept through her as he thrust inward, filling the yearning core of her need. She fiercely embraced him, her legs goading him into a hectic rhythm, harder, faster, deeper, revelling in the explosive action, feeling it drive her closer and closer to the exquisite splintering chaos of intense pleasure he had given hcr earlier tonight.

He took her there again.

With even more shattering intensity.

Ivy heard herself cry out at the incredible peak of tension before it broke, flooding her with a tsunami of sweet sensation. Some loud unintelligible sound broke from his throat, too, and he collapsed on top of her, breathing hard. She hugged him tightly, wallowing in the possessiveness of the moment, loving him for the gift of this marvellous experience.

He rolled onto his side, carrying her with him, hugging her just as tightly. Her head was tucked under his chin. He kissed her hair, rubbing his mouth over it as though he had to taste that, too. Ivy felt drained of all energy, yet beautifully replete. *A perfect feast,* she thought contentedly. It had been right to give in to temptation. She would never forget this as long as she lived.

He started stroking her back, lovely, long, skin-tingling caresses. She sighed with pleasure. He knew exactly how to touch a woman. She wished she could always have a lover like him. It was a pity a relationship with him wouldn't last, but Ivy was not about to fool herself on that score. She was a temporary episode in the life of Jordan Powell, and it was best for her to cut it short and not get too attached to him.

One night.

That was what she had decided.

It was a very sensible decision—one she would definitely keep.

'This time we are going to do it nice and slow, Ivy,' he said in a tone of determined purpose.

She smiled, wondering if it annoyed him that he hadn't managed to completely control the pace. She stirred herself enough to say, 'I liked it fine the way it was, but carry on as you like.'

If he wanted to do more, she was not about to object.

The night was still young.

She was happy to pack as much into it as he was capable of giving her.

CHAPTER SEVEN

IVY'S BODY-CLOCK WOKE her at six. It was her usual rising time at the farm. Still feeling tired from the night's unusual activities, she could have easily gone back to sleep, but looking at the man lying beside her—the absolutely yummy and extremely seductive man—she decided this was the time to leave, before he woke up and used his very persuasive powers on her to stay with him for the weekend.

Which would be terribly tempting.

However, she was half in love with him already. What woman wouldn't be after the night they had just spent together? Any longer with him would be getting in too deep and being dumped when he'd had his fill of her could hurt a lot. Better for her to do the dumping right now.

Her curiosity about him had certainly been satisfied. She hadn't seen much of the house he lived in but that was relatively unimportant. Her gaze roved quickly around the bedroom as she eased herself off the bed. Everything was black and white, like the en suite bathroom she had visited during the night.

There were two paintings on the walls she hadn't noticed before—both of them from Sydney Nolan's Ned Kelly series. It seemed a strange choice to have the legendary Australian bushranger on display in his bedroom. Ivy had imagined there'd be something more erotic—nude scenes or whatever—but the black frames and the famous black armour Ned Kelly had worn did suit the decor.

The thick white carpet muffled any sound her footsteps might have made on her way to the bathroom. Very quietly she closed the door and had a quick wash. A black silk wrap-around robe hung from a hook near the shower. She borrowed it to wear down to the car—easier than redressing in the sequinned stuff, which she could put in the trunk where her normal clothes for driving were stowed. A quick change into them and she would be on her way.

Jordan was still sound asleep as she swept up her high-fashion gear and underclothes from the floor. Having crept out of the bedroom and closed the door on the scene of her surrender to temptation, she found herself on an inside balcony overlooking the foyer. It was easy to spot the staircase. She was bolting down it when a woman emerged from a room to the left of the foyer—smallish, grey-haired, wearing a white uniform.

They both halted in surprise at seeing each other.

The woman looked Ivy up and down, the expression on her face clearly saying, Here's a new one.

It had to be the housekeeper, Ivy thought, trying to fight a hot tide of embarrassment.

'Good morning,' the woman said. 'I'm Margaret Partridge, Jordan's cook and housekeeper. You can call me Margaret. We don't stand on ceremony here.'

'Hello,' Ivy blurted out, grateful for the matter-of-fact tone of the other woman's greeting though her heart was still thumping madly over being discovered in the act of doing a runner. 'I'm Ivy…Ivy Thornton. I…uh…need to get some day clothes out of my car.'

'I'll unlock the front door for you,' Margaret said obligingly, moving to do so. 'I was just on my way to the kitchen. Would you like a cup of coffee? Jordan rarely rises before nine on a Saturday morning so there's no need to hurry over anything.'

'Thank you, but I won't wait. I have to get home,' Ivy explained in a rush, quickly resuming her descent to the foyer.

Margaret's eyebrows lifted quizzically. It was probably something else new to have one of Jordan Powell's women leave his bed before he did. Ivy was superconscious of the housekeeper's firsthand knowledge of her employer's affairs. The flush she hadn't been able to stop was burning fiercely on her cheeks as she walked briskly to the opened front door.

'I'm happy to cook you breakfast before you set off,' Margaret offered, obviously curious about her.

'That's very kind.' Ivy managed a polite smile. 'But it's only an hour's drive. I'll eat at home.'

'You should have coffee before you go. It will perk you up for the drive. I'll make it while you dress and have it ready for you in the kitchen.'

The uncritical manner of the housekeeper did ease some of Ivy's embarrassment. Nevertheless, while there might be no danger of Jordan waking up any time soon, the situation was too uncomfortable for her to delay her departure any longer than she had to.

'You probably don't know where the kitchen is,' Margaret ran on. 'Last door on your right at the back of the foyer leads into the breakfast room. You walk through it to the kitchen. And there's a powder room under the staircase where you can change if you don't want to go back upstairs.'

'Right! Thank you,' Ivy said firmly, not committing herself to anything though she welcomed the information about the powder room. The handyman/chauffeur might be roaming around outside the house.

'There's no need to hurry,' Margaret repeated, apparently sensing Ivy's urge to bolt and wanting to reassure her that time wasn't a problem.

Which might be true, but Ivy still didn't want to risk having a clean escape foiled.

The housekeeper left the front door open for her. Ivy made a quick trip to her car, unlocked the trunk, dumped the clothes she was carrying, grabbed the blue jeans, white top and flat navy sandals, and was back inside the house with the door closed within a few minutes. The powder room was smaller than Jordan's en suite bathroom but just as classy in grey and white and silver. Having dressed in her casual clothes and plaited the messy cloud of her hair, she looked for a hook to hang the black robe on. There wasn't one. After dithering for several moments, she folded it up neatly and placed it on the vanity bench.

The seductive aroma of freshly brewed coffee hit her as she stepped out of the powder room. Again she dithered, aware it would be very rude to the helpful housekeeper to simply walk out without acknowledging her efforts to please. It was also very ill-mannered not to thank Jordan for the pleasure he had given her last night. Being dumped without a word was really quite nasty.

Deciding to risk staying a couple of more minutes, she followed Margaret's directions to the breakfast room, which had such a fantastic view it momentarily stopped her. Beyond a wall of glass, a tiled patio surrounded a glorious blue swimming pool. Past that was the harbour, sparkling in the early-morning sunshine and already busy with water traffic.

Her gaze quickly swivelled around to take in the whole room. White tiles on the floor were largely covered by a beautiful thick rug in shades of blue and aqua. On this stood a glass-topped table surrounded by white leather chairs. Two Pro Hart paintings dominated the back wall—bushland scenes with vivid blue skies. This was how a billionaire enjoyed breakfast, she thought, pushing herself on to the kitchen.

It, also, was predominantly white and with the same view as the breakfast room. A quick glance around from the doorway revealed an extremely professional set-up with top-of-the-range appliances which would have seduced a master chef—a dream working area for any cook.

The housekeeper was pouring freshly brewed coffee into a mug. She smiled a welcome at Ivy and waved her to the stools on one side of an island bench. 'Milk? Cream? Sugar?' she inquired.

'Please excuse me. I can't stay. I must get home,' Ivy said firmly. 'I've left Jordan's robe in the powder room. I hope you won't mind returning it for me.'

'Is there some emergency?' Margaret cut in with a frown of concern.

'I just have to go,' Ivy replied, not wanting to be drawn into conversation. 'I'd be grateful if you'd tell Jordan from me…thank you for the lovely night.'

Margaret nodded slowly. 'All right. I'll pass that on.'

Ivy flashed a smile of relief. 'Thanks again for everything. Bye now.'

A quick wave of her hand and she was on her way out of Jordan Powell's life, satisfied she had left with some grace.

Jordan was conscious of a sweet sense of well-being as he drifted up from sleep. Memory clicked in. Ivy. He opened his eyes, his mouth already curving into a smile. It was a jolt to find her gone from his bed, a further jolt to see her clothes were no longer on the floor. He darted a glance at the clock—8:27 a.m.

Maybe she was an early riser. People who worked on farms usually were. Margaret was always up early, too. Possibly she was giving Ivy breakfast. Feeling an urgent need to check, Jordan hurtled off the bed and strode to the bathroom.

His black robe was not on its peg.

It brought the smile back to his face.

Ivy would look very fetching in it with her glorious hair.

Feeling more confident of her presence in his home, Jordan had a quick shower, shaved, grabbed another black robe from his dressing room and went downstairs with a bounce of happy anticipation in his step. He actually grinned as he wondered what Margaret thought of Ivy—very different to his usual run of dates, and both women were quite direct in saying what was on their minds, nothing evasive or deceptive about either of them.

No one in the breakfast room.

Jordan frowned as he strode through it, not hearing any conversation coming from the kitchen and the door to it was open. He found Margaret sitting at the island bench—alone—sipping a mug of coffee.

'Where's Ivy?' he snapped.

Margaret viewed him with sharp interest as she delivered her answer. 'Gone. And you needn't speak to me in that tone of voice, Jordan. I did try to keep her here. Offered her breakfast. Pressed her to have a cup of coffee, but she wouldn't have it. Nothing was going to make her stay. She was determined to leave.'

'Did she tell you why?' he shot at her, his mind too fraught with disappointment to monitor his voice tone.

'No. But she did ask me to thank you for the lovely night. I must say she had beautiful manners, unlike some of the other women you've dated.'

Jordan burned with frustration. Never had a woman left him before he wanted her to, and for it to be Ivy… no, he could not, would not respect her decision to reject what they could have together. She had been with him all the way last night, and *lovely* fell far short of what had happened between them.

A hard, cynical thought flashed into his mind. Was this some deliberate move to test how keen he was to have her in his life? A clever power game? Being the only one who didn't throw herself at him had worked to hold his interest last night. Running off might be the goad for him to give chase.

A billionaire would be a great catch for a farm girl.

Except the billionaire had no intention of being caught.

But he did want more of Ivy Thornton. A lot more. And he could not believe she didn't want more of him. So he would give chase, ensuring their connection would only end when *he* wanted it to end.

'Did she tell you where she was going?'

'Home.'

He grimaced with impatience at the short reply. 'Can

you be more specific, Margaret? I know Ivy works on a farm, but I don't know its location.'

'An hour's drive from here, she said.'

He threw up his hands. 'Too vague!'

'Sorry. I can't help on that point. If you want my opinion, I think she was deeply embarrassed at being found in your home and couldn't get out fast enough. Very different to others I might mention who were positively smug about being here with you. And since she didn't give you any contact details, it doesn't look like she wants you to pursue her.'

He frowned. Maybe this wasn't a calculated move. Margaret was very good at reading character. Possibly Ivy was shocked at herself. He'd taken advantage of her shock last night, sweeping her along with him. But she'd been fine in his bed. Fantastic in his bed! However, if she wasn't used to having sex with a man on a first date...was she ashamed of herself for crossing some moral standard?

Which might mean...oh, hell! If she was a *good girl,* not on any contraceptive pill...he'd totally ignored that issue last night, deciding to deal with it later. If taking that risk had hit her this morning...if there was a very real possibility she had fallen pregnant...she might have been overwhelmed by a sense of panic.

'I have to find her, Margaret.' He started tramping around the kitchen, raking his hair in agitation. 'I have to!' It wasn't just the pregnancy question, he couldn't tolerate the idea of never seeing Ivy again, never having her again.

'Not that it's any of my business,' Margaret said with an air of making it hers this once. 'But it's my observation that you're not into having serious relationships with women, Jordan, and Ivy Thornton didn't strike me as a sophisticated playgirl. It might be a kindness to respect her decision and let her go. Simply write her off as the one that got away.'

'No! No!' The emphatic negatives exploded off his tongue. He glared at Margaret, who looked stunned by the explosiveness of his reaction. 'I can't!' he added decisively, not wanting to explain why. 'I have to find her,' he repeated in teeth-gritting determination.

'And then what?' Margaret asked, critical brown eyes putting him on the spot, holding judgement on his motives.

Ruthless purpose swept straight past the uncertainties in his mind. 'Then she can tell me to my face that she doesn't want anything more to do with me.'

Ivy wouldn't be able to do it, not with any honesty.

'Fair enough,' Margaret conceded. 'What would you like for breakfast this morning?'

She slid off her stool, ready to get down to business.

Jordan was infuriated by her matter-of-fact dismissal of his intense frustration with the situation. And breakfast was the last thing he wanted to consider right now. He shook a finger at her and fiercely declared, 'Ivy Thornton is not going to be the one who got away!'

Margaret stopped and stared at him as though he'd suddenly metamorphosed into a stranger. 'Sorry if I spoke out of turn,' she said with uncharacteristic meekness. 'It was just...I liked her, Jordan. And I wouldn't like it if you hunted her down and hurt her.'

'I have no intention of hurting her.'

Margaret pressed her lips together, buttoning up against offending him with any further comment, but her eyes definitely challenged him to keep that stated intention. He would be the lesser man in her estimation if he didn't.

Ivy had clearly made a more strongly positive impression on her than any of the other women he'd brought here.

'I like her, too, Margaret,' he said more quietly. 'Very much.'

She nodded, still tight-lipped.

He sighed.

Battle lines were drawn.

He now had to win over Ivy—and make her happy to be with him—in order to win over Margaret or he'd be getting burnt breakfasts. Possibly even worse! She might walk out on him, too!

A burst of adrenaline raised his fighting instincts.

Jordan was not a man to back down from a challenge.

One way or another, he'd have what he wanted!

CHAPTER EIGHT

IVY kept telling herself she'd been absolutely right to get out of Jordan Powell's life, but her body was still fired up by the memory of him, and it was quite impossible to get him out of her head. Being home on the farm didn't really help. She couldn't stop imagining how it might have been if she'd spent the weekend with him in his beautiful Balmoral home.

It was a hot morning and shaping up to be an even hotter day. A quick dip in his gorgeous swimming pool would have been lovely, not to mention…

The ringing of the telephone was a welcome distraction. She dived on the receiver, hoping the caller would ground her in real life again. No such luck! It was her mother, who instantly recalled everything about last night.

'Ivy, I've just had Jordan Powell on the line.'

Her heart kicked into overdrive. 'What did he want?' she asked, her voice uncharacteristically shrill. With fear or excitement?

'Well, I thought it was rather odd. You did go out with him last night and you looked as though you were enjoying his company, but since you obviously didn't give him your address…was that an oversight, dear, or don't you want to see him again?'

A bomb of anxiety exploded in her mind. 'Did you tell him where I lived?'

'No. He was very charming. Always is. But I thought I'd better check with you first.'

Relief poured through Ivy. She didn't have to face Jordan again, didn't have to battle against her attraction to him. Her decision to leave had definitely been right and it was much easier to hold on to it from a distance. This call proved how shaky her resolution could be, given his immediate presence.

'I'm glad you did,' she said in a calmer tone. 'He's not for me. Good for a night out, but I'd rather leave it there.'

'Are you sure, dear?'

'I'm sure. Thank you for protecting my privacy. I really appreciate it. And congratulations on the show. Lots of sales last night.'

'Yes. Very gratifying. And it was lovely to see you looking so stunning, Ivy. Living right up to your full potential. I felt so proud of you.'

It was a nice feeling to have pleased her mother. Ivy relaxed enough to smile as she remarked, 'Well, I didn't want to let you down again and it felt really good when Henry's jaw dropped at seeing me. He's such a snob!'

'But he's very adept at wooing the right crowd at his gallery, dear, bringing in people with the money to buy. It's a pity I have to disappoint a good client like Jordan Powell...' She sighed. 'Are you absolutely certain you wouldn't like to see him again, Ivy?'

'Yes, I am. I don't fit into his kind of life and he wouldn't fit into mine. End of story,' she said emphatically, ignoring the flutters in her stomach and forcefully remembering the way Jordan's housekeeper had checked her over—the latest candidate for her employer's bed.

'Well, in that case, my lips are sealed. Such a shame!' Sacha muttered and disconnected.

By Monday morning Ivy was more settled into the idea that her night with Jordan was a one-off experience which she could look back on with pleasure and no regrets. Heather, of course, wanted to know everything, the moment she swept into the office.

'Did he zero in on you?'

'Yes, he did,' Ivy answered, and even managed to smile at her friend's whoop of triumphant excitement.

'Tell me all!' Heather demanded.

Ivy confessed that she had succumbed to the temptation of enjoying Jordan's company at the gallery and described the follow-up dinner date in great detail, much to Heather's salacious enjoyment.

'And then? Did you go and look at his paintings?'

'Some of them,' Ivy teased. No way was she going to confide what actually led to the trip to Balmoral! Some things were too intensely private.

'If you came straight home after that, I'll kill you!' Heather ranted. 'I want to know if he's a fantastic lover.'

Ivy laughed, needing to keep the whole episode light and unimportant. 'He is. I'd have to say he's very, very good at sex. I'm glad I stayed the night.'

'Only the one night?'

'That was enough, Heather. You know he's a playboy. I left while he was still asleep and ran into his housekeeper on my way out. If you'd seen the way she looked at me...'

'Another notch on his bedpost?' Heather interpreted with a sympathetic grimace.

'It didn't feel good. I was glad I skipped out when I did.'

'Fair enough!' Heather grinned. 'Marvellous that he

was great in bed, though. I think you needed to be taken down from the shelf and dusted off. Hopefully it will get you more interested in looking for some real action in your life.'

'I shall hope for it,' Ivy replied, grateful that Heather had already relegated the experience with Jordan Powell to the realm of fantasy. Where it belonged. 'Now let's get down to work.'

Occasionally, throughout the day, Heather questioned her further, but it was mainly curiosity about the Balmoral house, what Ivy had seen of it, nothing really personal. Orders for roses came in. The courier was loaded up and sent to the designated addresses. By late afternoon, Ivy was satisfied that her brief encounter with Jordan Powell had been dealt with and would quickly slip into the past. A memory. Nothing more.

Until he struck again!

'Uh-oh!' Heather muttered and swung her computer chair around to face Ivy, rolling her eyes for dramatic effect. 'You're not going to like this!'

'What?'

'Jordan Powell is ordering roses and double chocolate fudge to go to your mother.'

'My mother!'

'With a message attached. For you, Ivy.'

For one gut-twisting moment, she thought he knew the rose farm was hers.

'It says... "Please tell Ivy..."'

No, he was still trying to get to her through her mother!

The relief was so intense she didn't hear what the message was.

'Say that again, Heather?'

'"Please tell Ivy I need to talk to her. I'll be at the

Bacio Coffee Shop under the clock in the Queen Victoria building between noon and two o'clock on Saturday and Sunday. I'll wait until she comes."'

He wanted a face-to-face meeting, counting on his charm to win her over to what *he* wanted. She wasn't going to risk it. No way! She might fall victim to it again.

'What do you want me to do?' Heather asked.

'Put the order through. It's business as usual. I'll speak to my mother about it.'

'Okay.'

But it wasn't *okay*. The same order came through on Tuesday and Wednesday and Thursday and Friday, constantly reminding Ivy of the man.

'Maybe you should go and talk to him,' Heather said as she was leaving on Friday.

'No!' Ivy answered firmly.

But her weekend was totally wrecked, thinking about him waiting for her, wondering if he had something to say she would actually want to hear. Which was ridiculous, given his track record with women.

He didn't give up.

The order was repeated on Monday and every day of the next week. Her mother complained she was drowning in roses and putting on weight with all the double chocolate fudge.

'You don't have to eat it,' Ivy cried in sheer frustration with Jordan's determined campaign. 'Give it away. Give the roses away.'

'I don't see why you can't go and talk to him,' her mother argued. 'It's not as if he's asking you to come into his parlour, Ivy. It's a public place. You can walk away any time you like.'

'I don't want to see him. Full stop.'

However, her refusal to meet Jordan did not stop him.

Her mother was inundated with roses and fudge for the third week running. Even Heather, with all her Rose Valentino knowledge, started doubting Ivy's decision.

'You must have made a big impact on him, Ivy. To be this persistent…and waiting two hours at a coffee shop for you to turn up…' She frowned and shook her head. 'I don't think a dilettante would do that.' Her eyes gathered a look of fantastic possibilities as she added, 'What if it's a serious attraction? Maybe you should give it a chance. You did say he was a great lover.'

'How could it work between us? I'm here. He's there,' Ivy pointed out with considerable vehemence, needing to hang on to common sense.

'Distance wouldn't be a problem for a billionaire. He probably owns a helicopter.'

'I bet it's no more than an ego thing and I'm not giving in to it,' Ivy declared with fierce determination.

Heather said no more, keeping her thoughts to herself, but Ivy could see the glint of pro-Jordan speculation in her eyes as the orders continued through the fourth week. Which was downright persecution!

Heather no longer supported her stance.

Her mother was ranting and raving.

On the fourth Saturday morning after Ivy had walked out of Jordan Powell's life, she decided she had to meet him and give him a piece of her mind—an angry, outraged, totally damning piece which would rock him back on his billionaire-playboy socks and make him leave her alone!

She braided her hair back into one thick plait, minimising its impact. Blue jeans, a royal-blue T-shirt and navy sandals helped give her a fairly nondescript appearance. Without any make-up she was satisfied that

Jordan would not find her particularly attractive today. It had to be impressed upon him that he was wasting his time with her.

She drove to Sydney and used the parking station under the Queen Victoria Building, which was expensive but handy for a quick getaway. The big clock inside the shopping mall was showing ten minutes past midday as she kept herself inconspicuous amongst the crowd of shoppers passing by the tables belonging to the Bacio Coffee Shop. They were set out in open view, most of them occupied by people wanting a lunch break.

Her heart kicked into a gallop when she spotted Jordan at one of them, a pen in hand, apparently working on a crossword in the newspaper spread out on his table. He wasn't looking out for her, but he was there all right, all set up to wait patiently for her arrival. The relentless pressure for this meeting sent a bolt of panic through Ivy, quickening her pace as she walked straight past where he was sitting, too agitated by the sight of him to be in control of this encounter. Her righteous anger had just been swallowed up by a scary sense of vulnerability.

She stopped at a safe distance and turned to watch him surreptitiously. The back view of him was not so nerve-joltingly handsome, but it was impossible to set aside the fact she had gone to bed with this man, knew his body intimately, had run her fingers through his thick black hair, nestled her face contentedly into the curve of his neck and shoulder—sharp memories raising a terribly acute sexual awareness, both of him and herself. The moment she looked into his bedroom-blue eyes she would see them there, too, and how was she going to ignore or dismiss that once she sat down with him?

Ivy dithered, the need to stop Jordan from inserting himself into her life losing all its furious momentum in the power of his presence. She saw other women glancing at him from nearby tables, probably wishing they could catch his attention. Even though he seemed oblivious of their interest, he still had the charismatic magnetism to draw theirs. It kept tugging at her, too. Coming here had been a mistake—a big mistake.

He would stop sending the roses eventually.

She didn't have to say or do anything.

Except tear her gaze away from him and go back home.

So go, she told herself, but before she could bring herself to act, Jordan's head jerked up as though reacting to something. He rose swiftly to his feet, turned, shooting a questioning gaze around his vicinity. Ivy froze, couldn't move a muscle, the certainty of no escape now seizing her mind, making another encounter with him inevitable.

He saw her. The smile that instantly spread across his face turned her insides to mush. It wasn't a smile of triumph, more one of sparkling pleasure, inviting her to share it—share all the things that had pleasured them both. He lifted a hand in an open gesture of welcome, encouraging her to join him at his table.

Her heart started pumping again. Hard. She wondered if he would chase her if she turned and ran. But there was no dignity in that. Besides, she wasn't sure her wobbly legs were capable of racing anywhere. Somehow she had to firm up her mind—as well as the rest of her body—and directly address the situation with Jordan Powell.

She concentrated on forcing her feet forward and putting a glowering expression of reproach on her face, smiting his treacherous smile as she made her way to his table. He held out a chair for her. She sat down. He quickly folded the newspaper and slipped it under his chair as he resumed his seat, the blue eyes more serious now, appealing for her patience.

'It's good to see you, Ivy,' he rolled out in his deep, sexy voice.

'I only came to stop you from pestering my mother,' she declared, keeping her face tight with disapproval.

He leaned forward, elbows on the table, speaking with quiet urgency. 'I had to talk to you. The night we spent together...I didn't use any protection and I didn't ask if you were on the pill. I've been worried that you might have fallen pregnant.'

'Oh!' Her chest loosened up as her lungs expelled a gush of air in a sigh of relief. This was reasonable. It wasn't a mad pursuit of her. In fact, it was really nice of him to care about serious consequences from their mutual recklessness. 'It's okay,' she assured him. 'That was a safe time for me. You don't have to worry any more.'

'A safe time?' he queried, frowning as though he didn't quite understand.

'In my monthly cycle,' she explained.

'You don't normally use any contraceptive device?'

He sounded incredulous, as though any woman in her right mind shouldn't be protecting herself against *accidents*. Undoubtedly the women he mixed with did.

She leaned forward to make her position very plain, flushing with the violence of her feelings on his fly-by-night attitude. 'I told you I wasn't your type. I told you I wouldn't fit into your scene. I don't do sex on a casual basis and I haven't been in a relationship for over two years so I have no reason to be always ready.'

'Ah!' A smile of satisfaction tugged at the corners of his mouth. 'Then I'm glad you found me as irresistible as I found you. Which is the second thing I want to talk to you about.'

Ivy rolled her eyes and sagged back in her chair, feeling under attack again. 'Haven't I made my point, Jordan?' she cried in exasperation.

'No. Because it's based on assumptions about me which I don't think are fair,' he argued.

They weren't assumptions. His orders to the rose farm provided hard evidence of how he conducted his sexual affairs. However, she couldn't lay that out to him without revealing how she had such inside knowledge and she didn't want to give him any more information about herself. 'You're a notorious playboy,' she said accusingly, folding her arms in defensive belligerence.

He grimaced. 'Because of what I am, who I am, a lot of women throw themselves at me, Ivy. I wouldn't be human if I didn't find some of them attractive. Unlike you, they're intent on making themselves attractive to me, but the effort wears thin after a while. Their real selves emerge.' He shook his head as he ruefully added, 'And it's never what I want.'

'What do you want?' she asked, privately conceding what he said could be true. A handsome billionaire would be a target for most women.

The blue eyes burned into hers. 'Honesty,' he said, which he'd previously told her was the rarest commodity in his world.

Maybe it was. The more Ivy thought about it, the more she could see this could be a real downside in being obscenely wealthy...people cosying up to him for what they could get out of being close to big money. She didn't need what he had. Being happy in her own world, she didn't covet his kind of life at all. The only thing missing for her was…a loving husband, family, a shared future.

She couldn't see Jordan Powell in that picture.

Though she certainly wouldn't mind sharing her bed with him.

No denying that.

Her entire body was humming with tempting memories and sympathy for his situation with other women was sneaking into her heart, undermining her resistance to the strong attraction of the man.

'Well, I want honesty, too, Jordan,' she said, struggling to maintain a defensive line. 'Why don't you admit I was nothing more than an amusing challenge to you on the night of my mother's exhibition? Someone different to play with. And you simply didn't like it when I finished the game before you did.'

'Not a game, Ivy.' He shook his head over her choice of words. His mouth quirked ironically. 'A game doesn't spin out of control as that night did.'

The trunk of the car…the front steps of his house… her vaginal muscles contracted sharply at the pointed recollection of control being totally lost.

'That has never happened to me before,' he added quietly. 'Which does make you different, Ivy. Not in an amusing sense. In a very unique sense. And you've just told me it was extraordinary for you, too. So I don't think we should walk away from it. I think it's something we should explore a lot further. Together. With honesty. No game-playing.'

There was no trace of glib charm in his voice, no seductive twinkle in the blue eyes boring into hers. He looked completely serious, sincere, emitting a forceful energy that silently attacked and demolished any argument against what he was proposing.

Ivy suddenly found herself thinking of her parents. They'd led separate lives for as long as she could remember, but they'd never divorced and had always shared a bedroom when they'd spent weekends together. They'd each pursued their own interests, respecting the needs that drove them to take different paths while still maintaining an affectionate bond.

It wasn't what she wanted for herself.

But what if there was nothing better?

Never would be anything better.

She stared at Jordan Powell and knew she wanted more of him. Whatever that meant…wherever it led… she did want to explore how much they could have together.

CHAPTER NINE

JORDAN concentrated fiercely on willing Ivy to agree. The idea that she had been playing a power game with him had been whittled away by the sheer length of time it had taken her to respond to his message. Her attitude today—everything about her—indicated that inspiring a chase had not been the intent behind absenting herself from his life. She was fighting the attraction between them with all her willpower.

Or was all this a clever act, designed to draw him more firmly into her female net?

She *had* turned up.

And was forcing him to argue for a chance with her.

Throw out the challenge...hook the man like he'd never been hooked before!

Her fascinating green eyes had savaged him, mocked him, transmitted hard unyielding judgement, but now they were strangely blank, focussed inward, giving no sign of what she was thinking.

He couldn't deny his many affairs—most of them very short-lived. Ivy had plenty of reason to believe she would be no more than a brief addition to the long list. It could actually turn out that way. He wasn't about to promise it wouldn't. How could he know, at this stage, how long the attraction would last, whether familiarity would eventually breed contempt, as it so often had with other women?

All he knew was his gut was in knots, waiting for her reply. And that hadn't happened before. None of it had…sensing her presence before he even saw her, the mule-kick to his heart when his instincts had proved correct, the intense flare of desire which owed nothing to her outward appearance which was obviously meant to express lack of interest in him.

He *was* hooked.

But that didn't mean he was caught.

The instant zing between them told him she wasn't immune to what they had shared. He had to tap into that again, make her want what he wanted. Regardless of what was going on in her mind, Jordan was determined on drawing her into *his* net. Even more so now that she was here with him.

'Would you like a cup of coffee while you think about it?' he asked, intent on forcing her into active communication.

The blank shield on her eyes snapped open to reveal deep wells of vulnerability—a host of fears swirling through wishful possibilities. 'Yes,' she said huskily, sucking in a quick breath to firm up her voice. 'Cappucino, please.'

He signalled a waitress, ordered two coffees and a plate of toasted sandwiches to tempt Ivy into eating. There was nothing like sharing food to put people more at ease with their company, and it seemed—from the wildly swimming look in her eyes—that Ivy was wound up in an emotional dilemma about becoming more involved with him.

Unless she was a brilliant actress.

He was reminded of what Margaret had said...*I wouldn't like it if you hunted her down and hurt her.*

He had hunted her, with good reason, Jordan told himself. Nevertheless, being hurt by him could be high on the list of fears in Ivy's mind. A playboy...

To him it was a pragmatic lifestyle, given his circumstances. He was quite happy going along for a ride, hated the idea of being taken for one. He was beginning to think this was a different situation with Ivy, more a journey of discovery than the usual ride.

Her lashes had swept down, hiding her thoughts again. He leaned forward, pressing for her attention. 'Ivy, you're not a trophy woman to me.'

The green eyes flashed wildly amused sparks at him as she burst into a peal of laughter. 'Anyone seeing us together today would think you had rocks in your head to consider me one, Jordan.'

He relaxed into a laugh himself. 'Which proves my point. I want your company, regardless of trappings.'

'Mmmh...' She cocked her head consideringly. 'I'd have to say I enjoyed your company, too. Though I'm not sure how well that would wear over time. I don't think we have much in common.'

Oh, yes they did! Fantastic sex together. Unforgettably fantastic!

Maybe she read that thought in his eyes. A tide of heat whooshed up her neck and burned her cheeks. She wriggled in her chair, probably discomforted by an attack of hormones charged-up with the same memories he had. He had to shift a bit himself to accommodate his own charged up anatomy. If they weren't in a public place... but the sex hadn't kept her with him last time. He had to make more inroads into her psyche.

He tried a disarming smile. 'I like it that you don't see *me* as a trophy.'

That was a good, testing line.

She shot it down in flames, instantly firing derision at it. 'Too tarnished by a lot of careless wear.'

'I care about you,' he shot back at her, throwing all cynical caution aside. 'We have something special going between us. Too special to dismiss. I've never waited for a woman as I've waited for you. And don't tell me you don't feel it, too, because you do, Ivy. This is *us* and it's not like anything in the past. Face it. Give it a chance. It might be the best thing either of us could ever have.'

A chance…

Yes.

Ivy's whole body yearned to feel again the pleasure he could give her and the intensity he was transmitting made his arguments too persuasive for her to fight any further. It *had* been special. Unique for her as well as him. Of course there was no guarantee it would last but what guarantee could be attached to any relationship these days?

'How do you see it working?' she blurted out.

He leaned forward eagerly. 'We could start with weekends. This weekend.'

Her heart instantly kicked into a gallop. She hadn't come ready for this. 'I didn't bring anything with me. And I'm still not on the pill.'

'You don't need anything. I don't want to share you with anyone. Not today or tomorrow. And I'll take care of protection while you're arranging your own.'

Panic seized her. This decision felt too rushed. 'You forgot last time.'

'I promise you, I won't forget again.'

No, he wouldn't, not after being worried about getting her pregnant. Having a child with her was not on his agenda. It might never be. She had to think of this as a trial period and not get too…too…stuck on him. He'd been a playboy for so long, it was best if she didn't let herself believe their affair might turn out any different to his previous relationships. All she was committing herself to was giving it a chance.

She eyed him with fierce intensity. 'Don't send me any roses. Ever!'

'Sending them to your mother did bring us back together. It got the right result, Ivy,' he reminded her seriously.

'I don't mean *them!*' she said in emphatic dismissal. 'I mean the roses you send as a matter of rote to all the women who have held your interest for a while.'

He frowned, puzzled by her knowledge of intimate details of his past affairs.

Ivy gritted her teeth and revealed the truth. 'You order them from me, Jordan. It's my rose farm you deal with over the Internet. From this moment on, I'm writing you off as a client. When it's over with me and you find someone else, find yourself another rose source. Okay?'

He looked totally gobsmacked.

Ivy didn't care. Involving herself with Jordan meant there was no way of continuing to hide her business and she simply couldn't bear the idea of him resuming his Rose Valentino modus operandi with other women in the future. Not through her farm anyway.

The waitress arrived at their table with their coffees and the plate of toasted sandwiches. Ivy was too churned up to eat anything but she was grateful for the coffee. It was hot and sweet and strong and her shredded nerves needed soothing. She sipped it, covertly watching Jordan gradually recover from his shock and wondering how he would react to her revelation.

It was actually a good test of his feelings towards her. He wanted honesty. She'd just laid it out to him. He didn't reach for a sandwich or his coffee. He sat completely still, eyes lowered, a pensive expression on his face, probably reflecting on how much business he'd done with her farm over the years.

'I see,' he finally murmured, an ironic tilt to his perfectly sculptured mouth. Twin blue laser beams targeted Ivy's eyes. 'I now understand how sceptical you must have been over my intentions and how reluctant you still are to get involved with me. But you're here thinking about it, and I'm here fighting for a chance with you because we connected so strongly we'd always wonder what might have been if we didn't pursue it. That's the truth of it, isn't it, Ivy? The honest truth.'

'For me, yes,' she answered, her own mouth quirking with irony as she added, 'Where you're concerned, it requires a leap of faith I'm not sure I can make.'

He nodded. 'Make it. Take the risk. It's worth a try.' He flashed her a dazzling smile. 'Remember how good it was. Think how good it can be again.'

She hoped it would be, because the decision was already made. The buzz of anticipation was in her blood and she was no longer physically capable of backing away from this man.

He made a flip-flop gesture, unsure of where she was at. 'You can always end it if I let you down.'

She smiled, her eyes mocking the off-hand offer. 'I don't think you're too good at accepting an end you don't want, Jordan. My mother can testify to that.'

'But I hadn't let you down, Ivy,' he reminded her. 'You just assumed I would. Let's be fair now.'

She laughed, giddy with the sense of taking an even more dangerous step with this man. 'Okay. I promise I'll be fair.'

One black eyebrow arched in appeal. 'No harking back to my past?'

'I'll take you as I find you until you do let me down.'

'Done!' His hand smacked down on the table in triumphant satisfaction as he rose from his chair, emitting an electric energy that sent Ivy's pulse zooming into overdrive. 'Take me to wherever you've parked your car,' he commanded, his eyes blazing with the desire to move her with him to a far less public place.

The car...images of wild sex bloomed in Ivy's mind, flustering her into a hot flush. She waved at the plate of sandwiches in a rush of agitation. 'What about this?'

'Not what I'm hungry for. Are you?'

'No.' Impossible to eat anything with lustful thoughts running riot and there was no point in delaying what she'd decided to do. 'You haven't paid,' she said, trying to sound in some control of herself as she pushed up from her chair.

He took out his wallet, removed a fifty-dollar note, anchored it on the table under the sugar bowl, then reached for her hand. She gave it to him, consciously feeling every sensation of his touch: the power of the fingers entwining hers, the tingling pleasure from the rub of his flesh, the seductive caress of his thumb. Why he, of all men, could evoke this acute sexual excitement in her, she didn't know, but strangely enough it was a relief to simply surrender to it.

'The elevator,' she directed. 'Level two of the basement car park.'

They walked together, moving like an arrow of purpose that could not be diverted. The crowd of shoppers milled around them, no one blocking their path even minimally. Ivy was barely aware of other people. The connection to the man beside her virtually obliterated everything else.

Worries wormed their way through her mind. Had she given in too easily? Was she a fool for giving in at all? Were there other things she could have said, should have said before letting him lead her back into his life? Was there any real possibility of a relationship with Jordan developing into something solid?

Yet…did any of that matter when he could make her feel like this?

They reached the elevator just as its doors opened. A family—mother, father, child in a pram—stepped out, an ordinary family, what Ivy had hoped to have herself. Nothing with Jordan was going to be ordinary. Was she totally mad to involve herself with him?

They moved into the elevator. No one followed them. Jordan pressed the button for L2. The doors closed. They were alone together in the small compartment. Jordan erupted into action, scooping her into his embrace, kissing her with a hunger that found an instant, overwhelming response. Weeks—a whole month of repression burst under a wild surge of need to taste him again, feel him again, have him stoke the excitement that made everything else irrelevant.

Their mouths meshed in feverish passion. Their hands seized, travelled, pressed, dragged, dug in, feeding the fierce desire to take possession. They were so immersed in each other, they didn't notice the elevator coming to a halt, its doors sliding open.

'Sorry to interrupt you guys, but…'

The voice brought them back to earth with a heart-thumping shock.

'Right,' Jordan muttered, and swept Ivy past the amused onlooker into the cavernous car park.

Her legs were wobbly. She tried to catch a breath, get her wits in order, orientate herself enough to find her car. 'Where's yours?' she asked.

'My what?'

He looked as distracted as she felt. 'Your car.'

He shook his head. 'Didn't bring one. Had Ray drop me off.'

'Who's Ray?'

He stopped, sucked in a deep breath, obviously regathering himself as he turned to face her, lightly grasping her upper arms, the blue eyes boring into hers, his voice gruff with emotion. 'Are you okay, Ivy? You're not about to do another runner on me?'

'No.' Tearing herself away from him now was unthinkable. She wanted him too much. When or if he let her down…somehow she would deal with the fallout. Until then…she summoned up a shaky smile. 'Though let's not lose our heads again. At least, not here.'

His smile poured out relief and reassurance. 'I can wait a bit longer. And to answer your question, Ray is my handyman and he'll drive in to pick me up at two o'clock if not instructed otherwise. We can be home before he leaves if we go in your car.'

'Okay.' She opened her shoulder-bag to get out the keys. 'It's probably better if you drive. You're more familiar with the route to Balmoral.' Besides which, it was doubtful she could concentrate on the road.

He released her arms to take the keys, dryly commenting, 'It will make it easier to keep my hands off you.'

She laughed, giddily light-hearted with the tense burden of decision lifted. A quick glance around located her car and she hooked her arm around his to haul him in the right direction. 'This way. And we both need to exercise some care, Jordan.'

'Don't worry. I *will* take care of you, Ivy. In every sense there is.'

That was a big promise. Ivy wasn't sure she believed it. But she was willing to take this journey with him. It was probably an *Alice in Wonderland* kind of adventure and one day she would wake up from it. She hoped she would be able to treasure the good, shake off the bad and remember it as a risk that had been worth taking.

CHAPTER TEN

AT the first red traffic light Jordan whipped out his mobile phone, making a quick call to his handyman who promptly answered.

'No need to come, Ray. I'm heading home now in Ivy's car. Would you please tell Margaret it will be dinner for two tonight. Maybe a late lunch, as well.'

'Will do. And…uh…congratulations, boss.'

'Thanks, Ray,' Jordan said dryly, aware that his campaign to make contact with Ivy was well known to his household staff, with conflicting degrees of support. Ray had been rooting for him to win while Margaret reserved judgement on the outcome.

He closed the phone and slid it back into his shirt pocket, throwing a glance at Ivy to check all was well with her before turning his attention back to the bank-up of traffic waiting for the light to change. 'Why are you frowning?' he asked, wanting to wipe the tense expression from her face.

She heaved a sigh and shot him an anxious look. 'Your housekeeper…I guess she's seen a lot of women come and go in your life, Jordan. It's just kind of embarrassing. I know I shouldn't care what she thinks, but…'

'Don't worry.' He grinned as he reached across and

gave her hand a quick reassuring squeeze. 'Margaret likes you. In fact, I have a strong suspicion I'll be damned to perdition if I don't treat you right.'

'How could she like me?' Ivy queried in amazement. 'I only spoke to her for a few minutes. And that was when...well, it was obvious I'd spent the night with you.'

'Oh, I got the blame for that...having my wicked way with a nice girl.'

'How does she know I'm a nice girl?'

'According to Margaret, you have beautiful manners. Believe me, as long as you treat her with respect, you'll get the same respect back. Respect and honesty are Margaret's prime standards. Cross those lines and you're in her black books. An honest bit of sex between a man and a woman does not worry her one bit. Okay?'

Ivy relaxed, a happy relief in her smile. 'Okay. She sounds like quite a character.'

'She is. Hiring her was one of the best decisions I've ever made.'

And Jordan had the strong feeling that pursuing Ivy had been one of his best decisions, too.

The car behind them honked—a warning that the light had turned green and the traffic was moving again. Satisfied that he'd removed any fretting from Ivy's mind, Jordan drove on, revelling in the anticipation of having her to himself for the rest of the weekend, which gave him plenty of time to sort out any other concerns she might have about being involved with him.

It was highly vexing to find his sister's silver Porsche parked in the driveway of his Balmoral home. Apart from the fact that he didn't want any visitors taking his attention away from Ivy, Olivia was a self-centred snob whose manner could be very off-putting to anyone who wasn't used to her. Besides, she wouldn't be here unless she wanted him to *fix* something for her, which meant she'd want his undivided attention.

'Damn!' he muttered as he brought Ivy's car to a halt behind the Porsche.

'You have a visitor?' Ivy enquired, a wary look on her face.

'My sister, who only drops in on me when she has some problem to unload, so I won't be able to get rid of her until I hear her out.'

'If it's a private problem, Jordan, she won't want a stranger listening in.'

'No, she won't.' He grimaced an apologetic appeal. 'Would you mind very much chatting to Margaret while I deal with it? I'll ask her to make you some lunch. Or you could browse through the newspaper. I'm sorry. This is an awkward start, not what I...'

'It's okay,' she quickly assured him. 'Family should come first, especially if there's a problem.'

He heaved a sigh of frustration. 'Olivia makes trouble for herself. My father spoiled her terribly...his little princess. Don't be upset if she's dismissive of you. It won't be personal. She'll just be so full of herself, no one else counts.'

The green eyes filled with wry self-mockery. 'Well, I don't count for anything in her life.'

'You do in mine,' he said emphatically, feeling the question mark over his involvement with her and hating it. He turned in his seat to reach out and cup her cheek, his eyes boring into hers with forceful intensity. 'You do in mine, Ivy. Give me time and I'll prove that to you.'

He kissed her, wanting their desire for each other to obliterate everything else, leave no room for doubts. Excitement surged through him at her fierce response.

She didn't want to doubt him. She wanted to lose herself in the same passion he felt. It was hell having to restrain himself to a kiss when he was so hungry for her. He mentally cursed his sister for being an obstacle to the rampant urge to sweep Ivy straight up to his bedroom. A month of waiting and still he had to wait.

'Later,' he promised, breathing the word against her lips as he forced himself to break the kiss. 'You have to meet my sister now, Ivy.'

'Yes,' she whispered huskily.

He had to fight down his reluctance to separate himself from her, move away. It took an act of will to curb the rebellious needs of his body and alight from the car, taking the steps demanded by Olivia's unwelcome presence in his home. Ivy swayed a little as he helped her from the passenger seat. He tucked her arm around his for the walk inside, governed by the strong instinct to support and protect his woman.

His...

Strange...he couldn't remember feeling actually possessive of a woman before. Probably it was the long waiting that had made him uncertain of having Ivy again. And *that* was yet to happen. Olivia had better behave herself, he thought grimly. If she gave Ivy any cause to skip out on him...

'There you are!'

The words were flung at him the moment he and Ivy entered the foyer—Olivia emerging from the lounge, a highball glass in hand, obviously in a state of intoxication, her usual perfect grooming having taken a slide today: eye make-up smudged, her shoulder-length hair dishevelled, silk blouse crumpled, linen trousers badly creased.

She had the same blue eyes and black hair he did.

Tall and voluptuously curved, she could and usually did make a striking impact on people, but she was not about to make a good impression on Ivy at this meeting. He closed the front door behind him, eyeing his sister with stern displeasure. Getting drunk didn't fix anything, and driving a car while over the alcohol limit was downright irresponsible, let alone illegal. Not acknowledging Ivy's presence and addressing him as though he'd put her out by his absence was more than he could tolerate.

'Why are you here, Olivia?' he threw back at her.

She ignored the question, eyeing Ivy up and down with a supercilious look on her face. 'Who is this? Taking up with Cinderellas now, are you, Jordan? Been through the whole socialite pack?'

'Keep a civil tongue or go,' he said cuttingly. 'I don't have any patience for your rudeness today.'

'Sorry. I just haven't seen her before,' she rolled out with a shrug. 'Will I recognise the name?'

'Ivy. Ivy Thornton. Unfortunately, I have no pleasure at all in introducing you, Olivia.'

'Tough!' She sneered. 'I'm family and you can't get rid of family. The good old tie of blood is always there. Whereas Ivy…no doubt she will turn into Poison Ivy in due course. They invariably do, don't they?'

She was right, but due course hadn't been run yet, and he wasn't about to let Olivia spark off another bout of resistance from Ivy when he'd just brought her to the starting line. 'You've been warned!' he threw at his sister, stepping back to open front door. 'I'll call Ray to drive you home.'

'Oh, for pity's sake! Why take offence when you carry on about being honest and calling a spade a spade?' She flicked another look down her nose at Ivy. 'I have to concede you have the good sense not to marry any of them. I, on the other hand…' The jeering spite suddenly crumpled into tears and the eyes she turned back to Jordan were wretched pools of despair. '…was fool enough to hitch myself to a sleazy, cheating scumbag who plans on blackmailing me for all I'm worth.'

'Blackmail?' This was serious business. Jordan frowned over it as he quietly closed the door again. 'What does your husband have to blackmail you with, Olivia?'

Her *third* husband, who fell in the toy-boy range—twenty-three years old to her thirty-four—sweet, loveable Ashton whose gym-toned body promised sex on legs and had obviously delivered it beyond the marriage bed, which had always been predictable. But what had Olivia done to put herself in a blackmailing situation?

She shook her head, choking out words between sobs and shuddering intakes of breath. 'You've got to help me, Jordan. You've got to. Daddy would have fixed it.'

Jordan gritted his teeth. His father had always freed his darling daughter from the consequences of her follies, which, of course, meant Olivia had never learnt any hard lessons from experience. His own upbringing had been designed to teach him the strong hand required to run a business empire, to anticipate the consequences of any decision and make careful provision for them before acting.

Although well aware of why Olivia was the way she was, he was sorely tempted to let her stew in her own juices this time, make her count the cost for once, but blackmail was a dirty criminal act, and he couldn't allow anyone to stick his sister with it. Nevertheless, some lessons had to be hammered home right now.

'Okay, you want something from me, Olivia. I want something from you,' he said in a hard relentless tone, totally unsympathetic to her blubbering tears in the face of the insults she had flung at Ivy—a woman she didn't know and didn't care about knowing—putting his win at risk.

'What?' Olivia asked sulkily.

'Firstly you will apologise to Ivy for your ignorant remarks about her. Take a deep breath now and do it with some grace, please, or you can take your trouble to the cemetery and tell it to Dad's tombstone.'

Her jaw dropped in shock. She goggled at him and then at Ivy who hadn't said a word, despite the nastiness that had been directed at her. God only knew what she was thinking! Probably that any connection with him was fast losing its desire-power!

'Sorry,' Olivia finally mumbled at Ivy in a woebegone fashion. 'I'm just so upset. I wanted you to go so I could have Jordan to myself. I…I shouldn't have said those things.' She dashed the tears from her eyes with her hand, lifted her chin and looked belligerently at Jordan. 'Is that enough?'

'No, but it will do for the present. The next time you meet Ivy, you'd better take the trouble to make her acquaintance in a decent fashion. You could learn good manners from her for a start.'

'All right! All right!' She snapped, throwing up her free hand, then dropping it into a plea for him to stop browbeating her. 'I'm sorry. Okay?'

'None of this is okay, Olivia. Go back into the lounge and wait for me. Don't drink another drop of alcohol. If you have a serious problem we need to talk about it seriously. Soberly. Without any more theatrics. I'll take Ivy to Margaret, who I'm sure will make her feel more comfortable, and I'll bring you some strong black coffee.'

She flounced off into the lounge, slamming the door behind her in protest at being treated to some discipline instead of oodles of indulgence. Jordan reined in the angry resentment stirred by the whole scene with Olivia and turned quickly to draw Ivy into his embrace, searching her eyes for reactions to it, anxious to erase any damage done.

'I apologise for my sister's behaviour. It's beyond my control, Ivy. She just lashes out indiscriminately when she's upset. Not that that's any excuse…'

To his intense relief she gave him an ironic little smile. 'I thought you did a fairly impressive job of taking control.'

He heaved a rueful sigh. 'My parents spoiled Olivia rotten. All she had to do was throw a tantrum and she was given anything she wanted. It used to drive me around the bend. Still does. But she could be in real trouble with this blackmail business. I'll have to deal with it.'

'Of course you do,' she said sympathetically, reaching up to smooth the frown from his brow. 'What your sister said to me doesn't matter, Jordan. I know I'm not a Cinderella and I've never been poisonous to anyone. It seems to me it's your family wealth that's the poison.'

True, but…he needed to find out how profitable Ivy's rose farm was, whether it was on shaky ground, check that she wasn't a Cinderella in hiding as Biancha had been, because he knew only too well that it was the Cinderellas of both sexes who brought poison to his family's wealth.

'It does attract con-artists and fortune-hunters and Olivia invariably falls for them,' he replied with an unguarded touch of bitterness.

'That must be really nasty for her when she finds out she's been fooled.'

Being fooled was always nasty. Only once had he fallen into that trap, and not even the promise of fantastic sex forever would blinker his eyes to it again.

'It's about time she exercised some judgement,' he said grimly. 'At least testing the waters before blindly wading in.'

'Like you do?'

Her eyes reflected a mental reviewing of his many brief affairs in a different light. Not so much the playboy but the billionaire with a cynical part of his brain alert to anything false.

'Ivy, we can continue this conversation later. We should move on now. I don't trust Olivia not to hit the bottle again.'

'Yes. Better get the coffee coming.'

He was grateful for her quick understanding. No selfishness, no sulky pouts at being put aside for a while, just a fair assessment of the situation and a reasonable reaction to it. He liked her all the more for it. He hoped she spoke the truth about not being a Cinderella.

They found Margaret in the kitchen. As usual, she had anticipated what would be needed and already had the coffee brewing. Margaret was no fool. She was always aware of everything in this household. Regardless of her former reservations about his pursuit of Ivy, she welcomed her with a smile and instantly offered to take care of her needs, too. The Saturday newspaper was spread out on the island bench, the travel section uppermost, and Ivy slid straight onto a stool, obviously prepared to wait for him and acquaint herself with his housekeeper.

Feeling sure that this issue was settled, Jordan switched

his mind to dealing with Olivia and her problem. She was pacing around the lounge in nervous agitation—thankfully without a glass in her hand—when he took in the coffee, advising her to sit down, sip it and compose herself.

He waited until she did so, quelling his own impatience to get on with it, knowing that calm, cool deliberation had to be brought to damage control. He seated himself on the armchair adjacent to the sofa where Olivia had flung herself and thought about how to counter a blackmail threat until his sister could not contain herself any longer.

Having taken one sip of coffee, she threw a look of angst at him and blurted out, 'He's got a video of me having sex with him and he's going to post it on the Internet if I don't pay up.'

'Did you agree to the video or did he film it without your permission?'

Her gaze dropped. She plucked at her trousers. 'I…uh…thought it was fun at the time. Something…intimate…to watch together.'

Jordan shook his head. How many girls and women fell into that trap, letting their boyfriends take naked shots of them, only to find the photographs were not kept private—were posted on the Internet or flashed around on mobile phones? It was rotten behaviour by the guys, but with today's technology at everyone's fingertips, the women should wise up to the risk of being put out there.

'It's happening all the time, Olivia,' he said, exasperated by her foolishness. 'Why not tell him to publish and be damned? There's nothing shameful about having sex with your husband.'

'But anyone can look at it,' she cried, appalled at his

solution. 'It's humiliating, Jordan. I can't bear the idea of lots of people having a peepshow of me.'

'You've got a great body. You don't mind showing it off. You won't be the first heiress who's had to weather baring all on the Internet,' he said dismissively. And just maybe she'd be wiser next time around.

She grimaced and muttered, 'It's not just that.'

'Then stop pussyfooting around and give me the real dirt, Olivia.'

She erupted from the sofa, throwing up her hands, flouncing around to avoid looking at him. 'I was out of my mind. Ashton had a friend there, another gorgeous hunk. We were snorting cocaine, high as kites. Anyhow, it got to be a threesome. *That's* what he's got on the video.'

'All of it? The cocaine, as well?'

'Yes,' she hissed at him, eyes blazing hatred at having to confess her own sins.

'Are you in the habit of doing coke, Olivia?'

She stamped her foot at his inquisition. 'Everybody does at parties. You know they do,' she shouted at him.

He stared back at her in silent, burning reproof. Many did, but he didn't and she knew it. Apart from alcohol in moderation he never touched recreational drugs and he didn't want to see his sister take the downward spiral that so commonly ended in depression and disaster.

'I didn't do it much until Ashton started getting regular supplies,' she said, trying to mitigate her usage.

Possibly it was true. It would obviously serve Ashton's purpose to get Olivia hooked. 'Okay,' he said calmly. 'I have the picture now. Sit down while I think about how to get you out of this mess.'

Relieved that she had finally loaded it off onto his

shoulders, she dropped onto the sofa and resumed sipping coffee while darting anxious little glances at him.

Jordan mentally plotted the moves that had to be made. Call his lawyer to enquire about all the legal angles. Call his security guy. Olivia would have to be wired and rehearsed into how to get Ashton's blackmail threat on tape. Once he could be threatened with criminal prosecution, Jordan was fairly sure a reasonable settlement could be reached. Pretty-boy Ashton wouldn't enjoy a spell in jail. Olivia had to get stone-cold sober and stay sober until the situation was resolved, and then agree to a month in a rehabilitation centre.

He took out his mobile phone and called his mother. Fortunately she was home and, having been apprised of the problem, agreed to look after Olivia and ensure she was sober for a management meeting tomorrow morning. That gave him the rest of today and tonight with Ivy before he had to act for his sister who certainly deserved to stew overnight for being so damned stupid and careless.

He then called Ray to get the Bentley out to drive Olivia to his mother's Palm Beach residence. He would drive the Porsche there himself in the morning. Having dumped her problem in her brother's hands and now sure he would *fix* it for her, Olivia meekly followed his orders.

Jordan silently determined she would follow a few more in the very near future, like getting her head together enough to make sensible decisions and not take mind-blurring drugs.

It was all so bloody nasty, he thought, as he saw Olivia off in the Bentley. At least taking care of it could wait until tomorrow. Ashton was not about to go anywhere, not until he had milked the golden goose for all he could get.

And Ivy was waiting for him.

Ivy, who'd told him repeatedly she wouldn't fit into his social world: the parties, the gossip, the competitive status thing with its bitchiness and back-biting, the high-flying celebrities who did dabble in cocaine or ecstacy or marijuana for their sensory hits. Part of his mind stood back from it all, like a spectator rather than a participant. But if he took Ivy into it…

No, she didn't fit.

He didn't want her to fit.

It was the difference in her that he found so beguiling.

Somehow he had to keep her out of it, yet keep her in his life.

And his bed.

Determined on making that happen, Jordan headed back into the house, the adrenaline surge of desire kicking in as he went to collect the woman he wanted.

CHAPTER ELEVEN

IVY found Margaret surprisingly easy to be with. Aware that the housekeeper had to be curious about the decisions she'd come to in regard to a relationship with Jordan, she'd told her straight out that she owned the rose farm he used for gifts to his girlfriends and hadn't thought the attraction was worth pursuing, given her inside knowledge of his track record with roses.

'Good Heavens! And he kept sending them to your mother!' had been her stunned reaction.

'Yes, it was great for business, but I had to stop it.'

Margaret had burst into laughter, vastly amused by the piquancy of the situation, her eyes twinkling merrily as she'd commented, 'So you're giving him a chance.'

'I do like him.' Not to mention wanting him so intensely it was almost frightening, which the housekeeper probably realised anyway. Ivy couldn't imagine any woman not wanting to experience Jordan Powell in bed. It was his world, not his bed that was the problem.

'Yes, he's very likeable,' Margaret had replied with a fondly indulgent smile. 'I wouldn't work for him if he wasn't.'

This recommendation of Jordan's character from an employee's point of view, added to the masterly way he had handled the scene with his sister, had assured Ivy she wasn't making too big a mistake in getting more involved with him, even if it proved to be a brief affair in the end. Besides, maybe his previous affairs had been littered with fortune-hunters and she wasn't one. That might make some difference.

Margaret had produced a platter of nibbles, suggesting it might tide Ivy over until Jordan had finished with his sister and they could then have lunch together. The brie cheese and dates, little balls of fresh melon wrapped in prosciutto ham, marinated sun-dried tomatoes and olives were all very tempting and without any electric sexual tension knotting her stomach, Ivy suddenly found an appetite.

While picking at the platter, she'd asked Margaret what kind of tours she was interested in since the newspaper was open at the travel section. It turned out that the housekeeper had 'done' most of Europe, saving up all year for an annual trip overseas. The Americas were next on her list, specifically California and Mexico.

'I've never travelled anywhere,' Ivy had confessed. 'Friends of mine were raving about a cruise down the Rhine, and I thought I might try that next year.'

'Why not this year?'

Her heart instantly leapt at Jordan's voice and started banging around her chest as he strode into the kitchen, his face animated with interest. Whatever had transpired with his sister was obviously not lingering in his mind. The blue eyes twinkled with happy speculation as he pursued his point.

'I think they start running those cruises in May. It's only March now. In two months' time, we could be sailing down the Rhine together, Ivy. I'd love to share that part of Europe with you.' He stopped at the island bench, picked a melon ball off the platter, popped it into his mouth, raised his eyebrows at her stunned reaction to his enthusiastic suggestion as he ate the fruit, then asked, 'Can you get away from the farm to do it with me?'

He helped himself to some cheese, slicing up a date to accompany it while Ivy tried to catch her breath. Her mind spun around his extraordinary offer. She could imagine a billionaire on a super-luxury cruise ship like the *Queen Elizabeth II,* or a magnificent chartered yacht, but… 'Is it your kind of thing? I mean…travelling with ordinary tourists?'

'I'll enjoy whatever you enjoy, Ivy.'

Would he really? There was not a hint of doubt in his voice and Ivy could well believe he had schooled himself to be master of any situation. He would probably charm all the other passengers on the ship, make his presence a highlight of their cruise. As for herself, it would be great to have Jordan as her travelling companion, and so much time together would certainly sort out their differences, test how compatible they could be. Make-or-break time for their relationship, she thought.

However, there was one problem he was overlooking. The pipe dream of a marvellous trip together deflated as the reality of her world kicked in. Jordan was undoubtedly accustomed to travelling wherever he wanted whenever he wanted, but…

'We can't do it,' she said with a rueful shake of her head. 'Not this May. You have to book about a year ahead to get on these cruises.'

Determined purpose flashed in his eyes. 'There are always cancellations. Leave it with me and I'll see if I can find us a berth on one.'

He was intent on going and taking her with him. So intent, Ivy suspected he would *buy* a cancellation. It made her feel uncomfortable about it. Why did it matter so much to him? Was he so used to getting his own way nothing was going to stop him? How ruthless was he in wielding his wealth to get what he wanted?

So many questions…and he kept munching away on the hors d'oeuvres as though everything was already settled, his eyes teasing her with the confidence of solving any problem she might still raise. She had succumbed to the power of the man without knowing nearly enough about him, yet the lure of knowing more of him was too strong for her to back off now.

'Okay,' she said slowly. 'I can arrange time off from the farm, but if you do manage to get us on a cruise, Jordan, I insist on paying for my own plane ticket there and back and my share of the tour package.'

No way would she let him think he was *buying* her. Besides, she needed to be independent of him, in case she ended up disliking how it was between them and wanted to walk away.

He grinned, triumphant delight dancing in his eyes. 'Whatever you say, Ivy. I just want us to have this time away together.'

She did, too. It provided a relatively quick proving ground. Not like two years with Ben before finding out he would let her down when she most needed him to be there for her.

'Had enough to eat?' Jordan asked, and her stomach instantly clenched.

No more food.

He wanted sex with her.

'What have you done with your sister?' she asked, sure that he would have already ensured no further interruptions, but curious about the outcome of that meeting.

He grinned and held out his hand to help her off the kitchen stool. 'Sent her home to Mother. Come on. I'll show you the rest of the house. Do you want Margaret to prepare lunch or shall we have an early dinner?'

She took his hand, acutely aware of it enfolding hers as she slid off the stool, wanting to feel him touching her all over, remembering how it had been and eager to experience it again. 'I've had enough to eat for now,' she said, flicking a quick grateful glance at the housekeeper. 'Thank you, Margaret.'

'An early dinner then,' Jordan swiftly instructed.

'Give me a call when you want it,' Margaret drily replied.

Of course she knew what they were about to do, Ivy thought. It was probably a very common scenario with Jordan and she couldn't help wishing it wasn't so. Needing to block out his past and concentrate entirely on the present, her mind snatched at the distraction of his sister and her problems.

'Have you passed the blackmail business over to your mother, too?' she asked as they walked back into the foyer.

'No. I'll deal with it tomorrow when Olivia is sober.' He shot her an apologetic grimace. 'Which means cutting our weekend together short. I'll have to go to Palm Beach in the morning for a family meeting.'

'I hope you can sort something out,' she said sympathetically, thinking it would be horrible to be blackmailed by one's own husband, a man whom Olivia had obviously trusted, however unwisely.

'Don't be concerned about it, Ivy. It will be sorted, one way or another,' he said dismissively. 'In fact, it should be a good lesson for my sister. I intend to make it one, that's for sure,' he added in a tone of determination that would brook no nonsense.

He led her straight to the staircase, no detouring to 'show her the house.' That would come later, after…

Her pulse drummed a faster beat as they mounted the stairs.

'Olivia won't speak to you like that again, either,' he tagged on.

She sighed, relieving the tightness in her chest before slanting an ironic little smile at him. 'I guess all your social set will think the same things about me, Jordan.'

He squeezed her hand hard. 'What *they* think isn't important. Only what *we* have together matters.'

The intensity in his voice sent a quiver of excitement down her spine. She wanted what they could have together, wanted it as much as he did. They reached his bedroom and *nothing* else mattered. They were both insanely lustful, kissing as though there was no tomorrow, removing clothes in urgent haste, falling on the bed in a tangle of legs and arms, reaching for each other, gripping, clinging, caressing with fierce possessiveness, passion pumping through their bodies, fuelling the need to take, to give.

Jordan muttered a curse as he remembered protection, tearing himself away long enough to grab it from a drawer in a bedside table and sheath himself. A weird stab of sadness went through Ivy's heart. No baby with Jordan. That would never happen. It wasn't what this relationship was about. But she had accepted that, hadn't she? And she accepted him now with an intense shaft of pleasure as he came back to her and thrust deeply, driving to the edge of her pulsing womb.

Wild excitement coursed through her with each repeated plunge, the rhythm of it rolling through her in euphoric waves, cresting in marvellous peaks, finally carrying her to an explosion of utter ecstasy and a flood of sweetly lulling peace. *Yes,* she thought blissfully. It was worth any hurt later to have this with Jordan now.

She lay with her head resting over the strong beat of his heart, smiling as she listened to its pace gradually lessen to a quiet, steady thump. *Peace for him, too, after the long waiting,* she thought, and was glad she had surrendered to his patient pursuit. His hands started gliding over the curves of her back and her skin tingled with pleasure. He picked up her plait, removed the rubber band that kept it fastened, and slowly unwound the skeins of her hair, fluffing it out with his fingers when it was freed of its constriction.

'With your hair and skin, you could have posed for Botticelli's *Birth of Venus,*' he murmured. 'It's a wonderful painting, displayed in the Uffizi Gallery in Florence. We could go on to Italy after the cruise and…'

'I don't think so,' Ivy stirred enough to protest. 'We'll be away for a month as it is.' She lifted her head to give him a teasing look. 'And you haven't even shown me all the paintings in this house yet.'

He laughed, raking her hair out on either side of her face. 'You outshine them all, but when I summon up the energy and the inclination I'll give you a tour.'

'Mmmh…I'm not in any hurry.'

'Good, because I don't want to hurry anything this time.'

He kept every kiss and caress deliciously sensual. They moved around each other in a long, languorous dance of gliding, nestling, touching, feeling—a glorious sexual wallowing that simmered with excitement without blazing into imperative need.

He spoke seductively of the fantastic sights they would see and the pleasures they would share in Europe: the amazing array of statues in Prague, the magnificent Schonbrunn Palace in Vienna—'I'll dance you around the gold ballroom'—the vineyards climbing the hills in the Wachau Valley—'We'll go wine-tasting'—the amazing amount of castles along the Rhine, the totally eye-popping quantity of gold decorating the cathedral at the Melk monastery.

'You've seen it all before,' Ivy commented ruefully at one point.

'Not since I was in my teens. My parents took Olivia and me on a world tour as part of our education.'

Not with another woman then, Ivy thought with a rush of relief. It was ridiculous wanting something exclusive to herself, knowing how very experienced he was, yet she instantly felt happier in her anticipation of their travels together.

'Besides, I'll enjoy it so much more being with you,' he said, smiling into her eyes, making her heart melt with longing for that to be true.

'Talking of paintings, why did you choose to hang Sydney Nolan's Ned Kelly images in this bedroom?' she asked, wanting to understand more of the man. 'Do you feel some affinity with our famous bushranger or do they simply complement the decor with him wearing his black armour?'

He sidestepped the question, asking, 'Do you like them?'

'They're great, but I thought you'd be more into nudes in here.'

He grinned. 'I don't need that kind of stimulation.'

She laughed, well aware that he had no problem

with impotence. 'You still haven't told me why Ned Kelly?'

His eyes were hooded as his fingertips feathered her lips. 'He reminds me always to be armoured. Especially in the bedroom. Only you have ever made me forget that, Ivy.'

He kissed her, as though wanting to draw that power from her soul, be the man who never lost control again. The simmering excitement instantly escalated, compelling them into another climactic union. It wasn't until long afterwards that Ivy thought about what he'd said about always being armoured.

A billionaire's son, a billionaire in his own right—a target for people who wanted a piece of him for their own ends, in the bedroom and out of it. She imagined very few people would ever fool him in business, but there was a natural vulnerability with intimacy, a wish to trust. Jordan had seen his sister be a victim of it three times because of her wealth.

Was it any wonder that he'd chosen a playboy lifestyle?

Essentially a lonely life, Ivy thought, *always armoured.*

And she was lonely, too.

She enjoyed his company on the tour of his house, enjoyed his company over the delicious dinner Margaret served them, enjoyed the seductively sensual skinny-dipping in the solar-heated pool later in the evening and revelled in the lovemaking that followed. She didn't feel lonely with him and she hoped he didn't feel lonely with her.

Before Jordan had to leave for his family meeting the next morning, they had a happy, relaxed breakfast together and made plans for him to spend the next weekend on the rose farm with her. Ivy drove home feeling brilliantly alive, hoping they could make a lovely self-contained world together that nothing could spoil.

She knew it was a rather silly hope.

Other things would inevitably intrude.

But she was determined to enjoy what she could with Jordan while she could.

CHAPTER TWELVE

On Monday, Heather was cock-a-hoop over Ivy's capitulation to a relationship with Jordan Powell, insisting that his persistence proved he was really, really attracted, and the fact that Ivy had enjoyed her time with him showed it to be the right step to take. And when he came to the farm next weekend, could she please, please, please meet him.

Sacha called late in the afternoon to report that no roses had come and what did that mean? Had Ivy met Jordan? Had he persuaded her into seeing more of him? Given an affirmative reply, Sacha was delighted, bubbling over with a list of advantages to be had in associating with such a man, uppermost of which was experiencing a far broader and more civilised way of life than Ivy had been leading on the farm.

Ivy didn't mention the cruise to either woman, thinking it was probably too far in the future to count on, even if Jordan did manage to get them places on it. Who knew what would happen between now and then? She was confident that Heather and Barry could take over running the farm and managing the business on short notice and would be happy to do it for her, if and when required. She simply couldn't shake the fatalistic feeling that this harmony with Jordan was too good to last.

Each night during the week he called her to chat for half an hour or so, just normal conversations about what they'd done throughout the day. Without going into nitty-gritty details, he told her the blackmail threat to his sister had been dealt with, a reasonable divorce settlement agreed upon and Olivia was off to a health spa for some recovery time. And hopefully she would grow some armour against being taken for a ride again.

There was definitely a downside to being incredibly wealthy, Ivy thought. On the other hand, when Jordan arrived at the farm on Friday evening and presented her with confirmation that a stateroom had been secured for them on a cruise in May, she couldn't ignore the suspicion that he'd used the power of wealth to obtain it.

'Did we luck into a cancellation or did you bribe someone to give up their trip, Jordan?' she asked, searching his eyes for the truth, wanting an *honest* answer.

He shrugged. 'I made an offer. Someone took it. What other people choose to do doesn't concern us, Ivy. What matters is we're going.'

It didn't feel right. 'You've spoiled their plans. They would have been looking forward to the cruise. Don't you have any conscience about that?'

He frowned. 'I didn't force their choice. I guess they thought they'd have a lot more spending money for another trip.'

'How much more?'

He waved a dismissive hand. 'It's irrelevant. It's done.'

'But I should pay half of what you paid,' she argued, unable to shake a sense of guilty responsibility.

'No!' He shook his head emphatically. 'I made the decision. I pay the price.'

'We didn't have to go,' she protested, still uncomfortable with how it had been arranged.

'I *want* to.' He scooped her into his embrace, one hand lifting to stroke away her frown as his eyes bored into hers. '*You* want to. Let it be, Ivy.'

Looking at him, feeling him, wanting him, the temptation to let the issue slide pounded through Ivy's mind. *Let it be.* Only a last little niggle made her mutter, 'I wouldn't have minded waiting.'

'This is our time, Ivy,' he murmured seductively, his lips grazing over hers as he added, 'Let's make the most of it.'

Our time...

Her heart sank a little at those words, carrying as they did the implication that he expected their time to be limited. By the end of the cruise their relationship would have lasted four months—long enough for Jordan?

But didn't she have the same expectation?

Her body craved what he could give her.

*Make the most of it...*yes.

She couldn't fault Jordan over anything else that weekend. He showed a keen interest in the operation of the rose farm—how it all worked, the standard orders from florists, hotels, big business houses, the more random number of private clients like himself, though he was never to be again, the greenhouses, the packaging room, the refrigerated store of fudges which were supplied by a local woman who'd made an at-home business out of cooking them, the computer system for sales. She enjoyed explaining it all to him.

Graham and Heather came to lunch on Saturday, and Jordan impressed both of them with his appreciation of their contribution to the success of the farm. He didn't present himself as a playboy at all, talking of his own experience with employees, saying how much he valued those he trusted to get the job done. Graham was quickly at ease with him and Heather barely stopped short of drooling—Jordan was so gorgeous!

When the cruise was mentioned, both of them were enthusiastic about a break from the farm for Ivy and assured her they would look after everything.

Ivy let herself relax and enjoy every minute with Jordan. He made it easy, being the perfect lover in every sense.

Again he telephoned her every night during the week, keeping their connection strong. He arrived by helicopter on Saturday morning and flew her to Port Macquarie, a beach resort on the north coast of New South Wales where he was building a new retirement village and nursing home. He shared his vision for it with her, impressing her once again with his caring for the elderly. They ate in the best restaurants the town had to offer and slept in a luxurious apartment that overlooked Flynn's Beach.

He never seemed bored by the weekends he spent on the farm with her, and on his alternate weekends he invariably took Ivy somewhere special—to the Blue Mountains and the amazing Jenolan Caves, to Port Douglas and the Great Barrier Reef, to the Red Centre and Uluru, to the Hunter Valley vineyards. Cost, of course, was no object to Jordan and Ivy decided not to quibble about it. He was taking her on a fantastic ride—the ride of a lifetime—and even if it only lasted six months, which was his uppermost limit for an affair, she was certainly living brilliantly for a while.

More and more she shied away from thinking about the end. Her pleasure in Jordan's company was so intense, the idea of coming to an end was too frightening to contemplate. She loved him, loved everything about him. She lived for the next time they'd be together.

The week before they were due to leave for the cruise, Ivy decided to treat herself to a shopping day, wanting to dress up for the dinners on the ship. Her mother suggested she trawl through the boutiques at Double Bay and meet her for lunch at a bistro she named, since they hadn't seen anything of each other since the gallery exhibition. Having been told of this plan, Jordan invited her to stay overnight with him at Balmoral at the end of the day so she could parade her purchases, which would be fun for both of them.

Ivy was in a happy mood, wandering around the Double Bay shopping centre, looking at the window displays before deciding what might suit her. She was trying on a slinky violet pantsuit in the Liz Davenport boutique, admiring the cut and line of it in the wall mirror, when Olivia Powell walked in with another woman, both of them dressed in high-fashion gear.

Having not met Jordan's sister since the unpleasant scene in his house, she hesitated over whether to acknowledge the brief acquaintance as it would remind Olivia of things she probably wanted to forget. On the other hand, this was the sister of the man she loved. It didn't seem right to ignore her presence.

While Ivy was still dithering over this social dilemma, Olivia glanced around, her gaze picking up Ivy's direct stare at her in the mirror. Her perfectly plucked black eyebrows arched in surprise. Then a look of amusement settled on her face.

'Well, well, if it isn't Jordan's farm girl,' she drawled.

Her companion's attention was instantly drawn to Ivy. 'Who?' she asked.

'Darling, you are looking at the reason why Jordan has been shunning the social scene.'

The other woman goggled at Ivy with avid curiosity. 'A farm girl?'

'Mmmh…so my mother told me when I asked about his new interest.'

'Then what is she doing here?'

'Good question. Maybe he's decided to bring her out of the closet and wants her decently clothed.'

There was no attempt to lower their voices. Ivy heard every word and the unfriendliness of Olivia's attitude, the scorn in her tone, made her stomach churn with a sense of sick vulnerability. Jordan wasn't here to fend off his sister's nastiness and Ivy knew, even before Olivia started strolling towards her, knew from the malicious glint in her eyes, that she was about to be subjected to a humiliating public attack.

Pride made her stand her ground.

Olivia closed in, her mouth curling with a savage mockery. 'Did you stick Jordan for a dress allowance, Ivy?'

Embarrassment was burning her cheeks. Her mouth was dry. She quickly worked some moisture into it, lifted her chin, and answered. 'No. I've taken no money from Jordan at all, Olivia.'

'Oh? Investing in yourself, are you? Showing him if you can look the part, you might get further than his bedroom?'

Ivy shook her head, finding it difficult to counter such virulence. 'Why are you gunning for me like this, Olivia?' she blurted out. 'I've never done anything bad to you.'

'Your kind has taken too many bites out of me. No doubt you're as sweet as pie to Jordan, just as Ashton was to me, but let me tell you, my brother is the clever one. You're wasting your time and your money on him. You can crawl into his bed, but you won't get past his head which is screwed on very tightly. Put one foot over the boundaries he's set and you'll get dumped, just like all the rest.'

Boundaries…keeping her in his closet…no social contact with *his* friends…the realisation that Olivia was telling exactly how it was hit into Ivy's heart like a sledgehammer. She couldn't protest. It was pointless even carrying on a conversation. She looked into Olivia's blue eyes—Jordan's eyes—and knew what she had known all along but this time much more painfully. She was not of their world, never would be.

'Thank you,' she said. 'I appreciate your caring.'

At least Olivia's startled look at her response was some balm to her pride.

'Please excuse me,' she went on with as much dignity as she could muster. 'I need to change back into my own clothes. Rest assured I'll be out of your brother's life very soon.'

She didn't wait for a reply, heading straight for the change room, no longer interested in buying stylish clothes. Thankfully Olivia and her companion were gone when she emerged. Not wanting to run into them again and grateful that the bistro Sacha had named was in a back street, she hurried there, sitting over a cup of coffee while she waited for her mother, silently berating herself for falling in love with a man who should have always remained a fantasy.

Sacha arrived, beaming pleasure in this outing together until she saw there were no shopping bags at Ivy's feet. 'You haven't found *anything* you like?' she wailed in disappointment.

Ivy managed an ironic smile. 'I met Jordan's sister and lost the plot.'

Her mother frowned and sat down. 'What do you mean?'

'I mean I realised how big a fool I was for falling in love with him and I should end it right now.'

Sacha gaped at her in horror. 'But, darling, you're going on this marvellous cruise with him next week.'

She couldn't, not feeling so torn up inside. Tears welled into her eyes. She hadn't cried since her father's death, but this was like a death, too, the killing of hopes and dreams she should never have let into her heart. Embarrassed at breaking down, she covered her face with her hands and tried desperately to choke off the heaving sensation making her chest unbearably tight.

'Oh, Ivy!'

She barely heard the anguished cry from her mother, but she felt the warm hug around her shoulders and the stroking of her hair. The caring gestures made it more difficult to bring herself under control but she finally managed it, hating the thought of making a spectacle of herself in a public place.

'I'm okay,' she bit out. 'Sorry. Please…do sit down again.'

'Ivy, I know I haven't been the kind of mother you probably wanted but…let me help.'

'There's nothing to help. It was a mistake.'

Sacha resumed her seat on the other side of the table as Ivy blotted her face with a hastily grabbed tissue from her handbag. Aware that her mother was viewing her with anxious concern, she took several deep, calming breaths and forced a rueful little smile.

'I should have kept my head. That's all,' she said with cutting finality.

'Love isn't about keeping one's head,' Sacha said wryly. 'It wasn't sensible for your father and I to fall in love with each other—a hippie artist and a Vietnam veteran who needed a colourful butterfly to give him some zest for life again. It was even less sensible for us to get married, but you know, Ivy, I've never regretted it. Robert was the only man I've ever loved and I'm glad I had that experience.'

Ivy sighed, remembering how she'd argued herself into the affair with Jordan…as an experience worth having. 'I guess the difference is…Dad loved you back.'

'Are you sure Jordan doesn't love you?' Sacha queried. 'He has been very, very attentive to pleasing you.'

'More in lust with me than loving me, I'd say.'

'Love and lust can be intertwined.'

Ivy shrugged. 'On his weekends at the farm we went to a couple of dinner parties at my friends' homes. They wanted to meet him and he was always a charming guest.' She looked bleakly at her mother. 'On my weekends with him, we always went away somewhere. I've never been introduced to any of his friends. Only to his sister by accident. What does that tell you?'

'Maybe that he wanted you to himself.'

'That's not what Olivia thinks. Fit for the bedroom but not for being a partner in any public sense.'

'What she thinks does not make her an authority on what her brother feels,' Sacha retorted with an odd look of determination. 'You should confront him directly about this, Ivy. All those roses he sent me…he wanted a chance with you. At least give him the chance to explain how *he* sees your relationship.'

Ivy remembered Jordan's insistence on her being fair,

not making assumptions about him, despite all the evidence that painted a very clear picture.

He hadn't actually let her down.

She had let herself be blinded by her growing love for him, wanting what was special between them to encompass much more than it did. Nevertheless, her mother was right. It was only fair to tell Jordan face to face why she had decided their time was over.

'Don't worry. He won't be sending you any more roses,' she said dryly. 'He's expecting me at Balmoral this afternoon. I'll go and see him, speak to him.'

'Make sure you listen, too, Ivy,' Sacha advised, still looking as though she wanted to argue Jordan's case.

Because of who he is, Ivy thought. The billionaire tag *was* blinding and the power of wealth was seductive, providing all the luxurious living she had done over the past two months, which she had undeniably enjoyed.

Because she had been with him.

Weaving foolish dreams.

'I'll listen,' she promised, picking up the menu from its stand on the table. 'I don't want to talk about this any more, Sacha. Let's order lunch.'

She had no appetite.

Her stomach was cramped with tension.

She simply wanted some distraction from what she had to do later in the afternoon. They could talk about her mother's paintings—the life she had made for herself apart from her marriage. It was what she had to do without Jordan—make a life alone because there would be no other man. There couldn't be another man like him. It just wasn't possible.

CHAPTER THIRTEEN

HIS mobile telephone rang just as Jordan was about to go into a meeting with a consortium of property developers. *Ivy,* he thought, smiling as he whipped the phone out of the breast pocket of his suit. It was almost three o'clock. Possibly she had finished shopping and was about to drive over to Balmoral. No doubt she'd chat with Margaret until he arrived. He motioned for his aide-de-camp to go ahead and settle everyone in the boardroom as he answered the call.

'Jordan, it's Olivia.'

A frown replaced the smile. What did his sister want of him now?

'I think I might have made a mistake,' she went on.

He rolled his eyes. Indulging his sister by listening to her troubles was not on at the moment. 'Olivia, I have people waiting on me for a business meeting,' he said curtly. 'I'll call you back when it's over.'

'No, wait!' Urgent anxiety was in her voice. 'It's about Ivy.'

His impatience was instantly ejected by red alert signals going off in his brain. The only time Olivia had met Ivy she had been extremely nasty to her. 'What mistake did you make?' he asked, needing to know the worst.

'I was with Caroline Sheldon and we went to Double Bay to do some shopping.'

Tension whipped through Jordan's body at the mention of Double Bay and Caroline Sheldon, who could be as bitchy as Olivia about other women. This was shaping up to be a bad scene.

'Anyhow, we walked into the Liz Davenport boutique and there was Ivy, trying on a pantsuit I know was priced at over seven hundred dollars.'

'So?' he snapped.

'Well, naturally I thought you'd given her the money to make herself look fashionable enough to fit into our crowd. I did the same thing with Ashton.'

'Ivy is nothing like Ashton,' he grated out, furious with Olivia's assumption.

'How was I supposed to know that? You've kept her to yourself all this time. Mum told me she worked on a farm and that fitted what I saw of her with you.'

'Ivy *owns* a very profitable rose farm. It's a solid business. I've checked it out,' he almost shouted in his chagrin. 'She can afford to buy whatever clothes she likes.'

'Well, it's your fault for keeping so mum about her,' came the typical defence. Everything was always someone's else's fault in his sister's life.

He sliced straight to the vital point. 'What did you do, Olivia?'

She huffed. 'I've had to ask you to rescue me. I liked the idea of saving you for once.'

'Saving me from what?'

'A fortune-hunter! Except...I don't think she is one. What she said back to me...the way she looked...it didn't fit at all. And the more I thought about it, the more I felt I should 'fess up to you about making a mistake, because I think she means to walk out of your life and you might not want her to.'

'You're quite right. I don't,' he said grimly, knowing he could very well lose Ivy because of Olivia's interference.

'At least give me credit for telling you, Jordan. I'm sure you can fix it up now that you know.'

Removing all guilt from herself.

Jordan unclenched his jaw enough to say, 'Thank you, Olivia. You might also call Caroline Sheldon and correct the false impression you gave her of Ivy who happens to be the most genuine and delightful person I've ever met.'

It was the truth. Not once had she ever given him reason to doubt the character she had shown him throughout the whole time they had spent together.

'Then why haven't you introduced her around?' came the swift retort, loaded with self-justification.

'Because I'm still in the process of winning her over to wanting to be in my life.'

'Why wouldn't she want to?'

Unimaginable to Olivia.

'Because she doesn't feel she belongs with people like you,' he answered harshly, unable to contain his anger. 'And you know what, Olivia? She doesn't!'

He pressed the disconnect button and stood still for several moments, needing to calm himself and assess the situation. His heart was thumping like a battle-drum. What the hell could he do to counter what Olivia had done! Some things couldn't be fixed. Ivy would be all the more convinced now that she wouldn't fit into his world. That conviction had taken her away from him once. He had to fight it again to keep her.

Ivy had brought more joy into his life than any other

woman. It was always a pleasure to be with her, in bed and out of it. He'd had more fun at her friends' parties—relatively uncomplicated people, satisfied with their lives in the country—than he did at the parties revolving around who's who with the socialite A-list. He knew where she was coming from, knew what she would go back to and, although he understood why, somehow he had to stop it because he was not prepared to accept the hole she would leave in his life.

He quickly tapped in her mobile number, needing communication.

No answer.

She'd turned it off.

Was she on her way home?

No, he decided. Ivy would not skip out on him as she had before. There'd been too much between them to go without a word. She'd promised to be fair, which surely meant facing him with whatever Olivia had said. Therefore, she would be at Balmoral later this afternoon, as arranged. He would have the chance then to employ every hold he could think of to sway her into staying with him. Whatever it took, he was not going to lose her.

Feeling more confident he could do it, one way or another, Jordan switched his mind to the business meeting, determined to get through it as fast as possible. Two frustrating hours later he was out of it, trying to call Ivy again. No answer. He called Margaret, needing to know if Ivy had arrived.

'Yes. About twenty minutes ago. But…' She left the word hanging, as though in two minds whether to express the thought.

'But what?' Jordan pressed, wanting every bit of information he could get about the situation. Forewarned, forearmed.

'Not that it's any of my business…'

'Make it your business, Margaret.'

'Well, she's not herself. You know how much I like Ivy and we always have a nice chat. She's never been uppity or off-putting like some I could mention. I actually look forward to her visits because she's so nice and natural and funny, and I'm quite sure she enjoys my company, too. But not today. I think something's upset her. Badly. She declined a cup of coffee and said she'd wait for you out in the pagoda.'

Not in his house. Withdrawing…

'She didn't bring in an overnight bag, either,' Margaret went on worriedly. 'I checked.'

No intention to stay.

'And if she'd been happily shopping, which you told me was the plan, I'm sure she would have been all bubbly about what she'd bought. So, since you've asked my opinion, I think something's very wrong, Jordan, and I don't like it.'

Neither did he.

'Her phone is switched off. Would you please take your receiver down to the pagoda so I can speak to her?'

'Okay. Doing it now.'

His whole body was tight with tension as he waited, his mind zapping through an array of opening lines, wanting what might be the most effective one.

'Hello…' Her voice was dull, no joy in it.

'Ivy, Olivia called me,' he rushed out. 'She's very sorry for what she said to you.'

Silence.

Then flatly, 'I'd rather not discuss it on the phone,

Jordan. We'll talk when you get home. Thank you, Margaret.'

Cut off.

But at least she was waiting for him.

Peak-hour traffic slowed his journey to a crawl. Jordan applied several relaxation techniques to keep tension at bay. Nothing worked. At one of the many red lights delaying his progress, he removed his suit coat and tie, flicked open the top buttons of his shirt and thought about how to get Ivy naked. Bodies spoke a better language than words. The sex between them was still fantastic. She couldn't deny that.

But it hadn't stopped her from walking away in the past.

He clamped down on the negative thought. He'd win her over. He'd done it before. He'd do it again. That determination rode with him the rest of the way home.

Margaret intercepted him as he strode through the house to the back terraces. She handed him a tray which held a wine bottle in an ice-bucket, two glasses and a selection of savoury dips and crackers. 'This might help,' she said.

'Thanks, Margaret.' He took the tray. 'Ivy still out there?'

'Hasn't returned to the house,' she threw over her shoulder as she moved quickly to open the exit door for him.

'It's Olivia's doing,' he tossed at her as he passed, too vexed with the situation to accept the blame shooting at him from his housekeeper's eyes. Damn it all! He'd done the best he could, keeping Ivy away from the gossip-mill of the socialite world, the jealous snipes, the boozy parties, the self-destructive fools who indulged in recreational drugs. He shouldn't be shot down over his sister's transgression.

A wave of anger crashed through him.

There was so much good to be had in his world. Hadn't he shown Ivy that side of it? And he could keep on showing her if she'd just let him. Ending it here and now wasn't fair. He'd make her see that. Make her *feel* it!

Ivy had her gaze trained on the brilliant view of Sydney Harbour from her cushioned seat in the pagoda, but the images of boats and white-crested blue water barely impinged on her consciousness. Waiting for Jordan was like being in a suspended state of animation, knowing she couldn't go back to what they'd had together, yet unable to move forward until after she had laid that out to him.

In a way it was a relief that Olivia had told him about their encounter. At least she wouldn't have to explain that scene. Whether his sister was sorry or not didn't matter. It was best to end the relationship anyway.

Footsteps clacking down the path from the pool terrace, fast and purposeful.

It had to be Jordan.

Ivy tensed, feeling the power of the man coming closer and closer. He stepped into the pagoda, carrying a tray of refreshments and a ruthless air of command that instantly sent tingles of alarm down Ivy's spine. There would be no gracious letting go. Jordan was intent on fighting for what he wanted and exploiting every bit of vulnerability he could use.

As he had before, she reminded herself.

Except she wouldn't fall for it this time.

Her mind was steel on that point, even though her body quivered weakly at his nearness.

'A glass of wine?' he asked, setting the tray on the table, laser-blue eyes searching hers for some chink of giving.

'No, thank you. I'll be driving home very shortly, Jordan. I was thinking…maybe you could contact the people you bought the cruise package from and give it back to them. I won't be going and if you don't want to go without me, it will be wasted.'

He left the table, took a seat on the cushioned bench facing hers, and leaned forward, elbows on his knees, transmitting a patience that had a belligerent edge to it. 'What's behind this decision, Ivy?' he shot at her.

'Our time is up,' she answered with direct simplicity

He shook his head. 'That's not true. What did Olivia say to make you think that?'

'She made me see what I am to you.'

'Olivia doesn't have a clue what you are to me,' was his emphatic retort. 'She only sees things through her own eyes.'

'No. It rang all the bells. You have been a great lover, Jordan, and I thank you for all the pleasure you've given me. I wish I could have been more to you than your closet mistress, but…'

'My *what?*'

Ivy's heart kicked into a gallop at the violence of feeling exploding from his mouth, zapping from his eyes, shooting him to his feet in furious outrage, his hands clenched. She'd never seen Jordan angry and it was frightening.

'Please…will you sit down and hear me out?' she

quickly begged, scared that he might use physical force to bring her back to him.

'You're talking garbage, Ivy.'

'No, I'm not.'

He glared his impatience with her denial, saw the determined jut of her chin, the rejection of what he might do in her eyes, and resumed his seat, stretching his arms out along the backrest to defuse any sense of threat, watching her with an intensity that shredded Ivy's nerves. One hand flipped a dismissal as he said, 'It hasn't been an easy three hours since Olivia's call to me. I would have corrected what she said to you a lot sooner if you'd contacted me. Whatever you're thinking now is wrong, Ivy.'

'Then why have you never introduced me to your friends, your social circle?' she bored in.

'Because you claimed, right from the start, that you wouldn't fit into my scene, and I wanted the pleasure of your company without anything negative taking you away from me.'

The calm, matter-of-fact reply confused Ivy for a few moments. She *had* used their different worlds as a point of resistance to Jordan, but he had proved he could fit into hers. He hadn't given her the chance to come to terms with his. And hadn't planned to. Ever. He had set out to keep her happy in his bed because that was where he wanted her. There'd been no intention to see if she could be his partner in life.

'That's not how a real relationship works,' she said with conviction. 'You have been keeping me in your closet, Jordan, distracting me from that truth by taking me on a lot of marvellous out-of-the-way rides.'

'Wouldn't you say we got to know each other very well on those rides? And enjoyed being together?'

'Of course, I enjoyed it. Who wouldn't? You swept me off my feet in every sense, made a perfect fantasy of our time together. And you would have kept doing it with the cruise, as well, and I would have been too besotted with you to notice.'

'Notice what?'

'How it was simply getaway time for you. Not real time. And when the pleasure of it finally wore thin, I'd be jettisoned from your life, like all the rest.' She gave him a bleak little smile. 'Without the roses.'

He stared at her in silence.

No quick comeback.

No rebuttal.

She remembered the emphasis he'd placed on honesty and realised he couldn't lie to her.

The hope for some different outcome died in her heart.

He didn't love her as she loved him.

Their time was up and there was no point in any more talking, no point in staying another minute. She felt totally spent. It was an act of will to pick up her handbag and rise to her feet. A spurt of tears blurred her eyes as she looked at Jordan for the last time. She had to force herself to say the final words.

'Goodbye. Don't come after me, Jordan. It's over.'

CHAPTER FOURTEEN

'No!'

The shock of absolute finality from Ivy catapulted Jordan from the bench, the need to bar her exit from the pagoda slicing straight through the conflicts raging in his mind.

He couldn't let her go.

That was the bottom line.

He stood in her way, hands held up in a commanding appeal to stop. She did, actually reeling back a step to keep distance between them, clutching her handbag as a defensive shield, her lovely green eyes awash with tears, drowning pools of despair begging him to let her pass without interference.

It screwed up his thoughts and emotions even further. He cared about this woman, didn't want to give her pain, hated her distress. The urge to sweep her into his embrace and give her every physical comfort he could—kiss her tears away, cradle her head on his shoulder, stroke her hair—stormed through him. Only the absolute certainty in the saner part of his mind that it would be a mistake held him back. She would fight him, hate him for not respecting her decision.

He had to fight the decision, change it around. But what with? She had spoken the truth. All the weekends with Ivy *had* been a getaway from his normal life. It had made them special. *She* had made them special. He hadn't wanted anything she might not like to intrude on what they had together.

He'd deliberately spun that strategy out, using the cruise to keep it going, because he had expected their relationship to hit a snag somewhere along the line and come to an end. It was a perfectly rational expectation. He had actually anticipated his *real life* becoming one of the snags, not the omission of it.

'I simply wanted you to be happy with me, Ivy,' he explained. 'Happy with where we were and what we were doing.'

'Happy to be in your bed,' she retorted fiercely, dashing the tears from her eyes, her chest heaving as she scooped in a deep breath and faced him with what she believed. 'It's just sex with you, isn't it, Jordan? You're not looking for a life partner. You certainly don't see me as one. So why don't you *simply* admit that and let me pass because we are not going anywhere any more.'

A life partner…

No, he hadn't been looking for one, had been determined on not going down the marital road with all its pitfalls to suck a man down. Yet, might they not be avoided with a woman like Ivy?

Why not try it?

The thought zapped into Jordan's mind and grew powerfully persuasive tentacles. Margaret approved of her. Having the two women in his household sharing an easy bond was a very positive plus. Besides, a marriage proposal was the strongest possible way of rebutting the reasons Ivy gave for walking away.

It proved he wanted a real relationship with her. He wouldn't lose her today. That was certain. As for the future, if it didn't work out, Ivy was not the kind of person who would milk him for all she could get. He was as sure of that as it was possible to be. Besides, right now he didn't care if there was a price to be paid down the line. He wasn't ready to let her go.

A public engagement would make the transition to sharing his world much easier. People would be currying favour from her, not wanting to upset her in any fashion. It gave her protection from the gossips, from the guys who might want to hit on her, and the mean-spirited women who might be jealous of her success with him.

Most critically, it bought more time.

'You're wrong, Ivy,' he said, his conviction that this was the right move already cemented in his mind. 'I was keeping you to myself because what we have together was and is the most important thing in my life and I want it to go on being the most important. I hadn't planned to ask you at this point but I will because I believe we do and can have a great relationship, regardless of our different worlds.'

He saw the outright rejection of him begin to waver in her eyes, felt an exhilarating burst of adrenaline at the sure prospect of winning. *Seal the deal,* he told himself. Then he could take her in his arms and make her happy with him again.

'Ask me what?' Even her voice was furred with uncertainty.

'To marry me.'

She looked totally stunned.

He spread his hands in open appeal as he nailed home what he was offering. 'To become my wife, Ivy. To be my partner in life. To share everything, the good and the bad.'

He took a step towards her.

She didn't move. Her eyes were glazed with shock.

'To make a future together, have children,' he went on, surprising himself with what was coming out of his mouth, but not caring, intent on pursuing the need to have this woman, moving closer, reaching out, curling his hands around her upper arms, his eyes boring a determined hole through her shock, to engage her mind, her heart with a completely different scenario to the one she had brought to him today.

'Ivy, you're the right woman for me,' he pressed. 'Don't you see that? Don't you *feel* it?'

She stared at him, her gaze swallowed up by deep green pools of vulnerability. He saw her struggling with the wish to believe. There was no resistant strength in her hands when he took her handbag and tossed it onto the bench, no resistance in her body as he drew it against his. He gently cupped her face, the fire in his belly blazing from his eyes.

'I won't ask you to give up your farm. I won't demand that you do anything you don't want to do. We'll sort out how best to work our partnership as we go along, find a balance that we're both comfortable with. We've been good at that so far, haven't we?'

She was listening, still wary of believing but weighing up what he was saying, wanting it to be true.

He had to make it ring true.

'And if you're ready and willing to mix in with my usual social scene, we can start that this weekend,' he went on, driven to rid her of all doubt. 'I haven't been hiding you in my closet, Ivy. I've been waiting for you to feel confident at my side, confident enough to take on anything with me because I'm your man. Not a playboy. Your man,' he repeated emphatically.

Tears welled into her eyes again, but there was hope

shining through them, hope and something that twisted Jordan's heart, making him want to wrap her tightly in his arms and hold her safe from the whole world and any hurt in it.

She lifted her arms and wound them around his neck. Her lips quivered invitingly. The tension inside him eased. He had won. She wanted him to kiss her and he did with a passion, determined on making her feel she was the right woman for him, the only woman. And the way she kissed him back made him feel it, too. Excitement sizzled through him, urging him to go further, take all he could of her, complete possession.

No. Better not to risk it. Not when she'd thought he only wanted her for sex. There had to be some talking first. Her body had always responded to him, but he had to be sure her mind was clear of all bad thoughts, clear on where they were now heading. She hadn't agreed to it yet. Not verbally. Though one thing was certain. She was not about to leave him now.

He forced himself to check the desire that could so swiftly consume good intentions and slowly managed to control himself enough to murmur against her lips, 'Say yes, Ivy. Say yes to us having a future together.'

'Yes,' she said on a sigh of surrender that was blissfully sweet to his ears.

She lifted her head back and gave him a tremulous smile. 'I'm sorry I got it so wrong, Jordan.'

'Not your fault.' He stroked the lovely tilted corner of her mouth. 'I did straighten Olivia out on how I felt about you. What we'll do now is make it very public so there'll be no mistake from anyone about where our relationship stands.'

'Public?' Heat rushed into her cheeks at the thought of being thrust into the kind of limelight that had never shone on her life. 'Jordan, are you sure about this? Maybe we should wait awhile.'

He shook his head. 'Yes means yes, Ivy.' He wanted to get her tied to him as irrevocably as he could at this point. If either of them had doubts about marriage later, they could back out of it then. 'You planned on staying here tonight. Before you go home in the morning, I'll take you shopping for an engagement ring.' He grinned. 'What would you like? A diamond? An emerald to match your eyes? A ruby? Sapphire?'

She burst into nervous laughter. 'I haven't thought about it, Jordan. This is so…so…not what I expected from you.'

'You can look at the ring on your finger and know it's real. What's more, I'll have an announcement of our engagement put in Saturday's *Morning Herald* so everyone will know it's real. And an engagement party. I'll ask my mother to put one on.'

Plans were racing through his mind. He'd sweep Ivy along with him so fast, she wouldn't have time to have second thoughts; he'd open the closet door with a vengeance, plunge her into the society circus with his ring to make her sparkle at his side, then straight off on the cruise where he could keep reminding her of how good they were together. No negative comeback from that course of action.

'It will have to be this Saturday night because we leave for our cruise next Wednesday.'

She looked dazzled. 'What has to be this Saturday night?'

'Our engagement party. Come on, Ivy…' He dropped his embrace to take her hand and draw her with him. 'Let's go up to the house and break the news to Margaret.

Ask her to cook us a celebration dinner. Call my mother. Call your mother.'

He grabbed her handbag and passed it to her, then saw the tray he'd set on the table. 'Better take that with us. We can swap the bottle of wine for champagne. This is definitely the night for it.'

Champagne… Ivy felt as though she had imbibed a whole bottle of it already. Her head was fizzing from the sheer rush of Jordan's proposals…marriage, children, introduction to his family and friends…all unimaginable an hour ago. He had suddenly presented her with a dream life and it didn't feel quite real. Maybe they could make it real. Certainly he was brimming over with confidence, pouring out his vision of their future together as they walked up to the house.

The weird part was she had been about to walk out of his life because he had avoided making a public show of their relationship, and now she felt frightened of what that show might entail. Jordan was probably the most eligible bachelor in Australia. Another girlfriend was not big news, but the notorious billionaire playboy getting married would instantly beam a spotlight on the fiancée whom no one knew anything about. How was she going to handle it? This was a huge leap from her normal, quiet life.

She tried to calm her wildly skittering heart by telling herself Jordan would be at her side. He was used to handling everything, master of any situation. And being with the man she loved…wasn't that what she most wanted? Nothing else should really matter.

It suddenly struck her that Jordan hadn't spoken of loving her.

But he must.

Why ask her to marry him if he didn't?

Besides, she hadn't said it, either.

It didn't really need to be put into words.

She followed him into the kitchen where he set the tray on the island bench and whipped the bottle of wine out of the ice bucket, brandishing it at Margaret who looked relieved to see them together. 'This is not good enough for us tonight,' he said with a happy grin. 'Congratulations are in order, Margaret. Ivy has just agreed to marry me.'

Her mouth dropped open in surprise. She goggled at Jordan for a moment, then looked at Ivy as though wondering if she'd heard right.

'It's true,' Ivy said with a wry little smile, thinking they were probably going to get this reaction from everyone. After all, she hadn't expected it herself.

'Oh!' Margaret cried, suddenly clapping her hands in delight. 'You've made a wonderful choice, Jordan! You're the best, Ivy. The very best.'

'Glad to have your approval,' Jordan rolled out, clearly riding a high. 'You have an hour to whip us up a splendid dinner. I'll take this tray of titbits, minus the wine, into the lounge room and get a bottle of champagne from the bar there. Ivy and I have some calls to make.'

Margaret ignored him, walking over to Ivy, taking her hands and pressing them with pleasure. 'I'll do everything I can to see that you're happy here, my dear.'

The kind acceptance and welcome from Jordan's housekeeper brought a lump of emotional gratitude to Ivy's throat. She could only manage a husky, 'Thank you.'

'Go on now. You'll be fine,' Margaret assured her.

The housekeeper's confidence in her settled some of Ivy's nerves, but the sense of being on a roller-coaster ride persisted, especially as she listened to Jordan's side of his conversation with his mother.

He'd poured them glasses of champagne, made a toast to a happy future together, saw her seated on a sofa, and was walking around the room as he talked, giving out a crackling energy that was not about to be dampened by anything.

'Mum, I need you to do me a favour. I've just asked Ivy Thornton to marry me. She's said yes. And I want you to throw us an engagement party this coming Saturday night.'

His vivid blue eyes sparkled wickedly as he listened to what was undoubtedly a tirade of disbelief at the other end of the line. 'Mum, I'm thirty-six years old and in full possession of all my faculties. I do not need your stamp of approval on my bride-to-be.' He grinned at Ivy. 'I love everything about her, and you will, too. That's all you have to know.'

Love...

Her love for him poured into a smile that beamed with happiness. It was okay to marry him. As long as they loved each other, they could make it work.

'No, I don't want to wait. We're buying the ring tomorrow and we're flying off to Europe next week. I know it's short notice but I'm sure you and your personal assistant can make it happen. Get Olivia to help with the guest list. She owes me big-time.'

He grimaced at whatever his mother said next. Then his face set in a look of ruthless determination. 'No. No meeting beforehand. I won't have Ivy subjected to any uneasiness caused by you or Olivia, who did her worst today. We'll turn up on Saturday night and I expect both of you to be very warm and welcoming. As you should be.'

It was strange seeing this formidable side of him—the

exercise of unrelenting power—though she had glimpsed it before when Olivia had turned up with her blackmail problem. This was how he dealt with his world, she realised, the other side of the charm he had brought into her world.

She needed to know a lot more about Jordan's life. Her instincts said he was the right man for her, but experiencing a *real* relationship with him would definitely make her feel more confident that a marriage between them could work. However, what she needed most was for this current sense of *un*reality to leave her.

'All set,' he said with satisfaction, having ended the call. 'Would you like to contact your mother now? Tell her the news and invite her to the party?'

'Yes, I will.'

Sacha's reaction would surely lift her spirits, generate the excitement that Jordan's proposal should be generating. She fossicked in her handbag for her mobile telephone, found it, switched it on, took a deep breath and set about correcting the false impression of Jordan she'd given her mother earlier today.

Sacha was ecstatic at the marvellous turnaround from break-up to marriage, babbling on about being right about the roses and how happy she was for Ivy. Of course she would attend the engagement party. With bells on! She finished up with, 'I've always wanted the best for you, darling, and I'm sure with Jordan, you'll have it.'

It left a more relaxed smile on Ivy's face as she put her phone away. Margaret had said she was *the best* for him. Her mother thought Jordan was *the best* for her. She remembered at their meeting in the Queen Victoria Building, when Jordan had been pushing for a relationship, he'd argued, *It might be the best thing either of us could ever have.*

All she had to do was believe it.

Jordan took her hands and drew her up from the sofa, a teasing twinkle in his eyes. 'Happy now?'

Her heart swelled with love for him. She wound her arms around his neck, her eyes sparkling with the wonder of what had happened between them. 'Very happy,' she answered.

He kissed her forehead and murmured, 'No more bad thoughts. We're good together, Ivy, and everyone is going to see that. We'll show them.'

'Yes,' she said. It was true. They were good together.

And her whole body pulsed happily with that truth as he fitted it to his and kissed her with more than enough fervour to drive it home. An exultant joy danced through her mind. This was her man. Regardless of what the future held for them, she was never going to regret having him.

CHAPTER FIFTEEN

THE first clash over Jordan's world came at the jeweller's when they were looking at a fabulous array of rings. Ivy had never seen such beautifully cut and crafted gemstones. They were light years above the usual diamond engagement rings one saw in shop windows. She was so dazzled by them, she looked at Jordan in disbelief when he asked her to choose what most appealed to her. They were simply beyond anything she had imagined and her mind cringed at what any one of them might cost.

'You choose,' she pleaded, realising he was intent on having her wear a ring that reflected his buying power and gave her instant status as his fiancée.

Without the slightest hesitation he reached for a brilliant square-cut emerald mounted in the centre of two rows of diamonds, the first row square cut like the emerald, the second shaped like tear drops. 'Let's try this one,' he said, smiling as he took her left hand and slid it on her third finger. 'Perfect fit, too. Do you like it?'

'It's…it's magnificent, Jordan.' What else could she say?

'Great! We'll take it,' he said with satisfaction.

'A fine choice!' the jeweller approved. 'May I show you the accompanying pieces, sir? A matching diamond and emerald necklace and earrings.' He smiled at Ivy. 'I'm sure they would look splendid on Miss Thornton.'

She was speechless, appalled at the suggestion.

'Please do,' Jordan said, obviously enthused by the idea.

The jeweller swiftly removed himself to some back room to fetch them and Ivy seized the chance for a private protest. 'You mustn't buy them for me, Jordan,' she cried anxiously. 'The ring is enough. More than enough.'

He smiled indulgently at her. 'Ivy, I can afford to spoil you with some fine jewellery. And if it does look splendid on you, we'll go shopping for a suitable dress to show it off at our engagement party.'

'No!' She shook her head vehemently. 'They'll all know you bought it. They'll think…' Just like his sister did, that he was fitting her out to be introduced to his social scene—Cinderella striking it rich. 'I don't want it, Jordan,' she said with a fierce surge of pride. 'I'll dress myself and if I'm not good enough for you as I am…'

'Hey, hey!' he cut in, frowning at her reaction to his plan. 'I only meant to give you the pleasure of outshining everyone on the night.'

She glared at him. 'I'm not a trophy woman, remember? It's not me.' She looked down at the ring on her finger, beginning to feel uncomfortable about that, too.

He put his hand over it to prevent her from taking it off. 'You're going to be my wife, Ivy. This ring is part and parcel of that position. I want you to have it. Okay?'

He spoke with soft persuasion but there was inflexible purpose in his eyes, demanding that she surrender to his will on this issue. She heaved a sigh to ease the tightness in her chest and nodded. 'Okay to the ring. But not to you buying me anything else.' She was absolutely inflexible herself on that point. The memory of yesterday's encounter in the Double Bay boutique was too fresh to forget. No way would she invite rotten assumptions to be made about her.

He raised his hand to gently stroke her cheek, which was burning with the ferocity of her feeling. 'You're more than good enough for me and I hope you never change,' he said with what looked like genuine appreciation in his eyes. 'Wear whatever you like on Saturday night, as long as you also wear this ring because it says what I feel about you for the whole world to see.'

Her pride splintered into a quick apology. 'Sorry for being so prickly.' Her eyes pleaded for understanding. 'I guess it's a lot to take in all at once. I won't let you down at the party. I *can* look presentable, you know.'

'Don't let it be too important, Ivy. It's not,' he assured her.

But somehow it was. She was about to be publicly linked with Jordan Powell, and she needed to look like a match for him, not feel out of place at his side. After the purchase of the ring had been made, she delayed her return to the farm, driving over to Double Bay and not leaving until she was satisfied that her wardrobe had been suitably replenished with clothes which would not raise a critical eyebrow anywhere.

The sheer extravagance of what she'd bought nagged at her on the drive home. She was not used to spending so much money on herself. There'd only been the one wild spree for Sacha's exhibition, motivated mostly to avoid criticism, which was what she was doing again now. Jordan was right. She shouldn't let what others might think become too important, nor should she let her pride prevent him from giving her whatever he wanted to give her. If it gave him pleasure to adorn her like a queen, she should accept it gracefully, especially when she was his wife.

She wanted to fit into his world. For him. She needed to learn how to do it, not buck at every entry point. It was important to be more open-minded now, adapt to whatever company she was in. He'd done it for her. Loving him, having his love…keeping that at the heart of everything would surely smooth the path to the future they wanted together.

It was almost four o'clock—Heather's leaving time—when Ivy arrived home. She hurried into the office, carrying her shopping bags, knowing her friend would want to see everything.

'Hi! You're not going to believe this!' Heather exclaimed, swivelling her chair around from the computer table. 'Jordan has just ordered twenty dozen red roses, without the fudge, to be couriered to a Palm Beach residence on Friday afternoon.' Her brow furrowed over this departure from form. 'What do you suppose this means?'

Ivy grinned at her. 'I guess they're to decorate his mother's house for our engagement party on Saturday night.' She held out her left hand. 'Look!'

Heather squealed and erupted from her chair, pouncing on Ivy's hand, her eyes goggling at the ring. 'Oh, wow! That's the best Christmas tree I've ever seen!'

Ivy laughed. 'It does look a bit like one.'

'And marrying Jordan Powell!' She grinned in delight. 'All your Christmases have come at once, Ivy. Why didn't you call me, tell me? It's such fantastic news!'

'*Fantastic* is the operative word,' Ivy answered dryly. 'It didn't seem real at first. I wasn't expecting it. You know why, Heather.'

'That's all in the past,' was Heather's blithe dismissal. 'I thought he was seriously attracted to you and this proves it. Let's go out to the kitchen, pour ourselves a celebratory drink and you can tell me all the marvellous details.' Her eyes sparkled gleefully. 'Did he go down on bended knee to propose?'

Ivy shook her head. 'It wasn't like that.'

She didn't mind revealing the truth to Heather, who knew all the background. They sat at the kitchen table and Ivy poured out her feelings, how Jordan had turned them around, and confiding that she was still coming to grips with the new situation and would be grateful for any input that might help with it.

'Let Jordan be your guide into his world, Ivy,' Heather advised. 'Trust him to decide what's best for both of you. I think he's been doing that already, and he'll go on doing it because he loves you and doesn't want to lose you. Just keep that straight in your mind and don't let other people mess with it. Not his mother, not his sister, not anyone.'

'Yes, you're right,' Ivy agreed, the load of worries lifting from her heart. She could do this—be Jordan's partner in life. Anything worth having was worth working at. With experience would come more expertise in handling whatever had to be handled for them to be happy together.

'Now about this engagement party. Are Graham and I invited?' Heather asked hopefully.

'Of course! And all our other friends, as well.'

'Oh, good! We can hire a minibus for the night and have the fun of going together.'

There were calls to be made, arrangements to be put in place, and knowing she had the happy support of her friends made the prospect of the engagement party much less intimidating. As for the rest, she would have Jordan at her side—her man, proclaiming to the whole world that she was his woman.

It should be—would be—the most wonderful night of her life!

Jordan left no stone unturned to ensure there would be no upsetting incident for Ivy at their engagement party. The roses were a good talking point. Not only did they identify Ivy as a clever businesswoman, but it would undoubtedly amuse people to hear he'd been ordering them from her farm for years and she had initially rejected him because of them. Laughter was always an effective icebreaker and they would look at Ivy with the respect she deserved.

Having dealt with the business of the day, he drove to Palm Beach, intent on checking what his mother and sister had done so far. It was already Wednesday. Much had to be accomplished in three days, but where there was a will, there was a way, especially when cost was no object. Jordan didn't care what was paid out for this occasion. It had to be right for Ivy.

'I'm exhausted,' his mother complained, the moment the butler had shown him into the lounge room where pre-dinner drinks had been served. 'I've been on the telephone all day, letting people know, begging my favourite caterer to drop everything for me…'

'Which, of course, he did,' Jordan dryly remarked. No one refused Nonie Powell.

She set down her glass of sherry and threw up her hands in exasperation. 'Why the hurry? She's not pregnant, is she?'

'No. I just don't want Ivy in any doubt as to where she stands with me,' he replied, his gaze moving to his sister who was nursing a large Scotch on the rocks. 'Before you dull your sensibilities with alcohol, I'd like you to give me your support in doing that, Olivia.'

'I deserve a drink,' she retorted, her chin lifting belligerently. 'I've been on the phone for you all day, too.'

'Thank you. I hope it wasn't too much of a hardship.' He was quite sure she'd had a ball, getting the gossip-mill going as well as spreading the happy news. 'What I want now is for you to write Ivy a letter, apologising for your behaviour towards her yesterday and expressing the hope you can be friends in the future. If it's posted tomorrow for next-day delivery, she'll receive it before the weekend and feel more comfortable about meeting you again on Saturday night.'

Olivia huffed, grimaced, then lifted eyes full of confusion. 'I honestly thought she was getting into you, Jordan. How was I to know that you loved each other? You've never been serious about a woman. Certainly not since Biancha Barlow almost had you fooled.'

Ivy's character was light years away from Biancha's. 'Ivy doesn't want me for my money,' he said with absolute certainty. 'I've known that for quite a while. This morning I wanted to buy her some jewellery to match the engagement ring. She recoiled from it as though I'd offered her a snake. I think you've poisoned her mind against accepting any expensive gifts from me, Olivia, and I need you to put that right. I want her to be happy about what I can give her, not feel branded as a fortune-hunter.'

Olivia frowned. 'What jewellery did she knock back?'

'A necklace and earrings in emeralds and diamonds to match the ring.'

Her eyes almost popped. 'Wow! That's big!'

Jordan bored in. 'I wanted her to have them, Olivia. If you hadn't interfered…'

'Yes, yes, I see your point. I made it nasty instead of nice.' She set her drink down and rose to her feet with an air of decision. 'I'll go to the office and write the letter now. And Jordan…' She gave him a crooked little smile. 'I'm glad for you. I really am. At least one of us might have a happy marriage.'

He smiled back. 'Thank you.'

It was the first time he'd actually felt a sympathetic bond with his sister. Maybe, if Olivia made the effort to be friends with Ivy, he and she could become closer in the future, set their usual antagonism aside and be warmer towards each other.

Strange how suddenly his whole life now seemed centred on Ivy. Marriage to her had not entered his mind until it had burst into it as the only way to stop her from leaving him. Yet it was beginning to feel more and more right, so much so he was determined to prevent any possible snag that might stop it from happening.

'It's only been three months since Sacha Thornton's exhibition,' his mother commented, viewing him with sceptical eyes. 'You're rushing into this, Jordan.'

He raised challenging eyebrows. 'I was told it was only three weeks after you met Dad that he asked you to marry him.'

She waved a dismissive hand. 'They were different times.'

He shook his head. 'People have the same feelings now as they had then, Mum.'

That earned a hard look. 'You're sure she's right for you?'

'Yes.' Doubts could come later, but Jordan was now bent on not entertaining them until they bit him.

'Different backgrounds,' his mother pointed out.

'Doesn't matter.'

'It will in the future.'

'Not if we don't let it.'

She sighed. 'Well, I see you have your mind set on it, Jordan, but it is a different world now and women won't put up with what they used to. Do you honestly think you'll be faithful to her in a long-term relationship?'

He hadn't put that question to himself yet he answered without the slightest hesitation. 'Yes, I do. I've had lots of women in the past, Mum. I know I've got the best with Ivy. I won't even be tempted to look elsewhere.'

She sighed again. 'Yes, I guess you do know that.' Her eyes had a wry look as she added, 'Your father didn't. I was a virgin when we married and I was never really comfortable with what he wanted in bed. In some ways it was a relief when his mistresses supplied it. I knew he would never leave me, but...it wasn't the happiest of marriages, Jordan. I hope you have a better one with your Ivy.'

Jordan found himself deeply touched by this confession and sad that his mother had never known uninhibited joy in sex. 'I'm sorry it was like that for you, Mum. And for Dad. Do you think it was right for you to stay together all those years?'

Nonie's pride answered him. 'I had a wonderful life with your father. I wouldn't have given it up for anything. Besides, we had our family. And your father wouldn't have given that up for anything.'

Family...no, he wouldn't give that up, either, if he and Ivy had children. He had to make this marriage work, on every level. Sex was no problem. He was sure it never would be. If they could strike the right balance with the living part, if Ivy would ease up over fitting into his scene…

'This party is important to me, Mum,' he confided, appealing for her understanding, as well as her help. 'I want Ivy to believe she can have a wonderful life with me. Please…will you ask your friends to be especially kind to her? Olivia did quite a lot of damage to her confidence. If you give her your approval…'

'Jordan, I don't know the girl. I've barely met her.'

'I'm asking you to do it because it's important to me. I can handle the rest but I *need* this from you. Use your power, your influence, to make it a great night for Ivy. I know you can do it.'

Reluctance flashed in her eyes. 'You're putting my judgement of character on the line. What if she lets you down later?'

'Do it out of respect for *my* judgement.'

She stared at him, will clashing against will. Jordan poured every atom of forceful energy into his stare back. 'I've never let you down, Mum,' he said quietly. 'Anything you've asked of me…'

'All right,' she snapped. 'I'll do it. I just hope she lives up to your judgement, Jordan.'

He smiled.

The groundwork was laid.

All that remained was for Ivy to come to the party.

CHAPTER SIXTEEN

THE story of Jordan Powell's engagement to a rose farmer was front-page news in Saturday's newspapers. Jordan had warned Ivy he'd been asked for a press release, and she was safely installed at his Balmoral home before details of their romance were publicly released, escaping from the attention of the paparazzi, who subsequently swarmed to the farm to photograph everything in sight, and a bunch of reporters wanting more personal stories about her.

Heather and Graham held the fort, declaring she was a wonderful employer, there was no dirt to dig up and everything in the garden was rosy. Sacha was also approached for comment, to which she had no comment apart from saying her beautiful daughter deserved a beautiful man and she confidently expected them both to have a beautiful marriage.

After the umpteenth call telling her what was happening, Ivy rolled her eyes at Jordan and wailed, 'Please tell me this is a one-day wonder.'

He laughed and drew her into a reassuring embrace. 'It's a one-day wonder. Truly. Just the surprise element sparking it off. There's nothing to get their teeth into. And we'll be in Europe next week. Nothing to follow up with.'

She sighed and nestled closer. 'That's a relief.'

'There will be a society columnist and photographer at the party tonight, but I'll be right at your side and they won't cause you any unpleasantness. They're my mother's pet media people. Okay?'

She looked him in the eye and solemnly promised, 'I'll do my best to get used to being publicly connected to you, Jordan. I'll learn how to handle it.'

'Don't worry about it, Ivy. The trick is not to let it really touch you. We live our lives regardless of what people print or say.'

She smiled as she reached up and touched his face. 'I'll have to grow some armour like you.'

The Ned Kelly paintings in Jordan's bedroom reflected her comment as Ivy dressed for the party. She'd chosen to wear black, like the armour of the famous bushranger. Black was safe. No one was going to criticise an elegant black dress, and it *was* elegant. The bodice fell from a beaded yoke to a beaded waistband, leaving her shoulders and arms bare. The crepe fabric was cut on the bias for the long skirt so it clung to her hips, then dropped in graceful folds to her feet. She did not have to wear killer shoes with it, which was also safe. And pain-free. It was important to her to feel comfortable tonight. In every sense.

The style of the dress didn't need a necklace. The long jet earrings she'd bought for the sequinned outfit looked right with it. The diamond and emerald earrings Jordan had wanted to buy her would have looked spectacular, but to her mind, they would have distracted people—perhaps unkindly—from the ring, which was spectacular enough on its own.

A last check of her appearance assured Ivy she was suitably armoured for the role of Jordan Powell's fiancée.

Black was the best foil for her pale skin and the riot of wavy red hair fluffed out around her bare shoulders. In fact, she couldn't remember ever looking better than she did right now.

Having fastened a small black beaded evening bag containing repair make-up around her wrist, she headed downstairs to parade for Margaret who wanted to see her in her finery. Jordan's housekeeper had seen him in a formal black dinner suit many times, but Ivy had always worn casual clothes at Balmoral. Tonight was different in so many ways, Ivy's heart started skittering nervously as she saw both Margaret and Jordan waiting for her at the foot of the staircase.

They both looked up. Ivy held her shoulders straight and descended with as much aplomb as she could muster, determined to look as though she was born to be at Jordan's side. Margaret clapped her hands at the performance, grinning from ear to ear in delight.

'Will I do?' Ivy asked, wanting to hear their approval in words.

'You'll do perfectly!' Margaret answered emphatically.

'Perfectly!' Jordan echoed, the blaze of desire in his eyes flooding her with warmth.

She wanted him, too. Which was what all this was about...wanting each other for the rest of their lives. It was easy to keep that in the forefront of her mind as they travelled to Palm Beach. Ray drove them in the Bentley, and sitting beside Jordan in the back seat, his fingers tightly interlaced with hers reinforcing the strong sexual connection between them, Ivy began to feel confident that nothing would separate them.

She had never been to his mother's home. Jordan's house was big and impressive but nowhere near on the same scale as the Mediterranean-style mansion at Palm Beach, with its three storeys of columns and balconies. It screamed opulent wealth, making Ivy super-conscious of stepping into a different world. But she had Jordan as her guide. And partner. She didn't have to be dreadfully nervous about it.

Security guards flanked the entrance gateway, ensuring that only invited guests passed by them. Jordan had planned to be the last to arrive, preferring an informal meet-and-greet as they moved around the party, which was now obviously in full swing. As they alighted from the Bentley, dance music and a distant babble of voices could be heard. Ivy hoped her friends were enjoying themselves.

A butler met them at the front door. They stepped into a grand foyer where a magnificent display of her red roses stood on a marble pedestal. It put a smile on Ivy's face, her eyes twinkling at Jordan, who she knew had organised that, too. The butler ushered them into an incredibly fabulous ballroom: massive crystal chandeliers, mirrored walls, gorgeous sofas, chairs and ornamental tables ringing the dance floor, and doors opening out to a balcony at the end of it.

A live band was playing from a dais in one of the far corners. Most of the younger guests were kicking up their heels on the dance floor. Ivy spotted Heather and Graham amongst them. The rest of the crowd were sitting or standing around chatting, helping themselves to whatever was being offered on the trays of food and drinks being circulated by an army of waiters.

Nonie Powell rose from a chaise longue and came forward to greet them, her royal-blue satin evening dress adding to her queenly air. Sacha detached herself from a group of people, trailing eagerly after her, very much the colourful butterfly in a bright orange silk pantsuit with a long split jacket in shades of violet, blue and turquoise and printed with orange and red flowers. She wasn't actually wearing bells but lots of gold necklaces and bangles were jingling.

The contrast between the mothers was huge.

Totally different backgrounds, Ivy thought, hoping it would never become a divisive issue. Congratulatory kisses were bestowed. Jordan's mother drew them over to a seated group of her closest friends to introduce Ivy. They were all very gracious to her, amused that Jordan had finally been *caught,* saying Ivy must have many admirable qualities to make him drop his playboy mantle, and wanting to hear their plans for the future. The conversation was easy, fun, and Ivy began to relax and enjoy herself.

After they'd posed for the society photographer for a few happy snaps, Olivia dragged them away, declaring her friends were insisting on an audience with the newly engaged couple. Ivy instantly seized the opportunity to thank Jordan's sister for her letter, saying she hoped they could be friends in the future, too.

'Just don't bring any poison into my brother's life and you'll have my respect forever,' Olivia replied, bubbling over with high spirits.

Champagne was flowing and all the introductions were carried out with good humour. Jordan fed it with his charm, satisfying the curiosity about their relationship with amusing stories of how hard he'd had to work to win her. The women admired the ring. The men admired her as a woman. Ivy felt herself being scrutinised from head to foot by both genders but there was no real discomfort from it. The general flow of approval put her at ease.

'The pair of you look fantastic together,' Heather whispered to her in passing. 'You're slaying 'em, Ivy. No worries.'

The only worry was in trying to remember the names of so many people. Jordan helped by repeating them throughout the conversations. On the whole, Ivy thought she was coping fairly well, but she was glad when Jordan insisted they be excused because he couldn't wait any longer to dance with her.

It was a relief to be alone together for a little while, to simply sink into Jordan's embrace and feel at one with him. The slow beat of the jazz waltz thumped through her heart, giving her a dreamy sense of contentment. This was her man and he was the best partner she could ever have to spend her life with.

'Happy?' he murmured, dropping a hot kiss on her hair.

She lifted her head up from his shoulder to shoot him a brilliant smile. 'Very happy.'

He smiled back, the sexy simmer in his eyes giving her a buzz of pleasure. Making love tonight was going to be extra special. She wished they could leave now, but…

'Please excuse me, Mr Powell. I have a message for Miss Thornton.'

It was the butler, startling them both with his intrusion on the dance floor. What message couldn't wait a few more minutes until the music ended?

'Some problem, Lloyd?' Jordan asked, frowning at him.

'Mrs Powell sent me to tell Miss Thornton her father has arrived.'

'My father?' Ivy cried in astonishment. 'There must be some mistake. My father died over two years ago.'

The butler shook his head in dismayed confusion. 'I have no knowledge of this. The man was not on the guest list but he showed identification and explained that he'd been in Melbourne on business and didn't think he could make it to the party on such short notice. However, he'd managed to get an evening flight and didn't want to miss such a special occasion for his daughter. It seemed reasonable...'

'He's an imposter,' Ivy insisted, appalled that anyone would try such an offensive stunt.

'We'll very quickly sort it out,' Jordan assured her. 'Thank you, Lloyd. Not your fault you weren't aware of Ivy's family situation. Though my mother should have been. I told her.'

His frown deepened as he steered Ivy off the dance floor. 'Let's find Sacha first,' he muttered. 'Confront the guy with both of you.'

'Yes,' she agreed, her stomach churning at having to face the disgusting con-man. She wanted her mother there for back-up.

They found her out on the balcony with a group of her friends. Ivy quickly collected her for a private discussion with Jordan. As they joined him she was anxiously explaining, 'A man has come here claiming to be my father, presenting some identification that has to be false. I need you to...'

Sacha stopped dead, shock draining the colour from her face. 'No! No!' The fierce denials exploded off her tongue. Her eyes glazed over.

Ivy grabbed her around the waist to support her, worrying that she was going to faint. It was awful, someone stepping into a dead man's shoes to make some sensational situation, especially when her real father had been dearly loved. 'I'm sorry,' she blurted out. 'It was a shock to me, too. He's with Jordan's mother, and we have to denounce him, Sacha, before he makes more mischief.'

A shudder ran through Sacha. The limpness was shaken off by a surge of outrage. 'How dare he!' She looked at Ivy with wildly ferocious eyes. 'How dare he after all these years! The rotten snake in the grass!'

'Who?' Ivy asked, feeling a flutter of fear.

Sacha turned to Jordan in fighting determination. 'We have to get rid of him. For Ivy's sake. Order your security people to take him away and keep him away.'

'But who is it?' Ivy pleaded, not understanding anything.

'Your father's brother! Dick Thornton! Tricky Dicky!' It was a snarl of hatred. 'I haven't seen him since before you were born, Ivy, but I know him to be a total bastard without any conscience whatsoever. You can bet he's come to try and make some capital out of your connection to Jordan. It's the kind of lousy thing he'd do.'

An uncle! Her father had never mentioned having a brother. His parents—her grandparents—had died before she was born, and he'd told her they were on their own, just the two of them, plus Sacha when they had weekends together.

'Right! Let's go and undo the mischief he's already made,' Jordan said grittily, his handsome face instantly settling into a look of formidable power.

He hooked his arm around Ivy's to carry her along with him. She felt too dazed by the idea of having a wicked uncle to even begin to comprehend what it might mean to her. Sacha marched ahead of them, the panels of her split jacket flying out with the furious energy driving her forward.

The man standing beside Nonie Powell near the entrance to the ballroom had the gall to smile at their approach, not the least bit alarmed at the prospect of being unmasked as an imposter. He cut quite a fine figure in his formal black suit. He'd certainly made himself presentable. There were still some threads of ginger in his greying hair. The straight line of his nose was very similar to her father's, as was the distinctive slant of his eyebrows. Ivy sucked in a sharp breath as his eyes—green eyes—targeted her with dancing delight.

It was easy to understand why Nonie Powell had not denied him entry to the party. The family resemblance, the name of Thornton, would have given her pause for further investigation. However, she had discreetly held him aside from the known guests, waiting for confirmation of his claim, for which Ivy was intensely grateful.

'Well, well, I didn't know what a beautiful daughter I had,' the man rolled out as they arrived to deal with him.

'She's not yours! She was never yours!' her mother declared in towering outrage.

'Still as exotic as ever, Sacha,' he tossed at her, his smile broadening, not dimming at her rebuttal of his claim. 'You make me remember now why I couldn't resist you.'

'Don't think you'll get away with anything this time,' she fired back at him. 'Robert's gone so I don't have his feelings to consider.'

'Poor Robert, who was left sterile from his stint in Vietnam,' he drawled mockingly. 'You must have had to 'fess up to him that it was me who got you pregnant. And you know and I know that DNA will prove it. So let's cut to the chase, shall we? Our lucky daughter has hit the jackpot and I'm here to collect my share of it or the skeletons will come out of the closet with a vengeance.' He smiled at Jordan. 'I can't imagine the high and mighty Powell family would like that.'

'Jordan?' his mother bit out in tight disapproval. 'I did bring up background to you.'

'We all have skeletons in the closet, don't we, Mum?' he answered blandly. 'Let's take this to the library for a more in-depth discussion out of the public eye.'

'Yes,' she snapped, turning haughtily to escape the threat of embarrassing scandal. 'If you'll accompany me, Mr Thornton?'

'With pleasure, Mrs Powell.'

All five of them left the ballroom in Nonie Powell's wake.

Ivy's mind was reeling over the revelations of the last few minutes. Her whole being recoiled from accepting this man as her biological father. Was it true? Did his story have some substance? He'd seemed totally confident that a DNA test would prove his claim of paternity.

Sacha had called him a rotten snake in the grass and clearly that was what he was.

Poison.

And she had unwittingly brought him into Jordan's life.

Poison Ivy.

Her heart sank.

If she was the illegitimate daughter of a blackmailer, how would Jordan feel about this? Would he still want her at his side? He hated blackmail and dealt ruthlessly with it. Maybe he would see separating himself from her as the only way to stop the flow of more and more poison.

CHAPTER SEVENTEEN

THE library was another enormous room; its walls lined with books, a collection of decorative globes of the world adding interest, a huge mahogany desk at one end, two black leather chesterfields facing each other across a parquet coffee table, several black leather armchairs grouped in front of the desk as though ready for a conference.

Jordan led Ivy to one of these and saw her seated, murmuring, 'Don't worry. I'll take care of this.'

She lifted anguished eyes. 'I didn't know anything about this man.'

'We must get to the truth now, Ivy. Bear with it,' he advised her, relentless purpose stamped on his face.

She cringed inside, frightened of what else was to be revealed. As Jordan insisted they all be seated and rounded the desk to take the chair behind it, she stared at her mother who had kept this background hidden from her all her life. Sacha was glaring at Dick Thornton with utter loathing. Her blood-red nails were digging into the leather armrest as though wanting to claw him to death.

He sat at perfect ease, his legs casually crossed, a smug little smile lingering on his mouth. Nonie Powell ignored both of them, sitting straight-backed and stiff-faced as she watched her son take what must have been his father's chair and adopt the air of a formidable chairman who was not about to tolerate any nonsense from anyone at this gathering.

'Sacha, Ivy believes that her father is dead,' he started, boring straight to the vital point. 'Is that true or not?'

'Robert *was* her father,' she insisted vehemently. 'Ivy could not have had a better one. From the day she was born, he loved her and wanted to take care of her. And he did. No father could have been more devoted to his daughter.' She shot a pleading look at Ivy. 'You know that's true.'

'Yes,' Ivy agreed, the word coming out huskily as a lump of grief lodged in her throat.

'Was he her biological father?' Jordan asked.

Sacha sucked in a deep breath and shot another look of loathing at the man seated beside her. 'No, he wasn't. This disgusting rat raped me when I thwarted his plan to talk his brother out of his inheritance. I was left pregnant, and when I couldn't hide it from Robert any more, he insisted on marrying me and bringing up the child as his.'

'Hey, hey, hey!' Dick Thornton protested. 'You didn't yell rape at the time, Sacha. There was a lot of free love going on in that house, as you well know.'

'Free love?' Nonie Powell queried waspishly.

'Only between consenting adults,' Sacha shot at her before turning back to the bad brother in bitter accusation. 'You knew why I didn't call the police. None of us could afford to go anywhere else. We were barely scraping along on part-time jobs in between attending college or uni and studying for our courses. I couldn't risk having us all evicted.'

'Why would you be evicted?' Jordan asked.

Dick Thornton gave a bark of derisive laughter. 'Because they were squatters. A whole bunch of hippie squatters living it up in a deserted mansion.'

'We weren't doing any harm,' Sacha fiercely declared.

'Squatters,' Nonie Powell said in a tone of horror.

Sacha rounded on her. 'Most of us were poor students without any family money to support us. And before you turn your nose up at us, let me tell you, one of them is now the top medical expert in the world in his field. Another is a highly regarded barrister. Yet another went on to become a famous film-maker. I can name names if you feel it necessary to check up on them.'

She turned her gaze anxiously to Ivy. 'Robert was adrift when he came back from Vietnam. No one wanted to know about what our soldiers suffered there. No one wanted to help them. We should never have been in that war in the first place. Robert was a conscripted soldier, sent to do his duty by his country, then treated like dirt to be swept under the mat when he returned. He found refuge in that house of free-spirited students. He tended the garden and grew vegetables for us. He wanted to nurture life, not destroy it, and we were happy there...'

Tears glittered in her eyes. She dashed them away to glare her hatred at Dick Thornton again. 'Until his brother came, preying on Robert's sense of family, saying he didn't need his part of their inheritance to build a future because he was sterile and had no future.'

'If you'd kept your big mouth shut, Sacha, Robert would have turned what our parents left him over to me and you'd have gone on your own merry way, just smelling the roses,' he said mockingly.

Sheer rage erupted. 'You sick bastard! You set out to make Robert feel worthless and he wasn't. He had the right to build a life for himself and I wasn't going to let you take the money he could buy a farm with.'

'So you stuck your oar in and I stuck mine in,' he retorted in a crass jeer.

'By raping her as payback for interfering,' Jordan inserted quietly.

'Gave me a lot of satisfaction,' Dick Thornton admitted with relish, then quickly checked himself. 'Her word against mine in any court of law. Besides, it's all water under the bridge. What counts now is you wanting to marry my beautiful daughter and me wanting a slice of her good fortune.'

'Jordan, you cannot submit to a blackmailer,' Nonie Powell stated in high dudgeon. 'This marriage is clearly unsuitable. Best that you walk away from it right now.'

'Ivy is totally innocent of any wrongdoing!' Sacha snapped at her. 'Can you say the same of your own daughter, Nonie?'

Although it had to be a blind hit, it caused Nonie Powell to press her lips together. She looked at Ivy in angry reproof, as though Sacha had learned of Olivia's problems from her. Which wasn't true. She hadn't spoken a word to anyone about Ashton's attempt at blackmail.

Jordan flicked a querying look at her.

She shook her head, but the implication that she might have blabbed sickened her. No relationship could work without trust. As it was, she wasn't sure their relationship could survive tonight's revelations.

Her mind was awash with the flood of information about both her parents and the situation which had brought them together and led to their marriage—a marriage of need and compassion and love which she hadn't understood until now. Robert and Sacha were good people but that didn't matter, any more than her own innocence of any wrong-doing mattered. There was no escaping the fact that she was the daughter of a rapist, and would be forever tainted by this rotten man.

Jordan sat in silence, weighing up what he'd heard so far. He had instinctively dismissed his mother's solution—*walk away from it*—though that would, of course, extract him from this nasty mess. If it was only lust driving him to keep Ivy in his life…if he still actually anticipated a marriage that only lasted as long as their passion ran hot…why bother dealing with this scum?

He looked at Ivy.

She shook her head as though she'd already given up on the idea of a future together, her eyes sick and despairing, her face totally stricken by all she'd been hearing.

His heart went out to her.

He knew in that instant that this woman meant more to him than anything else in his life. No doubts. No doubts about their future together, either. Nothing on earth could make him walk away from her. He had to fight the urge to get up and take her out of all this right now. The situation had to be resolved first or she'd be haunted by it. He would not let it come between them. Ever.

He turned a stern gaze to his mother. 'In our family, there have been private matters which we've preferred not to bare, Mum. Let's not make hasty judgements on others. I see no fault in Sacha. And certainly not in Ivy. I'd appreciate it if you'd refrain from any further reactive comment and take into account the nobility of decisions made for the good of others. That deserves respect and admiration, not criticism.'

Nonie frowned at him, not used to being chastised for her behaviour and affronted that it be done in front of others, but she hadn't given any consideration to Ivy's feelings and it was well past time she started giving some consideration to how he felt, too.

'While we're on the subject of noble sacrifices, let's get to how much you'll sacrifice for my silence,' Dick Thornton said cheerfully. 'Make it good and you can all play happy families again.'

Jordan wiped everything else from his mind and concentrated on drawing out what was needed. 'How much do you think your silence is worth?' he asked coldly.

'Well, I'm sure parts of the media would gobble up a story like this. Hippie headquarters in a deserted mansion, free love amongst the squatters, brother pitted against brother by our gorgeous butterfly artist, the baby she dumped on one brother to be free to pursue her own career....'

'I did not dump Ivy!' Sacha cried, unable to contain her fury at the malignment. 'She was happy with Robert.' Her gaze turned pleadingly to her daughter. 'I tried living on the farm. I helped Robert start it and worked along with him, but it wasn't the kind of life I wanted and Robert knew it. The artist in me craved much more of the world but he had seen too much of it in Vietnam and the farm was the only world he wanted. He insisted that I go, said I'd given him his life and he wanted to give me mine. We still had weekends together, at the farm or in the city. I didn't dump you, Ivy. I simply couldn't take you away from Robert. You were so much *his* little girl.'

'Except she wasn't,' Thornton mocked. 'And that

lie makes *my* story all the more credible and valuable, doesn't it, Mr Powell? Lovely fruity fodder for gossip.'

Jordan held up a warning hand to Sacha, not wanting her to interrupt again. 'Name your price, Mr Thornton.'

'Oh, I won't be too greedy,' Dick Thornton drawled, believing he was in the box seat. 'Given the fact that you're a billionaire, I think five million dollars is a relatively modest amount.'

'You want five million dollars from me or you'll make your version of the past public. Is that what you're threatening?' Jordan bored in.

'In a nutshell, yes,' Thornton replied, grinning from ear to ear.

'Thank you.'

'No!' Ivy leapt up from her chair, anguished eyes begging him to understand. 'You mustn't do it, Jordan. This will only be the start.' She tugged at the ring he'd put on her finger as she headed for the desk. 'Whatever he says won't be worth anything if I don't marry you. Take this ring back.' She laid it on the desk. 'You can say it was a mistake ever to get involved with me.' Tears pooled in her eyes. 'It was. I always knew it was...just a fantasy.'

'That's not true,' Jordan answered her firmly, picking up the ring and rising to his feet. 'It was right! It was always *right,* Ivy. And I'm not about to let you down.'

'But...' Her hands fluttered in despair as the tears trickled down her cheeks.

Jordan caught her hands and slid the ring back on her finger, his eyes burning through her tears with an intensity of purpose that could not be broken. 'We're going to be together for the rest of our lives.'

And if it hadn't been clear to his mother before

why he loved this woman and wanted her as his wife, it should be crystal-clear now, as she witnessed Ivy's anguish over this situation and her willingness to free him from it.

'Bravo!' Thornton crowed, clapping his hands at what he believed was his triumph.

Jordan shot him a sharply derisive look. 'Bravo, indeed, Mr Thornton. You could not have done a better job of incriminating yourself.'

'So what?' Thornton retorted, totally unruffled. 'It's in everyone's interests here to keep this private.'

Jordan hugged Ivy's shoulders, tucking her close to him, wanting her to feel both comforted and protected as he confronted the slime who so richly deserved some comeuppance.

'My father occasionally held business meetings in this library. He installed a mechanism in his desk to record them. I switched it on when I sat down. Should you go to any section of the media to sell your story, the first action they will take will be to check with me. I will then take the tape to the police and proceed with criminal charges.'

'The story will still get out,' Thornton countered belligerently.

'No one will buy it, and you, sir, will go to jail without any money.'

'Oh, bravo!' It was Sacha this time, clapping her hands with sweet relief at some justice finally being done to the man who had tried to swindle his brother and raped her because she'd frustrated his scheme.

Jordan directed a commanding look at his mother. 'Time to call in a couple of your security men, Mum. Best that our uninvited visitor be discreetly escorted from the premises.'

Nonie was up from her chair and sweeping out of the library before Dick Thornton had fully processed the fact that his scheme was defeated and *he* was about to be evicted.

'Now look here!' he blustered, rising from his chair to fight his corner. 'I can still cause you embarrassment, turning up at your society events and telling all and sundry I'm Ivy's dad. It must be worth something to you to have me stay away. That's not blackmail. You can't have me jailed for that.'

'I can have you arrested for harassment,' Jordan answered, not the least bit concerned by his threat. 'I doubt a dad who deserted his daughter before she was born will be seen as having any rights at all. Why invite trouble when there'll be no profit in it for you?'

That salient point gave the slimy con-man a momentary pause for thought. He then shot a vicious look at Ivy. 'What about her? I can get to her when you're not around. Buy me off and you can live in peace.'

Feeling Ivy shiver, Jordan hugged her more tightly and spoke with totally ruthless determination. 'Do you want to be put under surveillance for the rest of your life, every dodgy move you make watched and reported on? As you pointed out, I'm a billionaire and I will go to any lengths—regardless of cost—to protect the woman I'm going to marry. I'll pay whatever price I have to in order to preserve her peace, but not to you, Dick Thornton. I will never pay you a cent, and I'll make you pay if you ever give Ivy any further distress. You can count on that.'

The extent of Jordan's power and the relentless threat of it finally penetrated. The man stared back at him, the fight draining out of his face. He threw up his hands in defeat as Nonie Powell led two security guards into the library.

'Okay. Call your dogs off,' he snarled. 'I won't bother you again.'

'Oh, I think I'll have them stay on your tail, at least until you move to another city and make a life for yourself away from all of us,' Jordan said to reinforce what he was prepared to do to ensure freedom from this man's poison. Having cast the con-man a look of towering contempt, he addressed the guards. 'Take this man to wherever he is currently housed and arrange to have him kept under constant surveillance until further notice.'

'I told you I won't bother you again,' Thornton cried in panicky protest.

'No, you won't. I'll see that you don't,' Jordan promised him. 'I'd advise you to go quietly now. The idea of putting you on trial and sending you to jail is becoming more compelling by the moment. In fact…'

'I'm going! I'm going!'

He went, closely escorted by the two security guards. Jordan was confident that Thornton would drop out of their lives as abruptly as he'd come into them. Nevertheless, he would keep a check on the con-man's movements, just for extra assurance.

As soon as the door closed behind them he turned to his mother. 'Mum, you and Sacha should return to the party now, preferably arm in arm, presenting a united front. I suggest you indicate you've had a happy chat about the forthcoming wedding. Any questions about Dick Thornton you dismiss by saying he was simply a brash party-crasher pretending to be someone he wasn't. Which is true. Robert Thornton was Ivy's father.'

'Yes, he was,' Sacha agreed with feeling, turning an apologetic face to Nonie. 'I'm sorry this was all such a shock, Nonie, but the past is the past and I've put it behind me for so many years, I never imagined it would…'

'We'll move on,' his mother cut in with her lofty air. 'We must do as Jordan says to save any unpleasant tattle.'

His mother was well-practised at sweeping unpleasantness under the mat and keeping it there. He had no doubt she would handle the situation with her usual queenly aplomb and guide Ivy's mother into following her lead.

'Yes. Yes, of course,' Sacha agreed distractedly. She threw an anxious look back at Ivy as they moved towards the door. 'Robert and I…we never meant you to know how you came to be born. I'm so sorry you've heard about it like this, but it doesn't really matter, Ivy. You've always been loved. Very much.'

Ivy nodded. She couldn't speak. Tears had welled into her eyes again and emotional turmoil was still churning through her. The horror of Dick Thornton, the circumstances of her birth, the background of her parents' marriage, her upbringing on the farm, Jordan's determination to rid her of the nightmare of her biological father and fix every problem that could mar their life together…her mind was jammed with so many feelings it was impossible to think of what she should say or how to say it.

The two mothers made their exit together.

Jordan turned her towards him. 'And you're loved even more now,' he said in his richly charming voice, the bedroom-blue eyes promising her it was true as he gently stroked the wetness from her cheeks. 'I love you, Ivy, and come what may in our lives, I'll never let you down.'

The sickening sense that what she had believed about her life had shifted into something else, and was still shifting as she gained a clearer understanding of how everything had come about, lost its grip on her. Jordan was making the present and what they shared in it far more important.

Faced with a situation that could have shattered everything between them, he had not let her down.

She believed he never would. He was a rock of solid support. She could trust him to be always there for her, no matter what.

Their relationship wasn't a mistake.

It wasn't a fantasy that would come crashing down to earth.

Her heart trembled at the amazing commitment Jordan was giving her. Had given her throughout this terrible showdown with Dick Thornton. Had been giving her all along, from his patient waiting in the coffee shop. She lifted a hand to stroke his cheek in awe of his masterful determination to make what felt right…really right.

'I love you, too,' she said huskily. 'Thank you for…for standing by me. I'll always stand by you in the future. I promise you that, Jordan.'

He smiled teasingly. 'No more giving me up to save me from trouble.'

'No.' She managed a shaky smile back. 'Wild horses won't tear me away.'

'Good!'

A lingering niggle of anxiety remained in her mind. 'I didn't tell Sacha about Olivia's blackmail problem. Please trust me on that, Jordan. I wouldn't gossip about anything so private and hurtful. Your mother obviously thought I had, and you looked at me as though you wondered.'

He shook his head. 'Not because I was wondering about that, Ivy. I was thinking how very wrong about you my mother was, and how very much you suited me, in every sense.'

'Oh! ' It was wonderful to have the trust issue so summarily dismissed. Jordan believed her as absolutely as she believed him.

'And don't be worrying about our respective mothers coming to open blows about their differences,' he went on, speaking very dryly as he added, 'I'm sure they're both strong-minded enough to put them aside as it suits them. They'll think about the future and they'll want to be part of our lives when the grandchildren come along.'

She laughed in sweet relief, realising how well he'd read their mothers' characters. 'How many children would you like to have?'

'As many as you want, my love.' He grinned and added, 'I'm certain to have immense pleasure in making them with you.'

Keeping the rose farm on didn't seem important any more. She would, though, at least through Heather and Graham, but becoming a mother, sharing parenthood with Jordan…that was the future she most wanted…a world of their own making.

'Now let's go and dance,' he said. 'Show the whole world we are one, you and I. Because we are, Ivy. You're my woman and I'm your man and we're going to celebrate our union in front of everyone. That's what this party is about and we're not going to let anyone spoil it.'

'No, we're not,' she agreed, winding her arms around

his neck, her tears completely dried up by the warmth of his pleasure in her, the warmth of his love so manifestly shown to her tonight. 'But kiss me first, Jordan.'

He did.

If eyes followed them to the dance floor, Ivy was totally unaware of them. She was blind to anything but her love for the man who was partnering her…her *life* partner, whose world was her world, just as her world was his. They fitted together. And nothing—nothing whatsoever—was ever going to part them.

THE SECRET MISTRESS

Emma DARCY

To Lew Pulbrook, whose INCA TOURS of South America inspired this book and provided all of the background material in it. Many, many thanks to Lew and Kristy for sharing their knowledge and experience, while showing me and all 'The Amigos' a fantastic and fascinating part of the world.

CHAPTER ONE

LUIS ANGEL MARTINEZ was feeling good as he rode the elevator up to his hotel suite. He'd completed the business he'd come to La Paz to do, he'd dined well, the current crisis in the city provided him with the perfect excuse for missing his own engagement party, and his mother—widely regarded as the wealthiest and most powerful woman in Argentina—couldn't do one damned thing about it.

He couldn't help smiling.

The two young women who were sharing the elevator—their accents and clothes marking them as tourists from the U.S.A.—turned interested, hopefully inviting eyes on him. Luis instantly killed the smile. Black scorn blazed from his dark eyes, shrivelling their speculation, and his whole body stiffened in proud rejection of whatever fantasies they nursed.

He despised the foreign women who tripped around, looking for sexual adventure, and he most particularly hated being viewed as a possible Latin lover. He might look the part, having the dark olive skin and black hair of his Spanish heritage, with the added attraction of a taller, more powerful physique than the average South American male, but he sure as hell would never get drawn into playing the part.

He'd been burnt once. Once was more than enough for him.

The elevator halted. He glared balefully at the back of the two blonde heads as the women made their exit. Not that their fairness compared in any way to the silky sun and moon mixture of Shontelle's hair, but the minds under the hair probably held the same attitude towards sampling one of the natives for the pleasure of a new carnal experience.

Not me, ladies, he savagely beamed at them before the doors shut and the elevator resumed its upward climb. His mother was right on one score. Best to tie himself to a woman of his own race, own culture, own background. No nasty surprises with that kind of matchmaking. All smooth sailing. Especially with Elvira Rosa Martinez at the helm, steering everything as she saw fit.

Except she hadn't counted on this little squall blowing up in Bolivia, causing him to miss the engagement party she had planned behind his back.

Unavoidable circumstances.

The absolutely perfect excuse.

The thought restored Luis' good humour. He was smiling again as the elevator opened onto his floor and he headed for his private suite. No one could validly question his staying right here. It was literally impossible for him to get out of La Paz without running into trouble.

After yesterday's violent march of the farmers through the streets, Bolivia was boiling up to yet another change of government. The airport was closed. A curfew had been imposed. The military had taken over the city.

Safely and comfortably ensconced in the Plaza Hotel, Luis was not in the least perturbed by these events. Bolivia was Bolivia, renowned for having more changes of government than any other country, five in one day in recent history. The volatile political situation would eventually blow over and life would go on as usual.

He entered his well-appointed suite, closed the door on all the outside problems, and moved to the mini-bar, deciding one or two more celebratory drinks were in order.

Of course, a second engagement party would be arranged, although he'd insist on doing it himself—*his* way—next time. This minor reprieve was only a postponement of the inevitable. He was thirty-six years old, time for him to marry, time for him to start a family. It was also time for his mother to step right out of his affairs.

She'd undoubtedly be stewing with frustration over this further delay to a public announcement of her most cherished ambition—the tying of the Martinez fortune to that of the Gallardo family. Do her good, Luis thought with intense satisfaction. She was far too fond of pushing.

She'd picked Claudia Gallardo out for him very shortly after his brother's death. Luis had scoffed at the idea—a schoolgirl! She'd be groomed to suit him, to grace their social position, to uphold all the traditional virtues of a wife, his mother had argued. I'll choose my own wife, he'd tossed back at her at the time, but he really didn't care anymore, not since Shontelle—that green-eyed witch—had chewed him up and spat him out.

He took ice and a lime from the refrigerator, lined up the bottle of *Caipirinha,* and wished he could blot the memory of Shontelle Wright right out of existence. Because of her…after her…he'd wanted more than just a *suitable* wife. He'd wanted to feel…

But maybe he didn't have any passion left in him, so what did it matter if his marriage bed wasn't as warm as he'd like it? Stupid to keep holding out for something he might never experience again. He would make the commitment to Claudia soon enough. She was willing. He was willing. Together they'd beget another line of heirs and heiresses. Surely he'd feel something for his children.

Nevertheless, it was one thing resigning himself to the destiny mapped out for him, another to be relentlessly pressed into it. Although he'd finally put his rebellious years behind him and shouldered the responsibilities that would have been his older brother's, had Eduardo lived, Luis did not want his mother thinking she could rule his life. He was glad—yes, glad—he couldn't fly back to Buenos Aires to keep *her* timetable, however *reasonable* it was.

Claudia would undoubtedly wait submissively.

She did everything…submissively.

Luis grimaced. Sometimes he suspected it was an act, deliberately put on to give him the sense of being on top. Respected. Honoured. King of his kingdom. But, so what? At least he knew where he was with Claudia.

He dropped the wedges of lime into his glass, mashed sugar into them, added the ice and drowned the lot with *Caipirinha.* Sweet and sour—like life, he thought. The telephone rang as he stirred the drink. Carrying the glass with him, he moved to pick up the nearest receiver, cynically wondering if his mother had found a danger-free way out of La Paz for him.

"Luis Martinez," he rolled out carelessly.

"Luis, it's Alan Wright. Please...don't hang up. It's taken me hours to track you down and I desperately need your help."

The quick, taut plea stilled what would normally have been an automatic reaction. Luis had no wish to see, hear, or have any contact with the man whose sister had taken him for no more than a lump of tasty Latin meat. The heat of deeply lacerated pride instantly burned through him.

"What kind of help?" he snapped, angry with himself for even hesitating over cutting off his former friend.

"Luis, I have a tour group caught here in La Paz. We were due to fly to Buenos Aires yesterday. God knows when the airport will be reopened. They're frightened, panicky, and some are suffering from altitude sickness. I need a bus to get them out. I'll drive it. I thought you might be able to provide it.''

A bus.

It conjured up old memories—a much younger, wilder Alan, driving a beaten-up bus through the Amazon jungle to the mining operation where Luis had been sent for safekeeping, away from the troubles in Argentina. Alan had worked there for six months, more or less swapping his mechanical skills for the spare parts he needed to get his bus roadworthy enough to set up his own tour business.

An Australian, in love with South America—nothing was going to stop Alan Wright from selling it to tourists back home. Camping trips to start with, he'd decided. Then gradually he'd build up to the bigger money stuff. Luis had admired his initiative and determination, liked his cheerful good nature, and enjoyed his company. For nine years they'd maintained an infrequent but always congenial contact with each other. If Alan hadn't introduced his sister…

''Is Shontelle with you?''

The question slipped out, unconsidered and loaded with a long, pent-up hostility that hissed down the line.

No denial. Nothing but a fraught silence that emphatically underlined the division of their interests.

''Is she?'' Luis demanded harshly, uncaring of what the other man thought, knowing he had the power to ruthlessly cut their connection without any comeback.

"Goddammit, Luis! I'll pay you for the bus. Can't you just deal with me?" Alan exploded, tension and urgency ripping through every word.

She was with him.

More than pride started burning through Luis Angel Martinez. Every cell of his body was hit by an electric charge. Adrenalin shot through his bloodstream. Even the sense of his sexuality leapt into powerful prominence…sharply revitalised, wanting, needing, craving the satisfaction of wringing something more from the woman who'd dismissed all they'd shared as a brief bout of lust, come to the end of its run.

"Where are you?" he asked.

"At the Europa Hotel," came the quick, hopeful answer. "As luck would have it, just around the corner from the Plaza."

"Very convenient!" Luis smiled. It was a smile that would have chilled the heart of anyone who saw it. "What's the size of your tour group, Alan?"

"Thirty-two, including me."

"I can get you a suitable bus…"

"Great!" A gush of relief.

"…And have it at your hotel, ready to go in the morning…"

"I knew if anyone could do it, you could." Warm gratitude.

"…On one condition."

Silence. On edge again. "What is it?" Wary.

Luis didn't give a damn about Alan's feelings. His

friendship had probably been as self-serving as his sister's association with him. After all, for a foreign tour operator, Luis Angel Martinez was a contact worth having in South America. He could open doors.

And shut them.

"Shontelle will have to come to my suite at the Plaza to negotiate the deal with me," he stated blandly. "The sooner the better, for your purposes."

"You can't be serious!" Alan burst out. "There's a curfew on. Army tanks are trundling around the streets and trigger-happy soldiers are everywhere. A woman alone, breaking curfew…it's too dangerous, Luis."

So was driving a bus out of here, Luis thought. The farmers were in revolt. They'd be blockading all the roads from La Paz. Alan was obviously prepared to take risks to get his people out, probably counting on his skill as a good talker with a dab hand at appropriate bribery. Which he could use tonight, as well, if need be. His plea on Shontelle's behalf left Luis totally unmoved.

"You can escort her from hotel to hotel, if you like. The distance is very short and the road that links us is a cul-de-sac, hardly the place for a tank or soldiers on guard duty," he pointed out.

"I can't leave the group. Shontelle can't, either. The women need her to…"

"There is a side entrance to the Plaza from the steps leading up to Prado 16 de Julio. I'll have a man posted at the door to let her in. Let's say...half an hour from now?''

Luis set the receiver down with firm decisiveness. He smiled again as he jiggled the ice in his drink. A responsibility to others often led to paths one wouldn't take, given an absolutely free choice. Because he was his mother's son, he would end up married to Claudia Gallardo. Because Shontelle was Alan Wright's sister, she would end up in this suite tonight.

With him.

And he would take a great deal of pleasure in stripping her of more than her clothes!

CHAPTER TWO

SHONTELLE saw her brother's jaw clench. He literally gnashed his teeth as he slammed the telephone receiver down. The violent action caused her heart to leap out of the frozen stasis that had held it for the duration of the call. The resulting pump of blood kicked reason into her mind, clearing it of the dark cloud of memories.

''What did he want?'' she asked. It was obvious from the conversation that Luis had at least considered procuring the bus. It was certainly possible for him to do so. The Martinez family had fingers in many pies right across the continent; agriculture, mining, cement works, oil and gas, transport…

''Forget it!'' Alan's hand sliced the air with negative vehemence. ''I'll try something else.''

There was nothing else. Shontelle shook her head over the mess of notes on the table. They'd already been down every other avenue. The usual help Alan could tap into was not forthcoming.

She watched him steam around the sitting room of the suite they were sharing, a big man chopping up the space around her, making it feel claustrophobic with the sense of failure. Getting accommodation in The Europa, a relatively new five-star hotel, had been a coup for this tour. Now it seemed like a prison. Everyone in the tour group had lost their pleasure in its luxury, anxieties building with being trapped here. More bad news could make soothing fears and frayed tempers a very difficult, if not impossible exercise.

Alan always fought against imparting bad news to his tour groups, especially when there was no good news to make it more palatable. Normally he was a very cool operator, highly skilled at lateral thinking whenever a crisis arose, as it frequently did in South America. The ability to be flexible was paramount to bringing off a successful tour and Alan was always prepared to come up with an alternative schedule. But this time he'd found himself blocked at every turn.

He was the kind of man who hated being thwarted.

Or found wanting in any way.

So was Luis Angel Martinez, Shontelle remembered.

The two men were very alike in that respect. Kindred spirits. They'd been friends…the type of friendship where time and distance and social standing had no relevance. They might not meet for long intervals but such separations hadn't made any difference, not over the nine years before…

Guilt wormed through Shontelle.

She had ruined it. For both of them. Blindly, wantonly, foolishly. Alan had warned her it wouldn't work between her and Luis. Couldn't. But she had refused to listen, refused to see…until Elvira Rosa Martinez had so very forcefully opened her ears and eyes. Then she'd been too wrapped up in her pride to realise how her exit from Luis' life might have a bitter fallout on his friendship with her brother.

Not that Alan had told her of the consequences of her decisions. She had overheard Vicki, his wife, dryly informing an office associate they were no longer welcome on Martinez territory. The popular day trip from Buenos Aires to the ranch run by Luis' younger brother, Patricio, had been struck from the tour.

When she'd tackled Vicki about it, the forthcoming explanation had been devastating. ''Shontelle, did you really expect Luis Martinez to keep up the connection? You and Alan are not only of the same family, you even look alike.''

It was true. Alan was ten years older than her but the family likeness was unmistakable. The bone structure of their faces was the same; wide brow, high cheekbones, straight nose, clearcut chin. Alan's top lip was thinner than hers and his eyes were not a clear green—more hazel in colour. The streaky blonde hair of his youth had darkened over the years but the variation in shade was still there. Either one of them was a physical reminder of the other, and that reminder would not be welcome to Luis Angel Martinez.

In her pride, Shontelle knew she had wounded his. It hadn't seemed to matter at the time. But it did. She had the strong conviction it especially mattered now.

''You were talking to Luis about me,'' she said, drawing Alan's attention.

He flashed her a pained look. ''He asked about you,'' he answered dismissively.

''No. It was more than that.'' She frowned, trying to recall what she'd heard. The call had ended abruptly, just after Alan had said it was too dangerous for a woman to be out during curfew. ''Tell me what he wanted, Alan.''

''I said, forget it!'' he snapped impatiently.

''I want to know. I have a right to know,'' she argued. ''I'm just as responsible for this tour group as you are.''

He paused in his pacing but aggression still pumped from him. His eyes glittered with a fury of frustration. ''I will not have my little sister grovel to Luis Martinez for anyone!'' he bit out.

Morc pride.

It was heart-thumpingly obvious that Luis had turned the deal for the bus into something personal. Very personal. Which again was her fault. Shontelle took a deep breath to calm a host of skittish nerves. She couldn't let this pass. It wasn't fair to Alan. Besides which, the tour group was depending on them to rescue them from the situation.

''I'm not little,'' she pointed out determinedly. ''I'm twenty-six years old and I can take care of myself.''

Alan rolled his eyes. ''Sure you can! Like you did two years ago whcn you talked me into leaving you with Luis.''

"I'm over that. I can deal with him," she insisted hotly.

Too much personal knowledge sliced back at her. "You didn't want to come back to South America. You wouldn't be on this trip but for Vicki getting glandular fever. And you were as nervy as hell while we were in Buenos Aires."

Her cheeks burned. "I came to assist you. That's my job." She pushed her chair back from the table which was littered with the evidence of failed attempts at solutions. Resolution drove her to her feet. "I'll go and talk to him."

"No, you won't!"

"Luis Martinez was your last resort, Alan. Two years ago he would have got you the bus, no problem. I caused the problem and I'll deal with it."

He argued.

Shontelle stood firm.

Nothing was going to stop her; not the curfew, not the danger—which she considered very limited with the Plaza Hotel being virtually next door—not any of Alan's big-brotherly concerns. She'd lived with guilt and shame too long. She'd spent two years being eaten up by memories she couldn't change or bury. Luis Martinez wanted a face-to-face meeting with her. Then let it be. Let it be.

Maybe something good would come out of it.

The bus, if nothing else.

She owed Alan that.

CHAPTER THREE

GOOD intentions were all very fine when made from a safe distance. Shontelle stared at the door which led into the suite occupied by Luis Angel Martinez and her heart quailed. A suite contained a bed…

She wasn't over him. She doubted she ever would be. Luis Angel… She'd even been besotted with his name. Dark angel, she thought now, barely suppressing a shiver. It took all her willpower to raise her hand and knock on the door.

In the next few stomach-knotting moments, Shontelle tried to steel herself against revealing the vulnerability she felt. This meeting would only be a matter of pride to the man she had to face. He undoubtedly wanted to rub in that she was the loser, not him.

Somehow she had to let that wash over her, do a bit of grovelling if need be. Remember the bus, she fiercely told herself. She had to get the bus.

At least Luis couldn't mistake the fact she was dressed for business. Her dark red T-shirt was printed with the *Amigos Tours* logo and her khaki trousers with pockets running down both legs were plainly practical, as were her sturdy shoes. This was strictly a business visit.

The door opened.

And there he was, hot flesh and blood, simmering in front of her. His thick, wavy black hair was brushed away from the beautifully sculpted features of his face, as always, framing them with a kind of dark, savage splendour. His skin gleamed with almost a magnetic vitality. His deeply set eyes, lushly outlined by their double rows of lashes, projected more power than any one man should ever have.

Shontelle stood rooted to the floor, speechless, breathless, mindless, her good intentions instantly zapped out of existence. Her scalp tingled. Every millimetre of her skin tingled. Her fingers curled into her palms, nails biting into flesh. Her toes scrunched up in her walking boots. Her heart swelled, throbbed, its heavy beat of yearning echoing through every pulse point.

She wanted him.

She still wanted him.

''Welcome back to my part of the world.''

His voice jolted her back to the chilling reality of why she was here. She'd loved his voice—its deep, rich, flowing tones—but there was no caress in it now, nothing warmly intimate. No welcome in his smile, either. The full-lipped sensual mouth that had once seduced her with such passion, was curled into a sardonic taunt, and the dark blaze of his eyes held a scorching intensity that shrivelled any hope of reviving good feelings. Or even a workable understanding.

He stepped aside to make room for her to enter,

derisively waving her into his domain. For one nerve-jangling instant, the highly civilised Plaza suite blurred in Shontelle's mind and the Amazon jungle leapt into it—its overwhelming sense of the primitive pressing in on her, vampire bats biting for blood, big black tarantulas hiding in trees, ready to pounce on their prey…

"Scared?" Luis mocked, his eyes raking her with contempt.

It goaded her forward. "No. Should I be?" she tossed at him as she passed by, determined on holding a brave front.

He closed the door behind her.

The metallic click felt ominous.

"Spurned Latin lovers are notoriously volatile," he remarked, still in a mocking tone.

"A lot of water under the bridge since then, Luis," she answered, shrugging off the implied threat and walking on through the sitting room of the suite, aiming for the big picture window on the other side of it.

The spectacular view of La Paz at night was not the drawcard. She desperately needed to put distance between her and the man who'd deliberately raised memories of their affair. And its ending.

"I must say you look as dynamic as ever," she threw at him, forcing herself to attach a conciliatory smile. "I'd say life has been treating you well."

"It could be better," he replied, watching her move

away from him with a dark amusement that raised Shontelle's sense of danger several notches.

"I expect you're married by now," she added, trying to drive a moral wedge between them.

His white shirt was half unbuttoned, revealing a provocative arrowhead of his broad muscular chest, dark skin tipped by a glimpse of the black curls she knew spread across it. His forearms were bare, too, sleeves rolled up, flaunting his strong masculinity. She hated the thought of his wife knowing him as intimately as she had.

"No. As it happens, I'm not married."

The cold, hard words were like nails being driven into Shontelle's heart. Had she made a mistake? A flood of hot turmoil hit her. Fortunately she'd reached the window. She swiftly turned her back on him, hiding her wretched confusion, pretending to be captivated by the spectacular view.

Surely to God he was lying! He'd been betrothed to another woman—the Gallardo heiress—before and during their affair two years ago. He'd lied then, by omission. He'd left Shontelle blindly believing she was the only woman who counted in his life when there were two others who had a longer, deeper claim on him.

How could anyone not count Elvira Rosa Martinez?

More to the point, it had been totally unconscionable of Luis to remain silent about the young woman designated as his wife; the sweet, convent-raised, beautifully mannered Claudia Gallardo.

His silence had spelled out where Shontelle stood in his life—a handy bit of foreign fluff on the side, out of his mainstream, suitable only for fun and relaxation. But then he hadn't made any promises, she savagely reminded herself.

''I assume you're not married, either, since you're travelling with your brother,'' he drawled, each word sounding closer.

He was coming after her.

''I'm here on business, Luis,'' she said tersely, wishing she hadn't raised anything personal. He couldn't be believed anyway. He'd undoubtedly say—or not say—whatever suited his purpose.

''Do you have a lover tucked away at home, waiting to serve your inclinations?'' His voice had the stinging flick of a whip.

''I'm all out of lovers at the moment,'' she answered flippantly, disdaining even a glance at him.

''Which is why you came on this trip, mmh?''

The silky taunt hit her on the raw. The urge to swing around and let him have the sting of her tongue almost blew her mind off her purpose here. She gritted her teeth, folded her arms to hold wayward impulses in, and stared fixedly at the myriad of lights beyond the window.

''It looks like a fairyland outside, doesn't it?'' she remarked as lightly as she could.

It was true. La Paz was the highest capital in the

world and it appeared to be built in a moon crater. From where she was viewing it from the low downtown area, the lights of the city rose in a great circular curve, going up so high they seemed to be hanging in the sky. Incredible there were actually people living behind them.

''You need a magician to get you out of it,'' Luis mocked, standing right behind her now.

''We need a bus,'' she said quickly, fighting her intense awareness of his nearness.

''The curfew doesn't lift until six in the morning.''

Her heart skittered. What was he implying? They had all night to negotiate?

''I don't like your hair constricted in a plait,'' was his next comment, confusing Shontelle further.

Her spine crawled at his touch as he lifted the rope of hair away from her back. She knew what he was going to do but her mind couldn't accept it. He couldn't still love her hair. He couldn't still *want* her!

Or maybe he didn't.

Maybe he was playing some cruel cat-and-mouse game.

She wanted to look at his face but she was frightened to. What if he was waiting to feed off her feelings? Pride insisted she deny him the satisfaction of knowing she was rattled. Could he hear the mad thumping of her heart? Stay calm, stay calm, stay calm, she recited feverishly.

He'd worked off the rubber band and was separating the twisted swathes, seeming to take sensual pleasure in the feel of her hair. Impossible to ignore it. Impossible to stay calm.

"What do you want from me, Luis?" she blurted out.

"What I had before."

Her mind fragmented under the force of her own desire to have him again, and his apparent desire to recall and repeat the passion they'd shared. Some tattered shreds of reason shrieked that he was only playing with her, using his power to make her succumb to him, but she had to know, had to see.

As she jerked around to face him, her arms flew out of their protective fold and lifted into an instinctive plea for truth. "What do you mean?" she cried.

He still held a skein of her hair and he wound it around his hand as his eyes blazed their dark purpose into hers. "I mean to seize the day, Shontelle. Or to put it more graphically...the night. You want a bus. I want one more taste of you."

Shock waves slammed through her.

One more taste...

Only *one...*

Payment for the bus.

"Not such a difficult deal, is it?" he taunted. "Just a matter of giving me what you gave of yourself two years ago...in your desire to get what you wanted of me."

"I didn't get what I wanted then," she protested, her voice thin and shaky under the appalling weight of devastated hopes.

A savage fury flared into his eyes. "Was I not all you wanted of a Latin lover?" His mouth curled with cruel intent. "Well, let me try not to disappoint you tonight. We have many hours ahead of us. I promise you a feast of hot-blooded sensuality."

Hot and hard and ruthless.

The awful part was, Shontelle could not stop her body from pulsing with excitement at what he offered. Only with him had she ever known intense physical ecstasy. She hadn't even felt a twinge of attraction towards anyone else in the past two years. Just the thought of touching Luis again, feeling him…quivers of anticipation shot through her.

But he was treating her like a whore, laying it out that she could only get the bus in return for sex.

Sex…not remotely connected to love. Not even the slightest semblance of love. It was wrong, wrong, wrong! Her heart twisted in torment as he twisted her hair more firmly around his hand and tugged her closer to him. Then his other hand slid over her breasts, his palm rotating caressingly, his eyes glittering their triumphant knowledge of what had pleasured her in the past, and to prove him right, her nipples instantly stiffened into begging prominence.

"Stop it!" she hissed, hating his power to arouse her even as she revelled in the sharp sensation that stimulated a host of nerves, arcing from her breasts to the innermost core of her sexuality.

One black eyebrow arched mockingly. "You no longer like this?"

He was the devil incarnate, tempting her. The truth was, she didn't want him to stop. She didn't want him to ever stop. But he would. This was only to be one more taste. Unless…

Something deeply primitive stirred in Shontelle.

He wasn't married, so he said.

And he still wanted her.

He also wanted a payback for his wounded pride.

Well, so did she. So did she!

"I don't normally go for one night stands," she said.

"But these are special circumstances," he returned silkily.

"Just let me understand you clearly, Luis…"

With her heart thumping to a wild beat, Shontelle flicked open the shirt button over his chest curls and slid her hand inside, seeking and deliberately tweaking one of his nipples. His sharply indrawn breath was music to her ears. She had power over him, too. It wasn't a one-way street.

Her eyes flirted challengingly with his as she spoke through the provocative, physical teasing. "…If I stay with you the night and let you have your…" She lowered her gaze to his mouth, regarding it assessingly. "…taste of me…" She let the words linger for a moment, then flicked her gaze up, raising her eyebrows in pointed questioning. "…I get the bus? Is that the deal?"

"Yes," hc hissed at her.

"Then make your calls now, Luis. Let me hear you

arrange the delivery of an appropriate bus to The Europa Hotel as soon as the curfew is lifted tomorrow. When you've done that, I'll call Alan to assure him everything's all right and I'll be staying with you until morning.''

His jawline tightened. His eyes narrowed. He didn't like her calling the shots, but he'd dealt her the cards, made the rules of the game, and Shontelle figured he couldn't fault her over playing them. A sense of triumph poured a burst of adrenalin through her veins. No one was a victim unless they allowed themselves to be.

She pursed her lips into a considering little smile. ''A feast of hot-blooded sensuality sounds good. I do hope you're up to it, Luis.''

The moment the words were out, she felt a swell of danger—a dark and fierce emanation from him swirling around her, sending shivers down her spine. He smiled right back at her as he released her hair—a smile that promised himself a deep well of satisfaction. He plucked her hand from inside his shirt and drew it slowly down, palm against him, fingers splayed.

''Feel for yourself how *up* to it I am, Shontelle,'' he drawled, his other hand gliding up her throat to cup her chin.

He was fully erect, his arousal straining against the barrier of clothes. He guided her into stroking him as he tilted her head and bent his own. ''Just to make sure I do want the taste,'' he murmured, then covered her mouth with his, not giving her any chance of reply.

Shontelle didn't even think of trying to deny him. The urge to taste him, too, was far too strong for any denial. And his mouth was soft, sweetly seductive, at first, his tongue merely flicking over the soft inner tissues of her lips, sensitising them with delicious tingles.

She responded, wanting to know if the passion they had once shared could be triggered again, beyond pride, beyond all the differences between them. Her free arm instinctively curled around his neck to hold him to her and the kiss deepened, pursuing a more erotic, more exciting intimacy.

Her body started clenching with a need it had all but forgotten. She grasped the hard proof of his desire, fingers digging around it, revelling in the feel of him. She was so caught up in her own strong responses, it came as a shock when he abruptly ended their kiss, removed her hand from him and broke out of her embrace.

''You must be hungry for a man, Shontelle,'' he mocked, lifting the fingers that had been squeezing him to his mouth. He lightly nipped them. ''Definitely an appetising taste. Please excuse me while I execute my half of the deal. I look forward to the rest of the night.''

He walked away from her, seemingly completely in control of himself. Shontelle was left feeling shattered, her legs trembling, drained of strength, her stomach churning so much she wanted to be sick, her heart aching, her mind zigzagging helplessly through a maze of fierce contradictions.

She loved him…and hated him.

She craved more of him…yet wanted to cut out his callous heart.

Was it to be a night of intense life…or a night of heart-killing desolation?

She didn't know…couldn't decide…couldn't tear herself away from whatever might pass between them.

He picked up a telephone, pressed a sequence of numbers, spoke with the arrogant authority of his name, his position, the power that came automatically with great wealth…Luis Angel Martinez…the only man who'd ever moved her like this…and maybe the only man who ever would.

Was there anything to win by staying?

The bus, her mind answered.

But the bus had no relevance to the question.

She wanted…needed…to win something for herself. So she had to stay and see this night through, even if she lost everything.

One night…one night…unless she could turn it into something more.

CHAPTER FOUR

LUIS was rock-hard and in pain but the shattered look he'd left on Shontelle's face was worth every second of the discomfort. No way was she going to turn the tables on him! He hoped the witch was burning with frustration.

He deliberately kept his back turned to her while he talked on the phone to Ramon Flores who could organize any form of road transport in La Paz. It was local courtesy to speak Quechua, the old Inca language, and Luis did so with perverse pleasure, knowing Shontelle would not be able to follow it. Her grasp of Spanish was good, but she only had a sketchy knowledge of the native dialects.

Let her stew in uncertainty, he thought. She was too damned sure of her power to get what she wanted. Before this night was out she'd learn who was master of the situation, and he'd kiss her goodbye with the same brutal finality she'd shown him two years ago.

''The bus is not a problem, Luis,'' Ramon said predictably. ''But...''

The pause sharpened Luis' attention. ''But what?''

''It would be useless to ask any of my local drivers to deliver it. They would be stopped and arrested before the bus got to The Europa. The military edict is no gathering of crowds. They consider three people together a crowd. A local man taking out a bus…it would not be allowed. Too suspicious.''

Luis frowned. He hadn't thought of that. Yet if he didn't deliver…no, he had to. He refused to look weak and ineffectual in front of Shontelle Wright. There had to be a way.

''Your Australian friend…he might get through, being a foreigner,'' Ramon suggested. ''Since he is prepared to risk his tour group in trying to get out of La Paz, tell him to come to the depot and take the bus himself. It will be fully fuelled, ready to go.''

It made sense, but it wasn't the deal he'd agreed to with Shontelle. Her words, not his, he reasoned. He didn't have to toe *her* line. The essence of the deal was the same. The bus would be available for Alan to take. That was all his erstwhile friend had requested.

''Someone will be at the depot to hand over the bus?'' he asked.

''Curfew lifts at six. I'll have a man at the gates at six-thirty.''

''Thank you, Ramon.''

''Your friend is a fool, Luis.''

''His choice.''

''It's our bus. This could bring trouble kicking back to us.''

''I'll wear it. You are simply following my orders, Ramon.''

''As you wish.''

Luis slowly lowered the receiver, his mind engaged in hard reappraisal. This whole enterprise was stupid, inviting trouble. Alan's tour group was safe at their hotel. What was another week or two out of their lives? Better locked away in luxury than dead. It was just as stupid for him to get involved, putting the Martinez reputation for finely balanced political sense on the line.

For what?

A woman who had used him...a woman worth nothing!

Madness to have been tempted into wreaking some sweet vengeance. It was beneath him. He should dismiss her from his suite right now, send her off with a bitter sense of failure. That was vengeance enough.

He turned to do it.

She stood framed by the blackness of the night beyond the window, the twinkling stars of light from the city surrounding her, lending her an air of etherial mystery. Her long hair gleamed like a stream of moonlight and her golden skin glowed, the perfect foil for eyes that shone like emeralds. Her full lips were slightly apart, as he'd left them, waiting it seemed for another kiss, insidiously beckoning him.

He forced his gaze down the long graceful line of her neck to the blood-red T-shirt. She had no heart, he told himself. No heart. But the lush softness of her breasts moved as though to the beat of one, a beat that tugged on him with inexorable and tormenting strength.

How was it possible, he wondered, to feel such desire for a woman...yet hate her with equal ferocity?

"Is the bus assured for tomorrow morning?" she asked, her voice strained.

The conviction swept into Luis' mind. This was no

fun for her. Which was only right and just. She'd had her *fun* last time. It was his turn tonight. He could send her away right now, defeated, but what satisfaction was there in that? He wanted—needed—the same physical satisfaction she had taken from him, over and over again.

"Yes," he said. "You'll get the bus."

Which put their deal on the line.

Luis watched her take that in, and all it implied. Her gaze dropped from the hard challenge in his. Her hands interlocked in front of her waist, as though testing how much strength she had, fingers flexing…and he craved their touch on him again. Her breasts and shoulders lifted slightly as she drew in a deep breath. He found himself holding his own breath, waiting for her decision, willing her to concede to him, his whole body focusing energy on her, determined on drawing her into the ring with him.

She spoke, still with her eyes downcast. "If you have a wife, Luis, this is a rotten game you're playing and I won't be a party to it."

Luis clenched his teeth. It was because of her he didn't have a wife, but he'd rot in hell before she dragged that admission from him.

"If I had a wife, you would have had no access to me, Shontelle," he stated bitingly.

Her lashes slowly lifted, her eyes meeting his with an oddly poignant expression of irony. He caught a sense of fatalism, yet there was no resignation to defeat in it, more a feeling of being ready to ride whatever outcome ensued from the situation. It disturbed him. It wasn't what he expected from her. Not what he wanted, either.

"What time should I tell Alan the bus will be at our hotel?" she asked. "He'll want to have the tour group ready to go."

The hotel! It was on the tip of his tongue to state that Alan would have to collect the bus from the depot. A surge of pride stopped him. If he didn't win his ground with this woman, he would always feel whipped by her. Which was totally intolerable. No way would he give Shontelle Wright any cause to scorn him again.

It might be sheer madness to risk his own skin to balance the scales, madness to risk blotting the Martinez reputation for steering clear of trouble, but he would get the damned bus himself rather than give Shontelle a loophole out of this deal. She had to be his for this one night. Somehow it was a need that drove to the very core of his manhood.

"Seven o'clock," he answered tersely. "Given that it's not stopped by the military. That I cannot control."

A sigh whispered from her lips. She nodded acceptance. "Fair enough! I'll ring Alan now."

Done!

Yet Luis' triumph had a bittersweet taste. She had wrung more from him than she was worth. But she would pay, he promised himself. He would strip her of every bit of power she had over him before dawn came. Then he would be free of her. Finally free of her.

CHAPTER FIVE

SHONTELLE tried desperately to focus her mind on how to tell Alan she was spending the night with the man who'd stolen her heart two years ago and hadn't valued it…a man who'd used her for pleasure…and when she'd taken the pleasure away, had vindictively taken out his displeasure on her brother. There was simply no way Alan was going to understand.

One more night…

With any luck she should at least win something from this encounter. It would either set her free of Luis Angel Martinez…or…give her hope of something more from him, more than she had believed possible.

He *wanted* her…perhaps as badly as she wanted him. It was what she was gambling on. Plus the fact he hadn't married. The Gallardo heiress hadn't got him. And maybe—just maybe—Elvira Rosa Martinez didn't know her son as well as she thought she did.

''The telephone is free for you to use,'' Luis dryly reminded her, gesturing to it with a casual grace that belied any tension on his part over her decision to stay.

He looked so arrogantly sure of himself.

But he did want her.

Shontelle pushed her legs into action and a wry smile onto her mouth. "This is not going to be an easy call."

He returned a derisive look. "Did you think it was easy, looking like a fool for ordering a bus out in this volatile climate?"

He had a point.

Both of them fools.

For some reason, that thought boosted Shontelle's morale.

Luis did not move away from the telephone to let her speak privately to Alan. He propped himself against the edge of the writing desk, apparently intent on hearing every word. She had no choice but to stand next to him, which heightened her awareness of the strong force field coming from his dominating maleness.

She turned her back on him once the call was put through. She didn't want him witnessing her awkwardness in explaining her decision to Alan. It was bad enough knowing he was listening without him watching her every nuance of expression.

"Where are you calling from?" Alan demanded, the moment she announced herself.

"I'm still with Luis in his suite. He's got you the bus, Alan."

"What did he want for it?"

"It's no problem. You can tell everyone to be in the hotel foyer, ready to leave at seven o'clock, all going well."

''All going well?'' Suspicion sharpened his voice. ''What's Luis up to, Shontelle?''

''Alan, he's ordered the bus. He can't guarantee the military won't stop it before it reaches the hotel.''

She heard him expel a long breath. She also heard Luis straighten away from the desk, moving to stand behind her.

''Right! That's it then,'' Alan decided. ''I take it you've finished talking and you're ready to leave. Give me five minutes and I'll be at the side door into the Plaza to bring you back here.''

Hands slid around her waist, distracting her. Luis was standing close behind her, very close, but not touching except for his hands. Her buttocks clenched in sheer nervousness. Her heart leapt into her throat when he started unbuckling her belt.

''Shontelle?''

She dragged her attention back to Alan, belatedly recalling he'd been offering the protection of his escort back to the hotel.

''Uh…no. No, we haven't finished here,'' she rushed out.

''Just starting,'' Luis murmured, darkly purred words that set her pulse pounding. The buckle undone, he unbuttoned the waistband and drew down her zipper.

Shontelle held her breath. Her mind blanked out on all active thought, waiting, poised on the edge of an explosion of sensation should he move his hand inside her clothes and…

''What's going on there?'' Alan demanded, his voice getting edgier.

She gulped, forced herself to think. An answer was needed. Fast. ''I'm going to spend the night with Luis, Alan,'' she gabbled, almost yelping as her trousers and underpants were pulled down to her thighs.

''What?'' Alan squawked.

Her brother's shock was nothing to Shontelle's at being so summarily stripped. Exposed. Vulnerable to anything Luis might choose to do with her. This was going too far, too fast. The urge to drop the telephone and yank up her clothes was muddled by Alan's yelling at her.

''I'm coming to get you right now.''

''No!'' She jerked around to face Luis, wanting to stop his actions, too. ''No!'' she repeated for him.

Wild, reckless and wicked intent blazed at her. He ignored her protest, picked her up, sat her bare bottom on the desk, lifted one of her legs, propped her foot against his thigh and proceeded to undo her bootlace. Shontelle lost track of what she should be doing. Luis was undressing her with ruthless efficiency. His powerfully muscled thigh was bent towards her, reminding her of how magnificently perfect his physique was. But shouldn't she stop this…this taking? If she moved her foot up…

''Shontelle…'' Alan bellowed in her ear. ''…If this is the bargain he's struck with you…''

''Alan, I've done your business,'' she cut in, frantic to be free of the argument. ''This is mine and Luis' business and it's completely personal. Personal! Got that?'' she snapped.

Her shoe and sock were off. Luis was lifting her other leg.

''Are you off your brain? Luis will chew you up and spit you out again,'' Alan thundered at her.

Once both her feet were free, he would remove her clothes and…there was no time for appeasing Alan. Couldn't be done anyway. Just watching Luis' deft, ruthless movements, she was torn between excitement and fear, yet swamping both feelings was a compelling need to know all she wanted to know.

''Let him do it then!'' she cried recklessly.

''Is he holding the deal with the bus over you?'' Anxious now…

Better for her to sound sane…though her trousers and underpants were being tugged down her calves, over her ankles. She struggled for breath, struggled for some final words.

''Do me a favour, Alan, and pack my bags so they're ready to go. I'll come back when the curfew lifts in the morning.''

Luis stepped in between her legs, his eyes glittering at her, exultant, revelling in seizing the moment, the night, her, everything…making it his.

''Shontelle, for God's sake! Will you…''

Luis seized the telephone. ''Stay out of this, Alan!'' he commanded. ''Your sister and I have much to work through and it's very, very personal.''

There was no argument with Luis. He simply didn't

allow it, cutting the connection by slamming the receiver down. Without so much as a pause, he grabbed the bottom of her T-shirt and hauled it off her. Shontelle's arms were still coming down as his hands whipped around her back to unclip her bra. No fumbling. Snap, and her last piece of clothing dangled loose and was swiftly consigned to the pile on the floor.

She was completely naked, dazed by the speed of its happening and the total lack of any sensuality accompanying the stripping of clothes. She stared at Luis' face and saw a mask of hard pride…dark, dark Angel.

He gave her no time to think, speak, question. He gripped her rib cage, hoisted her off the desk and carrying her virtually at arm's length, he strode through the suite to the bedroom. Impossible for Shontelle to find purchase for her arms or legs. They flapped uselessly. She was so stunned at being held like some distasteful object, any sense of coordination was utterly lost. He tossed her on the bed and she bounced into an abandoned sprawl.

"That's where I want you," he said, his voice harsh with the effort expended. He lifted his shoulders back, holding an imperious, superior stance by the bed. "Where you should be…" he went on with savagely mocking emphasis, "…on the playing ground you use so well."

Scathing words, scathing eyes as they travelled slowly over her. They spurred Shontelle into a clear recognition of his fierce drive to pay her back for having regarded him as no more than a good lay. Even lower than that…a transient lay who'd worn out his novelty value. The Latin lover tag had remained a burr under his skin.

But deeper than that…was *she* still under his skin?

He was holding control, determined on keeping the upper hand, but how much feeling for her lay behind his armoured pride? If she could break through…

She moved sinuously, provocatively, arranging herself more comfortably on the bed, looping her hair over one shoulder so it streamed across her breasts. "You were quite a masterful player yourself, Luis," she said with a reminiscent smile, idly moving a tress of hair back and forth over one of her nipples. "A pity you seem to have lost your touch." She deliberately ran her gaze over his body as she added, "Brute strength is rather a sad step down."

A mirthless laugh scraped from his throat. "In your search for variety, I'm sure a bit of rough has featured somewhere." His eyes glittered challengingly at her as he stripped off his shirt. "I thought it might give you a kick since you grew bored with my kind of lovemaking."

"I was never bored with you," she said truthfully. "I thought what we shared was very special."

A flash of derision. "So you left before it got spoiled."

It was spoiled *before she left*. "The writing was on the wall, Luis," she said quietly, remembering how naive she'd been not to even see it until it was pointed out to her. "I got out before it fell on top of me."

"What writing?" he jeered, bending to remove his shoes and socks, his body language clearly contemptuous of any excuse she might offer.

"Your real life in Buenos Aires," Shontelle said, testing for some flash of guilt from him for what he'd kept hidden.

There was no sharp glance at her. He finished taking off his footwear and when he straightened up, his dark eyes gloated over her with unmistakably sexual intent…such burning intent Shontelle squirmed inside.

"I see," he drawled. "Our romantic idyll on the Amazon was over. I had work to do in Buenos Aires so you did not get my full attention there. Rest assured you have it tonight, Shontelle."

He proceeded to unfasten his trousers.

"Why?" she shot at him, frustrated at being relegated to a sexual object. Though that might be all he'd ever thought of her. The urge to sting him as she was stung slid straight off her tongue. "Your other women not delivering any spice, Luis? You need a taste of me to supplement your diet?"

It stung him all right. His mouth thinned for a moment and there was a flare of anger in his eyes, giving her a glimpse of a banked inner rage that promised no quarter given tonight.

"You think you're special, Shontelle?" He left the lilt of mockery hanging while he finished undressing.

Then stark naked, powerfully naked, aggressively naked, he gave her a smile that curled with vengeful satisfaction. ''Well, yes you are,'' he drawled. ''A rich, erotic indulgence...so special I think I should make a banquet of you.''

And spit me out in the morning.

Shontelle's stomach was suddenly a hollow pit. All the cards looked black in this game—clubs and spades—no hearts, no diamonds. Even so, she could not give up all hope. Not yet.

''Taking a risk, aren't you?'' she slung back at him. ''People get addicted to rich, erotic indulgences.''

He laughed, and despite its being dark amusement, his face was suddenly transformed into the lighter, more lovable Luis she had known, and Shontelle's heart tripped over itself. Her body wantonly buzzed with anticipation as he prowled onto the bed, looming over her, sweeping her hair away from her breasts, raking it into a fan around her head, his eyes simmering with lustful heat.

''A substance has to be readily available for one to become addicted,'' he murmured, sipping seductively at her lips. ''I'll just take all I can get of it tonight.''

Readily available...the phrase echoed in Shontelle's ears as Luis fully engaged her mouth with his in a long, devouring kiss, stirring her hunger for him, a hunger that had been starved for two miserable, empty years. If she'd stayed, maybe he would have defied his heritage to keep her. Foolish pride... walking out on him without confronting him with what she'd been told, what he'd withheld. An open choice would have been better, cleaner.

Maybe with this second chance…

She raked her fingers through his hair, revelling in the feel of it, a huge surge of possessiveness welling through her. This man was *hers,* had to be. There was no other like him. And he had to feel the same about her. It had to be mutual, this passionate craving.

Then suddenly her hands were snatched away, slammed onto the bed and pinned above her head as he levered himself up. "It's *my* night, Shontelle."

She looked into eyes seething with dark turbulence.

"And the playing will be all mine."

He bent and licked her lips as though collecting the lingering evidence of her response to his kiss, then trailed his mouth slowly down to the pulse at the base of her throat, pausing there to apply a heated pressure that kicked her heart into wilder pumping.

Satisfied, he moved lower to the taut mounds of her breasts, tilted up by the lifted position of her arms. He subjected them to exquisite torment—teasing tongue-lashing, voluptuous suction, sharp little nips—orchestrating such a varied rush of sensations, Shontelle had no mind to protest the ruling he'd made. She was awash with rippling excitement, too enthralled with experiencing Luis again to care how or why he was feasting on her…as long as he kept doing it.

Even when he took one imprisoning hand from hers, she didn't try to touch him. He was touching…tantalising, circular caresses over and around her stomach, dipping lower, lower, fingers sliding through the silky mound of hair, stroking, parting, slowly seeking the sensitive moist place that yearned for his touch.

And he was so good at it…softly sensual, as though he was acutely attuned to how much arousal her nerve-ends could take at a time, and he matched the rhythm of his stroking to the tug of his mouth on her breasts, building a momentum that held Shontelle utterly enthralled, focused so intensely on what he was making her feel, there was no room for anything else, no time.

All vestige of control over herself slipped away under the sweet onslaught of sensation. Muscles quivered. The ache of need soared into an urgent scream for the ultimate path to be taken. She was more than ready for him. The inner convulsions were starting and he wasn't there yet. Not the part of him she wanted most, the intimate connection that would take her with him on the final climb to ecstasy.

''Luis…please…'' The cry burst from her throat, shamelessly begging.

He reacted fast, so fast she didn't even begin to comprehend what he intended to happen. He flipped her body face down, pushed her legs apart with his knees, curled one arm around her stomach and hauled her backwards, her thighs sliding past his as he rocked back on his ankles, her bottom pressing up against his stomach. She felt him position himself for entry, felt her own flesh quiver in eagerness for the promise of him, a totally out-of-control response. The penetration came hard and fast and incredibly deep as he pushed her down on him, taking an angle he'd never taken before, making her feel the passage of every inch of him rushing further and further inside her. Then he arced her body back with his to make her feel it even more intensely.

He rocked her with him—forward, back, up, down—Shontelle was both shocked and shaken by the sheer animal wildness of this coupling, yet acutely aware of sensations she'd never felt before, bombarded by a physicality she hadn't even imagined, and hopelessly distracted by the sheer strength of him both enveloping and invading her.

Every time he drew back he left one strongly controlling arm around her waist, hand splayed across her stomach, pressing in, keeping her hugged tightly to him as he moved almost to the point of losing intimate contact. Then came the hard thrust forward again, the weird, sweet sense of shattering inside her as he drove himself back to the inner centre, and the hand on her stomach held the fullness of him there as though emphasising a claim of absolute possession, relishing it, filling her with the sense of him filtrating every cell of her body.

He repeated the action—Shontelle had no idea how many times. Occasionally when he paused at the innermost point, he slid his other hand over her breasts, cupping them, squeezing them, fanning her nipples, rubbing her hair over them, or he kissed the nape of her neck, making her shiver from the sheer intensity of his *tasting,* while deep within her a storm of ecstatic waves flowed and ebbed, wild, turbulent, impossible to stop.

She didn't care that he controlled everything. The incredible chaos he wreaked on her was beyond anything she'd ever known. It didn't matter when he carried her forward to kneel underneath him, taking the freedom to drive to his own climax in a fiercely pummelling rhythm.

She was so soft and mushy inside, she welcomed the fast stirring of more sensation, the feeling of violent desire being answered by what he found in her, the surging power of it, coming and coming and coming until he spilled the essence of his strength into her and she exulted in receiving it because there was no taking this back. He was hers as much as she was his.

He scooped her to him spoon-fashion as he dropped onto the bed to rest. There was no parting, no letting go. Her head was tucked under his chin, his arms around her. It didn't occur to her that he had used her as his plaything. Her mind was completely fuzzed with the sense of being one with him.

Luis Angel…dark, light…it didn't matter. He was her man. And as he began stroking her again, arousing both of them to a pitch of needful excitement, she thought only that he wanted more of her.

But…he stopped her from making love to him. He

blocked every initiative she started to take. He controlled the moves. He chose how, when and where he tasted her. And Shontelle gradually lost all sense of being one with him. The realisation came like cold claws creeping around her heart, squeezing out the hope she'd nursed.

This was, indeed, his feast. It wasn't mutual. He hadn't meant it to be mutual. She was the food and he was taking it as he liked, sampling whatever appealed to his fancy, sating himself with every aspect of her sexuality. He didn't care what she was feeling, except in so far as it increased his pleasure, his satisfaction, his sense of being master of the situation, master of *her*.

The answer she'd sought was staring her in the face.

There was no future for her with Luis Angel Martinez.

There was nothing for her here.

Nothing.

With that absolute conviction, Shontelle found the strength to fight free of him, jabbing her elbows into his body, kicking and shoving herself out of contact, scrambling off the bed. She heard him curse in Spanish but she didn't stop. Choosing the bathroom as the safest refuge, she sped into it and locked the door behind her.

She was a tremulous mess, a hopeless tremulous mess. Nevertheless, there was one thing she could and would hold firm—the fierce resolution to deny Luis Angel Martinez any further chance of using her as he willed. Regardless of anything he said or did, she would not return to *his* playing ground.

CHAPTER SIX

SHONTELLE'S fast and frantic evasion of him took Luis completely by surprise—a decidedly unwelcome and frustrating one. It came without any apparent reason—compliance suddenly exploding into rejection. However, the slamming of the bathroom door was so jarring, it propelled him into a swift review of what he'd been doing.

She hadn't cried out, hadn't complained or protested. He couldn't have hurt her physically. Every step of the way her body had responded positively, not once baulking at submitting to his pursuit of every desire he'd harboured when thinking of her. No…he shook off the niggle of concern…he had not hurt her.

So why had she cut and run?

He'd certainly stopped her from weaving her seductive power over him. No way would he allow her to treat him as her toy-boy again. He'd made that clear from the start. Though she probably hadn't believed him immune to her charms. More than likely that had finally bit in—no leeway given for Shontelle to get her hooks into him.

He shrugged, dismissing the annoyance of having his game-plan thwarted. Let her sulk in the bathroom. Let her rage. If she thought she was making some stand against his domination of proceedings, she'd soon find out it was impossible to wring any concession from him. Besides, he'd already done what he'd set out to do, and enjoyed every second of it, too. He wasn't about to beg for more.

He smiled with grim satisfaction as he swung his legs off the bed.

She'd begged.

And he'd given it to her.

Right to the hilt.

He hoped she'd remember that to her dying day. Luis Martinez was not a man to trifle with.

The clock on the bedside table read 11:47. Not even midnight yet. So much for Shontelle's agreeing to give him the night. Another cheat from her. All promise…no staying power. Typical.

He collected the hotel's complimentary bathrobe from the cupboard, put it on, wrapped it around his nakedness to ward off the night chill, and headed for the sitting room and the minibar.

As he passed the bathroom he heard the shower running. Trying to wash him off, he thought sardonically. If there was any justice in the world, she'd be no more successful than he'd been in washing her off the past two years.

The lights were still on in the sitting room. Shontelle's clothes were on the floor. Luis viewed the litter of female garments with a sense of black humour as he moved past them to pour himself a drink. Shontelle wasn't going anywhere without dressing herself first. Sooner or later, she'd come out of the bathroom and collect her clothing. That should be an interesting moment.

He heaped more sugar than usual over the slices of lime for his drink. Vengeance was supposed to be sweet, but it wasn't, Luis decided. It reinforced the bitter taste of knowing what was really wanted was beyond reach. Hopelessly beyond reach.

He took his drink over to the picture window and stared out at the lights of La Paz—quite stunningly beautiful, a fairyland, as Shontelle put it. Just like her, Luis thought savagely, a deceptive facade, offering magic, hiding the power to blow him apart.

Tomorrow morning he'd have to face the streets down there, walk them unprotected in order to get to the bus depot. It would be more dangerous once he was behind the wheel of the bus. A stupid deal…all for the sake of one more experience of Shontelle, with him ending up the winner.

Utterly stupid…when there was nothing to win. She'd made that clear last time. No love in her heart for him. Just sex. Sex he'd once believed was entwined with something much deeper…so deep it was still playing hell with him. What joy now in his vengeful drive to expunge that tormenting residue of feeling? He shook his head in self-derision. A brief savage pleasure…leaving him empty.

He sipped his drink and decided he didn't care if he died on the streets of La Paz tomorrow.

He just didn't care.

CHAPTER SEVEN

SHONTELLE switched off the bathroom light, turned the knob as quietly as she could and slowly eased the door open, listening acutely for any sound coming from the rest of Luis' suite. She held her breath. Her heartbeat seemed to be thumping in her ears but she couldn't hear any other movement going on.

Had Luis given up on her and gone to sleep?

Shontelle vehemently prayed it was so. She'd been in the bathroom over an hour, trying to get herself back together, vigorously cleaning off every possible vestige of Luis' tasting, even washing and blow-drying her long hair in a compulsive need to rid it of any touch of him. She would replait it, as well, once she found the rubber band Luis had taken off.

Clutching the top edge of the bath towel she'd fastened around her nakedness, she plucked up a brave front, slid out into the short passageway that linked the bedroom to the sitting room, and headed swiftly into the latter. The lights had been left on. She had no trouble spotting her clothes.

As distasteful as she found having to dress in the same things Luis had stripped off her, there was no other choice in these circumstances. She wanted a barrier established fast, one Luis couldn't fail to recognise, and she'd fight him tooth and nail if he tried to tear it away.

Pants, trousers, bra, T-shirt…she hastily pulled them on, discarding the towel as she donned more protective gear. Rather than waste a second in fully covering herself, she sat on the floor to put on her socks and shoes. Then feeling more in control and less at risk, she climbed to her feet and turned to assess the supposedly comfortable seating near the window, intending to spend the rest of the night there.

Her swinging gaze didn't get that far.

It halted, very abruptly, at the passageway to the bedroom.

Shock ripped through her, throwing her into chaos again; every nerve-end twitching with agitation, every muscle tensing, every logical thought in her head jamming into confusion. Her eyes stayed glued to the man dominating the space she had desperately wanted to stay empty, the man whose presence could only mean more trauma for her, the man who'd systematically destroyed what had once been good between them.

He hadn't just arrived. Shontelle knew instantly he'd been watching her, standing there watching her as she'd scrambled to get into her clothes…another humiliation added to the humiliations he'd heaped on her. It was some relief that he was no longer naked, though the white bathrobe—so pure and clean-looking—formed an ironic contrast to the dark, satanically beautiful face of Luis Angel Martinez. There was no relief, however, to her fear of what was brooding behind it.

There was a less controlled air about him now, hair mussed, wavy strands dipping over his forehead, curling around his ears. The brilliant dark eyes no longer burned with purpose. They were shadowed by his thick lashes but seemed to emit a sardonic gleam—mocking her, mocking himself, mocking the world and everything in it.

"I take it you don't intend to rejoin me in my bed," he drawled.

"You've had your pound of flesh, Luis," she flashed at him, too worked up to temper her words.

He shrugged. "I've lost my taste for it anyway."

She burned under the contempt implicit in his words, contempt for what she had tried to give him, however misled she had been. "Good!" she snapped. "I've lost any taste for you, too."

He waved carelessly towards the door that led out of the suite. "Do feel free to leave anytime you like."

Her fury at his treatment of her sliced straight into bitter scorn. "Oh, sure! So you can welch on the deal."

"Your staying here any longer is now quite irrelevant," he said in a bored tone. "If you're afraid to brave the streets, by all means call your brother. I assume he's prepared to escort you back to your hotel."

"No!" she retorted vehemently, hating him with the same force as she had once loved him. "I'll stay until curfew lifts in the morning, as I agreed. Having been used by you as no better than a whore, I will not give you any loophole to weazel out of paying what you promised.''

She'd hold him to the damned bus if it killed her. He wasn't going to get away with taking her as he had for nothing.

The cold mask of pride resettled on his face. ''I gave you my word.''

''I'll see how well you keep it in the morning.'' Her eyes blistered any worth in his *given word.* ''Since you're finding no more pleasure in my company than I am in yours, I suggest you go back to your bed and I'll settle myself here.''

''Thank you,'' he mocked. ''Do sleep well with your choice of discomfort.''

He strolled off to the bedroom, leaving Shontelle feeling wretchedly deflated. Clearly he now saw her as a waste of his time, not even worth arguing with. For several moments she teetered on the edge of going after him, flaying him with her own contempt for his lies and double-dealing, but what was the point?

He didn't care.

That was the bottom line.

He simply didn't care.

Even if she stayed until the curfew was lifted, it was no guarantee he would follow through on his word, but at least she would have fulfilled her part. If she took nothing else away from this night, she would take her own integrity intact.

Nursing this shred of pride, Shontelle walked over to the window and searched the floor for the rubber band Luis had taken from her plait. Somehow it was important to restore her appearance to what it had been before she'd come here. She looked everywhere without success and finally concluded Luis had pocketed it. Which defeated her.

Defeat all round, she thought despondently, moving back to the writing desk. She picked up the telephone and made a request for a 5:45 wake-up call. It would mean Luis being woken, too, which she'd have to weather, since it served the purpose of letting him know she had stayed the full night.

Reassured of not oversleeping the mark, she proceeded to switch off the lights. The window provided a dim glow, enough to see her way by. She pulled two armchairs together, curled up on one and rested her legs on the other. Hoping fatigue would be her friend tonight, she closed her eyes and prayed for sleep.

But tears welled out of the devastation in her heart. Tears oozed through her lashes and trickled down her cheeks. Silent tears. Lonely tears. Tears that needed to be wept now because tomorrow she had to be strong again. It was a long time before sleep wiped them away and gave her some brief peace.

''Shontelle...''

The sharp call of her name brought her awake. Her

eyelids felt glued together but she dragged them open and looked up blearily.

Luis was standing by her chair, frowning at her.

Her brain was sluggish. Why was he waking her? Then her nose picked up the tangy scent of male cologne and she suddenly realised he was freshly showered, shaved, and fully dressed! Which had to mean she had somehow overslept and he was annoyed at finding she was still here.

She pushed the leg-rest armchair away and scrambled to her feet, crying out, ''What time is it?'' panicking at the thought of Alan waiting for her, worrying...

''Time enough,'' Luis answered brusquely. ''It's not quite five-thirty. I've ordered breakfast. I thought you might like to refresh yourself before it arrives.''

''Breakfast...for me?'' she repeated dazedly.

''For both of us.''

A knock on the door heralded its arrival and he turned away, moving quickly to let the waiter in. Shontelle stared at his back, flummoxed by this turn of events. He wore a navy shirt, navy trousers, navy Reeboks. What was he ready for this early in the morning?

The question nagged at her as she headed for the bathroom, needing to use its facilities to get herself ready for the day ahead. When she looked at her face in the mirror, she fiercely wished Luis had kept to himself in his bedroom. The whites of her eyes were red-rimmed and the skin around them was obviously puffy. Hating the thought he might have noticed this evidence of prolonged weeping, she did all she could to diminish it, splashing the area copiously with cold water.

Her hair was a flyaway mess but that didn't matter. She finger-combed it into reasonable tidiness. Having straightened up her crumpled clothes and composed herself to face Luis this one last time, she hurried out of the bathroom, anxious to know what his plans were.

Breakfast was laid out on the table in the sitting room. Luis was already seated and helping himself to the food he'd ordered. He glanced sharply at her face as she approached, his dark eyes uncomfortably penetrating.

''I've poured your coffee,'' he said matter-of-factly.

''Thank you.'' The reply was automatic, though she hated the reminder of how intimately acquainted they had once been and nothing would induce her to accept anything he offered at this point.

He gestured to the chair opposite his when she made no move to sit at the table. ''Don't stand on ceremony, Shontelle. You might as well eat what's here.''

''I'm not hungry.'' Which was true. ''I put a wake-up call in for 5:45. I didn't expect you to be up so early.''

''I'll be leaving the hotel as soon as curfew lifts,'' he answered offhandedly.

Alarm jangled through Shontelle's mind. Was Luis skipping out so he couldn't be called to account on the bus? ''To go where?'' she asked. ''La Paz is shut down.''

He shrugged. ''Personal business.''

She watched him crunch into a croissant and her stomach churned over his indifference to Alan's and her urgent concerns. ''What if the bus doesn't come at seven o'clock? Where will you be?'' she demanded testily.

He gave her a devil-may-care look. ''Who knows?''

''That's not good enough, Luis,'' she shot at him, incensed by his blasé attitude.

His mouth tilted into an ironic curl. ''It's as good as it gets, Shontelle. Take it or leave it.''

No...she couldn't. She just couldn't. The pain and frustration she'd been holding in reached overload and streamed out over everything else, sweeping pride aside, demolishing any reasonable common sense, demanding an outlet. Her mouth opened and her voice shook with the force of feeling he'd brought her to.

''I never used you as you used me last night. I don't know why you think you have the right to play with me as it suits you, but I will not walk away from your lies and evasions this time.''

That jolted his appetite. He stopped eating and glared at her.

Shontelle's throat felt scraped raw but the compulsion to throw down the gauntlet kept the words coming. ''I'll follow you when you leave this hotel. I'll haunt you until the bus you promised turns up on The Europa doorstep. I'll...''

''What lies?'' he demanded tersely.

''Don't you dare pretend you haven't lied!'' His question was like a fire bomb going off in her brain. Old wounds ruptured and demanded to be aired. ''Very convenient for you, wasn't it, to forget Claudia Gallardo while you were with me.''

''I am not married to her,'' he bit out.

''*Betrothed* was the word your mother used. Your mother, whom you so carefully screened me from all the time I lived with you in Buenos Aires. Your mother, who explained your *real* life to me.''

''When was this?'' he snapped.

''The day before I left you. After you excluded me once again from your family life, Luis, evading the invitation your mother extended.''

He erupted from his chair, dark menace emanating from him so strongly, Shontelle almost shrank from him. But she would not be intimidated. It was she who had the high moral ground, he who had to answer for his actions.

''You kept this from me,'' he accused.

''You kept it from me,'' she retaliated.

''You let my meddling, manipulative mother lay it waste. Without consulting me. You let Elvira have her way without so much as raising a question.''

His seething fury rattled Shontelle.

"No heart!" he roared at her. "No faith! No trust! And for *you* I risk my life!"

She stared at him, mesmerised by the powerful surge of energy pouring from him, understanding nothing of what was causing it.

"Your life?" she echoed dazedly.

His chin jerked up. Pride emerged in a fierce blaze. Not cold pride. Not arrogant pride. Shontelle sensed this was his entire manhood on the line.

"Go back to your hotel," he commanded in a tone that brooked no opposition. "Wait with your brother. If I do not arrive with your bus, it will not be for the want of trying."

"You? You'll be driving the bus?"

He'd already turned his back on her, striding towards the door. Her disbelief was unanswered. He did not so much as pause.

"Luis!" she cried, suddenly torn by the feeling she would never see him again and there was too much left unanswered. Far too much.

He opened the door, stepped out, and was gone, the door closed firmly between them.

Shontelle struggled to get her shell-shocked wits together.

Nothing made sense to her anymore.

She didn't know what to believe.

If Luis turned up with the bus…what then?

Go back to your hotel. Wait with your brother.

That command made sense.

Besides, there was nothing else to do here.

Luis was gone.

CHAPTER EIGHT

ALAN was in the foyer of The Europa, obviously watching out for her while keeping an eye on the progress of checkouts at the desk. He was at Shontelle's side the moment she cleared the front door.

''Are you okay?'' he asked, sharply scanning her face.

''I'm fine.'' She kept walking, making a beeline for the elevators, determined on not discussing anything personal with her brother. ''Are my bags still in our suite?''

''Yes. I thought you'd want to change clothes.''

''I do. I'll need the door key.''

He handed it to her.

''Thanks. Won't be long.''

''Shontelle…''

''Luis has gone to get the bus,'' she cut in, blocking what might have been an unwelcome inquiry.

''Luis has?'' Stunned surprise.

''He said if it's not here by seven, it won't be for want of trying. Where is everyone?''

Alan was still shaking his head over Luis' personal involvement. ''Those not paying their accounts at the desk are having breakfast in the dining room,'' he answered distractedly. ''You'd better grab some, too, Shontelle. Long day ahead.''

She pressed the up button on the elevator. Luck was on her side. The doors opened immediately. ''Did you get the hotel to pack some food for us?'' she tossed at Alan as she stepped into the compartment.

''Yes. Everything's organised. Shontelle...''

''Be down soon,'' she promised, activating the control panel.

The doors closed, shutting out Alan's frowning face.

Shontelle breathed a sigh of relief. She'd told him everything pertinent to the tour group situation. As for the rest...Luis might have some justification for thinking badly of her...if his mother had lied...and if Claudia Gallardo had conspired with Elvira Rosa Martinez to give a false impression. Where the truth actually lay was impossible for Shontelle to sort out.

Two facts stood out very starkly from all the grey areas. If she had told Luis of his mother's intervention two years ago, there would be no confusion about his feelings now. The blame for that was fairly and squarely on her shoulders. Nevertheless, even granting he had reason to think of her in the worst possible light, Luis should not have treated her as he had last night. That was unforgivable.

So there was no point in agonising over this encounter with him. Any future they might have had together was well and truly dead. It was time to lay the whole affair between them to rest. It was doubtful she'd ever forget her regrets, but she could accept he was gone from her life.

Though if he brought the bus himself…Shontelle felt her nerves tighten. He would only be here for a few minutes, she told herself, just long enough to hand the bus over to Alan. He'd walk away then. No trauma. It would only be a few minutes at most. *If* he came with the bus.

The elevator stopped and opened to her floor as she was frowning over this scenario. It wasn't until she was in her suite and digging into her bag that she attached Luis' claim about risking his life to the procuring of the bus. Yet was it what he'd meant? Was it so dangerous in the streets? Surely Alan wouldn't have decided on this course if the risk was truly grave.

She knew her brother expected to deal with some trouble on the way out of La Paz, but he was confident of steering them through it. Surely with the clout of the Martinez name, Luis could deal with any problem he ran into.

Risking his life for her… It made no sense. Why would a man who felt the utmost contempt for her, put his life on the line to get the bus she'd requested? He could probably snap his fingers and people would fall in to do his bidding. It made no sense at all.

Shontelle found the fresh clothes she wanted and changed into them, glad to feel clean from the inside out. Not that she looked any different, except for wearing a dark green shirt with the Amigos Tours logo, instead of red. She gave her hair a quick brush, plaited it, and felt considerably better, more equipped to handle whatever came.

Having checked the suite in case anything had been left lying around, she took her bags down to the foyer and left them in Alan's care. ''Breakfast,'' she said and zipped off to the dining room. Maybe by tonight she might feel up to fielding sensitive questions, but she felt too raw to start answering them now.

Most of the tour group was moving out of the dining room as she entered it. Time was getting short. She exchanged quick greetings and hurried to the buffet bar, not that she had suddenly found an appetite but sheer practicality dictated she replenish her energy.

Having picked up a fruit juice, a couple of bread rolls, some slices of cold meat and cheese, she headed for an empty table, not wanting to be drawn into conversation with anyone. The ploy succeeded. She was left to eat her breakfast in peace.

At ten minutes to seven she returned to the foyer to help Alan settle the tour group, answering concerns as best she could and preparing them for the long journey ahead. It was ten hours by road from La Paz to Santa Cruz…if nothing went wrong. Once there, it would be possible to catch a flight to Buenos Aires, then home to Australia.

The mood of the group was jumpy. Those suffering from altitude sickness didn't care what other discomforts they might have to suffer, so long as they were getting away from here. Some were fearful of what lay in wait beyond the hotel.

Australians simply weren't accustomed to a military presence. Apart from a formal parade of war veterans on Anzac Day, soldiers did not feature in their lives, and a tank was only seen in a military museum. There were mutterings of never leaving home again. They had a new appreciation of Australia being called "the lucky country."

The minutes ticked by. A nervous bustle started with people rechecking their luggage, making sure they had everything to hand. Having instructed everyone to stay inside, Alan left them to go out to the street where he could watch for the bus which would have to back in to the cul-de-sac.

Shontelle fixed a patient smile on her face, projecting calm confidence to the group. It took quite a lot of concentration. Her stomach was in knots. As more minutes passed, worries mounted in her mind, becoming impossible to set aside. If the bus didn't come, would that mean something bad had happened to Luis?

Despite the deep hurt he had inflicted on her last night, she did not want him physically injured. She certainly didn't want him dead. Though if he was risking his life by getting the bus for them, it wasn't her fault, was it? It was *his* choice. *He'd* made the deal.

Her mind skipped to what Luis had once told her about his older brother, Eduardo. During the political troubles in Argentina, the military police had simply scooped him up off the street one night, supposedly rounding up young dissidents, and Eduardo was never heard of again, becoming one of the disappeared whose deaths were never recorded.

In Buenos Aires, she had seen for herself the Thursday march of the women now called The Mothers of May, protesting the disappearance of their children. It didn't matter how many years had gone by. They turned up each week to parade their banners with photos in front of Government House because they still had no answers. Rumour had it that many of the lost ones had been taken off by helicopter and dropped in the sea.

Shontelle shivered. Could that happen here in Bolivia? No, surely not. This was a land-locked country, no coastal territory at all. Even if Luis was imprisoned for some reason, Elvira Rosa Martinez had the power to have him freed. Eduardo had probably not been identified before he was killed.

Another dreadful thought hit. What if Luis didn't have time to identify himself? What if some trigger-happy soldier…

Alan burst into the foyer. "It's here!"

Shontelle's knees almost buckled in relief.

"Collect your belongings and come outside now," Alan commanded. "Remember what I said—women to board the bus immediately, men stand ready to load the suitcases in the luggage department. The sooner we get going, the better."

Action seemed to buoy everyone's spirits. There was a buzz of excitement as thirty people headed for the door, carrying their bags. Shontelle lingered behind the rest, ostensibly to check that nothing was left in the foyer. She could see the bus being backed into position in front of the hotel and it *was* Luis in the driver's seat.

Her heart lifted. He was safe. He could return to the Plaza Hotel from here and be absolutely safe. The bus came to a halt, the luggage compartment hatches were unlocked, the door was opened, and Luis rose from the driver's seat. He'd go now, Shontelle thought. This was the last she'd ever see of him.

Strange how torn she felt. Absurd after last night. It shouldn't matter to her. Yet her legs moved faster, wanting to get outside, closer to him before he left. She virtually herded the stragglers of the group past the front door.

Luis was rounding the front of the bus. He saw her at the back of the crowd and for one sizzling moment, their eyes locked. Somehow it was as though everything else ceased to exist and there was only the two of them, tied by a bond that went beyond any other reality. The tug on her heart was so strong, her chest felt ready to burst. Then he tore his gaze away and addressed Alan.

Shontelle was so shaken she could barely put two thoughts together. What did that look from Luis mean? He'd shut the door on her before. There was nothing left of what they'd once shared. Couldn't be.

She tried to collect her scattered wits. Her job was to usher the women onto the bus while Alan supervised the loading of the luggage. Somehow that task fell by the wayside. While she was vaguely aware of the women heading into the bus by themselves, she couldn't drag her attention away from Luis and Alan who were clearly having a tense exchange of words. She walked straight over to them and broke into their conversation.

''Thank you for bringing the bus, Luis,'' she said with genuine sincerity.

Alan shot her a searing look. ''He says he's staying with it.''

''Sorry...'' She showed her confusion to both of them. ''What do you mean?''

''He's not handing it over. He insists on driving it,'' Alan tersely explained.

''To Santa Cruz?'' She looked at Luis in bewilderment.

''To hell and back if necessary,'' he answered with grim purpose.

''But why?'' she cried.

His mouth curled. His dark eyes flashed a derisive gleam at her. ''Because you'll be on it, Shontelle. And I'm not finished with you.''

She should have said, yes, he was. Or at least said *she* was finished with him. But the words stuck in her throat and she just stared at him, feeling the power of his will swirling around her, tying her to him again. It was crazy. Nothing good could come of this.

They'd scarred each other too badly. Yet the feeling coming from him was different now...not contempt, not dismissal or rejection and certainly not indifference.

''Luis...'' Alan started in a tone of protest.

''It's my bus,'' Luis cut in ruthlessly. ''Get your people off it if you won't accept my driving it.''

The luggage compartments were being slammed shut. The women were already in their chosen seats and the men were proceeding to join them.

''Goddammit, man! Let my sister go!''

Luis' gaze hadn't shifted from Shontelle's. The black resolution in his eyes was not going to be moved by anything. It was either stay here in La Paz where he would be, as well, or take this journey to Santa Cruz with him. Whichever choice was made, Shontelle knew intuitively Luis did not intend to let her escape him until he *was* finished with her. Whatever that meant.

It certainly wouldn't mean more sex, Shontelle thought with fierce determination. Besides which, on a busload of people she wouldn't be alone with him. Better to let him get his ''unfinished'' business with her over with in the relative safety of numbers, she decided.

''Better to go with Luis than not go at all, Alan. Everyone's on the bus,'' she said pointedly. ''I'll go and do the head count.''

''You can't drive a bus as well as I can, Luis,'' Alan argued as she moved around them.

"From what I've seen on the streets, you'll have your hands full keeping your people calm," came the grim retort. "This is no picnic trip. You can take over the wheel once we're clear of La Paz."

"So you can have time with Shontelle and tear her into more little pieces."

Already on her way around the front of the bus, Shontelle paused, wishing Alan would keep his mouth shut about her.

"I tell you, it's not right, Luis," he went on. "She hasn't picked herself up from her last affair with you."

"Neither have I, my friend," came the cold reply. "Neither have I."

Shontelle frowned. Was that true?

"What's the point, man? You're never going to marry her. I told her so from the start, but she wouldn't listen."

"You, too, Alan?" His voice was ice. "Then some of those pieces can be laid at your door."

"What the hell does that mean?"

"It means stay out of my business on this journey. You don't know a damned thing about what I feel or what I'll do."

Neither did she, Shontelle thought as she moved on to board the bus. It was difficult to focus her attention on completing an accurate head count but everyone had responded to the list of names by the time Alan and Luis had joined them.

Luis took the driver's seat. Alan occupied the tour

guide seat adjacent to it, activating the microphone so the whole group could hear him clearly as he introduced Luis and outlined the planned trip for them. Shontelle settled on the seat left vacant for her, directly behind the driver.

The bus started moving.

She didn't listen to Alan.

The physical trip they were about to take meant nothing to her. It was the journey with Luis that preyed on her mind. What did he want of her now? Where could it lead? How would it end?

CHAPTER NINE

THE streets of La Paz were unnaturally quiet. Traffic was minimal and very few pedestrians were civilians. The eerie sense of moving through a war zone was strong and oppressive. There was no buzz of conversation in the bus. If the passengers spoke at all, it was in whispers.

Shontelle noted that Luis avoided driving along the main thoroughfares, detouring around them through a series of side streets. It was obvious he was highly aware of the danger of being stopped, accelerating past groups of soldiers before they had time to react to a busload of people going by.

Alan instructed the tour group to remain seated naturally, not to duck down or to act in any way which might appear suspicious. Tourists were not targets in the current political conflict. Shontelle hoped her brother was right in his reading of the situation.

They were travelling along what appeared to be a deserted stretch of road, when a tank emerged from a cross-street, directly in their path. Luis had to brake or collide with it. The bus came to a screeching halt and ominously, the tank halted, as well. Slowly, terrifyingly, its turret swung towards them. So did the long barrel of its gun.

Agitation broke out amongst the tour group, screams from the women, shocked cursing from the men.

"Be quiet and sit still!" Alan barked into the microphone.

They settled down but the atmosphere in the bus was thick with fear. The gun did not move. Neither did the tank. Shontelle suddenly realised the barrel was trained directly on Luis. Her mind was jolted into two quick leaps—the driver—who had the colouring of a local man.

She was out of her seat instantly, throwing her arms around Luis' neck, and lowering her head next to his so her fair hair could be seen. She was so clearly not a native South American, it seemed logical that whoever was sighting them from the tank would have second thoughts about attacking them.

"Shontelle…" Alan started to protest.

"Luis is dark, Alan. Could be taken for a Bolivian. Show yourself. Tell them we're tourists and we have sick people on board."

"Right! Open the door, Luis."

Alan waved at the tank to draw attention to himself as he rose from his seat. Luis activated the door. It hissed open.

"Stay near the bus, Alan," Luis sharply advised. "Don't look threatening."

The next few minutes were extremely tense. Alan stood just outside the door, waving and explaining in a quick stream of Spanish. No verbal reply came from the occupants of the tank. Alan kept talking, emphasising Australia and foreign relations.

The gun started to move, swinging back to the direction the tank had originally been taking. Then the tank started to move, proceeding on its route, unblocking their way forward. The relief in the bus was palpable. Alan jumped back on board. Some of the group cheered him, grateful that the crisis was past. Shontelle belatedly realised she was still hanging on to Luis and started to withdraw her arms.

He caught her right hand, his strong fingers wrapping around hers, squeezing, transmitting a quick jolt of electric heat. It lasted only a moment or two before release came. Other actions had to be carried out, closing the door, getting the bus moving again. There was no glance, no word, just that quick squeeze, then total concentration on the job of driving them out of La Paz.

Alan clapped her on the shoulder. ''Good thinking,'' he said with a wide grin, the zest of having won this round beaming from his face.

She nodded and returned to her seat.

Alan gave a morale-boosting speech over the microphone but Shontelle didn't listen to it. She stared down at the hand Luis had gripped, using her other hand to stroke away the feeling of his touch. Her mind fretted over how strongly he could still affect her. It was as though somehow he was imprinted on her—mind, body and soul—and it was an indelible imprint she couldn't wipe out no matter how hard she tried.

He touched her and instantly triggered a chemical reaction through her entire body. How could he do that after last night? And the look he had given her earlier—just one look—and she was drawn to him. Fatal attraction, she thought bitterly.

But she would not let him take her again. If he wanted something more from her it had to be on a very different basis. Respect, for a start. And the truth had to be told from both sides…no more prideful holding back. She recalled Luis' fierce words to Alan…

You don't know a damned thing about what I feel or what I'll do.

One thing he wouldn't do, Shontelle vowed to herself, was seduce her into accepting him as her lover again. Her jaw firmed in resolution. He would not shake her on that.

Then she silently laughed at herself. Unfinished business didn't have to mean sex. It more likely meant getting his facts straight. Then he could move on, satisfied he knew where all the pieces fitted. And maybe the same knowledge would help her put this in the past, as well.

The bus was almost at the top of the long hill that led to the airport, though it was not their destination. They had to go past it to get out of La Paz and on their way to Santa Cruz. However, the area around the airport was sure to be heavily guarded. Alan had anticipated there might be trouble there, if anywhere.

He'd already underestimated possible problems, Shontelle thought, tensing in readiness for more as Luis drove past groups of soldiers who eyed the bus suspiciously. Military jeeps were parked alongside the road but none of them gave chase. It seemed like a miracle when they actually cleared the whole stretch past the airport without being stopped.

The tour group started to relax as the bus travelled on through the settlements on the outskirts of the city. People made jokes to lighten the atmosphere and an air of triumphant jollity started to develop. Alan told a couple of stories about tight spots he'd been in during other tours, making the escapes sound amusing. It really seemed the danger was past—behind them. The bus moved into open country, safely on their journey.

No one was thinking about the farmers' revolt.

At least, Shontelle wasn't. Her gaze was trained on the man sitting in front of her. She saw what Luis saw just as he spoke.

"Alan...ahead of us!"

Large groups of men were milling around what appeared to be a huge speed bump spread across the road.

"They've dug a trench," Luis said, no doubt at all about what the hump meant.

Shontelle's heart sank. A speed bump was passable, but a trench?

''Put your foot down, Luis,'' Alan advised quickly. ''We'll have to jump it.''

''No telling how wide it is,'' came the terse warning.

''If you don't want to risk your bus...''

''Prepare your people.'' It was a grim command.

''Men, up on your feet and put all the overhead hand luggage under seats or on the floor,'' Alan yelled, clapping his hands to encourage fast action. ''The farmers have dug a trench across the road. Our driver is speeding up and we're going to be airborne to cross it. Move, move...we don't want any injuries from flying bags.''

The acceleration in speed made the task more difficult but it was accomplished in a wildly lurching fashion. The hump hiding the trench was coming up very fast and looking bigger by the second. Which could mean the gap in the road behind it was too wide. Shontelle started praying it wasn't. This gamble could end in a very nasty accident.

''Sit, sit!'' Alan yelled. ''Brace yourselves in your seats for impact when we land on the other side...''

If, Shontelle thought darkly.

''...Anyone with a bad back, try to cushion yourself against the thump.''

Silence, except for the rustle of adjustments and much heavy breathing. They were hurtling towards the crisis point. Shontelle wondered what Luis was thinking. Why was he risking so much? What was at stake for him?

He stood up behind the wheel, bracing himself against his seat. Could he see beyond the hump? Impossible to stop now anyway. Was he regretting the risk he'd accepted? He'd be the first hit if the trench was too wide. Luis and Alan…*then me,* Shontelle realised. It could all end here and she'd never know…

The thought stopped there.

The bus hit the heaped pile of rubble dug from the trench and lifted, slightly skewing in the air from an uneven take-off. Shontelle looked frantically out the side window. The gap… Oh, God! Oh, God! It was too big…but the bus was soaring, reaching over the threatening maw of emptiness below them. They weren't going to crash into it. As the long vehicle started dipping forward on the other side, it shot through Shontelle's mind that the back wheels weren't going to make it across.

The front of the bus landed at an angle, half facing towards an open field. The left rear end wheel caught the trench but the right side made it onto the road. With a heart-stopping, wrenching manoeuvre, Luis somehow got enough traction to drag the trapped wheel out. The bus careered down the road in a wild zigzag as he fought for control of it, every muscle stretched to the task.

Shontelle was very, very glad there weren't any roadside trees or other obstacles, and no bends to negotiate—just a straight road and unfenced fields on either side. Hand luggage was sliding all over the floor. There were grunts and groans as the passengers were knocked around, but no one screamed. Shontelle felt they were all fiercely willing Luis to pull them through this nightmare.

How long it took she had no idea, but he finally did it, slowing the bus down, gradually easing it to a very ragged halt. The cessation of movement brought a shock of disbelief. It was hard to take in that it was actually over and they'd made it intact.

''Back left wheel's locked up, Alan,'' Luis muttered.

He jumped up from his seat. ''I'll go and have a look.''

The door whooshed open as Luis said, ''I'll come with you.''

Alan flashed him a grin. ''Great driving, man!''

''Born to survive,'' Luis retorted wryly.

''Shontelle, take over in here,'' Alan instructed.

''Will do.'' She rose shakily to her feet.

Luis paused, dark eyes sharply scanning hers. He said nothing to her, just gave a curt nod before following Alan outside. *She* should have said something, Shontelle thought crossly. At least thanked him. But the moment was gone and she had no idea what the look and nod from him had meant. Satisfaction that she was more or less fighting fit?

This was no time to concern herself about it. Moving quickly she picked up the microphone and turned to address the tour group.

''Is everyone okay?''

It stirred them all into taking stock of themselves. They reported probably a few bruises but no cuts or other injuries.

"How much more of this can we expect?" the chief trouble-maker in the group demanded.

"I don't know," Shontelle answered truthfully.

"Damned madness! Alan shouldn't have led us..."

"Now, hold it a minute, Ron," another cut in. "Alan gave us fair warning there could be trouble. You were the one who insisted he get us out of La Paz or you'd badmouth his tours when you got home, remember?"

"Yeah!" another chimed in. "Better keep your mouth shut, Ron. You not only asked for this, you roped us all into supporting you. We're here now with no broken bones so far. We've got no complaint. Right?"

"Besides, what an adventure to tell our grandchildren!" one of the women said, awed at having lived through the experience.

"Wish I could have videoed it all," another remarked with rueful humour.

Rebellion over, Shontelle thought with considerable relief. "Well, if you feel up to it," she began cautiously, "it would be a good idea to reorganise the loose hand luggage on the floor while Alan and Luis are fixing the wheel."

"Can they fix it?" someone asked.

"Alan's a highly skilled mechanic. He'll get us going again," Shontelle answered confidently.

The assurance encouraged people to start hunting for their belongings and securing them in a more orderly fashion than they'd had time to do so beforehand. The sound of hammering underneath the back of the bus started and continued while the interior tidy-up was in progress.

Shontelle wondered if Luis and Alan were settling some of their differences as they worked together. She hoped some of the hostility would be eased. Fighting Luis was difficult enough without having to fight her brother, as well.

One of the women suggested opening the thermoses provided by the hotel and having cups of coffee.

Shontelle vetoed the idea. They weren't so far away from the aggressive gathering of farmers to be complacent about time. They had to be off again, the moment Luis and Alan finished the repairs. Apart from which, they were barely an hour's journey out of La Paz. They had nine more hours on the road before they reached Santa Cruz.

No one protested.

At last the hammering stopped. Everyone perked up as Alan and Luis boarded the bus again…everyone except Shontelle. She immediately tensed, glancing warily at the two men's faces. Alan was obviously in high good humour. Her brother seemed to thrive on danger. Luis' expression was more guarded but she sensed a radiation of energy that put her nerves even more on edge.

Alan took the microphone from her. ''Any problems?'' he asked quietly.

She shook her head and he waved her back to her seat. Luis moved to the instrument panel and activated the closing of the door.

''Okay, we're about to roll again,'' Alan announced. ''We'll travel for two more hours before stopping for...'' he smiled ''...a refreshment opportunity. If anyone develops an urgent problem before then, let me know. I'll be taking over the driving now. Luis' muscles need a bit of relaxation...''

Shontelle frowned. Had Luis pulled something? He hadn't shown any strain in his movements.

''How about giving him a clap for a fantastic job of getting us this far in one piece?'' Alan suggested, starting off the applause.

Everyone joined in enthusiastically. Luis turned around and acknowledged them with a casual salute and a dry little smile. Alan set aside the microphone and took the driver's seat. The two men had a brief, private discussion. Then Alan gunned the motor and the bus started moving, in a straight line, much to Shontelle's relief. The back wheel problem had obviously been fixed.

She expected Luis to take Alan's seat, but he didn't. Without so much as a by-your-leave, he stepped back and settled himself onto the twin passenger seat beside her.

Every nerve in Shontelle's body jangled. Her hands clenched. She almost cringed away from him in fear of being touched. Which was ridiculous, she fiercely told herself. What could Luis do to her here in front of a busload of people? She was safe from any unwelcome touching. Alan was directly within call, too. Not that she wanted to involve him. She could cope with Luis by herself. Of course she could.

"Are you hurt?" she asked brusquely, not quite able to bring herself to look directly at him.

"No," he answered.

"Then why aren't you driving?"

"Because I want time with you."

Her heart squeezed tight. "Did Alan agree to this?"

"Yes."

Two hours, she thought, staring at the back of her brother's head. Was he listening? No, concentrating on the road, she decided. The drone of the engine was probably filling his ears, as well. The cushioned backrests of their seats closed them off from the passengers behind them. This was probably as good a place as any for a private talk.

Shontelle steeled herself to look at the man who had given her so much torment. Slowly she turned her head, met his waiting gaze, and at point-blank range, asked, "Why?"

The dark eyes had a black intensity of purpose that sent shivers down her spine. "Tell me about your meeting with my mother."

The words "my mother" were edged with acid.

Shontelle wrenched her gaze away, deeply disturbed by the force of energy he emitted. "Why dig around in the past?" she cried. "What point is there now?"

"As far as I'm concerned, the past is the present. And I shall deal with it," he stated with ruthless intent.

Shontelle shook her head, not wanting to relive the pain of Elvira Martinez's disclosures. "You deceived me two years ago, Luis," she accused bitterly.

"No. I didn't."

The rebuttal was instant and powerfully stark.

Shontelle closed her eyes. She couldn't bear it if he was telling the truth. She just couldn't bear it.

"Start talking, Shontelle," he commanded. "Tell me every detail of your experience with my mother."

Again the acid emphasis on "my mother" as though he was barely suppressing a violent flow of bitterness.

The truth, she thought. However much it hurt, whatever it might mean to her, she had to know it, too. So she cast her mind back to that fatal day…the day Elvira Rosa Martinez broke her heart and changed the course of her life…and started to recall it in all its painful detail.

CHAPTER TEN

TWO years had not faded the memory of her meeting with Elvira Rosa Martinez. Shontelle had tried to seal it into a hidden compartment in her mind, but once the locked doors were opened up, it flooded out so vividly, it could have been yesterday…visually, emotionally, physically.

''You said it was the day before you left me,'' Luis prompted.

''Yes. But it didn't really start then,'' Shontelle answered slowly, remembering back to the weeks they'd spent together, living in Luis' apartment which was wonderfully well situated in the Barrio Recoleta. This was considered the most chic neighbourhood in Buenos Aires and Shontelle had been more than happy to call it home. Except Luis kept his life there strictly separate from his *family* home which was only a short distance away from the apartment.

''My mother had contacted you beforehand?'' he asked sharply.

''No. But you avoided introducing me to her. You also avoided introducing me to any of your friends or social acquaintances in Buenos Aires.'' She turned to search his eyes. ''Why was that, Luis?''

He held her gaze unflinchingly. "I didn't want to share you."

"Did you ever plan to?"

He shrugged. "It would have become inevitable if you'd stayed."

"Were you ashamed of me?"

He frowned. "Whatever for?"

"Not measuring up in some way."

His eyes flashed black venom. "Are these my mother's words?"

"If you had not decided to keep me to yourself, her words wouldn't have had any power, Luis."

She turned her head away and stared blindly out the side window, remembering how she'd filled in all those days he'd spent at the Martinez company offices, working long hours. She'd filled them alone. No companions. Just waiting out the time until Luis came back to her.

Admittedly it had not been difficult. There was so much to do and enjoy; roaming around the famous and fascinating Recoleta cemetery where Eva Peron had finally been laid to rest, wandering around the plazas, watching the mime artists, listening to mini-concerts by street buskers, looking through galleries. Buenos Aires was called the Paris of the Americas for good reason. Even the architecture was fascinating.

She hadn't been bored.

Not at all.

But she had been alone. In a strange country. In a

strange culture. Even so, she hadn't felt really *foreign* until the day with Luis' mother. And Claudia Gallardo.

"You know...one of the hardest things to bear that day was her sympathy," Shontelle dryly remarked. "How sorry she was that I'd been so blind about what your relationship with me meant. How very wrong it was for her son to have deceived me about my place in his life."

"What place was that...according to my mother?"

"Oh, good for satisfying the desires men have. Not good enough to marry, of course," she answered flippantly. "Women like me get *used* so the fine men of Argentina can behave themselves with the properly brought up virgins they marry."

"You believed I had so little honour I would use a woman—any woman—*let alone the sister of a friend,* for such a purpose?" he bit out scathingly.

She swung fiercely condemning eyes on him. "You used me as a whore last night. Are you going to deny that?"

"You had a choice," he retaliated, hard black eyes denying any shame in his actions. "You chose the role. The same role you put me in two years ago. Someone to be used for sexual satisfaction."

"You were never that to me," she cried. "I only said so because..."

"Because my mother's words meant more to you than all we'd been to each other?" he interpreted savagely.

''Not just *words,* Luis,'' she retorted just as savagely. ''I met your bride-to-be, Claudia Gallardo.''

''Ah...'' His eyes glittered. ''Did Claudia actually say she was my fiancée?''

''Betrothed was the word used.''

''By Claudia?''

Shontelle frowned. She couldn't recall Claudia actually saying she was betrothed to Luis, yet everything she said and did had certainly implied it. ''*When I am married to Luis*...it was a kind of refrain she tossed at me over lunch, prefacing her plans for the future with you,'' she related, determined on being accurate in her recollections. ''It was your mother who used *betrothed.* Before Claudia arrived.''

''Where was this lunch?''

''At your family home in the Avenue Alvear.''

His jaw visibly tightened. His lips compressed into a thin line. She felt an emanation of wild, destructive violence before he brought it under control.

''How did this come about?'' he demanded, his voice thick with the unresolved conflicts inside him.

''Your mother came to the apartment that morning,'' she replied quickly. ''It was about nine-thirty. She introduced herself and invited me...'' A wave of nausea shot bile up Shontelle's throat. She swallowed hard and turned her head away from the sickening lack of sympathy in Luis' eyes. ''...To learn more about you and your life,'' she added dully.

This was hopeless...hopeless... No good was going to come from raking over the past. She tried to focus on the present, the journey they were on now. Alan was driving fast across the high Andean plateau. At least the weather wouldn't hold them up, Shontelle thought. It couldn't be a finer, sunnier day.

Like the day Elvira Rosa Martinez had walked into her life.

Alan had told her Luis' family was very wealthy. He had listed off their assets when he had grown concerned over her involvement with his friend. Though all the time she had spent with Luis, his wealth hadn't really seemed relevant to her. He hadn't pushed it in her face.

The boat he'd hired for their trip down the Amazon was more like *The African Queen* than a luxury cruiser. His apartment had certainly been comfortable, but not what she'd call showy. It wasn't until she'd opened the door to the woman who introduced herself as his mother that she saw serious wealth being flaunted.

Beautifully coiffeured black hair was artfully winged with white. The deep mulberry-coloured suit was very smartly trimmed with black, its classy elegance marking it as an Italian design, most probably Cerruti. Shoes and handbag were black with a mulberry trim, obviously made to complement the clothes.

Having toured the H. Stern workshops in Rio de Janeiro, Shontelle recognised the work of the famous jeweler in the fabulous geometric design of the woman's necklace and earrings; hexagonal wine-red rubellites set in yellow and black gold, costing a small fortune. The rings on her hands were equally fabulous.

Shontelle had instantly felt like a waif from the streets, wearing merely a loose button-through cotton dress designed more to hide a traveller's pouch for money and passport than to flatter her figure or give her a bit of style. The sandals on her feet were for practical comfort.

However, since her touring wardrobe did not contain fancy clothes, she had to accept her own appearance as being as good as it could be in the circumstances. Luis had never once criticised it. Though she'd thought afterwards he liked her best naked, anyway.

The plush chauffeur-driven car she'd been led to had made her feel even more self-conscious. The distance they travelled was easily walkable, a matter of a few blocks, but Shontelle was acutely aware that walking the streets with the common people was not the done thing in Elvira Rosa Martinez's world. They drove right to her front door, a semicircular driveway guarded by huge iron gates allowing this private access.

Front door was a misnomer for the huge, elaborate portico that embellished the entrance to a home which was far more than a home. It was probably impossible to explain to Luis, who'd grown up with it, how overwhelming that virtual palace in Alvear Street had been to her, the almost obscene wealth evident in every room she'd been shown, furnishings and furniture imported from Spain, Italy, France. The ballroom had featured all the unbelievable richness of the hall of mirrors in Versailles, reflecting over and over again how hopelessly unsuitable Shontelle looked in such a place.

Naturally, Elvira Rosa Martinez was far too gracious to say so. She didn't have to. Pointing out family heirlooms and portraits, recounting the achievements of Martinez generations in Argentina, she'd made it subtly clear to Shontelle that Luis had the responsibility of carrying on a heritage—an integral part of him no foreigner could even begin to comprehend.

Beside her, Luis stirred from his tense stillness, thrusting out his hand in an impatient gesture. "So tell me the judgment you made…of my *real life.*"

Shontelle sighed at his persistence. "You know it better than I, Luis."

"A conducted tour through the mausoleum must have been quite an experience for you," he went on sardonically. "All my forebears framed on the walls, the accumulated treasures of centuries of plunder and exploitation on ostentatious display. I'm sure my mother didn't spare you anything."

His disrepectful tone startled Shontelle. She glanced sharply at him. "Don't you value what's yours?"

His eyes mocked the value she'd placed on it. "It

cost too much. Did Claudia join you for the grand exhibition?''

''No.''

Shontelle scooped in a deep breath as that memory billowed into her mind—the perfectly presented Claudia wearing a spectacular silk dress in glorious autumn tones, highlighting her lovely, glowing olive skin, a lustrous fall of black curly hair, and dark velvet eyes. Fine gold chains and a gold filigree necklace and earrings added their rich touch to her young vibrancy. It was all too obvious she belonged to the same class that the Martinez home portrayed so tellingly.

''Claudia arrived about midday,'' she added, anticipating Luis' next question and deciding she might as well satisfy his curiosity and have done with it.

''Were you introduced to her as my secret mistress?''

A surge of hot blood scorched up her neck and flooded into her cheeks. She shook her head, trying to get rid of the painful flush. ''Your mother tactfully explained about your friendship with Alan and simply introduced me as Alan's sister who was staying in Buenos Aires for a while.''

''Tactful!'' Luis snorted derisively. ''That was for your benefit, Shontelle, not Claudia's. Who was clearly in on the game of getting you out of my life.''

Was that true? Even if it was, didn't Claudia have good reason to want to be rid of the woman sharing Luis' bed…his *secret mistress?* Having just returned from a tour of Europe, it must have been galling to hear that her man had been playing fast and loose with another woman.

Though the comments she had made over lunch about her future with Luis had seemed quite natural, artless. Impossible to tell if they were or not now. They had certainly robbed Shontelle of any appetite…any appetite for food, for staying with Luis, for remaining in Buenos Aires any longer than it took to get a flight home to Australia. The feeling was so sickeningly strong that she didn't belong with these people and never would.

She remembered staring at the centrepiece on the dining table, a magnificently crafted artwork in silver. It was a tree rising from a mound of grass and roots where three deer lay at rest. At the top of the trunk was a holder from which spread a beautiful array of fresh red roses, forming the foliage of the tree. Similarly, silver branches held other, smaller holders, containing more bunches of roses. The effect was stunningly sumptuous and the scent of the roses dreadfully insidious. Red roses for love. Shontelle had hated red roses ever since.

''Was Claudia wearing a ring on the third finger of her left hand?'' Luis asked.

''No. Though she talked about what she fancied. An oval yellow diamond surrounded by two rows of white diamonds.''

Louis muttered something vicious under his breath.

The Spanish was too fast or too colloquial for Shontelle to pick up the meaning.

"Yet even hearing all this," he said tersely, "you were still there for me in the apartment that evening."

"I didn't want to believe you'd used me like that. I thought there was a chance you had changed your mind about marrying Claudia," she explained ruefully.

"Then why did you not speak of this?"

Because it was too shaming if it was true. Because she still wanted him. Because she simply couldn't face it…until after the telephone call.

She heaved a sigh to ease the burden of all she'd felt, and still felt. "Your mother called you that evening. At the apartment. She said she'd call at eight o'clock. And she did, didn't she, Luis?"

"Yes."

"With an invitation for you to bring me to her next Sunday lunch."

"No," he answered vehemently.

"Luis, I heard the excuse you made. In fact, you sounded extremely vexed and impatient with her for suggesting it."

"She wanted me to be Claudia's escort at a welcome home party. It had nothing to do with you, Shontelle. Nothing!" He gave a derisive laugh. "Or so I thought at the time. I actually thought you were still safe from her. Safe! *¡Madre de Dios!*"

Confusion swallowed up Shontelle's understanding

of the situation. Was Luis afraid of his mother? How much power did Elvira have over him?

''My mother planned this call with you...as a test of my intentions?'' he probed in a hard ruthless tone.

She gave him her vision of the situation because she had nothing else to give him. ''I thought it was a woman to woman thing. A kindness to show me where I stood with you.''

''So when you heard my negative reply, you assumed this meant I was keeping you as my secret mistress...yes?'' he snapped.

''Yes,'' she acknowledged.

''And the fire of your love for me went out that night.''

She'd cravenly given herself one last night with him, but had found it impossible to respond to his lovemaking, impossible to block Claudia out of her mind, impossible to feel Luis really loved her.

''I felt...used,'' she repeated wearily.

''So you made me feel *used.*''

''Yes.''

''For you, it was marriage or nothing.''

He had no right to leap to that conclusion. Her love had been freely given, no strings attached. ''We hadn't got that far, Luis,'' she angrily reminded him.

''No, we hadn't. Which was why I did not throw you into the ring with my mother who had her own plans for me.''

''You must have known of them,'' Shontelle argued. ''There was too much...too much evidence.''

His hands sliced the air in a contemptuous scissor movement. "Talk. Deliberate, divisive talk. If you had spoken to me...but no, you decided I would marry Claudia and there would be nothing for us."

"Back then...your marriage to Claudia meant there was nothing for *me,* Luis," she fiercely corrected him. "Nothing I could feel happy with."

"Claudia Gallardo will never get her yellow diamond from me! Not from *me!* Never!" he declared passionately. "I see now she is every bit as manipulative as my mother and I will not be caught in either of their webs."

Shontelle retreated into silence. She had never been part of this *power* side of Luis' life. From what he'd said, it seemed now that she'd been a victim of it, but it was all beyond her experience.

The old saying...*power corrupts*...slid into her mind. It had never applied to her personal life. She didn't want it to, either. It felt dark and ugly. Luis had accused her of having no faith, no trust, but how could anything be trusted or believed in Luis' world if his own mother plotted behind his back?

The truth—if that was what she had now—did not give her any satisfaction. Only sadness.

Alan had been right.

Her relationship with Luis had been doomed from the start.

Love didn't always find a way.

Not when there was too much stacked against it.

CHAPTER ELEVEN

LUIS closed his eyes. He felt like a drowning man whose whole life was passing before him. And there was no rescue to be had. No going back to a more promising place. He'd killed any possibility of that last night.

The rage inside him was futile. What was done could not be undone. Shontelle—the Shontelle who had brought love and joy and laughter and the sweetest of pleasures into his life—was forever lost to him. No point in blaming her for it. She'd been an innocent, mangled by the forces that had ruled his world, forces he'd known all too well and had wanted to ignore with her. To be free of them with her.

Fool! he thought savagely.

He might have won her back last night. Instead, he'd driven her further away. Beyond reach now. He could feel the shield she'd wrapped around herself, blocking him out. And why not? He was pain…pain in all its forms.

He'd done wrong by Alan, too. Another innocent party. While the guilty ones had almost reaped the benefits of their self-serving conspiracy. Tonight, if there'd been no trouble in La Paz, he would have presented Claudia with the yellow diamond ring, and his mother would have beamed triumphant approval over the proceedings.

How the coin of Fate turns, he thought with an acute sense of irony. But for Alan's need for a bus, his mother would have succeeded in her drive to link the Gallardo and Martinez fortunes. He would have let her succeed, and in doing so, would have provided her with justification for sacrificing the one great love of his life. For that, there was no justification. None that Luis would ever accept.

Everything Shontelle had said to him last night made sense now. If he hadn't been so blinded by bitterness he might have picked up on her repeated references to marriage, questioned more closely.

No…on reflection, there'd been no chance of his being sensitive to what was going on in her mind. The damage had been well and truly done two years ago. Old scars didn't suddenly clear up. But those who'd delivered the wounds could and would still pay for the injuries.

The beautifully polished, submissive Claudia, offering her cold comfort, hiding a Machiavellian heart…she could kiss goodbye to whatever ambitions she'd nursed as an outcome of their marriage merger. The sly bitch hadn't turned a hair at making Shontelle bleed, delivering her poisonous little cuts. He could see her delicately picking through her lunch, sticking her knife in with sweet, loving smiles. She, who didn't know a damned thing about love. Not the kind of love Shontelle…

His heart cramped.

Forget it, he railed at himself. Alan was right. Let it go. God knew there were other things that had to be dealt with. Like his mother…

If only Eduardo had not been taken…Luis could mark the change in his mother from that terrible grief. Not even his father's death, five years before Eduardo's, had touched her so deeply, so traumatically. Perhaps because there'd been no body to bury, no answers to be drawn from anyone.

It was then that the woman she was today had emerged. Control had become everything. The more wealth she acquired, the more power she had, the more control she wielded. Loving anyone was a weakness that left one vulnerable. Better not to love. Better to hold what you had with an iron fist and never risk it, never allow even the possibility of risking it. Protect. Shore up the walls so they were impregnable. Keep a constant watch.

She didn't put her philosophy in such stark terms, but that was what it boiled down to. Luis had fought it for years, to no avail. She'd hung his heritage—Eduardo's heritage—around his neck like an albatross, and wouldn't listen to any point of view that differed from hers. He'd understood—to a degree—what drove her. He'd tried to fill the void she feared—within reason. But for her to take Shontelle out of his life with such ruthless efficiency, uncaring of the pain she gave to either of them…

She had to be stopped.

So forcefully she would never interfere in his life again.

Better still, if she could be made to realise how far she'd gone along a road that was intolerable to him, maybe she could be turned around. Shutting her out of his life was not the answer. She'd find a way to intrude, to interfere. She had to be faced with consequences she couldn't change.

But how to do it? How to hammer it home?

He knew what he wanted to do, what he'd love to do, but he also knew in his bones Shontelle wouldn't agree to it. She was probably longing for him to move away from her right now, have nothing more to do with him.

Yet he couldn't let the idea go. It was the perfect act of justice. No secret moves. No sly manoeuvrings. An act no one could stop, a public act in the spotlight of his mother's own choosing, an undeniable act that declared Luis Angel Martinez his *own man* against any force that could be rallied against him.

But he needed Shontelle's cooperation. Would she listen? Would she see it was an act of justice for her, too? Her response would almost certainly be she wanted no more to do with either him or his family. But it was worth a try. It was very much worth a try. It might just balance the scales so that Shontelle would look at him and see a man she could love again, a man who was free to love.

CHAPTER TWELVE

ALAN made good time to Caracollo, their first stopping place. To have achieved this distance without further mishap put everyone in a good mood.

"You have twenty minutes maximum," Alan warned. "Don't wander away. Use the facilities you'll find across the road, then come back to the bus. Shontelle and I will have coffee and cake and soft drinks ready for you."

The tour group alighted from the bus looking both relieved and happy. Shontelle was grateful for the opportunity to move away from Luis and get about her business of helping Alan with the refreshments. To her frustration, Luis offered his assistance, as well, hovering around her until everything was set up. She refused to look at him, knowing it would only upset her. She was tense enough as it was, feeling him watching her.

Maybe the message that his presence was unwelcome finally got through to him. He drew out a compact mobile telephone that had been clipped to his belt and walked away to make whatever calls he wanted to make in private. Shontelle insisted to herself she was not curious about them. Luis' life was no business of hers anymore. She was better off out of it.

"Are you okay?" Alan asked.

"Yes," she answered shortly.

"I was wrong about Luis, Shontelle. Sorry for thinking I knew better."

"Don't worry about it. We were all wrong. About a lot of things."

"Did you sort it out?"

"Yes."

"And?"

"And nothing. There's nowhere to go."

Alan frowned, not liking the answer, but people were trailing back to the bus and his attention was claimed by them. Shontelle's attention, too.

Cochabamba was their next stop, then the long stretch through the lowlands to Santa Cruz, hopefully arriving there by early evening. Alan had booked them into a hotel for the night, and on a flight to Buenos Aires tomorrow morning. All going well, they would arrive there in time to make the prebooked flight home to Australia. All going well…which it rarely did in South America. Keeping schedules ran on hope, never certainty.

A downpour of rain could block roads, holding up traffic for hours. Flights were cancelled or delayed with no apology or explanation. A gunfight had broken out in Rio on this trip, causing them to take a long detour around the trouble spot. Then a political upheaval in La Paz. Hopefully that problem was behind them, but who knew what they'd run into next?

On the other side of the ledger, was the sheer magic of this continent, so many incredible wonders: La Paz itself, with its fantastic Moon Valley, the Inca history in Cuzco and the strange, eerie atmosphere of the abandoned city of Machu Picchu, the splendid primaeval spectacle of the Iguazu Falls, the awesome Amazon Valley, the beauty of Rio with its Sugarloaf Mountain and the majestic statue of Christ the Redeemer, Buenos Aires…where the Martinez family lived.

Shontelle tried to sigh away the pain.

Whatever discomforts their tour groups ran into on tour, the trip was always worthwhile, the journey truly memorable. Especially this one, Shontelle thought wryly as they herded everyone back on the bus. She suggested to Alan she do a tour commentary over the microphone during this next leg of the trip.

"It will keep them entertained," she pressed, wanting to avoid sitting with Luis again.

Alan surprised her by replying, "I'll do it myself. Luis said he'd take the wheel to Cochabamba. We'll get along faster and more safely with us both coming fresh to driving after a spell."

So Luis *was* letting it go.

It was the inevitable outcome, Shontelle told herself, as they got under way again. She sat alone, which should have relieved the stress of being constantly aware of him, but now she found herself staring at the back of his head, wishing she could read his thoughts. The stress didn't diminish at all. She gradually sank into a black pit of depression.

No heart…no faith…no trust…

The words Luis had hurled at her earlier this morning kept pounding through her mind, making her head ache. She ached all over. The plain truth was she hadn't believed enough in his love for her. She'd let her own sense of inadequacy swallow it up, then spit it out. She had trusted his mother instead of Luis, put her faith in women she didn't know against the man she did know. He was right. Where was the heart in that?

Broken, she thought. Smashed. Bleeding to death.

And there was no cure for it. None at all.

Eventually they reached Cochabamba and stopped for lunch. Luis went off by himself, the mobile telephone in his hand ready to make more calls. Probably shuffling his business affairs around, Shontelle thought. She and Alan led the tour group into a hotel where a buffet spread provided instant self-service. Once everyone was fed and watered, it was back to the bus.

The next stretch of their journey to Villa Tunari was very picturesque and again Shontelle offered to carry on a commentary, aware that Alan would be doing this drive.

''Better to keep quiet and let them doze after lunch,'' he argued. ''Let's save it for when they get restless later on.''

Which meant she had to sit with Luis.

More torture.

She shrank into herself as best she could as he settled beside her. Anticipating a long journey of tense silence, she was surprised when he spoke to her, the moment Alan had the bus moving.

''Will you accept an apology for my behaviour last night, Shontelle?''

She glanced sharply at him, drawn more by the low intense tone than the question. There was no mockery in his eyes, not one trace of contempt for her, just deep unfathomable darkness. His face looked strained, absolutely serious. Shontelle's heart skittered nervously. Had she been wrong about his decision to let it all go?

''We've both acted regrettably, Luis,'' she answered stiffly. ''I'm sorry, too, for the pain I caused you.''

His mouth twisted into a rueful grimace. ''Saying *sorry* isn't enough, is it?''

She shook her head. ''There are too many other factors.''

''Yes,'' he agreed.

They were in tune with each other on that score, Shontelle thought, sliding back into bleak despondency.

''My mother is holding a grand reception tonight,'' he remarked. ''The guest list includes the most prominent people in Argentina. The Gallardo family will certainly be there. In strength.''

Shontelle fiercely wished he'd keep his family business to himself.

"I would be very honoured," he went on, "if you'd be my partner to this highly glittering occasion, Shontelle."

Shock addled her brains. He couldn't mean it. She was either dreaming or he'd taken leave of his senses. Yet he still looked perfectly serious.

"Why?" she blurted out, needing to sort through the ambivalence of such a suggestion.

His mouth curved into a whimsical little smile. "It is, perhaps, one thing I can right, out of all the wrongs I've done you."

"How could that make anything right?" she cried.

"Two years ago, I made you feel less than you were, Shontelle," he said quietly. "It was unintentional, but a very grave error on my part. I would like, at least, to correct that error. I'd be very proud to present you as my partner in front of my mother and all of Argentina."

Shontelle squirmed in anguish. "It's too late for that, Luis."

"No. It's never too late to give due respect. To restore pride and self-esteem. I shall do it tonight, if you'll allow me."

"It doesn't matter. These people are not part of my life. They never will be."

His face hardened. "It doesn't matter that they lied to you? That they lied about me to make you feel like *nothing?* You can forgive and forget that, Shontelle? Or will it not always burn a hole in your heart?''

''It's in the past, Luis.''

''No.'' His eyes blazed with passionate intensity. ''The past is never in the past. It lives with us. Always. I need…please, I beg you…let me give you justice.''

She wrenched her gaze from his, feeling the power of his will tugging on hers, intent on drawing her with him again. For what? Justice was a cold repast. It could never give back what had been taken. At best, all it did was balance the scales.

Nevertheless, there was an insidious attraction about turning up at a grand reception given by Elvira Rosa Martinez, being flaunted as Luis' chosen partner for the evening, right under his mother's and Claudia Gallardo's snobbish noses. Yes, there would be some satisfaction in that…robbing them of their mean triumph over her.

But it would also mean more time spent with Luis…time filled with painful might-have-beens. He'd be touching her, stirring memories, putting her through a make-believe situation, pretending all was right between them when it wasn't. She couldn't do it.

Besides, how did he expect to get to this reception? ''Have you forgotten we're in the middle of Bolivia, Luis? We'll be lucky to make it to Santa Cruz tonight.''

"A company jet will be waiting there to fly us on to Buenos Aires."

She looked at him in astonishment. "You've already made arrangements?"

"For me, yes. I hope you will accompany me."

His calls on the mobile telephone, Shontelle thought, and wondered when he had started planning this proposition. As early as before Caracollo, or had the idea grown on him while he drove to Cochabamba?

"Shontelle, I owe you this," he said softly. "You owe it to me, as well."

She stared at the steadily burning purpose in his eyes. "How do you work that out?" she challenged.

"You let them picture me falsely. Because they got away with it, they will go on picturing me falsely to others whenever it suits their purpose. That must be stopped, and the most effective way of stopping it is for you to bear witness for me in a court where it will count, in front of people who count to them. Together we can throw their game back in their faces."

She shivered at the ruthless intent behind his words. "As you did with me last night, Luis?" she said, reminding him of that wretched outcome.

"No. That was not justice. It was the vengeance of a man whose love had been robbed of all value. And it will always haunt me as a shameful act on my part. But there is no shame in seeking justice, Shontelle. Only shame in not pursuing it."

He was right in a way. It was wrong to let Elvira

Rosa Martinez and Claudia Gallardo get away scot-free with what they'd done. Justice...it gave a kind of closure to a crime. And it had been a crime...the premeditated murder of love.

It wouldn't take much, she argued to herself. Just one more night. For his pride. For her pride. But how could she carry it off? "I don't have anything suitable to wear, Luis. They'd all look down their noses at me and think you mad for bringing me into their midst."

"I'll provide you with appropriate clothes. I'll have a selection delivered to my apartment. With the finest accessories." He flashed a wicked smile that jiggled her heart. "Believe me, you will not be underdressed for this occasion."

Wealth, Shontelle sternly reminded herself, was one of the divisive factors she could not overlook. Obscene wealth. Luis could probably order anything to appear at the snap of his fingers. Or a telephone call. Though there were some things one couldn't buy... like love and trust and happiness.

"Is it worth it to you, Luis?" she asked. "Even if we manage to get to Santa Cruz by seven o'clock, it's then a three hour flight to Buenos Aires. Add on the hour time difference, plus time to dress ourselves appropriately. I doubt we could make it to the reception before midnight."

"Yes, it's worth it," he asserted strongly. "And I consider midnight perfect timing. Everyone will be there by then and no one would have left. It would be seen as rude to leave such an elite gathering before

3:00 a.m.'' Another flash of wickedness. ''We shall make quite an entrance, you and I.''

He relished the idea. And suddenly Shontelle did, too. Why not? ''You intend to turn the pumpkin into a princess at the stroke of midnight?'' she half mocked.

''You were never a pumpkin,'' he shot back at her, anger flaring from his eyes. ''Do not ever regard yourself in such a demeaning light. You are...'' His lips compressed, shutting off the line of thought he'd been about to give voice to. He shook his head in an anguished roll. ''It is wrong to hate one's mother. But I do hate much of what's she's done.''

The torment so clearly expressed moved Shontelle more than anything else he'd said. She thought of her own mother who was always there for her, ready to give any help or comfort, always looking to answer her needs without ever forcing anything. For all the wealth at his disposal, it had not been an easy life for Luis, always feeling the load of responsibility he'd inherited through his older brother's death.

She remembered all the things he'd confided to her when they'd been most intimate. He had never openly criticised his mother for the way she had ordered his life so he could take Eduardo's place, but she had sensed he sometimes felt trapped in a role that had been thrust upon him. Once he had said he envied Alan's freedom to choose his own path.

''I have to break the chains that have bound me for so long,'' he muttered. Then his hand reached across and took hers, interlacing their fingers in a tight, forceful grip that throbbed with intense feeling. ''Be my partner tonight, Shontelle. I will see that you catch your flight home to Australia tomorrow. But tonight is ours…one final stand together…for justice.''

''Yes,'' she agreed, barely aware of giving her consent.

She was overwhelmingly aware of the physical link he had just forged. Except somehow it was more than physical. It was like a current flowing from him and flooding every cell of her body. She stared down at their hands, not understanding, only knowing she ached with a terrible need to stay joined to him.

She forgot the other factors.

Suddenly they were meaningless.

If only Luis would hold on to her, she would stand with him to the end of time.

CHAPTER THIRTEEN

‘‘THE red,’’ Luis said decisively.

‘‘Are you sure?’’ Shontelle asked, her gaze clinging to the safer, black lace creation.

She still couldn’t quite believe the array of beautiful designer clothes and accessories laid out for her to choose from in the main bedroom of Luis’ apartment. It was difficult enough, coping with being hit by the familiarity of a room they had shared so intimately. Besides which, the prospect of returning to the Martinez mansion had her nerves in a jangling mess, despite having the promised security of Luis’ arm to support her. She was afraid of looking wrong.

‘‘Melding into the crowd is not what tonight is about, Shontelle,’’ Luis dryly reminded her.

Not the black then. ‘‘The gold one is very elegant,’’ she pointed out.

‘‘Wear the red.’’ No doubt, no reservation in his voice.

‘‘Luis, it hardly has any back to it,’’ she protested worriedly. The gown dipped right down to waist level, apparently supported by a silver Y-strap running down her spine and two shoestring red straps that joined it to hold the bodice firmly across her breasts.

''You have a beautiful back.''

The soft, thick words raised goose bumps all over her skin. Her heart thumped erratically. She knew she could still arouse desire in him. Last night had proved that. Even when he'd hated her the sexual chemistry hadn't waned. But tonight wasn't about answering those needs, was it? He'd given no indication of it.

''That doesn't mean I should bare it,'' she said, keeping her gaze fixed firmly on the dress, as though studying its potential to embarrass her.

Her mind was jagging off in wild directions. This togetherness project was bound to push them into more intimacy as the night went on…holding, dancing, continual linking with each other. What if it led back to this bed? What if they ended up making love? Would he ask her to stay with him…or would he stick to his promise to have her at the airport tomorrow in good time to join Alan and the tour group for their flight home?

''Your hair will veil most of it,'' he said, his voice even more furred with sensual overtones.

''I thought I'd put it up. It's more sophisticated,'' she almost gabbled in helpless agitation.

''No. Wear it loose. And wear the red, Shontelle.'' She heard his breath hiss out on a long sigh. ''I will leave you to dress. The bathroom is free for your use.''

His footsteps moved to the spare bedroom. Its door clicked shut. He was giving her complete privacy, removing any sense of lurking intimacy she might feel. And did feel. One night…for justice, he'd said. Did she dare reach for more? Was *more* possible?

Dear God! Hadn't she hoped the same last night? She'd be totally mad to lay herself on the line again. Just get on with what's been planned, she savagely berated herself, and grabbed the make-up that had been supplied to complement the red dress. The bathroom was free and there was no time to waste.

Nevertheless, as she took a quick shower and set about adding glamour to her face, she couldn't stop her mind from wandering over Luis' manner to her since she had agreed to his plan. Apart from the one strong hand grip, he hadn't touched her, nor said anything suggestive of a sexual interest or any interest in her beyond tonight.

Unfinished business, he'd told Alan when he'd asked they be dropped at the Santa Cruz airport before the tour group was driven on to their hotel. Alan had simply asked her, ''Is this your choice, Shontelle?'' and when she'd answered, ''Yes,'' he'd set the scene for her and Luis' departure, explaining to the group that Luis had supplied them with the bus as a special favour to the Amigos Tours Company and they were returning the favour in helping him to make an important business connection on time. Shontelle's accompanying him to Buenos Aires on a private flight would place her there to deal with any problems arising tomorrow.

No one had protested.

On their arrival at the airport, it had been all business. The moment the bus pulled up, a man from the Martinez company had been on the spot to escort them to the company plane. He'd handed Luis an attaché case which Shontelle had deduced contained important company documents, then taken charge of her luggage. The tour group gave them a rousing farewell, happy that their journey was almost over, Alan wished them well, and their escort whisked them away.

There was no delay in taking off. Once safely in the air, they were served dinner, after which Luis had urged her to get some rest and moved to another part of the plane, presumably to work on the papers in the attaché case. She'd actually slept for most of the flight, the toll of a long day's travelling following a wretched night of distress finally wearing out her too active mind. Luis woke her as they were about to land, awakening her senses, too, as she breathed in the cologne he'd splashed onto his freshly shaven face.

His shaving on the flight had probably been done to leave his bathroom free for her, she thought now, but right then, in her drowsy state, she'd almost reached up and touched his face, only just halting the movement and redirecting her hand to scrape an errant strand of hair off her own face. But the impulse had rattled her. She shouldn't still want him so… wantonly. She knew it was foolish.

The subsequent drive from the airport to this apartment had been fraught with tension on her part. They didn't talk. It was a company car with a chauffeur doing the driving. The silver-grey Mercedes with its plush interior was clearly executive class. The power of wealth was being demonstrated in full, ever since she'd agreed to standing with Luis tonight.

A final stand...

Final!

She had to get that through her head.

Tonight was the end, no chance at all of a new beginning.

Having emphasised her eyes with subtle earth tones and put a glow on her skin with the clever cosmetics designed for that purpose, Shontelle outlined her mouth with the red pencil provided and filled in the curves with a vivid scarlet lipstick, the perfect match for the dress Luis had insisted upon.

The thought occurred to her she'd certainly be a scarlet woman tonight to at least two people. Or a flaming sword, cutting their lies down and laying them waste. Which was what those wicked lies deserved, defaming Luis and deceiving her with such devastating results.

Justice...

Satisfied she'd at least done justice to her face, Shontelle put the lipstick down, unbraided her hair, and brushed it into a cloud of rippling waves. The plait had crinkled it and there was no time to wash and dry it into a straight fall, but it was still clean and shiny from last night's washing. Luis had always preferred it loose. She hoped it didn't look too untamed and casual to other eyes.

Wrapped in a towel, she collected her things and dashed back to the bedroom. Luis was nowhere in view. She hurried through the nervous business of dressing herself to the standard expected of a guest at a Martinez grand reception.

The red gown was spectacular. The fabric was soft and slinky and woven through with silver thread, creating a kind of oriental design of meandering vines and leaves that shimmered exotically on the scarlet background. It clung to every curve of her body, only flaring slightly from the knees so she could walk comfortably.

The silver shoulder straps extended down the outside curve of her breasts and joined underneath them, creating a bra effect with the fabric stretched above and between them. Shontelle worried over the cleavage on display until she added the fine filigree silver chains and necklaces that cascaded from her throat, filling in the expanse of bare flesh and adding that indefinable sense of class to sexiness.

Beautiful silver strappy high heels and an elegant little silver handbag gave the perfect touches of completion. Shontelle couldn't help staring at her reflection in the mirror, amazed by the transformation that could be wrought, given no expense spared for anything. Fine feathers certainly made fine birds. Even to herself she looked stunning. Which gave her a much-needed boost in confidence.

She quickly put the scarlet lipstick, a couple of tissues and some emergency money into the tiny evening bag. The bedside clock read 11:43. Luis' estimate of a midnight arrival at the reception was going to be very close, assuming he was also ready to leave now. Time to find out, she told herself, taking a deep breath and hoping the flutters in her stomach didn't get any worse.

He was waiting for her, just standing in the middle of the living room, nursing a drink in one hand. The sheer impact of him, dressed in formal evening clothes, brought Shontelle to a halt. His black dinner suit had the expensive sheen of silk, and its black satin lapels and matching bow tie added a sensual touch against the crisp whiteness of his finely pin-tucked shirt. He looked utterly superb and so handsome, Shontelle could hardly breathe, let alone walk.

The perfect man, she thought—tall, dark, handsome and loaded with a brooding, male animal appeal that was all the more enticing for being encased in the clothes of sophisticated civilisation. Her heart was going haywire, frantically signalling that *he* was the man for her, and if she let him go, she would be losing the mate of her life. But how could she make it right between them? How?

"The sun and the moon and the stars..."

The soft murmur from Luis seemed to feather down her spine. His eyes glowed the kind of warmth she'd all but forgotten, stirring memories of beautiful times together, times of tenderness and deep, inexpressible joy. Hope leapt into her mind and danced through her veins. Then his thick lashes lowered, shadowing the look that belonged to an idyll of blissful togetherness, and his mouth curved into an ironic little smile.

"You'll outshine them all tonight. As you should. Though I would have been proud to present you whatever you wore, Shontelle. I don't suppose you'll believe that, but it's true."

"I want to do you proud, Luis," she answered, feeling he was making light of the power of first impressions. Not that he'd care…if tonight was the end. First impressions would only be important to him if she were to stay in his social circle. But just this once, Shontelle wanted to feel acceptable in his world, and see acceptance in others' eyes. It was important to her that she didn't fail this test.

His brows drew together in a quick frown. "If you feel…not right…" He gestured an apologetic appeal. "I should not have pressed you to wear anything you prefer not to."

"No. I like the red on me," she quickly assured him.

His concern broke into a grin of sheer, wicked pleasure. "Good! It is absolutely perfect for you in my eyes. I shall enjoy being the envy of every man at the reception."

He set his glass down on a table as he moved to open the door with a flourish, his grin still alight with devilish anticipation. "Come, Cinderella. It is time to go to the ball."

A nervous laugh bubbled out of her throat as she forced her legs to move. Elvira Rosa Martinez wasn't exactly the wicked stepmother and Claudia Gallardo couldn't be described as an ugly stepsister, but Shontelle couldn't help hoping they'd get the shock of their lives when they recognised who had the Prince's arm tonight.

The silver Mercedes was waiting for them. The chauffeur saw Shontelle settled on one side of the back seat while Luis rounded the car and took the other side. They were closed in together for the final act.

Five more minutes and the players would be on stage, Shontelle thought, wondering just how many people would be shocked by her appearance with Luis Angel Martinez, the heir to a fortune, who was undoubtedly expected to be paying court to the heiress of a fortune. A worriesome thought struck her and she turned sharply to Luis as the car moved off.

"What about the Gallardo family? Will this make bad business between you?"

"I don't care, Shontelle. What will be, will be," he said quietly, firmly.

Reckless?

She studied him for a moment, but his expression was difficult to read in the shadows of the night. He sat back, apparently perfectly relaxed, yet she could feel the harnessing of power and purpose in him, the determination to sweep all before him, to stamp his own will on everything that happened.

''Don't fear anything on my account, Shontelle,'' he said softly. ''Whatever the consequences of to-night, I would rather be known as my own man than have others think they own me.''

''It's strange to me…this Martinez side of you…the public position you hold in Argentina. You never really showed it to me.''

''I preferred you to know the private person.''

''I don't think you can separate yourself out like that, Luis.''

''It was wrong,'' he agreed. ''You have made me see that very clearly, Shontelle. For which I am deeply grateful. A man cannot live another's life. He must be true to himself.''

Shontelle suddenly perceived tonight wasn't so much about justice to Luis. It was about freedom. Which made it a far more momentous occasion than she had realised. He was seeing this as a major turn-ing point in his life…and *she* had done this?

A shiver ran down her spine.

No, she argued frantically. I'm only the catalyst. He wasn't happy. He probably hadn't been happy for many, many years. Even in his mind, his love affair with her had been time stolen from a life he found oppressive, time for himself. Which was probably why he'd been so frustrated and embittered when she'd ended it.

Had he ever really loved her? Or had she repre-sented something he'd needed…a rebellion against the structure he'd been born into…an outlet for feelings he couldn't normally express…a refuge from pressures that seemed ultimately inescapable?

There were so many layers to him she didn't know. She had loved him instinctively. Still did. Impulsively she reached over and lightly squeezed his arm. "I'm with you tonight, Luis. Whatever you want to achieve, I'm on your side."

Before she could withdraw her hand he caught it, trapped it, transmitting a burst of energy that zinged up her arm and raced through her whole nervous system. "Is that a promise, Shontelle?" he asked, and even in the darkness his eyes blazed with an intensity that shot quivers through her heart.

"Yes," she whispered.

"Then the sun and the moon and the stars shine on me tonight," he said, and laughed, tilting his head back and giving vent to a peal of joyous, devil-may-care laughter.

Even as Shontelle stared at him in startled wonder, he lifted her hand to his lips and pressed a warm kiss across her knuckles. His eyes sobered, but a winsome smile lingered on his mouth as he said, "Thank you. Though I will not hold you to such an all-encompassing promise, Shontelle. I would not want you to rue it. You are free to choose whatever is right for you."

Free…her heart sank, taking with it the foolish hopes that had persisted in fluttering, despite a strong dose of common sense. He did not want her to tie herself to him. This partnership was mutual in so far as they had a common purpose in seeking justice, but there the mutuality ended. He could not have spelled the position out more clearly.

The car slowed, turned, and the huge black iron gates that guarded the Martinez mansion caught her eye.

They were here!

The impressive Graeco-Roman edifice with its massive columns and elaborate cornices was stage-lit from the gardens on either side of the driveway. Music drifted from the opened doors to the second-story balconies which led off the ballroom. The grand reception was clearly in full swing.

The Mercedes stopped at the flight of steps which was framed by a portico that would have done a temple proud. It was a temple, Shontelle thought with painful irony, a temple to all Elvira Rosa Martinez held dear. The question tonight was…which did she hold more dear, her son or his heritage? The choice was almost upon her.

Luis released her hand to alight from the car, quickly skirting it to lend his arm to Shontelle's emergence on the other side. The chauffeur held her door open. She gathered her skirt up carefully to avoid any problem with it as she stepped out.

Red…the colour of danger.

Too late to retreat now.

She'd given her word.

Luis took her hand again, and as she straightened up beside him he tucked her arm around his in a proprietary gesture that proclaimed their public togetherness.

"Ready?" he asked, his eyes gleaming some deep, personal satisfaction.

"Yes," she answered, resolved on facing the people who had brought her—brought both Luis and her—to this final act.

Arm in arm, they moved up the steps.

And somewhere in the distance, a clock tolled midnight.

CHAPTER FOURTEEN

"SEÑOR MARTINEZ!" The surprise on the elderly manservant's face was echoed in his voice as he ushered them into the foyer. "It was not expected..." He looked in confusion at Shontelle, who was undoubtedly even more unexpected.

"I had some luck getting out of La Paz," Luis explained.

"Your mother will be..." He choked on whatever word he might ordinarily have used—pleased, delighted, ecstatic—staring at Shontelle in a kind of dazed horror.

"May I introduce my companion, Miss Shontelle Wright. Shontelle, this is..."

"Carlos," she broke in. "We've met before." She smiled at the elderly retainer whose skin had gone quite sallow. "You served me with lunch here, two years ago, though you may not remember me."

"Sí, Miss Wright," he answered faintly, then swallowed hard. "I shall go and announce your arrival."

Luis reached out and stayed the man before he could move. "Let's pretend I let myself in, Carlos. I wish to surprise my mother."

"But, *Señor*..."

Steely authority instantly emerged. "I'd advise you

to look the other way, Carlos. Do I make myself clear?''

''Sí, señor.''

He backed off and Luis swept Shontelle onto the grand staircase which led to the long gallery bordering the ballroom; the gallery of gold-framed portraits and priceless objets d'art that had so overwhelmed her on her last visit here.

They mounted the stairs, meeting no resistance from other household staff. The music was louder now, an orchestra of master tango musicians playing traditional *porteno* arrangements on violins and the unique Argentinian version of squeeze-boxes, *bandoneons.*

''Remember dancing the tango with me?'' Luis murmured.

She glanced at him, flushing at the memories he'd evoked; the wildly erotic movements they'd practised in private, teasing each other with a pretence of discipline and control, throwing themselves into the beat of the music for the sheer dramatic fun of it...and always ending up making passionate love to each other.

His eyes caught hers, and she saw he was thinking of those times, too. ''It was good,'' she answered huskily, her pulse beat speeding up at the simmering look he returned.

''Poetry and fire...it is a dance of the soul, yes?''

She nodded, unsure what he wanted from her. Historically, the tango had evolved from a *darkness* of soul, more an expression of tragic pain than anything else…men without women, dancing alone, working off their despair with life. Was Luis feeling some parallel with that history now?

"Will you dance it with me tonight?" he asked.

A last tango? Her legs quivered at the prospect. To her the dance was associated with very raw, uninhibited desire. Was it sensible to tempt fate when there was no future in it? An unaccountable surge of recklessness overrode wisdom.

"If you think it's appropriate," she said.

"I find poetry and fire particularly appropriate in this instance."

Dante's *Inferno* slipped into Shontelle's mind. Were the devils in hell dancing tonight? Luis seemed intent on using every bit of firepower to blow his mother's ambitions for him apart. *I'm his torch,* she thought, and wondered if there'd be anything other than ashes left over when all the burning had been done.

He'd mockingly named this place a mausoleum, she recalled, as they stepped past the marble arch that marked the entrance to the gallery. It might contain treasures of the dead but Shontelle was made instantly aware of very alive people occupying it. Groups of guests were viewing items of interest or just chatting amongst themselves, taking a break from the ballroom.

The late appearance of Luis Angel Martinez with an unknown woman in tow was swiftly noticed. Conversation stopped. Heads craned. Shontelle was acutely sensitive to the wave of shock rolling down the entire showroom, and it was her presence causing it, or rather her being partnered by Luis. Eyes busily assessed her appearance. Whispers started. Shontelle imagined people hastily asking… *Who is she? What does this mean?*

One man broke away from his circle of companions and hurried towards them. Shontelle's heart did a little skip as she recognised him as Luis' younger brother, Patricio. He looked bewildered, unable to believe his eyes, yet driven to ascertain what the situation was.

''*¡Dios!* This is some entrance, Luis!'' he muttered, deliberately blocking their way.

His physique was shorter and leaner than his older brother's but there was a tensile strength about him that made him a formidable opponent if he wished to be. His moustache gave his handsome face a rather dashing, playboy air, which was deceptive. Shontelle knew him to be an exacting and shrewd businessman who managed the Martinez agricultural interests with a very astute reading of marketability. He occasionally showed off his brilliant horsemanship to tour groups who visited the main ranch outside Buenos Aires, but Alan had told her that was the only playing Luis' brother indulged in.

''Move aside, Patricio,'' Luis commanded in an equally low voice.

''You're supposed to be in La Paz,'' came the confused protest.

''Get out of my way,'' Luis warned. ''And please give Shontelle the courtesy of a greeting. You have met Alan's sister.''

''Shontelle?'' He did a double take, staring at her with suddenly enlightened eyes. ''I did not recognise you. And this...'' His long Spanish nose lifted haughtily as he glared back at Luis. ''...This I do not understand.''

''You don't have to,'' Luis tersely informed him.

''You yourself declared any member of the Wright family persona non grata,'' Patricio retorted fiercely.

''The betrayal of trust was not theirs. I did them an injustice I am bound to correct.''

''There's a time and place for everything, Luis. This isn't it,'' Patricio argued.

''There is none better in my opinion.''

''Are you mad? The Gallardo family is here in full force. You cannot flaunt another woman in Claudia's face.''

''Oh, yes I can.''

The venom in Luis' voice jolted Patricio. He turned a beetling frown on Shontelle. ''I mean no offence to you, Shontelle, but this is a situation of some delicacy. My mother intends to announce...''

''She will not,'' Luis cut in. ''I informed her it was not possible when I called about the situation in La Paz. I told her I would select a time of my own choosing.''

Patricio shook his head. ''Your supposed absence was not going to stop it, Luis. You gave your tacit approval before you left for La Paz. When the orchestra finishes their performance…''

''So she would force my hand…even to this,'' Luis grated. His face was thunderous as he shot out an arm to hold Patricio at a distance while he steered Shontelle around him with such alacrity, she almost tripped trying to keep up.

Patricio fell into step beside him, urgently pleading. ''Luis, this is tantamount to committing harakiri in public.''

''She leaves me no choice.''

''Let me take care of Shontelle. You can ride this through and…''

''No.'' Luis instantly secured Shontelle's hold on his arm by clamping his free hand over hers, deliberately emphasising their togetherness as he moved relentlessly forward. ''There will be no more riding anything through at my mother's will,'' he seethed at his brother.

''Luis, what is this about?'' Shontelle pleaded, agitated by the turbulent currents in the conversation. ''You said it was a glittering occasion but if it has some important meaning…''

''His engagement to Claudia Gallardo is about to be announced,'' Patricio shot at her.

''What?'' she cried in horror.

''No!'' Luis denied vehemently. ''It will not happen. I will not allow it to happen.''

Shontelle's feet faltered as she was hit by the enormity of what he had kept from her. ''But you knew…

Oh, my God! You brought me here, knowing...and last night...''

He halted to face her, his eyes blazing into hers. ''*I* have not given Claudia a commitment, Shontelle.''

''You let them think it was on the cards,'' Patricio sliced in, moving to close them into a private little circle.

''The cards got reshuffled today and they will never be the same again,'' Luis fired at his brother. ''I am reclaiming my life. Wear Eduardo's shoes yourself if all this means so much to you. They probably fit you a lot better than they do me.''

Patricio recoiled a step, his face reflecting intense inner turmoil. ''I don't want it, Luis.''

''Then don't shovel it on me.''

''Luis...this is wrong...you didn't tell me how it was,'' Shontelle cried, plucking at the hand holding hers, hating the feeling of being used.

''Did Claudia care for you? Did my mother let us be?'' he flashed at her with such violent feeling, it shook Shontelle from her bid to detach herself from him. ''You said you would stand by me,'' he went on passionately. ''Can I count on no one?''

His eyes burned with a terrible need that sucked relentlessly on Shontelle's heart, draining it of resistance to what he was asking of her. She was part of the pattern of deceit that had riddled his life and that guilt still remained, twisting inside her. Yet two wrongs didn't make a right and he had let her believe—led her to believe—there was no relationship with Claudia worth talking about.

"You repeat your own error in holding things from me, Luis," she reminded him, unwilling to let his fault pass without comment.

"The issue of justice was the same," he insisted.

Was it? Somehow the imminent engagement muddied everything. The thought of him courting Claudia, kissing her... "Have you made love to her?" she asked, riven by the stark memory of what he'd done last night with no love at all.

"*¡Cristo!*" Patricio expostulated. "She has no right..."

"*¡Silencio!* It is you who has no right!" Luis snapped, then swung his gaze back to Shontelle, urgently begging belief. "I was never even tempted to make love to her." His look of repugnance reinforced his claim. "There was absolutely no intimacy between me and Claudia Gallardo."

"Then how could this engagement come about?" she cried in torment.

"It was a matter of indifference to me whom I married. Claudia pursued it. My mother pushed it. *You* had left me to them."

Her fault? Was this justice or vengeance? A last tango with him...dark, dark angel.

"Luis, the music has stopped," Patricio warned.

"Shontelle...am I alone?" he pressed, still searing her soul with his eyes.

The tug was stronger than ever, despite the dreadful

confusion swirling around it. She gave up the fight to understand. If it meant so much to him—that she stand by him now—using her to gain his freedom—then why not do it? At least it would expunge her guilt over how she'd scarred his life.

"No," she whispered. "I'm with you."

He released a long shuddering breath and quickly acted on her consent, walking them both on. She could hear people gathering behind them, following them, drawn by the promise of scandal. The scarlet woman indeed, Shontelle thought, beginning to feel quite light-headed.

As they rounded the corner of the gallery to the shorter section which opened into the ballroom, Patricio slipped behind Luis and stepped up beside Shontelle so she was flanked by both men. The three of them walking abreast drew attention from the people they were approaching. More stares. Buzzing speculation.

"Better peel off, Patricio," Luis advised.

"No."

"This is my fight."

"I don't know what the hell is behind this, Luis, but if you're vacating Eduardo's shoes, she's not going to put me into them. I'll stand with you."

"This a highly personal affair, Patricio."

"Better we present a united front."

"A bit late for that, given your attempt to stop me."

"Not too late for the main event."

Stubborn resolve from Patricio, reckless resolve from Luis. Between them, Shontelle felt carried along towards some kind of Armageddon, a clash of power that promised the end of an era of domination. And here she was, dressed like a princess to be a pawn in the battle. No, not a pawn, she decided. A symbol. A weapon. A flaming sword for truth and justice.

She smiled at that thought…definitely light-headed. The words of the song—*Don't Cry For Me, Argentina*—flitted through her mind as they entered the ballroom. The aristocracy was all around her now, very distinguished-looking men, women lavishly bejewelled. She was being inspected by them. Shontelle held her head high—Cinderella at the ball, escorted by the Martinez princes.

Then from the other end of the ballroom, a voice rang out over a microphone, a voice Shontelle instantly recognised as belonging to the woman reputed to be the wealthiest and most powerful woman in Argentina.

''My friends…thank you for coming this evening. It gives me much pleasure to see you all here, to join with me in celebrating a very special event. Unfortunately, my son, Luis, has been trapped in La Paz, due to…''

''No, *Madre*… Luis has come,'' Patricio called out.

It was as though he had pointed a staff like Moses. The sea of people in front of them parted, fell back, and a clear path opened up down the length of the dance floor to the dais where Elvira Rosa Martinez stood like an all-powerful pharaoh in command of her world.

She looked magnificent, dressed in shimmering royal blue, with a fabulous collar of gold around her throat, gold falling from her ears and circling her wrists. The hand holding the microphone sparkled with ornate rings. But her handsome face lost its winning smile as she realised what was facing her.

Not Luis alone.

Not Luis with his younger brother.

Not Luis, miraculously arriving in time to pledge himself to the woman his mother had ordained he marry.

On his arm was another woman, possessively secured there by a hand that proclaimed her his in no uncertain terms.

Shontelle had no idea if Elvira recognised her but the message being telegraphed was unmistakable, to everyone looking on. This was a parade of proud defiance of what anyone thought. This was a statement of arrogant independence. The gauntlet had been thrown in front of every high-ranking person in the country and there was no turning back from it.

CHAPTER FIFTEEN

A SILENCE fell, and it seemed to Shontelle there was a freezing of time in the Martinez mansion. The huge gilt-framed mirrors in the ballroom reflected a scene that had stopped moving. Overhead the many-tiered chandeliers were brilliantly alight, glowing with a life of their own. Below them, she and Luis and Patricio walked in unison, a pace measured by dignity…no haste…no falter.

The sound of their footsteps on the parquet floor was eerie…isolated…echoing in a weird emptiness. Luis and Patricio were stepping into an unknown future, Shontelle thought, and risking all they'd had in the past for it. Was it worth it to them? Was it? She didn't know what it was like to be shackled by a heritage such as theirs. Impossible for her to weigh the prizes and penalties of great wealth.

Elvira…staring at them, her expression oddly glazed.

Open rebellion facing her.

Would she act to stop it?

Did she sense there was no stopping it?

Shontelle's nerves prickled as Elvira's gaze focused on her, her eyes suddenly sharp with recognition. Yes, she thought fiercely. Look at me. Look at your victim of yesteryear and feel the wheel turning. It's right that it should.

Elvira's head turned slightly, her gaze shooting to a group of people gathered to the right of the stage. And there was Claudia Gallardo, presumably surrounded by her family. Claudia, dressed in pure virginal white, a bridal beacon, masking the calculating mind that had sacrificed integrity in her ruthless push to an altar of greed. Claudia, staring at them in disbelief, not receiving whatever mental message her co-conspirator had tried to send.

Frustrated and aware of the electric curiosity aroused, Luis' mother sought to distract, as well as soothe the escalating tension, using the microphone to draw attention back to her. ''Well, this is a wonderful surprise! It appears nothing—not even a revolution in Bolivia—could keep Luis from joining us tonight. Please forgive a short delay while I welcome him home.''

She turned and gestured to the violinists to play. They quickly struck up a tune. Elvira set the microphone on its stand and moved regally to the left-hand side of the stage, away from the Gallardo family, a blatant directive to Luis to accommodate her wish to have a private word with him before he committed himself to what she undoubtedly saw as ultimate folly.

Luis did not oblige her.

Without hesitation, he aimed the three of them straight towards the Gallardo family. Patricio needed no signal. He adjusted his step to keep the united front. A march into the face of enemy lines, Shontelle thought, seeing a bristling start to run through the family who had expected to seal an important liaison this night.

Did they know what had been done in pursuit of it? The Gallardo men were older than Luis and Patricio. Much older. Had they viewed Luis Angel Martinez as a bunny to be taken for what he was worth?

Well, meet the rabbit in the hat, Shontelle thought with wild irreverence for their fortune-melding. She locked her eyes onto the dark, dazed gaze of the heiress who'd cut Shontelle's faith in Luis' love into irredeemable fragments, and all her grief boiled up into a blistering challenge.

How do you like it, Claudia, being faced with a partnership you thought you'd destroyed? Being faced with the woman you lied to? Seeing the future you'd hoped for dashed into dust?

The answer was not long in coming.

There was a sudden snap of recognition…the realisation of what Shontelle's appearance with Luis had to mean…then fury…sheer black fury. No broken heart in those eyes as they slashed down Shontelle's dressed-to-kill gown and whipped up to the man she'd almost won with the connivance of his mother. The fury switched to a haughty contempt. No way was Claudia Gallardo going to be bowed in defeat.

"I see you've taken up with your foreign trash

again, Luis,'' she attacked first, just as they halted directly in front of her.

Shontelle's hackles rose. It was difficult to treat such an insult with disdain, but she did her best to project unassailable confidence in her right to be at Luis' side. Apart from which, this was his fight. He proceeded to answer his erstwhile fiancée with icy control.

''I leave it to you to explain to your family why I do what I do now, Claudia. And may I suggest you curb your malicious spite. It will not serve you well.''

''Explain to *me!*'' the elderly man beside Claudia demanded brusquely. ''You serve us with a public humiliation. It is not to be forgiven, Luis.''

''Esteban, your daughter and my mother contrived to destroy the most precious thing in my life. Do not speak of forgiveness to me. I will see justice done first.''

For a moment, Shontelle's heart swelled painfully. Hearing Luis call the love they'd shared *the most precious thing in his life* made the loss all the harder to bear.

''What justice?'' the old man spluttered. ''Patricio…'' he appealed, ''…is this an act of honour?''

''You cannot divide me from my brother, Esteban,'' came the hard warning. ''We will have truth tonight and there is no dishonour in truth.''

''We had an understanding!'' Esteban protested fiercely.

''Built on deception,'' Luis accused.

"You can prove this?"

"Ask your daughter," Luis repeated with steely force. Then with a harsh edge of suspicion, he added, "If you don't already know of the lies she spun to engage me with your family."

The Gallardo patriarch flushed in anger. "To what are you referring?"

"Clean your own house, Esteban…as I now clean mine."

Luis inclined his head slightly, a token respect to the old man, then wheeled their small procession towards the other side of the stage where his mother was waiting.

"Foreign trash," Claudia sniped again.

"Hold your tongue, girl, and put your best face forward," Esteban commanded tersely. "You will not shame me in this company."

Luis Angel Martinez was no bunny and would never be taken by any of these people as anything but a man to be reckoned with, Shontelle thought with intense pride. She savagely wished she had given him the chance to stand up for her two years ago. She knew now, beyond a shadow of a doubt, he would have done it, would have challenged his mother then and there and fought to keep what was *precious* to him.

Tears pricked her eyes. She'd been so stupidly gullible. Yet looking at the woman—Luis' formidable mother—who had played her hand with such subtle but devastating force, Shontelle knew she'd had no defences against such cleverly harnessed power. She had needed a champion, such as Luis had shown himself to be tonight.

Stand by me…

Was he drawing strength from her support?

She willed back the moisture threatening to film her eyes. People were watching. Elvira Rosa Martinez was watching. To cover the snub by Luis, she had moved on to the group of people closest to the other side of the stage, smiling, chatting, as though there was nothing amiss—

"The sister of a very enterprising tour operator. An old friend of Luis'," Shontelle imagined her explaining. "They must have been in La Paz, too. They've obviously managed to get out together. Heaven knows how…"

But Elvira needed space to confront the only truth that mattered to her. She excused herself to meet her sons, and there could be no misreading the battle light in her eyes. The queen was not amused at having her act upstaged and sabotaged.

Shontelle braced herself. Elvira would certainly consider her the weak spot, the most vulnerable to attack. It was vitally important to show no weakness whatsoever. Luis was counting on her to play her part through. If this was a courtroom, the jury was all around her, judging her performance. She had to prove worthy of being championed by both the Martinez men.

"Could you not have faced me first, Luis?" she lashed at him in fury.

"You did not face me at all two years ago, Mother," he retorted.

"It was for your own good," she retaliated. "Which, if you had any sense, you would recognise."

"And for my good, you would wed me to a cold, lying bitch! Step aside, Mother."

"No. I will not let you throw all I've worked for away."

"Your needs are not mine. Accept me for the man I am or *you* throw it away. Who else have you got, Mother?"

The challenge could not be borne. She fixed a commanding gaze on her younger son. "Patricio..."

"No." His rejection was sharp and immediate. Then with quiet and resolute force, Patricio stated, "I will not carry the load you demanded of Luis. I am content with what I am."

Thwarted, she raked Shontelle with bitter scorn. "This woman...how can she be worth bringing us down?"

"Down from what?" Luis mocked. "The prison you have made for me out of Eduardo's death?"

She flinched. "How dare you..."

"How dare you abrogate my rights to my own life?" His voice vibrated with outrage.

Elvira's chin lifted in arrogant pride. "She is not even Argentinian."

Foreign trash...

"She is the woman I love, Mother."

Love? Shontelle's heart stopped. Had she heard right? Did Luis mean it or…

"You could try to remember how that feels," he went on with hard, driving passion. "The intense joy of it, Mother. The sheer exhilarating splendour of it. Look into the cold little coffin you call your heart and dredge out what you felt for my father. Or even more, for Eduardo."

"Stop this!" Her face was drained of colour.

"Just once. Do it! I'm your son, too. As is Patricio."

"It's because you are, I've done what I've done to protect you," she argued.

"We are men. We do not need or want your protection."

"Eduardo would not have died…"

"Eduardo is gone. And I shall lead my own life…with or without you. Your choice, Mother."

"Luis, you can't…"

"Watch me! Shontelle?"

The call of her name and the slight tug on her arm jolted Shontelle out of her absorption in the deep conflict between mother and son. She looked up at Luis, unsure what had been said in truth or for telling effect.

"It is your turn now," he said, his eyes burning with a purpose she didn't comprehend.

Did he mean her turn to say something to his mother? Surely he realised it was irrelevant.

"Patricio..." He glanced over her head at his brother. "...The stage is mine."

"We will stand by and watch," he replied. "Won't we, *Madre?*"

Shontelle didn't see or hear a response from Elvira. Luis swept her around his mother, heading for the steps at the side of the stage. "What do you plan to do?" she whispered urgently.

Surely there was nothing left to be achieved. The announcement his mother was to have made had been stopped and rendered impossible. Was Luis going to make some kind of public relations speech to cover the breech?

He bent his head closer to hers. "Shontelle, you are free to choose as you wish." His voice was low, intense, his eyes scouring hers. "Have I done enough?" he muttered, seemingly to himself.

His words made no sense to her. "You've set everything as right as you can," she assured him.

"No. I stripped you down to nothing last night. I know it is something you will never forget. But, Shontelle, I offer you now the chance to do the same to me. You can reject all I am in front of everyone, and I will not blame you for it. It is your just due."

"Luis..." He was frightening her. "I don't want this...this atonement."

"Then accept my gift for the spirit in which it is given."

"What gift?"

"You will see...and I hope...understand."

Already he was drawing her up the steps to the stage. Bewildered and apprehensive, Shontelle could barely respond to the smile he flashed at her as he unhooked their arms and caught her hand. He signalled to the violinists to stop playing, which they very promptly did.

The sudden cessation of music was like a clarion call to the crowd, galvanising attention on the stage which had been vacated by Elvira Rosa Martinez and now starred her son, Luis Angel, and the woman in red.

The general hush was loaded with fascinated anticipation. The Gallardo family had not walked out. Elvira Rosa Martinez stood with her younger son, Patricio, apparently at ease with this curious development. An announcement had been promised. A celebration was supposed to ensue. When Luis took hold of the microphone, one could have heard a pin drop in the ballroom.

Shontelle found herself holding her breath and forced herself to relax. As far as she was concerned, justice had been carried out. Whatever Luis did now was for himself. She had no further axe to grind.

Only his declaration of loving her remained a private torment. She wished it was true. But his reminder of last night's wretched travesty of intimacy…how could that equate with love?

He squeezed her hand, transmitting a bolt of tingling warmth, distracting her from her feverish thoughts.

She looked at him, craving all that his touch had once meant.

As though he'd been waiting for her gaze to lift to his, he smiled at her, a brilliant heart-tugging smile that mesmerised her into smiling back. And for that one incandescent moment, there was no darkness between them. None at all.

Then he turned to face the crowd and began to speak.

''Ladies and gentlemen…''

CHAPTER SIXTEEN

SHONTELLE hoarded that one lovely moment with Luis in her heart as she looked out at the elite gathering in front of them—*the ladies and gentlemen*—Elvira's guests, people who were important to the smooth running of Martinez interests, people of influence, people who mattered if Luis was to hold his stake in the family company. Their faces seemed to run together in a stream of avid curiosity.

She heard Luis take a deep breath before continuing, and tension screamed along her nerves again. Had he listened to her? Enough to put aside whatever plan he had to even the score for treating her badly? She didn't want some public humbling. She'd hate it. Please…let him satisfy these people and be content with his stand for personal integrity, she prayed with desperate fervour.

His deep, resonant voice seemed to boom through the ballroom. "…I am very proud to introduce to you, a woman of great heart and courage, Miss Shontelle Wright…"

Shontelle squirmed inside at the heightened interest he was stirring…spotlighting her. What was the point?

"Her brother, Alan, is a long-time friend of mine,"

Luis went on. "He worked with me at the Martinez mine in Brazil and has since built up a highly successful business, running tours of South America, using Buenos Aires as his base city." He gestured encouragement for approval as he added, "And, coincidentally, bringing a lot of tourist money into our country."

There was a buzz of appreciation from the spectators. Shontelle relaxed a little. She could see the need to publicly explain her connection to him.

"Last night, Shontelle braved breaking the curfew in La Paz to acquire a bus for Alan's tour group, some of whom were suffering seriously from altitude sickness."

The sympathetic murmurs around the ballroom did not soothe the alarm jabbing through Shontelle's mind. Luis wasn't going to reveal personal details, was he? She darted a sharp glance at him, eloquently appealing for discretion.

He smiled as though sharing something good with her, with everyone. "Today," he said, giving a time-frame which relieved her of her worst fears, "this amazingly resourceful lady saved me from one of the military tanks cruising the streets, just as I was looking straight down its gun barrel. Her beautiful fair hair provided the right distraction."

His blatantly admiring comments evoked a lighter humour in the crowd. There was a ripple of laughter as people visualised the scene he'd drawn for them.

Luis' smile widened to a grin. "I returned the favour later by jumping our bus over a trench which the farmers had dug across the road. It was a rather bumpy ride, but we survived it.''

Outright laughter, this time, and a burst of applause for their daring in getting out of La Paz. Shontelle found herself smiling, glad that Luis was turning what had been a nightmare into a tale to be enjoyed by others. It also neatly covered why they were together tonight, making his partnering her perfectly acceptable in the light of today's events.

The noise died down, the desire to hear more rising uppermost. Again Shontelle glanced at Luis, wondering where he would take them next. His expression had sobered. When he resumed speaking it was in a quieter, more confidential tone.

''I am happy to say there was more than survival involved in our long journey here to be with you tonight.''

He paused, galvanising everyone's attention.

''Two years ago, because of difficult, personal circumstances, Shontelle decided, much against my wishes, that she could not share her life with me.''

Oh, my God! He couldn't...he just couldn't reveal his mother's and Claudia's scheming in public! Shontelle could feel all her insides knotting up.

''Today, when both our lives were in danger, those circumstances no longer held any meaning,'' he went on.

How could he say that? Shontelle thought frantically. Their whole purpose here was to exact justice for those *circumstances!* And they'd done it. So what was he leading to now?

In sheer agitation she scraped her nails against his palm. He threaded his fingers through hers and gripped more tightly. It increased her agitation a hundredfold. She didn't know what he was tying her to.

He turned to look at her and all she could think of was…dark Angel…dark Angel… She sensed him reaching out through some critical mass, unsure of his way but bent on fighting every obstacle and suddenly the words he had spoken this morning burst into her mind—*for you I risk my life*—and she wanted to scream… *No!*…but her throat was too constricted to utter anything.

Then he spoke.

"To all of you I announce…this is the woman I love…and will always love."

The words vibrated through her, creating chaos. Impossible to sort out truth from need—either his or hers. Tears misted her eyes. She couldn't even see him clearly, let alone perceive what he meant by this public announcement.

"Shontelle…" His voice was husky. He poured more strength into it. "…Will you do me the honour of marrying me?"

Understanding came in a burst of anguish… *marriage or nothing.*

This was his offer…in atonement for last night…perhaps even in atonement for never having made their love public when it would have counted.

She wasn't *foreign trash* to him. He had paraded her as his partner into the highest of Martinez circles. Now he was offering her his name in front of these people…if she wanted it. And if she didn't…if she refused it publicly…he was prepared to have his pride sacrificed, just to give her the satisfaction of knowing he had paid her the highest compliment he could pay any woman.

To lay himself on the line like this…risking everything…as she had done last night, though differently, privately…was it an expression of abiding love…or an extreme expression of balancing the scales?

Panic coursed through her. He was waiting for her answer. Everyone was waiting. But the answer wasn't simple. Except…she was utterly incapable of humiliating Luis in front of these people. So there was no choice. And she had to speak.

"I…" Her mouth was hopelessly dry. Perversely, her eyes were awash with tears. She nodded to Luis as she tried to work moisture around her tongue, signalling the consent he had to want, for whatever reason he wanted it. Then in an explosive rush, she said what she had to say. "Yes, I will." Somehow it didn't seem enough, coming belatedly, so she quickly added, "I will marry you, Luis."

The words carried through the microphone for everyone to hear and they seemed to echo and echo, haunting her, until someone started clapping. The sound came from the side of the stage where they'd left Patricio and Elvira. Impossible to know who it was, slapping their palms in approval, but the action caught on and was repeated by others, more and more, building such a momentum, the ballroom seemed to thunder with the noise.

Luis released her hand and curved his arm around her shoulders, hugging her closely to him. Shontelle concentrated fiercely on blinking back tears, pasting a smile on her face. Unbelievably, she was being approved as Luis' wife-to-be and she still had to do him proud, regardless of her own tearing confusion.

"Gracias. Muchas gracias."

Maybe it was a distortion of the microphone but Luis' voice sounded thick with emotion. Shontelle reasoned it was huge relief that his public proposal had produced this result. Even she was stunned by this overwhelming acceptance of his choice. Was he a popular personage in Buenos Aires? Or had his presentation of a crossed love, revived in the face of possible death, struck some deep appeal?

Romance...

A fairy tale...

Cinderella claimed by the prince.

She was getting light-headed again, her mind dizzied by too many whirling thoughts. It was just as well Luis was holding her because her knees were trembling.

"In the hope..." he started again when the prolonged applause died down. "In my quite desperate hope...that Shontelle would agree to sharing her life with me..."

There was so much warm pleasure in his tone, Shontelle couldn't stop her heart from going mushy. If he really meant what he was saying...but what of his promise to have her at the airport tomorrow? How did that gell with this?

"...When we stopped on the road at Villa Tunari, this afternoon, I called ahead to Santa Cruz. As you know, Bolivia produces some of the finest emeralds in the world and there are some very fine jewellers in Santa Cruz. I wanted to present Shontelle with a ring tonight, an emerald to match her eyes."

He had been planning this...all those hours ago? From the moment she had agreed to accompany him to this reception? Shontelle's mind boggled. He'd been so...so businesslike in getting them here.

"So I had a selection brought to the airport..."

The attaché case!

"...And while Shontelle slept on the flight to Buenos Aires, I chose the one I now give her, as a token of my love, my commitment to her, and my belief in our future together."

Luis thrust the microphone into her right hand. In a helpless daze Shontelle watched him take the ring from his coat pocket, pick up her left hand, and slide onto the third finger the most amazing ring she'd ever seen—huge glittering emerald, set amongst an abstract cluster of baguette diamonds—like a perfect green pool surrounded by a pile of irregular rocks.

It won't fit, she thought wildly, but somehow it did, as though her finger had been measured for it. And it looked...totally incredible. She was still staring down at it—a fortune of precious stones displayed on her hand—on her engagement finger!—as Luis took the microphone again.

"I think I have surprised her," he said with such happy humour, people laughed indulgently.

Surprise was not the word for it, Shontelle thought, trying to struggle through a maze of shockingly unanswered questions.

"Since most of you have not yet met my wife-to-be," Luis raved on, "may I inform you Shontelle speaks fluent Spanish, probably knows more about our country than we do, and can dance a superb tango. Which I feel in the mood to demonstrate right now."

He waved to the orchestra to take their places on the stage in readiness, then appealed to the guests who were obviously enjoying his showmanship. "I invite you all to join us on the dance floor in celebration of a night to remember."

So now the tango, Shontelle thought, feeling helplessly entangled by decisions she had no hand in making. As Luis set the microphone back on its stand—the microphone that had made his proposal so terribly public—it struck Shontelle that he'd used it to virtually blackmail her.

Forcing his will?

Was this engagement really, truly what he wanted?

Nothing to do with justice?

Luis turned to her, his face alight with the exhilaration of having carried all before him, his eyes sparkling and his mouth almost dancing with a smile of wicked pleasure. He lifted her newly beringed hand to his lips, gave it a cavalier kiss, then slid his arm around her waist and swept her off the stage and onto the dance floor.

They were still very much on show, the guests

waiting for them to lead off, or watching to see if Shontelle could, indeed, dance a superb tango. Luis certainly exuded confidence as they positioned themselves in front of each other. Shontelle's heart was hammering, confusion still rife in her mind, but pride demanded she perform with all the skill she could muster, which meant she had to get her jelly-like legs in strong, agile order very fast.

It helped when she and Luis lifted their arms and settled into the initial embrace. Somehow his confidence flowed into her and his sheer arrogance in staging all this, sparked a gush of volatile energy. He might be the leader, she the follower in the sophisticated interrelation of steps in this dance, but the urge to challenge him with a few intricate improvisations of her own, tripping up his comfort zone, was very, very tempting.

The orchestra had chosen a 1950's song, setting a distinctive style and mood with its dramatic passion, which suited Shontelle's need for a little individual creativity. Luis had had a fine time manipulating her movements. He deserved to be pushed into meeting her initiatives.

''Just remember this dress doesn't have the mobility of a slit up the side,'' she warned him.

He laughed, his eyes very hotly wicked. ''My control will be masterly.''

It was a goad that fired Shontelle's blood. Luis Angel Martinez had taken far too much control upon himself. It was time to show him she had rights, too, including the right not to be boxed into a corner.

''Ready?'' he asked with a cock of his eyebrow.

"*You* had better be…this time," she retorted with a mocking little smile.

He grinned and started them into the traditional *salida,* the basic walking pattern. Shontelle gave him his head for a while, following his perfectly executed figure eights, turns, twists, sweeps, but after he threw in a masterful drag, making himself very much the leader with her trailing in a feet-together slide, she started challenging him with subtle little embellishments to the hooks and kicks, forcing him into very fancy footwalk.

He growled at her, his eyes taking on a very animal gleam as he engineered a *sandwich,* catching her thigh against his, leaning into her, arching her back, his arm circling her so his hand was virtually cupping the underswell of her breast.

"Taking again, Luis?" Shontelle fired, seizing the advantage of close range.

"Giving. Giving with all I've got," he answered, and the raw desire in his eyes had nothing to do with justice.

He really did want her!

Still!

Maybe always?

Excitement sizzled through Shontelle.

The controlled elegance of their tango swiftly acquired a slinky sexuality, a stalking sexuality, and Shontelle deliberately kept it simmering with artfully provocative wiggles and shakes.

No point in pretending she didn't want him. He had a lot of answering to do, but if this night could lead to sharing their lives in an acceptable way, Shontelle was not going to turn her back on the possibility.

Luis swept her into double-time steps, moving into a high lift and a dexterous curl around him, re-establishing his dominance. She countered with a full body downward slide that left her in no doubt of his state of excitement.

They indulged themselves in the dramatic rhythm of the music, communicating heat that became so steamy, Shontelle felt herself in danger of melting on the floor. Only the wild exultation of more than matching Luis kept her feet twinkling, her body sensuously supple, and her head proudly held.

They were breathing hard when the music ended, her breasts heaving against his chest, their lower bodies entwined in the traditional aggressive/resistant pose, her arms held back, hair still swinging, and Luis' face hovering over hers.

But this wasn't the end, Shontelle thought in wild elation. Not in Luis' eyes. And the hopes that had seemed so foolish, danced their own irrepressible tango through her heart.

CHAPTER SEVENTEEN

HAD he done enough?

The question gnawed at Luis' mind as he watched Shontelle dancing with Patricio—a waltz, not the tango. No way would he allow any other man to dance the tango with her. A waltz was bearable…just. He itched to have her in his arms—only his—though he knew it was appropriate she dance with his brother; obvious evidence of family support, reinforcement of approval.

His plan had worked…so far. Shontelle was still carrying through the role he'd thrust upon her, but what she was feeling…what she was thinking…he couldn't even begin to be sure of that until this reception was behind them. The words she'd spoken during the tango kept haunting him—*Taking again, Luis?* Could his giving tonight make up for the way he'd treated her in La Paz? Was it enough?

He had done all he could here, Luis decided. His need to have Shontelle to himself could no longer be suppressed. He had to know if she'd been co-operating with everything for his sake—saving him from social disaster—or giving him the chance to show he meant what he said. If it was the latter case, there was hope.

A check of his watch showed it was close to three o'clock, not too early to leave.

''Impatient, Luis?'' one of his friends asked, a knowing grin on his face.

''Who could blame him?'' another remarked. ''Such a woman would heat any man's veins. She is magnificent, Luis.''

''She is, indeed,'' he agreed, smiling to cover his gut-twisting need to keep her in his life.

He signalled to one of the household staff and requested a message be immediately taken to Carlos—their car and driver to be summoned and waiting at the door for them.

Most of the guests looked set to party on and might well remain until dawn, but Luis had no doubt that indulgent understanding for his and Shontelle's early departure would be readily given. After all, it had been a long and highly eventful day and they had clearly won the popular vote tonight. Benevolence was still running strongly.

The Gallardo family had effected a tactful exit during the past hour, Esteban undoubtedly exercising his patriarchal authority to ensure there was no open rift between the families. If there was any accounting to be done, it would be done in boardrooms, not here. Saving face was just as important as holding profitable business connections. Luis had banked on that. Esteban Gallardo was a very pragmatic man.

Shontelle could no longer harbour any fear of being ostracised or snubbed by Argentinian society. On the contrary, over the past few hours, she had been showered with admiration and genuine good wishes. At least this much had been achieved, Luis thought with satisfaction.

The public response to *his* announcement had been all he could have wished. Not that it had been critically important, but it was helpful—one less issue to argue, once he and Shontelle were alone. *If* they got as far as argument.

Her acceptance of his proposal had been so long in coming, he certainly couldn't count on its lasting beyond the doors of this house. She'd promised support and she'd given it, right down the line. Though he'd felt there'd been more than support in the fire of her tango dancing. Surely she couldn't have been quite so excitingly sensual if she felt no desire for him. Unless it had been an angry tease.

Yet if she was nursing anger, there'd been no hint of it since then. She'd been warmly gracious through all the introductions, her apparent ease in bantering with him, smiling, laughing, giving him every encouragement to believe their partnership was real. Or was she simply acting out what she thought he expected of her?

It was possible her manner stemmed from a need to prove herself a match for him, whether she saw any future in it or not, but Luis fervently hoped it was motivated by more than personal pride.

The waltz ended.

Luis moved aside from his friends, compelled by

the urge to gather Shontelle to himself as soon as Patricio escorted her from the dance floor. *Magnificent* was an apt description, he thought, watching her walk towards him, the red and silver dress enhancing her glorious femininity, her hair flowing like a river of light, her face alive with vibrant personality. Everything she was called to him…body and soul, and the primitive caveman inside him was severely testing his control.

I have to win…

The thought—the need—burned through his mind, through his entire body. He held out his hand to her. Without hesitation she placed hers in it, though she bestowed her smile on his brother, making Luis' stomach clench with uncertainty.

''*Gracias,* Patricio,'' she said huskily.

''We'll leave now,'' Luis announced, the inner caveman insisting on it. He couldn't share any part of her with anyone anymore, not even his brother. ''I appreciate your support, Patricio,'' he forced himself to add, sincerely grateful for his brother's stalwart defence of both their positions.

Patricio's eyes twinkled with understanding. ''I could do with more warning next time you're intent on bearding lions, Luis. Though I must concede you do it with style.'' He lifted Shontelle's left hand, which he'd retained while they spoke, and bowed over it with excessive gallantry. ''Forgive my trepidations, Shontelle. I am truly delighted to welcome you into the family. You do my brother proud.''

"It's kind of you to say so," she replied, leaving Luis acutely aware there was no commitment in those words.

Having finally released Shontelle, Patricio gave Luis an earnest look. "Don't go without speaking to our mother. It was she who began the applause after Shontelle accepted your proposal of marriage."

It surprised him. "I thought it was you."

"I very quickly joined in but she led."

"Face saving," Luis interpreted sardonically.

Patricio shrugged. "A public step into your camp. It could mean more than you think."

"We shall see," Luis said noncommittally. "Goodnight, Patricio."

"Buenos noches."

Luis waved to the friends he'd been waiting with while Shontelle danced, then drew her down the ballroom towards the exit to the gallery, mentally crossing off another confrontation with his mother. Why risk her saying something unpalatable to Shontelle? He needed every advantage on his side.

"I take it *court is adjourned,*" Shontelle remarked dryly.

His heart contracted. Had it all been an act on her part? "I hope you feel justice has been done," he answered, willing her to look directly at him.

She flicked him a derisive glance. "It could have been a bit tricky there, if you'd produced a yellow diamond."

Tricky...yes, she could certainly accuse him of that.

Though, to him it had been a gamble, pure and simple. The biggest gamble of his life. And still he didn't know if the outcome was positive.

''Was an emerald the right choice for you?'' he asked, almost begging for a hint.

Her mouth curved as she lifted her left hand and gazed down at the ring he'd put on her finger. ''It's a very extravagant gesture, Luis,'' she said with a wry twist. ''And it certainly served to persuade everyone you meant what you said.''

She didn't believe him.

Shock rattled his confidence. What more could he do or say? Had his plan been futile from the start? *¡Dios!* He ached for her. He could not let her go. Frantically he counted the hours before he had to take her to the airport. Thirteen. Another two before the flight boarded. He had to make every minute work for him.

''I do mean it, Shontelle,'' he stated quietly. ''I thought it was the only way to prove you could trust my word. In the circumstances…it seemed to me that actions would be more convincing than speech.''

He felt the fingers that had been resting lightly within his grasp, curl into her palm with knuckle-tight intensity. Her left hand dropped to her side. Her head lowered. Shutting herself off from him, Luis thought, and frenziedly searched for some opening which might turn her towards him.

His mother intercepted their path to the gallery.

He silently cursed her interference. If she'd kept out of their lives two years ago…

"Luis, Shontelle…are you leaving?"

"I trust you're not going to stand in our way," he answered tersely, in no mood for political appeasement.

Her eyes looked sick, her face strained, yet neither sign of stress touched him. The damage she'd done went too deep. She touched his arm, a tentative reaching out which was uncharacteristic of her. Still he could not respond to the gesture. Two years…two years of being twisted around at her behest, and if he lost Shontelle now…

"I'm sorry. I was wrong," she acknowledged, her gaze sliding to Shontelle in bleak appeal, finding no softening in his for the admission that had been wrung out of her. "Shontelle, I beg you…don't take Luis from me."

Shades of Eduardo… Luis gritted his teeth against a savage wave of resentment. Couldn't his mother comprehend his need to be free of that blight on her life?

"I would never have done that, Señora Martinez. Nor will I now," Shontelle answered gently.

No, she would just walk away and leave him, as she had before, Luis thought bitterly.

"You…shame me."

Such humbling made him restive. He stared at his mother, unsure if this was some ploy to regain favour or a genuine expression of regret. Her face looked older, seamed with lines he hadn't noticed before—tired, sagging lines. It struck him forcefully that the indomitable arrogance was gone.

''I hope you can find it in your heart to forgive me...in time,'' she said haltingly, as though treading an unfamiliar path where the end could not be seen.

''Patricio said you started the clapping after I accepted Luis' proposal,'' Shontelle said with a slightly quizzical air.

Ascertaining the truth? Luis wondered. Why would it matter, if she didn't care?

''It was...something I could do,'' came the rueful reply. ''I didn't know...no, I didn't allow myself to think...that Luis would...or could...love you so much.'' She looked back at him, openly pleading his forgiveness. ''Please believe now...I wish you both...every happiness.''

Virtually against his will, Luis found himself moved. Maybe an understanding could be reached with his mother if she was finally comprehending he was not her tool.

''Thank you,'' Shontelle murmured.

Polite to the end?

Luis tried to shake off the doubts plaguing him. ''We'll talk...another time,'' he promised brusquely. ''If you'll excuse us now?''

Elvira Rosa Martinez re-emerged. She nodded graciously and moved aside.

''Call Patricio to her, Luis,'' Shontelle whispered.

He frowned at her, hope warring with disbelief. Her

beautiful green eyes were filled with caring—sympathy, the wish to make things better. It stunned him.

''Now. Before we leave. Please?'' she urged.

He looked back to where they'd left Patricio and found him watching them. Luis nodded towards his mother. It was enough. His brother raised a hand in a salute of understanding and started walking.

He met the query in Shontelle's eyes with a crooked little smile. ''Done,'' he assured her.

His smile was returned. ''She *is* your mother.''

''And you? Are you my fiancée, Shontelle?''

Her lashes fluttered down. The slight curve of her lips disappeared as she sighed.

Luis held his breath.

''Let's get out of here, Luis.''

It wasn't a no!

''I've already ordered the car. It should be waiting at the door.''

She slid him an ironic look. ''So efficient.''

He laughed out of sheer relief that she hadn't handed him an outright rejection. Then he tucked her arm around his and swept her out of the ballroom, a full complement of newly vitalised energy coursing through him.

The reception had served its purpose.

Shontelle *wanted* to be alone with him.

He had thirteen hours to win her over.

CHAPTER EIGHTEEN

FIVE more minutes, Luis told himself as he settled into the car beside Shontelle. The desire to reach out and haul her onto his lap and hug her tightly to him, washing away whatever doubts she had with a passionate rain of kisses, was pumping through him. But *taking* might not be a good idea, particularly not in the car. The chauffeur would get them to his apartment soon enough. Then he wouldn't have to stop. Unless Shontelle…

He took a deep breath and looked at her, craving some sign that she felt the same urgent desire for him. Her gaze was turned back at the house, remaining fixed on it even as the chauffeur drove towards the exit gates. Worried that the whole wretched Martinez heritage it represented might still be a barrier between them, and determined on smashing all barriers, Luis seized Shontelle's hand to draw her attention to him.

Her head snapped around, her eyes meeting his, but with a faraway look in them that screwed up his gut again. His fingers dragged over her palm, the need to get under her skin burning through him. Her expression changed, inviting him into the rueful reflection in her mind.

"We've never had a tragedy in our family, Luis.

I'm sorry I didn't understand...didn't appreciate the toll it can take.'' She squeezed his hand. ''However hard it was, I'm glad it was faced tonight. I think it was good for all of you. And for me. It showed me things aren't always what they seem on the surface.''

Relief surged through him. There was nothing negative in that little speech. ''What things?'' he prompted.

She shrugged. ''I put your mother's rejection of me down to snobbery and I didn't think that would change. But it wasn't snobbery. It went much deeper...''

''It had to do with power, Shontelle,'' he supplied.

She nodded. ''Yes, I see that now.'' Her eyes searched his in anxious concern. ''Will there be a backlash from the Gallardo family?''

''I doubt it. In any case, there's little they can do to really hurt the Martinez company. It's not vulnerable to attack. There could be deals that won't now be made, but overall, it's not a make or break situation.''

With a satisfied sigh, she looked down at her lap where her left hand rested. Even in the dimness of the car the emerald and diamond ring glittered as she stretched out her fingers, apparently studying his gift to her.

Once again Luis was racked with uncertainty. Had he chosen wrongly? Was she preparing to take it off and return it to him?

''I thought...last night...it was all gone...what

there'd been between us,'' she said quietly, still gazing down at the ring as though unsure whether to believe what it stood for.

He winced, fiercely wishing he could turn back the clock and do it all differently. She might have told him the truth last night if he'd given her any leeway, shown her…what? His love for her had been buried under so much bitter fury and frustration, there was no way it could have been expressed. So why should she believe him now?

Despairingly he sought for an answer she might accept. His mind was a blank. The urge to just pull her into his arms was barely containable. Words were no good. He had to show her…make her feel all the positive flow inside him. Not like last night. Completely different.

''You'd better tell me,'' she went on, catching back his attention, pausing the wild train of thought. ''Was tonight…'' She hesitated. The corner of her mouth turned down into a grimace. ''Well, it served many purposes, didn't it?''

''No.'' The word burst from him with passionate vehemence, the built-up tension reaching breaking point. ''*¡Dios!* Look at me!''

She did, her eyes wide and questing and seemingly reflecting his own desperate need.

''I hated you last night, Shontelle. I hated you because for two damnably empty years I'd wanted and needed and craved the love I'd felt we'd shared. Then when I realised today we *did* share it…'' That dreadful moment of revelation rushed back on him, choking him momentarily. He swallowed hard and pushed out the truth. The only truth that counted. ''I'd do anything to have it again. *Anything!* Do you understand?''

The car stopped.

Luis couldn't bear to wait another second. Shontelle was just staring at him in a kind of awed daze. He was out of the car and around it to her side before the chauffeur had alighted. He easily beat the man to opening Shontelle's door. Without a pause, he scooped her off the seat and swung her up against his chest, one arm under her knees, the other cradling her close, the caveman inside him rampaging straight through any other considerations...his woman, *his!*

''Don't say no!'' he heard himself wildly muttering as he carried her to the door of his apartment.

Her warm breath fanned his ear as she wound her arms around his neck. ''Can I touch you tonight?'' she asked huskily.

''Yes,'' he hissed. ''Touch me all you like. Anywhere. Everywhere.''

''No holds barred?''

Was that a teasing note in her voice? He wasn't sure. Didn't care. ''None. None at all,'' he repeated gruffly. ''Hang on to me. I've got to get the door key.''

He felt like kicking the door in but some grain of sanity told him it was too solid. Shontelle didn't seem to mind him hoisting her over his shoulder as he fumbled in his pocket. She started to laugh. Laughter was good, wasn't it? His heart was thumping so hard he could hardly put two thoughts together.

He jammed the key in the door and one more barrier gave way. They were inside. A satisfying kick closed out the rest of the world.

"Put me down, Luis," Shontelle said in a breathless gurgle.

"Soon." He charged for the bedroom.

"Not on the bed," she managed more emphatically.

"Not?" It seemed a very good place to him.

"On my feet. Now!" she commanded, wriggling to break his hold.

It was against every raging instinct, but…somehow he managed enough control to pull himself back from falling onto the bed with her. He set her on her feet, though it was quite impossible to pluck his hands away from her waist. A hold was a hold and releasing her altogether was unthinkable.

"I don't want you to tear my dress," she said.

"I'll get you another."

"No, this one is special. Put the light on, Luis."

"Light," he echoed, telling himself "special" was good. It was okay to let go. For a few seconds. He did it to switch on the light.

She was grinning at him, her beautiful green eyes sparkling, dancing, teasing with wicked delight. "It's my turn to undress you," she said pointedly. "All touching permitted."

And the driving urgency inside him shattered into a brilliant burst of happiness. It was all right. Just like it used to be between them. The freedom of it bubbled through him…glorious, exhilarating, exultant freedom.

"Yes," he said, and he knew her grin was on his face…exactly the same…sharing…no barriers, no inhibitions, nothing coming between them except clothes. "How about one each? My tie, your necklace, my coat, your dress…" He cocked an eyebrow at her. "It'll go much faster."

She laughed and started undoing his bow tie, her eyes flirting deliciously with his. "I don't want it to go fast, Luis. I want to revel in every moment."

And suddenly, so did he, though there was one thing he needed to hear. "You do still love me." It came out more a statement than a question because he just couldn't accept a question, not with her hands on him, the look in her eyes, the pleasure humming through him.

She sighed. "Looks like I'm stuck on you, for better or for worse. Which reminds me, naked is fine, but if you think you're going to get this ring off me…"

"I want you to say it, Shontelle," he cut in, the yearning to hear the words too needy for playfulness.

She slid his tie out from his collar, linked her hands around his neck and raised her lashes, revealing the windows to her soul. "I love you, Luis Angel

Martinez. There never has been anyone else for me. And never will be.''

She carried that promise on her lips to his and Luis' heart seemed to pump liquid fire through him as they kissed, and kissed, and kissed, hungry for the giving of each other, the knowing, the certainty, the lifting of every last shadow on a love that should never have been shadowed.

He was so beautiful...so intoxicatingly beautiful... the feel of him, the smell of him, the sight of him...Shontelle felt as though her whole body was effervescing with happiness, her skin tingling like champagne.

Her man...her mate in every sense there was... and when they did move to the bed, it was together...together in all the ways she had craved last night, the giving and taking so excitingly, blissfully mutual, the sheer ecstacy of loving and feeling herself loved, the intense pleasure of touching, not just physically, but knowing how deeply it went, the wonderful, awesome flow of becoming one again, one in heart and mind and soul.

It was so incredibly special...this filling of all the empty spaces that had blighted two years of their lives...the unanswered needs and desires and hopes and dreams. It was as though everything they'd felt for each other had been waiting, trapped in a timewarp, and the release of it was heaven.

And when he entered her, slowly, both of them

treasuring the magical sensation of ultimate intimacy, his face hovering above hers, their eyes mirroring the rapture they shared...that was heaven, too, and she heard it in his voice as he murmured, ''Shontelle...'' and tasted it in his mouth as he kissed her, making the melding complete, and in her mind beat the one beautiful word... Angel...Angel...Angel.

It was goodness and light and joy and it moved into a rhythm that celebrated the life they would have together. She wrapped her legs around him in exultant possession and lifted herself to him, urging the feast of sharing that would always be theirs...the feast of love...free to soar into any future they decided upon, because the form didn't matter. This was the substancc of it, the essence of it, the fusion of their lives.

Then there was no thought...only feeling... powerful waves of feeling, obliterating everything but the sense of their oneness, peaking into a sublime climax, a pulsing flow that lingered on and on, permeating their embrace as they lay together in the harmony of utter fulfilment.

''Thank you,'' Luis whispered, his voice furred with deep emotion. ''Thank you for being you and loving me.''

''It was meant to be,'' she murmured, feeling that as a deep, unalterable truth. ''I felt only half alive without you, Luis.''

''And I without you.'' He raised himself up on his elbow to look into her eyes. His were dark velvet, glowing with lovely soft warmth. ''Where would you like our future to be, Shontelle? If you want me to move to Australia…''

''No!'' She was shocked he would even think of it. ''Your life is here, Luis. I'm happy to be here with you.'' Besides, she had more or less promised his mother she wouldn't take Luis away. She couldn't compound the tragedy of Eduardo's loss by removing Luis from all Elvira held dear.

''Away from your family?'' he softly reminded her.

Shontelle hesitated a moment, knowing she would miss them, wishing they were not so far away. But by air it was only a day's travel. ''We could visit them, couldn't we?'' she appealed hopefully.

He smiled. ''As often as you like, my love. And, of course, I shall fly to Australia to meet your parents and discuss our marriage plans with them.''

''Okay, master planner,'' she happily teased. ''What is your schedule for that?''

He grinned. ''Well, since I have to put you on the plane with Alan all too soon…''

He intended to keep his promise, which was only right, but it gave them such little time together just now when…

''…I thought I could follow next week.''

Relief and pleasure instantly swamped the little jab of disappointment.

''Which gives you time to prepare your family,'' he went on purposefully, ''and me time to deal with mine.''

''I thought your mother was...well, accepting tonight,'' she reminded him.

He nodded. ''I just want to make sure everything's ironed out before you come back with me.''

She smiled, joy bubbling through her. ''So you're flying out to Australia to fetch me, are you?''

His eyes sparkled. ''One week alone I can manage. But only with the promise I don't have to spend any more of my life without being able to reaffirm this.''

He kissed her, long and lovingly.

''I promise,'' she murmured, moving against him with languorous sensuality, happy to have absolutely everything reaffirmed as much and as often as Luis liked.

Which was how they spent the hours leading up to their departure for the airport, hours well used, deliciously used, and when they joined up with the tour group at the terminal, the glow of their love for each other was like a neon light to Alan and everyone else.

No one asked Shontelle to do anything. She and Luis were left alone to talk the talk of lovers soon to be separated, but knowing it wouldn't be for long. The promise was real, as real as the emerald and diamond ring on her finger, and every bit as lasting as all the precious stones in the world.

''One week,'' Luis said with passionate longing when he finally had to let her go to board the plane.

''I'll be waiting at Sydney airport for you,'' Shontelle promised.

''I'll call you every day,'' he vowed.

"Yes, yes."

She had to go. One quick last kiss and she ran to catch the others, her feet yearning to dance a wild and wonderful tango because she was coming back to Luis, coming back to Argentina, coming back to the love of a lifetime.

Nothing was banished forever.

Marriage was the final act.

CHAPTER NINETEEN

"I NOW declare you man and wife."

At last, Luis thought, a sense of triumph soaring through him. The commitment of marriage was sealed. Three months he'd waited for this, three months of wanting it every day, craving the security of knowing with absolute certainty that nothing could stop it. Now he could breathe easily. He and Shontelle were publicly, legally wed. Their future together was assured.

Brimming with elation, he turned to lift the veil from his bride's face. Shontelle's beautiful green eyes were shiny with tears, just as they'd been when he'd asked her to marry him in front of the very same people who now filled the church. But there was no doubting the emotion behind these tears.

Love…love and joy and sparkles of sheer blinding happiness.

"You may kiss the bride."

He took her in his arms. Heart of my heart, he thought, and kissed her, feeling a glorious sense of completion. Husband and wife—one in name—one in everything—and they would cherish each other for the rest of their lives, cherish all they were to each other.

''I love you, Shontelle,'' he whispered as he lifted his mouth from hers.

''I love you, Luis Angel Martinez,'' she answered with a wealth of feeling, rolling his name off her tongue as though it was the most magical name in the world.

''Well, *Señora* Martinez,'' he rolled back at her, grinning from ear to ear. ''Ready to face the world as my wife?''

''Anytime,'' she declared, sharing his grin.

Anytime... It was music to his ears. Shontelle at his side, standing by him, right down the line. Faith, trust, love, loyalty, boundless support...he had no doubt she would give them unstintingly, just as he would to her. All that was needed was to be honest with each other and that lesson had been learnt. Too painfully to recollect it now. Today there was no pain and he fiercely hoped it was forever in the past.

This was the real beginning of their lives together.

As they turned for the walk down the aisle, he tucked her arm around his, feeling a huge surge of love and pride. Patricio and Alan ranged up beside him. Alan's wife, Vicki, and his own young cousin, Maria, fussed over the train of Shontelle's beautiful bridal gown.

His mother rose to her feet from the front pew, looking very much the impressive figure she'd always been. Luis still found it difficult to forgive the two years she'd taken from him and Shontelle.

You see? he beamed at her with all the positive

energy pulsing through his mind. This is right. This is good. This is how it should be between a man and his woman.

She smiled and nodded, accepting his choice, and the scarring on his soul faded under a flow of contentment. He knew there would still be skirmishes over her way and his, but the war had been won. Elvira Rosa Martinez had conceded there was a power beyond her grasp. Wealth and influence could not buy love. He hoped she kept remembering that truth.

But it was irrelevant right now.

He and Shontelle were married.

Irrevocably married.

If problems arose they'd work them out. If they had differences of opinion, they'd talk them through. Nothing was ever going to tear them apart again.

His gaze was drawn to her parents rising from their pew, their blessing having been given to this marriage without any reservation at all. Their daughter loved him. And he silently vowed to them he'd return her love a hundredfold.

The organ began to play, filling the church with its rich, resonant sound. Luis hugged Shontelle's arm closer to him and of one accord they stepped forward, heading down the aisle to the exultant lilt of the last piece of ceremonial music, heading towards the life they would forge together.

A shining future, Luis thought, watching Shontelle bestowing a brilliant smile on all the guests they passed. She dazzled them, just as she dazzled him…always had, always would.

With her there was no darkness.

She was the sun and the moon and the stars.

Shontelle…his wife.

He'd won.

They were married.

Luis Angel Martinez smiled, too.

CLAIMING HIS MISTRESS

Emma DARCY

CHAPTER ONE

HER hair caught Carver Dane's eye first. Hair like that invariably did—a long lustrous spill of black curls. His mouth twisted self-mockingly. It was said that people were always attracted to the same physical type, but two relationship disasters really should have some deterrent effect on him.

He waited for a negative switch-off.

It didn't happen.

His gaze kept being drawn to her.

Of course it could be a wig since this masked ball was also a fancy dress affair. It was impossible to tell from this distance across the dance floor, especially with the glittery scarlet and purple mask she wore, disguising her hairline. Purposefully he moved his partner in a sequence of steps that brought him closer.

The hair belonged to a woman dressed as Carmen, the femme fatale gypsy from Bizet's opera. Warning enough to stay clear of her, he told himself. Her body was definitely packaged dynamite, poured into a slinky red gown with a provocative fishtail of red and purple frills. The front of the hip-hugging skirt was even more provocative with a thigh-high slit revealing a flash of shapely legs as her partner twirled her around.

Gold bangles on her arms, gold hoops dangling from her ears. A very sexy piece all around, Carver decided, keeping her in view, determined on claiming her for the next dance. The loose tendrils curling down in front of her ears proved her hair wasn't a wig. Third time lucky, he wryly argued, though he didn't believe it. He simply wanted to pursue the desire she stirred.

Katie Beaumont was enjoying herself. She hadn't let her hair down, in a fun sense, for a long long time. Being dressed as Carmen amongst a crowd of people she didn't know, and who didn't know her, was definitely liberating. There was no need to maintain a responsible image. This was a wonderful slice of freedom from any care, especially the care of what others might think of her.

Her toreador partner was sweating rather heavily by the time the dance bracket ended. "That was great!" he puffed, making a grab to pull her close. "Come and have a drink at the bar with me."

"Thanks so much, but I'm expected back at my table," she excused, smiling as she twirled out of reach. "Enjoy your drink," she tossed back at him, not wanting to leave him completely flat. He was an enthusiastic dancer, but she didn't want his company off the floor, and tonight was about pleasing herself.

It was easy to slip away through the milling crowd. She was actually placed on one of the official tables, next to her old school friend, Amanda, who'd set out to marry spectacularly well and had accomplished it with Max Fairweather, a leading stockbroker at Sydney's top financial levels.

Katie was glad to have met her again after so many

years of being out of contact—a lucky coincidence with Amanda placing her four-year-old son at the day-care centre where she'd been working for the past six months. While she had no ambition to slide into the high-flying social scene, having Amanda's amusing company from time to time, definitely put a bit of sparkle in her life.

She grinned at her friend's extravagant gestures as Amanda entertained her other guests at the table with some outrageous story. No doubt about it, she was a great hostess. And looked fantastic tonight, dressed as an exotic belly dancer in vibrant blues and greens, with a gold mask attached to a gold mesh cap, from which hung strings of glittery beads, winding through her long blond hair.

''So how was the toreador?'' she archly queried the moment Katie had settled on the chair beside her.

She grinned, knowing she was about to dash Amanda's devious plans to find her a *life* partner. ''Good on his feet but a bit too full of himself.''

''Mmm...we obviously need a better prospect,'' she mused with unabashed candour. ''The guy I fancy is the very sexy buccaneer. A pirate king if ever I saw one.''

''A pirate king?'' Katie effected a careless shrug. ''I haven't noticed him.''

''Well, he noticed you,'' came the loaded reply. Amanda always had ammunition ready to fire at Katie's single status. ''He was eyeing you off during that last dance.''

She laughed, aware that many men had been eyeing her off, so one in particular carried no real meaning.

The Carmen costume was blatantly sexy. Amanda lived by the rule—if you've got it, flaunt it—and she'd certainly pressed the principle on Katie tonight. Not that she minded. Tonight she didn't care how many men looked at her. It was harmless enough, letting herself revel in feeling desirable when there was no danger attached to it.

''You're not supposed to be fancying anyone, Amanda,'' she teasingly chided her friend. ''I'm here in place of your husband, remember?''

''Don't remind me. I'm seriously annoyed with Max for missing tonight's ball. Especially when I'm on the fundraising committee for this charity. Him and his golfing weekends,'' she muttered darkly, reaching for the bottle of champagne to refill their glasses.

''Didn't you tell me the contacts are good for his stockbroking business?'' Katie put in politically. ''This lifestyle does come at a price.''

''Don't I know it!'' Amanda sighed. ''Still, I'd rather be drinking the best bubbly than worrying my head about setting up a business. Are you sure you want to take on this taxiing kids around, Katie?''

''Yes. I've thought it all out and I've already set up an appointment with the investment company Max recommended.''

''I'm sure I could matchmake a suitable husband for you.''

Katie shook her head. ''I'd really rather support myself.''

Amanda heaved another exasperated sigh. ''It's not natural.'' She waved an arm around the ballroom.

"This is what's natural for someone with your looks."

"What? A masked ball in fancy dress? This is sheer fantasy land," Katie mocked laughingly. "But I do thank you for talking me into using Max's ticket. And finding me this costume."

"So you *are* having a good time!" Amanda pounced triumphantly.

Katie grinned. "Yes, I am."

Her friend handed her a glass of champagne and clicked it with her own. "To a night of fun and frivolity! May there be many more of them!"

Katie smiled and sipped, but didn't echo the toast. The occasional bit of fun and frivolity did provide a high spot, but a steady diet of it could soon make it lose its magic.

She suspected Amanda kept her life hectic because her husband, who was a truly nice man, tended to be somewhat staid, and exciting distractions kept a happy balance. She also suspected Max had arranged the golfing weekend because appearing in fancy dress was definitely not his style.

Still, the marriage seemed to work quite well, and Katie wondered if the years of working as a nanny in London had made her cynical about the permanence of any relationship. Observing the intrigues and infidelities that went on behind the superficial glitz of supposedly *solid* marriages had been an unpleasant eye-opener, and guarding the children from them had not been easy.

She loved the innocence of little children. She took more pleasure in their company than the company of most adults. The idea of providing a taxi service for children whose parents didn't have the time to ferry them around to activities had appealed very strongly to her. She was sure it was workable, given enough finance to back the venture.

In any event, she didn't want to be *fixed up* with Amanda's divorced acquaintances, and divorcees seemed to be the only unattached males for a woman looking down the barrel of being thirty years old. Not that Katie was madly interested in getting *attached* anyway. She was used to being independent. There'd only ever been the one great passion in her life, and unless someone, somewhere, could spark those same feelings in her, she'd rather stay single.

Making her own way seemed infinitely preferable to sharing her life with a man she didn't love, even if going into business for herself held more pitfalls than she could foresee at the moment. Just glancing around at the men sharing this table…not one of them was attractive enough to give her even a niggle of doubt about the decision she'd made to invest in a future which she could control.

They were pleasant enough people to spend a few hours with; intelligent, witty, accomplished people who could afford the astronomical price of the tickets to this ball. Maybe it was the effect of the masks and fancy dress, but none of them felt *real* to her. They were all play-acting. But then, she was, too. Silly to judge anyone when tonight was aimed at taking time out from their day-to-day lives.

Fantasy…

She sipped some more champagne and laughed at

the wickedly clever jokes being told. The band started up again and Amanda nudged her in the ribs.

''The pirate king is coming at a stride,'' she warned gleefully. ''To your right. Three o'clock.''

Katie turned her head obediently, curious to see the man who had stirred Amanda's interest.

''Now don't tell me he isn't seriously scrumptious,'' her friend challenged.

It was the wrong word, Katie thought. Completely wrong.

He was striding across the dance floor, a black cape lined with purple satin swirling from his shoulders. The purple was repeated in a dashing bandanna circling his head above his black mask. A white flowing shirt was slashed open almost to his waist, revealing a darkly tanned and highly virile chest. A wide black leather belt was fastened by a silver skull-and-crossbones emblem. His black trousers seemed to strain over powerfully muscled thighs, and knee-high boots accentuated his tall, aggressive maleness.

He looked…seriously *dangerous*…not scrumptious.

Katie's heart started thumping. He was coming straight at her with the lethal grace of a panther on the prowl…and he was not about to be diverted or fended off. She could feel his focus on her, feel the driven purpose behind it. A convulsive little shiver ran down her spine. Before she even realised what she was doing, she was pushing her chair back, drawn to stand up and be facing him properly before he reached her.

He emanated a magnetism that was tugging inexorably on her and she didn't know whether to fight it or succumb to it. All her instincts were on red alert, yet it was more a state of excitement than of fear, like meeting a challenge head-on, compelled to engage whatever the outcome.

She hadn't experienced anything like this since… since her ill-fated love for Carver Dane had swept her into the sexual intimacy that had been so terribly broken.

Shocked at being reminded of a time she had determinedly put behind her, Katie stiffened with resistance when the buccaneer halted a bare step away, holding out an open palm to her in confident invitation. She stared down at it, and the sharp memory of Carver eased back into the darker side of her mind. This man's palm was not rough or calloused from manual labour.

''Will you dance with me?''

The softly spoken question had a mocking lilt to it, drawing her gaze up to the eyes behind the mask. They were too shadowed to see his expression. His firmly etched lips were slightly curved, but she caught the sense that the half smile carried more sardonic amusement at himself than any attempt to persuade a positive response from her.

Resentment stirred at the thought he didn't really want to be attracted to the Carmen persona she was projecting tonight. Yet what was good for the gander was just as good for the goose, Katie argued to herself. His buccaneer costume was also blatantly sexy. In fact, his physical impact was so strong, he was probably well aware of its effect on women, and he was undoubtedly banking on her being an easy target for him.

A perverse streak in Katie urged her to pose a challenge to his overwhelming self-assurance. Instead of placing her hand in his in acquiescence, she propped it on her hip in languid consideration.

''Taking a risk, aren't you?'' she drawled. ''Men tend to fall desperately in love with Carmen once they give themselves up to her clutches.''

Amanda burst into giggles and the rest of the party around the table fell silent to take in this interesting encounter.

He tilted his head to one side, and the hand he'd offered gestured non-caringly. ''My life is littered with risks I've taken. One more is neither here nor there.''

''You come out...unscathed...every time?'' Katie queried disbelievingly.

''No. But I hide my scars well.''

She quite liked that answer. It made him more human, less invincible. She smiled. ''A fearless fighter.''

''More a survivor,'' he returned blandly.

''Against all odds.''

''Would you have me back off, Carmen?''

''That would spoil the game.''

She sashayed around him, swishing the frills on her skirt, the exhilaration of being deliberately provocative zinging through her as she turned and extended her hand to him in invitation. ''Will you dance with me?''

He'd already swung, following her movements as

though she was now the pivotal magnet. He took her hand in a firm grasp, and with slow deliberation, lifted it to his mouth.

''The pleasure...believe me...will be mine.''

He turned her hand over and pressed a hot, sensual kiss onto her palm, completely blitzing any reply Katie might have made to that subtly threatening claim. She stood stunned by the electric tingles running up her arm. Before she could recover any composure at all, he moved, sliding an arm around her waist and sweeping her onto the dance floor with a dominant power that enforced pliancy. He placed her hand on his shoulder and pressed the rest of her into full body contact with him.

''Now we dance,'' he murmured, his voice simmering with a sexuality that vibrated with anticipation. ''We shall see if Carmen can follow where a pirate leads.''

CHAPTER TWO

KATIE was swamped by his aggressive maleness. Hard muscular thighs were pushing hers into matching his every step and her feet were instinctively moving to his will. His body heat was seeping into her, arousing a highly sensitive awareness of her own sexuality, and the physical friction of dancing in such intimate proximity stirred feelings she hadn't had in years.

Occasionally a very handsome man with a well-built physique had inspired a fleeting moment of lustful speculation, but that had only ever been a mental try-on… *What would he be like as a lover?* She hadn't experienced any noticeable physical reaction. Her stomach certainly hadn't gone all tremulous. Her breasts hadn't started prickling with excitement. Her pulse rate had not zoomed into a wild gallop.

The pirate was doing all this to her within seconds of her being in *his clutches,* and Katie was so mesmerised by his effect on her, she was following him willy-nilly, taking no control whatsoever over what was happening. Deciding she probably needed a good dose of oxygen in her brain, she took a deep breath. The result was her nostrils tingled with the sharp, tangy scent of whatever cologne he'd splashed onto his jaw after shaving.

It seemed that all her senses had moved up several

intensity levels and were being flooded with some wanton need to pick up everything there was to know about this man. She couldn't get a grip on herself. She didn't even want to get a grip on herself. Her body was alive with all the feelings of being a woman who craved the primitive pleasure a man could give her…*this man,* who might be dressed as a fantasy but was most certainly flesh and blood reality.

"Gold rings on your ears, on your arms, but not on your hands," he commented.

"None on yours, either," she answered, very aware of the strong bare fingers wrapped around hers.

"I walk alone."

"So do I."

"No one owns Carmen?"

"I don't believe anyone can ever *own* another person."

"True. We're only ever given the pieces they choose to give us. Like this dance…"

"You're not counting on anything else from me?"

"Are you…from me?"

"You claimed the role of leader."

"So I did. Which begs the question…how far will you follow?"

"As far as I still want to."

"Then I must keep you wanting."

He executed a masterful series of turns that made wicked use of the front slit of her skirt, their thighs intertwining with every twirl, and the hand pressing into the pit of her back ensuring she remained pinned to him. The deliberately tantalising manoeuvre left her breathless, the surge of excitement so intense she had to struggle to think.

But this wasn't about thinking, she fiercely reasoned.

It was about feeling.

And the desire to indulge herself with what he was promising was too strong to question.

All the long empty years since Carver...nothing. There was a huge hole in her life and this might not be the answer to it but it was *something!*

Free and clear, Carver thought, and the sooner he turned this burning desire to ashes, the better. She was on heat for him. He could feel it. No need for any more talking. The provocative little witch wanted action. He'd give her action in spades.

It had been months since he'd been with a woman, preferring to remain celibate than enter into another affair that didn't satisfy him. But the need for sex didn't go away and the delectable Carmen had it roaring to the fore right now.

Her musky scent was a heady come-on, infiltrating his brain and closing out any reservations about taking what she was offering. The doors were open to the balcony that commanded the multimillion-dollar view over Sydney Harbour. Since it was a fine night, there could be no objection to going outside. She could pretend it was romantic if she wanted to.

He steered her through the dance crowd, revelling in the lush curvaceousness of the body so very pliantly moulded to his. She was ready to give all right. Ready to give and take. He whirled her out onto the balcony. The broad semicircular apron that extended from the ballroom held several groups of smokers but that didn't bother him. It was too public a place anyway.

He danced her down the left flank of the balcony that ran to the end of the massive mansion. The music was loud enough to float after them and there was no word of protest from her, not the slightest stiffening to indicate any concern. She wanted privacy as much as he did.

The light grew dimmer. Huge pots with perfectly trimmed ornamental trees provided pools of darkness. But he didn't want to take obvious advantage of them. Not yet. He took her right to the far balustrade, leaned her against it, and kissed her with all the pent-up need she'd stirred.

No hesitation in her response. Her mouth opened willingly, eagerly, and her hunger matched his, exploding into a passionate drive for every sensual satisfaction a man and woman could give each other. Her arms wound around his neck, pressing for the kissing to go on and on, a wild ravaging of every pleasure possible, a tempest of excitement demanding more.

No artful seduction in this. She was caught up in the same primitive urgency he felt. And that in itself was intensely exhilarating, the direct and open honesty of the craving in her kisses, the hot desire to explore and experience and tangle intimately with him. It reminded him of how it had been with…

No! He wasn't going down that track!

This was Carmen's lust, not Katie's love.

And love was a long-lost cause.

He ran his hands over the body he held. The clinging stretchy fabric of her dress left little to his imagination. He savoured the soft voluptuous curves of *Carmen's* buttocks, the very female flare of her hips, the almost hand-span waist. Her breasts felt full and swollen against his chest. He wanted to touch them, hold them.

Reaching up, he grasped her arms and pulled them down to her sides. Still kissing her, feeding the wanting, he slid his hands up to the off-the-shoulder sleeves and yanked them down, taking the top of her bodice with them to bare her breasts. It shocked her. Her head jerked back. He heard her sharply indrawn breath.

''No one can see,'' he swiftly assured her, smiling to erase any fear. ''The advantage of a cloak.''

He moved his legs to stand astride hers, holding her pinned against the balustrade for firm support while he cupped her breasts, lightly fanning her stiffly protruding nipples with his thumbs. She didn't speak. She stared at his mask for several seconds, as though wanting to see behind it. Then slowly she looked down at what he was doing, watching, seemingly fascinated at having her breasts fondled like this, out in the open.

She was still *with* him, still wanting, and her naked flesh was a delight to feel, to stroke, the different textures of her skin intriguing enough to draw his own gaze down. Either his caresses or the cool night air had hardened her nipples to long purple grapes—very mouth-tempting. He gently squeezed the soft mounds upwards, meaning to taste, but was suddenly struck by the size of her dark aureoles, the whole shape of her breasts…so like Katie's…

His rejection of the memory was so violent, his hands moved instantly to pull up her bodice and lift the off-the-shoulder sleeves back into position. It was the long black curly hair, he savagely reasoned, triggering memories he didn't want, playing havoc with what should be no more than a slaking of need. His heart shouldn't be thumping like this. Not for Carmen.

Yet as though she knew it, he saw her gaze fixed on his chest. She slid her hand under his opened shirt, spreading her fingers over the light nest of hair. Her touch on his skin was electric, his arousal almost painful in its intensity.

She was feeling her power over him, Carver thought, and acted again in violent rejection, lifting her off her feet, swinging her over to the shadowed area to the side of one of the ornamental trees, planting her against the stone wall of the house, snatching her hand out of his shirt, and kissing her to reassert his dominance over this encounter.

Again she wound her arms around his neck and kissed him back—following his lead. But Carver now wanted done with the game. He plundered her mouth while he took the necessary packet from his trouser pocket, freed himself and deftly applied the condom. The front split of her skirt had to be hitched higher, quickly effected. Much to his relief, his hand found only a G-string covering the apex of her thighs, easily shifted aside.

He hadn't meant to wait another moment, but the slick warm softness of her drew him into stroking, feeling, *claiming* this intimate part of her and driving her arousal to the same fever pitch as his own. Where he was rock-hard, she quivered, and he knew precisely when she couldn't bear any more excitement. She wrenched her mouth from his, gasping, moaning.

''Put your legs around me now,'' he commanded, hoisting her up against the wall, one arm under her buttocks as he inserted himself into the hot silky heart of her, thrusting hard, needing to feel engulfed by the female flesh welcoming him.

Her legs linked behind his hips, pressing him in, obviously needing the sensation of being filled by him, every bit as needy as he was for sexual satisfaction. It was more than enough permission for what he was doing. The only thought he had as he continued to revel in the freedom of unbridled lust was... *yes...yes...yes...*

It felt so good...better with every plunge...the tense excitement building faster...faster...his whole body caught in the thrall of it...and finally, a fierce pulsing of intense pleasure exploding from him...the sweet, shuddering relief of it...

He knew she had climaxed before him. Probably with him, as well. He would have liked the sense of fully feeling the physical mingling with her. Impossible with a condom. But protection was more important than any fleeting and *false* sense of togetherness.

Her legs were limply sliding down his thighs. Excitement over. Aftermath setting in. He separated himself from her and helped steady her as she stood once more against the wall. The clasp around his head loosened, her hands dropping to his shoulders. He was glad they were both wearing masks. He didn't want to see the expression on her face. For him, this encounter had run its course, and the sooner they parted, the sooner he could get it out of his head.

He'd wanted her.

She'd wanted him.

They'd satisfied each other and that was that.

The spectre of Katie Beaumont could now be put to rest again.

Katie was stunned out of her mind. It was all she could do to stand on her own two feet. The impression of Carver was so strong—the shape of his head, the texture of his hair, the broad muscular shoulders, the sprinkle of black curls across his chest, the whole feel of him—her head was swimming with it. Her entire body was swimming with the sense of having been…*possessed* by him.

It had to be sheer fantasy, driven by long unanswered needs, yet…

Who was this pirate king?

She could tear off his mask…but if he looked totally different to Carver, how would she feel then?

Wait, she told herself.

It was safer if she waited.

He might say something to reveal more about himself.

Her heart was still thundering in her ears. Impossible to think of anything to say herself. He was readjusting his clothes, all under cover of the cloak that had sheltered their intimacy. Her skirt had slithered back into place when he'd moved away from her. There was no urgent need to reposition the G-string panties. It made no difference to the line of her dress.

Besides, she didn't want to touch herself there... where he had been. Not yet. She wanted to savour the lingering pleasure of all he'd made her feel. Like Carver...

He straightened up. It was difficult to tell if he was the same height as the man she'd once loved, given the boots he wore and her own high-heeled sandals. Was the cloak making his shoulders look broader than she remembered? They *felt* right. She stared at his mouth. The light was dim here, but surely the shape of those firmly delineated lips were...

He compressed them, frustrating her study. He plucked her hands from his shoulders and carried them down, deliberately placing them on her hips as he stepped back.

"The dance is over, Carmen."

The cold, harsh statement was more chilling than the night air, bringing instant goose bumps to her skin.

Somehow she found her voice. "So what happens now?" It came out in a husky slur.

"I told you I walk alone."

Another chilling statement, striking ice into her heart.

He lifted a hand and ran light fingertips down her cheek. "This is one man who *can* take what you give…and leave. But I do thank you…for the pleasure.''

He took another step away from her, his hand gone from her face but still raised in a kind of farewell salute. He paused a moment, as though taking in the image of her—Carmen left against the wall, abandoned by him after he'd taken his pleasure of her…and after he'd given what she'd virtually asked of him.

She didn't move.

This was the end of it.

He was going.

''The pleasure was mine, too,'' she said, driven to match him even now. ''Thank you for the dance.''

He inclined his head in what she thought was a nod of respect, then turned and strode away, taking with him the spectre of Carver, the cloak swirling around his swiftly receding figure.

Fantasy…

She stood against the wall for a long time, needing the support as she fought the tremors that shook her. It was better this way, she kept telling herself, better to have the memory and not the disappointment that reality would surely bring.

It might be like an empty memory right now…but it *was* something.

He'd made her feel like a woman again.

CHAPTER THREE

As SHE rode the train from North Sydney to Town Hall for her all-important appointment in the city, Katie did her best to keep her nerves under control by thinking positively.

The facts and figures she had marshalled—costs and estimated profits—for her business proposition were neatly organised in the slim-line black leather attaché case she carried. References from previous employers attested to her good character and sense of responsibility. Trustworthy and reliable were tags that were repeatedly emphasised.

She was wearing her one good all-purpose black suit, having teamed a cherry red sweater with it since red was supposedly a power colour. Her hair was clean and shiny and as tidy as her curls ever allowed. Her make-up was minimal. She wore new stockings and sensibly heeled black court shoes.

There was nothing to object to about her appearance or preparation, so hopefully she would clinch a deal that would give her a more interesting and satisfying future than her current situation. Max Fairweather had told her this particular company matched investors to budding businesses. With luck, her bud of an idea could flower into a fleet of specialised taxis for transporting children.

Because of her fear of being rushed or late, it was

barely nine o'clock when she stepped off the train. Since her appointment wasn't until nine-thirty, she walked slowly along George Street, then up Market Street to the address Max had given her. It turned out to be a skyscraper with a very impressive facade of black granite and glass.

Big money here, Katie thought, even more determined to fight for the investment she needed. She took a deep breath and entered the huge lobby. The directory on the wall gave her destination as the eighteenth floor, with either elevator one or two providing an express ascent.

There were still ten minutes to go before her appointment. Reasoning that being overly punctual was not a black mark against her, and the company would surely have a reception area with chairs where she could sit and wait, she pressed the button to summon elevator two.

A few seconds later the doors opened…and shock rooted Katie's feet to the floor.

Standing inside the compartment, directly facing her, was a man whose identity was unmistakable. She hadn't seen him for almost ten years but she knew him instantly and her heart quivered from the impact he made on it.

Carver Dane.

Carver…who, in her heart of hearts, had been behind the pirate's mask…a fantasy, stimulated by a host of frustrations and the wild and wanton desire to feel what she had once felt with *him.* The mask had let her pretend. The mask had made a dream briefly come true. But that was all it had been. A dream!

The man facing her was the real person!

Shock hit him, too. No doubt she was the last woman in the world he expected to see or wanted to meet. His facial muscles visibly tightened. There was a flare of some violent emotion in his eyes before they narrowed on her in a sharply guarded scrutiny that shot her nerves into a hopelessly agitated state.

Only a few nights ago she'd been fantasising about the intimacy they'd once shared. The raw sexuality she'd indulged in—with a masked stranger who'd strongly reminded her of Carver—suddenly flooded her with embarrassment. Here was her first and only love—in the flesh—and she simply wasn't prepared to face him, especially when *that* memory was so fresh.

''Are you coming in, Katie, or would you prefer not to ride this elevator with me?'' he asked.

''I...I was wondering if you were stepping out.''

''No.'' His mouth curled into a sardonic little smile. ''I'm on my way up.''

She flushed, painful old memories rushing over her embarrassment, making it more acute. The expensive suit Carver was wearing was evidence enough that his status had risen beyond anything her father had predicted, but what he was doing here Katie had no idea. While she wrestled with her inner confusion the elevator doors started to slide shut.

Carver reached out and pressed a button to reopen them. ''Well?'' he challenged, a savage glitter in his dark brown eyes.

A surge of pride got her feet moving. ''I'm going up, too,'' she declared, stepping into the compartment beside him. She was not her father's little girl anymore. She was an independent woman, all primed to establish her own business, and she was not about to be intimidated by anything Carver could bring up against her.

He released the button holding the doors. As they closed her into sharing this horribly small space with Carver, Katie fiercely hoped the elevator lived up to its promise of being an *express* one. She couldn't bear being with him for long, knowing they couldn't ever be truly together, not how they'd once been.

''What floor do you want?'' he asked.

''Eighteen.'' It was easier to let him operate the control panel than lean across him and do it herself. ''Thank you.''

''You're looking good, Katie,'' he remarked as the compartment started rising.

She flashed him an acknowledging glance. ''So are you.''

''You're back home with your father?''

''No. I'm on my own. How's your mother?'' she retaliated, burning with the memories of how each parent had played a critical part in breaking up the relationship they saw as destructive to the best future for Carver and Katie.

''She has to take it easy now. Not as well as she used to be.''

And probably plays that to the hilt, too, Katie thought bitterly. Lillian Dane would never give up her apron strings. She wondered how Carver's wife coped with her mother-in-law, and was instantly prompted to add, ''And your wife?''

The supposedly polite interest question was not immediately answered. The tension in the silence that followed it was suddenly crawling with all the conflicts left unresolved between them, and the string of circumstances that had kept the two of them apart, preventing any possible resolution.

Katie gritted her teeth as the memories flooded back—the pressures that had forced the break-up, the timing that had been wrong for them, even years later when Carver had come to England looking for her, just when she'd been between jobs and back-packing through Greece and Turkey…the letter he'd left, asking if there was any chance they could get together again, a letter she didn't know about for six months…her phone-call, wild hope fluttering through her heart until the call was answered by *his wife*…then the confirmation from Carver himself that he was, indeed, married.

That was the cruellest cut of all!

Five years apart…then six months too late!

Though to be absolutely fair, maybe she'd read too much into his coming to London, too much into the letter, as well. It had only been an inquiry, not a promise. He might simply have wanted to put the memory of her to rest, and her apparent lack of response could well have effected that very outcome. She could hardly blame him for getting on with his life.

He wasn't hers.

He'd never be hers again.

"My wife died two years ago."

The flat statement from Carver rang in her ears,

then slowly, excruciatingly, bounced around her mind, hitting a mass of raw places she didn't want to look at. The sense of *waste* was totally devastating.

She wasn't aware of the elevator coming to a halt. She was blind to the doors opening.

It took Carver's voice to jolt her out of it. ''This is the eighteenth floor.''

''Oh! Sorry!'' she babbled, and plunged out of the compartment, without even the presence of mind to say goodbye to him.

She found herself in a corridor with a blank wall at one end, glass doors at the other. Her legs automatically carried her towards the doors which had to lead somewhere. It wasn't until Carver fell into step beside her that she realised he had followed her out of the elevator. She stopped, her head jerking towards him in startled inquiry.

''This is my floor, too,'' he informed her, his eyes flashing derisively at her non-comprehension. ''Are you seeing someone here?'' he went on, moving ahead to open the way for her.

''Robert Freeman.'' The name tripped out, though it was none of Carver's business. ''Are *you* seeing someone?''

He shook his head, holding one of the glass doors open and waving her through to what was obviously a reception area. ''I work here, Katie,'' he said quietly as she pushed herself into passing him.

Again her feet faltered, right in the doorway next to where he stood, shock and bewilderment causing her to pause and query this extraordinary statement.

What did a doctor have to do with an investment company?

"You work...?" was as far as she got.

He bent his head closer to hers, murmuring, "I'm one of the partners... Andrews, Dane and Freeman."

Not only was she stunned by this information, but she caught a light whiff of a scent that put all her senses on hyper-alert. Recognition of the distinctive male cologne was instant and so mind-blowing, she almost reeled away from it, barely recovering enough to hold her balance and move on into the reception area.

"How...how nice for you," she somehow managed to mutter, though she was totally unable to meet his eyes.

He couldn't have been the pirate, she frantically reasoned, but her gaze was drawn in terrible fascination to the mouth that now thinned at her lame response, and her heart was catapulting around her chest at the possibility that fantasy had crossed into reality.

It was the physical similarities that had got to her at the masked ball. Plus her own sexual response to them. But that didn't make his identity certain. Far from it. Neither did the cologne. It was probably a popular brand bought and used by many men. She was not normally close enough to most men to notice a scent. It was silly to get so rattled by a coincidence that could be easily explained.

"Life does move on," Carver remarked sardonically, responding to her inane "nice" comment.

''Yes, it does,'' she quickly agreed, hating herself for being so hopelessly gauche.

He hadn't become a doctor but he'd certainly moved up in the world, a long way *up* if this office building was anything to judge by. She didn't understand why he hadn't pursued a medical career, but he certainly had to have become a very successful businessman to be a partner here. His pride had surely been salved by such success. As for *her* pride...

Given the chance, would she have Carver back now that he was free again?

Could one ever go back?

He shut the glass door.

She screwed up her courage to look directly at him, to judge if there was anything left for them.

It was a futile effort.

''Laura will look after you,'' he coolly instructed, gesturing towards the reception desk.

Having dismissed her into another's hands, he turned aside and headed off down a corridor which ran off the reception area, striding fast as though he couldn't wait to get away from her...like the pirate king after declaring the dance was over.

Katie stared after him, any thought of taking some positive initiative utterly wiped out by the comparison pounding through her mind.

Had it been Carver in the buccaneer costume? A widower, who walked alone, feeling the same compulsive physical attraction she had felt because the chemistry was still there for them? Always would be?

A convulsive shiver ran down her spine.

Even if it had been Carver, he'd made it plain he

wanted nothing more to do with her…at least, not with the Carmen she'd been role-playing. He couldn't have known who she really was.

But the man who'd accompanied her to this office floor did know the woman he'd just left, making it equally plain he was finished with her.

She watched him enter an office and disappear from view, heard the closing of the door behind him, and knew there was not going to be any comeback. He didn't *want* any further involvement with her.

The dance was over.

It had been over for Katie Beaumont and Carver Dane years ago.

CHAPTER FOUR

ONCE inside the privacy of his office, Carver took several deep breaths, trying to clear the insidiously sexy aroma from his nostrils and haul his mind back from the chaos it had evoked.

It was definitely the same musky scent Carmen had worn… Carmen, so like Katie—her hair, her breasts, the whole feel of her, the intensity of her need for him.

Had it actually *been* Katie under that mask?

He shook his head, recoiling from the possibility and all it might mean, yet he couldn't banish it. She was back in Sydney. She certainly had access to the high society crowd anytime she wanted to move into it. Her father's connections and her old school network would open most doors. *It could have been her.*

The need to know drove him to the telephone on his desk. He snatched up the receiver, pressed the button to connect him to Robert Freeman and fiercely willed the other man to pick up. Instantly. Robert was the obvious conduit to immediate information about Katie Beaumont. She was here to see him. He had to know something.

"So how did the breakfast meeting go?" his partner inquired, not bothering with a greeting.

"As expected," Carver answered briefly, too caught up in more urgent issues to go into detail. "I just rode up in the elevator with a Miss Beaumont. I understand you have an appointment with her this morning.''

''In five minutes. Some problem with it?''

''Do you know her personally?''

''Never met her. Comes with a recommendation from Max Fairweather. Wants to set up a business and needs cash.''

''Needs cash? From *us?*'' Carver couldn't stop his voice from rising incredulously. ''Do you know who her father is?''

''Beaumont Retirement Villages. Max did mention it.''

''The guy is worth millions.''

''Uh-huh. Could be he disapproves of his daughter's business plans.''

As well as her choice of men, Carver thought acidly.

''Very wealthy fathers can get too fond of flexing their power,'' Robert went on. ''We could reap some benefit here if the daughter is as smart as Daddy at capitalising on a customer need.''

''An interesting situation...'' Carver mused, recalling Katie's assertion she was on her own, not back with her father. She'd worked as a nanny in England in years gone by but what she had done with her life in more recent times was an absolute blank to him. It could be that everything she chose to do was an act of rebellion against her father...including sexual encounters where she took what *she* wanted...like Carmen.

Every muscle in his groin started tightening at the

memory of her flagrant desire matching his. ''Any chance of your passing her over to me, Robert,'' he heard himself saying, not even pausing to consider the possible wisdom of staying clear of any involvement.

He'd once thought of Katie Beaumont as *his*. The temptation to re-examine the feelings that only she had ever drawn from him was too strong to let go. If she'd been behind the Carmen mask, they could still have something very powerful going between them. They weren't so young anymore and the circumstances were very, very different.

''I'm clear for the rest of the morning,'' he pressed, ''and I must admit I'm curious to hear Miss Beaumont's business plans.''

''Mmm...does she happen to be gorgeous?''

''You're a married man, Robert,'' Carver dryly reminded him, uncaring what his partner thought as long as he turned Katie over to him.

He laughed. ''Just don't be forgetting facts and figures in her undoubtedly delectable presence. Go to it, Carver. I'll let Laura know to redirect the client to you.''

''I owe you one.''

''I'll chalk it up.''

Done! He set the receiver down on its cradle, feeling a huge surge of satisfaction. Katie Beamont was his for the next hour or so. The only question was...how to play it to get what he wanted!

Katie was only too grateful that Robert Freeman was occupied on the telephone and not yet free to see her.

She was far from being cool, calm and collected after the run-in with Carver Dane. Her focus on business was shot to pieces, and she was in desperate need of time to get her mind channelled towards her purpose in being here.

The shock of the link between Carver and the pirate king had left her shaky, too, forcefully reminding her of how terribly wanton she had been with the masked man. She had believed that secret was safe. And surely it was. It had to be. She was not normally a wild risk-taker. To have that kind of behaviour rebound on her now…here…no, she was getting in a stew over nothing. Even if Carver had been the buccaneer, he couldn't know she had been Carmen.

It was good to sit down with the option of hopefully getting herself under control again. A few deep breaths helped. If she could just let the past go and concentrate on the future, managing this meeting shouldn't be too difficult. Only the future counted now, she fiercely told herself, and neither Carver nor the pirate king held any part in that. She was on her own.

Definitely on her own.

She had to go into the meeting with Robert Freeman and prove an investment in her business would be worthwhile. All the necessary papers were in her attaché case. She simply had to pull them out and…

"Miss Beaumont?"

Katie's heart leapt at the call from the receptionist, a pleasant young woman with a bright, friendly manner, obviously trained to put people at ease. She had auburn hair, cut in a short, chic style, and her navy suit, teamed with a patterned navy and white scarf knotted around her throat, looked very classy. The perfect frontline person for an investment company, Katie thought, and forced an inquiring smile.

Laura—that was the name Carver had given her—responded with an apologetic grimace. ''I'm sorry. Mr. Freeman is tied up with some urgent business.''

''That's okay. I don't mind waiting,'' Katie quickly inserted, relieved to be given more time to calm her nerves before she had to perform at her best.

''As it happens, that isn't necessary, Miss Beaumont.'' Her mouth moved into a conciliatory smile. ''One of the other partners is free to take over your meeting with Mr. Freeman. In fact, you came in with him… Mr. Dane.''

''Mr.…Dane?'' Katie could barely get the words out. Her tongue felt as paralysed as the rest of her at the thought of facing Carver across a desk, spilling out where she was in her life and asking *him* for money.

''He's very experienced at assessing presentations,'' Laura assured her. ''Your time won't be wasted with Mr. Dane, Miss Beaumont.''

''But I don't mind waiting for Mr. Freeman. It's no problem for me,'' Katie babbled, unable to quell a rising whirl of hysteria.

''The arrangement has already been made.''

Without any discussion with her? Didn't she have any right to decide whom she dealt with? Not that she actually knew Robert Freeman, so she couldn't claim an acquaintance with him. And Carver was a partner, so she couldn't very well protest on the grounds of being handed to someone of lesser authority.

Having announced this official decision, Laura came out from behind the reception desk, clearly intending to gather Katie up and deposit her in the appointed place. Katie froze in her chair, her mind in a ferment of indecision, her body churning with sheer panic as her future and past collided head-on.

A benevolent smile was directed at her, along with the words, "I'll show you to Mr. Dane's office."

What was she to do?

Somehow she levered herself out of the chair and picked up the attaché case, grasping the handle with both hands and holding the square of leather in front of her like some shield against the arrows of fate.

"This way..." An encouraging arm was waved towards the corridor Carver had taken.

The past was gone, Katie frantically reasoned. If she didn't take this chance, she faced a future of always being an employee without any prospect of really getting ahead in life. Besides, this was a business deal. There shouldn't be anything personal in it. If Carver turned it into something personal, she could walk out, with good reason to demand a more objective hearing.

"Miss Beaumont?"

Laura was paused in front of her, a slight frown questioning the delayed reaction from Katie.

"Sorry. I'm a bit thrown by the change."

An understanding smile. "There's no need to be, I

promise you. Mr. Dane follows exactly the same company policies as Mr. Freeman.''

Katie expelled a long breath to ease the tightness in her chest. ''Okay. I'm coming.''

Laura nodded approval as Katie pushed her feet into taking the path to Carver's office. The carpet was dove-grey. It felt like sand dragging at every step she made.

She told herself Carver wouldn't want this meeting any more than she did. He'd been landed with it because he was available and Robert Freeman was busy. Which surely meant he would keep it strictly business, totally ignoring the intimacy of their former relationship.

Or was the intimacy the buccaneer had shared with Carmen as sharply on his mind as it was on hers?

Katie instantly clamped down on that thought. But her stomach contracted at the memory and to her horror, some wanton rush of excitement attacked her breasts, just as Laura came to a halt, gave a courtesy knock on a door, and opened it.

''Miss Beaumont for you, Mr. Dane,'' she announced.

''Thank you, Laura,'' came Carver's voice.

It had the same deep timbre of the pirate king's! Why hadn't she noticed that before? Because she'd been in too much of a flap over running into Carver and she hadn't smelled the cologne until he was on the point of leaving her. But now…her heart started thundering in her ears.

Laura stood back and waved Katie forward.

She had to walk into Carver's office, face him, and

pretend everything they'd ever known together was water under the bridge, including a fantasy that was fast gathering too many shades of reality.

Having constructed a somewhat rueful smile to ease her over the next few moments which were fraught with pitfalls, Katie willed her legs to move without wobbling, thanked Laura for her services, then stepped into what she couldn't help thinking of as the torture room.

Like going to the dentist.

Only worse.

No one here was going to give her an anaesthetic to kill pain.

She heard the door shut behind her. Goose bumps rose on her skin at the realisation she was once again enclosed in a space shared only with Carver Dane. At least it was bigger than an elevator, she hurriedly told herself, and there was furniture to keep them separated.

''Hello, again.''

The greeting forced her to fasten her gaze directly on the man himself. He'd been on the periphery of her vision, standing to the side of his desk. She'd felt him watching her, probably assessing her reaction to the changed appointment, and a sudden surge of stubborn pride tilted her chin in defiance of any judgement he might have made.

''I wasn't expecting this, Carver,'' she stated bluntly.

''I do appreciate that, Katie,'' he returned, his quiet tone aimed to soothe frazzled nerves. His mouth quirked into whimsical appeal. ''Will it help if we pretend we're meeting for the first time?''

Impossible! He'd taken off his suitcoat. Her mind's eye was already measuring his shoulders, matching them to old and fresh memories, and her body felt as though it was pulsing to the imprint of every hard muscle in his very male physique.

''Why aren't you a doctor?'' she blurted out, totally incapable of putting him in a business frame.

He shrugged and moved to the front of the desk, propping himself against it in a relaxed pose that suggested he was prepared to be patient with her. ''That was a long time ago, Katie. I might well ask what you're doing here, seeking a business investment? Why didn't you pursue the course you were taking to become a kindergarten teacher?''

Because I couldn't bear being in the same city as you after the break-up. Not even in the same country! The words screamed through her mind but couldn't be spoken. As he said, it was a long time ago.

''It's just that I always thought of you as working towards that goal,'' she said to explain her intemperate outburst. ''To find you here...''

Carver stared at her, a hard bitterness coiling through him. How *much* had she thought of him? Certainly not enough to bring her back to Australia to find out if anything had changed for them. All those years he'd worked around the clock, needing to prove to himself—and her father—he *could* amount to something...had she given him anything more than a fleeting thought?

Even when he'd gone to England, she'd been off trekking through Greece and Turkey, spending her money on more travel away from him, and staying away so long he'd given up on any response to his letter—given up and trapped himself into a marriage that was bound to be sour before it had even begun, all because he'd been thinking of Katie.

Well, she could think what she liked. He wasn't about to tell her what he'd been through. And certainly not *why!* The sexual attraction was still strong, but he was never going to let Katie Beaumont into his heart again. He'd been there, done that, and any private intercourse between them now would be based on sex, which he very definitely wanted and would find very sweet...*with her.*

He enjoyed her obvious confusion of mind before cutting it off. ''So...you want my credentials before dealing with me,'' he drawled, and enjoyed it even more when a flush rose up her neck and spread into her cheeks, making them almost as red as her sweater...as red as the provocative dress Carmen had worn.

''I'm sure they're everything they should be,'' she rushed out, discomforted by the doubt she'd inadvertantly projected and retracting it as fast as she could. ''You wouldn't be in this position unless they were.''

''But it's difficult for you to accept,'' he taunted, cynically wondering if she'd come to accept her father's view of him—a guy who was screwing a rich man's daughter to make an easy track for himself to a better life.

''No. I...''

Words failed her. Her eyes flickered with confusion. Hazel eyes—grey and green with dots of gold, he remembered. Big, beautiful eyes to drown in… when he was much younger. Her face was still probably the most essentially feminine face he'd ever seen, its frame of black curls accentuating her pale creamy skin, the finely winged eyebrows, a delicately formed nose, and the very kissable, lushly curved lips.

Was she remembering how they'd once kissed?

Were the memories as recent as a few nights ago?

Right now she was boxed into a corner and struggling to get out, realising that referring to the past was a faux pas in these circumstances. She was the one in need of money, not him. Quite a delicious irony, given the background of their former relationship.

Carver noted that her mouth remained slightly parted, the full sensuality of her lips accentuated, and the kisses he'd taken from Carmen were vividly evoked, inciting the desire to taste them again.

She scooped in a quick breath and gestured an agitated appeal for his forebearance. ''I'm sorry. Of course, I accept your credentials. I hope you're prepared to accept mine.''

They would undoubtedly make fascinating listening, but Carver was not about to reveal any personal interest in them. ''I'm here to be convinced that your proposition is well founded and potentially profitable,'' he assured her, smiling his satisfaction in the concession to his obvious standing in the company. ''If you'd like to start…''

He waved an invitation to the chair he'd placed

handy to his desk for her to pass over papers. Without waiting for her to move, he straightened up and strolled around the large desktop to his own chair, a clear signal that he expected business to begin.

Control was his and he intended to keep it, right down the line.

Even when he kissed her.

Which he fully intended to do before she left this office…if Katie Beaumont reacted to the trigger of Carmen!

CHAPTER FIVE

KATIE burned with embarrassment as she took the client chair Carver had indicated. *Client* was the operative word and she fiercely vowed not to forget it again. Her logic had been spot-on before she'd stepped into this office. For Carver, this was strictly business, and if he had been the buccaneer at the masked ball, she could forget that, too. It had no bearing—none whatsoever—on this meeting.

In fact, she wished she knew what Robert Freeman looked like so she could mentally transpose his face onto Carver's. A mask would be very helpful right now. It would save getting distracted again by things that weren't pertinent to this time and place.

As it was, looking straight at the man behind the desk, she couldn't help seeing that ten years had given Carver's handsome face a more striking look of strength and authority. Success certainly sat well on him. But his dark chocolate eyes no longer had a melting quality. No caring in them, she thought. At least, not for her. Which made the past a hollow thing she should discard. Immediately.

''Best to start with a summary of what you're aiming for and why you think it would prove a good investment,'' Carver directed, making Katie acutely aware that she'd lost all sense of initiative.

''I need to know where you're coming from so I

can assess the probable outcome of where you want to head,'' he went on, spelling out what she already knew she had to do.

She'd practised it many times. There would be no difficulty at all in rolling it out if Carver was a stranger, so she had to pretend he was one, just as he'd initially suggested...meeting for the first time.

Setting that parameter in her mind as firmly as she could, Katie managed to pull out her rehearsed presentation, beginning with her background in childcare, her current employment at a day-care centre, and her observations regarding the need for a safe, reliable transport service to deliver and pick up children, thereby relieving the stress of working parents who were stretched for time to manage this themselves.

Carver nodded thoughtfully. ''You're talking about creches, preschool child-minding centres...''

Katie leaned forward in her eagerness to press her case. ''It's where to start distributing leaflets about the service but I envisage much more than catering to the very young age group. I'm thinking schoolchildren who have medical or dental appointments, swimming lessons, dance classes, after-school tutoring, birthday parties. Also picking up teenagers from movies or parties. Parents worry about them using public transport after dark.''

''This would encompass a very long working day,'' he remarked warningly.

Katie nodded and spelled it out. ''A 6:00 a.m. start for week days. Before and after school hours will be the busy times. I would expect most days to finish by

9:00 p.m. The weekends would be different—sporting activities and later nights for teenage parties.''

''You do realise the hours you're proposing leave literally no time for a social life of your own,'' Carver commented, watching her intently for some reappraisal of the situation.

''I have no social life,'' she rattled out, dismissing what was irrelevant to her without realising how unreasonable that might seem to him.

''Excuse me?'' His eyes were suddenly very hard and sceptical. ''On any measuring scale you're a very attractive woman, with, I imagine, the normal urges to mix socially. You surely attend the usual parties...*balls*...'

The subtle emphasis on that last word had the jolt of an electric prod. He *knew,* was her first wild thought, and her heart instantly pumped faster, shooting a horribly telling tide of heat through her entire body.

''Only when I want to and I don't often want to,'' she spilled out, frantically casting around for other words to convince him he was mistaken in his view of her. ''It's not important to me,'' she strongly asserted, her eyes flashing a fierce denial at him. He couldn't *know,* she assured herself. Stupid to get flustered.

Silence as he weighed her answer.

Katie sat it out, determinedly meeting his testing gaze, every nerve in her body strung tight, waiting in fearful anticipation of some revealing comment that reason insisted wouldn't come. Carver was intent on avoiding anything on a personal level, especially if it involved him.

''I take it you're currently unattached,'' he said blandly.

''Yes. And I don't see that status changing,'' she flashed back, a surge of pride insisting she make it clear that acquiring a man in her life was not a driving need to be relentlessly pursued, and it was her choice to channel her energy into a future of her own making.

His eyebrows rose inquiringly. ''You're not looking for marriage? Having children of your own?''

''Would you put those questions to a man, Carver? Are we getting into sexual discrimination here?'' she challenged.

''I'm simply questioning priorities, Katie,'' he answered in a quiet reasonable tone, deliberately defusing the dynamite she'd hurled into the ring. ''I'd certainly inquire of anyone seeking to set up a business what balance they envisaged between their private and working lives. I have to make a judgement on how stable an enterprise will be before recommending it for investment.''

Still seething over his presumption about her personal needs—of which he knew nothing—Katie eyed him with icy resentment. ''Then let me state there is no question that my priority is setting up this business and running it successfully.''

''Fine!'' He made a concessionary gesture. ''As long as you comprehend how demanding it will be. How big a time commitment you're taking on. You are virtually giving up any private life.''

What private life? she thought mockingly. Out loud she said, ''I expect it to *fill* my life until it grows enough to allow me to invest in more vehicles and employ other drivers.''

His eyes sharply scanned hers, assessing her strength of purpose. ''So this isn't a one-off enterprise,'' he said slowly. ''You intend to expand.''

''Yes,'' Katie confirmed without hesitation, and pumped more conviction into her voice. ''There is a very real need for this service. More and more these days, both parents are working. This is an extension of the caring a nanny can give their children. It takes away the guilt and gives peace of mind.''

He nodded. ''It's a very saleable idea.''

''I'm certain of it.''

''But you need the money to set up.''

''That's why I'm here.''

''Okay.'' He sat back, both hands gesturing his willingness to pursue the deal as he added, ''You've sold it to me so far. Let's see your fact sheets.''

Katie tingled with a sense of triumph as she lifted her attaché case onto her knees, opened it, took out the sheaf of papers, sectioned them, and placed three separate bundles on his desk.

''All the information on requirements and costs, the projected rates for permanent and casual bookings, and my references,'' she instructed, satisfied in her own mind that nothing had been overlooked in her preparation. Any fair-minded person would surely be favourably impressed.

Having set down the now emptied attaché case, she was finally able to relax while Carver meticulously checked the information she'd gathered. He obviously found the material comprehensive as he raised few questions and those were quickly answered to his satisfaction. Her confidence in his approval of the investment grew when he set her detailed planning aside without offering any criticism whatsoever and started perusing her references.

Knowing there could be no objection to anything they contained, Katie's concentration drifted, her gaze inadvertantly dropping to the strong male hands holding and turning the pages. No wedding ring. No sentimental hanging on to the symbol of his marriage, though perhaps he had never worn a ring. Some men didn't.

Were these the ringless hands that had cupped her naked breasts just a few nights ago? A widower for two years…needing sex but perhaps still grieving for his wife. It would explain an aggressive desire, burning briefly and quickly extinguished once satisfied. An anonymous encounter was probably the best answer for someone who wanted to walk away afterwards. It committed him to nothing.

Had he come to the masked ball with that in mind?

If so, why choose her?

She hadn't shown any interest in him, hadn't even seen him prior to his asking her to dance. Yet Amanda had said he'd been watching her. No, watching Carmen in her sexy dress, all inhibitions cast aside as she danced as Carmen would. The moment he'd targeted her, the only question left would be her consent. And because he'd reminded her of how she'd once felt with Carver…

Had he been the pirate king?

His mouth, his hair, the whole feel of him…she'd been totally captivated by the likeness at the time. And today, the same cologne…

''I see you've spent most of your working life in London,'' he commented, breaking into Katie's dangerously distracting reverie.

She snapped her attention back to the important issue that had to be settled. ''Yes. It was easy to get a job as a nanny there and one position led to another,'' she quickly explained. ''My mother was English and I was actually born in England so I have dual citizenship. No problem with staying there.''

''You've only been back in Australia for six months. How can you be sure you'll settle here?''

''This is the land of opportunity. I can establish something here that I wouldn't be able to in England.''

''So you came back with this business plan in mind.''

''And have been investigating its viability ever since.''

''You're totally committed to it.''

''Totally.''

''Ready to sign on the dotted line.''

''Unequivocally.''

''There are various forms for you to fill in and sign. We can go through them now and complete the deal or you can take them home for further consideration if you prefer to do so.''

Katie was stunned at this quick result. ''You're approving the investment?''

''Yes. The estimated profit margin comfortably covers the interest you'll have to pay. This is not a high-risk venture. It's simply a matter of how you wish to proceed now.''

''Let's go through the forms,'' she promptly decided, barely able to contain her joy and relief at this outcome.

''I take it you have photocopies of all this documentation?'' he said, restacking her papers into one pile.

''Yes.''

''I'll file these here.''

It was really happening, Katie thought in a daze of excitement. Carver laid out the forms and explained in careful detail what she was about to sign, making sure she understood each clause and what was involved if she couldn't make the repayments. He pointed out the places for her signature, which she duly wrote, then watched him attaching his own, making the agreement a legal contract.

''Is that it?'' she asked eagerly.

He smiled. ''The money will be forwarded to your account today. You can go shopping for your people-mover this afternoon if you like.''

She couldn't stop herself grinning from ear to ear. She'd done it! Her father had refused to lend her the money—unless she toed *his* line—and had derided her chances of getting it elsewhere, but she'd done it!

''Congratulations, Katie,'' Carver said somewhat whimsically, and rose from his chair.

''Thank you,'' she breathed ecstatically. Unlike her

father, *he* had been fair-minded, despite their past history and the bitterness of their break-up.

He came around the desk, offering his hand to her. Katie sprang to her feet, happy to put her own hand in his at such an auspicious moment, not thinking of the pirate king at all…until Carver's strong fingers closed around hers.

Suddenly she was back in the ballroom, feeling *claimed,* the heat of his skin sending highly charged sexual signals through hers. His thumb lightly fanned the inner side of her wrist, making her pulse leap at the sensitivity it raised. Her gaze got stuck on the shirt button that closed the fine white fabric over the hair she knew spread across his chest, springy black hair that arrowed down…

"Carmen…unmasked."

The soft, husky murmur was like a thunderclap in Katie's ears.

The pirate king!

No one else *could* say that!

The impact of certain knowledge rocked her mind and thumped into her heart. Her gaze flew up to his. The same certain knowledge was simmering in his eyes, mockingly challenging her to deny it. She felt utterly caught, stripped of any place to hide. But so was he, she thought wildly. No denial possible from either of them now, and that truth blazed between them in a sizzling silence.

He released her hand, lifting his to stroke tauntingly light fingertips down her cheek to her chin. "Will it taste the same…feel the same…knowing it's me…knowing it's you?'' he mused, his eyes locked on hers in burning challenge.

She couldn't move, couldn't speak. The question had been tantalising her from the moment the elevator doors had opened and she'd been faced with the real flesh-and-blood Carver Dane. It pulsed through her mind now with mesmerising force as he stepped closer, his arm sliding around her waist, the hand on her chin tilting it up.

She stared at him…the pirate king unmasked… watching his face—his mouth—come closer, closer, doing nothing to evade the kiss that was coming. The desire to know if it would be *the same* now was a wild rampant thing compelling her into this moment of truth. There was no thought of consequences, any more than there'd been on the night of the ball. Only need…demanding answers.

His lips brushed hers. She closed her eyes, focusing on sensation. He *was* tasting her, no forceful demand in the seductive sipping at all, more a slow and thorough exploration—touch, caress, the sensual slide of his tongue teasing rather than invading, exciting the anticipation for a more intense contact. Yet the very gentleness of this kissing was enthralling—soft exquisite pleasures spilling over each other, inciting a needful *tasting* of her own.

This wasn't a fantasy of Carver. This was the man himself, whom she'd once loved with all her heart, and her heart yearned for him to fill the void of that lost love, to turn back the clock and recapture the joy and wonder and the glorious passion they'd felt for each other. The hunger for it welled up in her. Her hands slid up around his neck, instinctively seeking to hold him to her, to press for a more intimate kiss.

His hand moved to the nape of her neck, his fingers thrusting up through her hair to cradle the back of her head. The arm around her waist scooped her lower body hard against his, instantly arousing the physical awareness of their sexual differences, and the urge to revel in them. She wanted to feel desire stirring in him, reaching out for her, blindly dismissing the years they'd been apart.

Whether she deepened the kissing or he did…Katie was beyond knowing or caring. It happened, just as she wanted it to, the sudden, fierce explosion of passion where they couldn't get enough of each other, the wild need to excite and be excited, abandoning all control in the craving rush to be satisfied, every primitive instinct running riot.

She felt the hard push of his erection and exulted in it, rolling her hips to incite his full arousal, loving the pressure of it against her stomach. His hand clutched her buttocks, increasing the physical sensation of feeling him…feeling her softness accommodate the strong force of a need he couldn't hide, didn't try to hide.

He wrenched his mouth from hers, sucking in a quick breath before he spoke, his words furring against her lips. ''We both want this.''

''Yes…'' The sigh of agreement whooshed from her with the same urgency racing through her body.

''Not here, Katie.'' The decision seemed to gravel from his throat. ''Wrong time, wrong place.''

''Oh!'' She'd forgotten they were in his office.

Even with his reminder, it was difficult to recollect the reality of their situation. The intoxicating haze of desire, reborn and rampant, still clung to her, reinforced by his unabated arousal. And hers.

He lifted his head back, his dark eyes burning a path to her dazed brain. ''Are you free tonight?''

''Yes...'' Sweet relief that he wanted to pursue what they were both feeling.

''I'll come to your place. Nine o'clock.''

''My place?'' How did he know it?

He cut through her bewilderment. ''Your address is on the forms you signed.''

''Oh!'' Belatedly registering the time he'd stipulated, she quickly offered, ''Come earlier if you like. I could cook dinner and...''

''No. I'm not free before then.''

''Not free?'' She was beginning to sound like a mindless parrot echoing his words.

''You won't be in the very near future, either, given you're serious about your business.''

''That's...that's true.'' It shocked her that she had even forgotten the commitment she'd just made to the investment he'd approved. Though time wasn't a problem for her tonight, there was no point in arguing this as Carver had already declared he wasn't free any earlier.

He eased his hold on her, one hand sliding to her hip as he moved back, the other raking lightly through her curls before dropping away. ''I always liked your hair,'' he remarked with a quirky little smile.

It piqued Katie's curiosity. ''Is that what attracted

you to Carmen?'' she asked, wanting it to be so as it would mean he had been reminded of her.

He shrugged, his eyes hooding slightly as he answered, ''Carmen presented a very sexy image.''

True, Katie admitted to herself, but she was disappointed in the reply. ''So did the buccaneer,'' she was prompted to comment.

''A fortunate coincidence. And today is another one. But tonight is about choice, isn't it, Katie?'' he said softly, his narrowed gaze glittering with anticipation.

Her stomach clenched over the emptiness he'd left when he'd moved back. ''Yes,'' she agreed, though it suddenly struck her it was sex they were talking about, nothing else.

But tonight would provide more time together, she hastily assured herself, hours of private time in which to come to a broader understanding of where they were and what they wanted of each other. The hope for a new start welled up in her…a chance to mend what had been broken.

Carver stepped past her, picked up the attaché case from beside her chair and set it on the desk. ''You'll need to take your copies of these documents you've signed,'' he advised, prompting her into action.

''Thanks again, Carver,'' she said self-consciously, quickly opening the case and laying her records inside. A nasty thought shot into her mind and agitated her into confronting it. ''You…you weren't influenced by…by…''

His face tightened, his eyes savagely deriding the

doubt in hers. ‘‘It’s not my habit to buy women, Katie.’’

‘‘No. Of course not. Why would you?’’ she babbled, inwardly writhing over another awful faux pas. Women were probably falling over themselves to climb into Carver’s bed. Desperate to explain the uncalled-for suspicion, she quickly added, ‘‘It’s just that my father…’’

‘‘I’m not your father,’’ Carver cut in coldly.

She was making things worse, referring to the man Carver had every reason to hate. Her eyes eloquently begged his forgiveness, even as she wondered if they could ever paper over the old wounds.

His mouth relaxed into a wry little smile. ‘‘The deal is on the level, Katie. Your idea is soundly based. It’s up to you to make it work.’’

She expelled a long, tremulous breath. ‘‘I appreciate your…your faith in me, Carver.’’ Determined not to put her foot in her mouth again, Katie quickly snapped her attaché case shut and picked it up, ready to leave. ‘‘I’ll see you at nine o’clock tonight?’’

‘‘I’m a man of my word,’’ he stated dryly and ushered her to his office door, opening it for her.

She paused, her heart hammering at the idea of leaving like this with so much unresolved between them. She looked at him, a host of questions clamouring to be answered.

‘‘Tonight,’’ he said firmly.

And she knew she had to be content with that promise.

Until tonight.

CHAPTER SIX

CARVER leaned over and pressed a soft goodnight kiss on his daughter's forehead. ''Sleep tight, baby,'' he murmured, his heart filling warmly with love for her.

''I'm not a baby, Daddy,'' she protested, her big brown eyes chiding him for not recognising how grown up she was. ''I'm Susannah and I'm three years old.''

He grinned at her. ''Of course you are. I keep forgetting you're a big girl now. Goodnight, Susannah.''

She huffed her satisfaction, rolled onto her side and closed her eyes. '''Night, Daddy,'' she mumbled contentedly.

He stroked her silky black curls—tight spirals like Katie's—except this child was no part of Katie Beaumont. She was his, and he'd gone through hell to keep her.

''Sweet dreams,'' he whispered, loving her innocence, wanting to keep it safe as long as he could.

His baby...she would always be that to him, Carver thought as he rose from the side of her bed, put the books he'd read to her on the side table and moved to switch off the light. He looked back at her—the light of his life—and the realisation struck him that Rupert Beaumont may well have felt this same overwhelming need to protect *his baby girl* and give her the best life had to offer.

Had he viewed her first love as a thief who'd stolen her innocence, alienating her from her father? Did that excuse the violence when he'd found them together, intimately naked? Carver remembered the hatred blazing from the older man's eyes, the raging tirade of accusations, the fist swinging, connecting with his jaw, breaking it, Katie's screaming…

He shook his head, sure in his own mind he'd never subject his Susannah to such an ugly scene. As she grew up, he hoped they would develop an understanding that would never encompass harsh judgements about the relationships she chose to have. She wouldn't have a mother to turn to, but he was determined to make up for that—to always be there for her when she needed him. *And* to let her go to be her own person when she was ready to take that step.

Parents could hold on too long, and fathers weren't the only ones guilty of that, he thought grimly, switching off the light and moving quietly along the hallway to his own bedroom, pausing there long enough to pick up his leather jacket before moving on to his mother's apartment—his mother who'd used emotional weapons which were just as powerful and destructive as fists.

Like the old insidious blackmail she had continually pressed—*how much she'd done for him.* It didn't work anymore. She knew that. Nevertheless, the damage done by it still lay between them—a line that was not to be crossed, ever again, if a relationship between them was to survive, given a reasonable amount of give-and-take.

She was in her sitting room, watching television,

already in her nightie and dressing gown, comfortably settled in the adjustable armchair, her walking frame in easy reaching distance. He felt sorry for her disability but he didn't feel guilty. She had chosen to do what she did. He would not carry the burden of her choices anymore. He'd paid too much on that account…was still paying.

"Mum…" he called quietly from the doorway, drawing her attention "…I'm going out."

She frowned. "You didn't say so at dinner."

"No. I didn't want to discuss it in front of Susannah. Would you check on her before you go to bed and leave your door open in case she wakes and needs you?"

He could rely on his mother to baby-sit at night, not that he asked it very often. Though he'd be asking more often if tonight worked out as he wanted.

"Will you be gone long?" she asked, still frowning over the unplanned request. Usually Carver did give her more notice.

He shrugged. "Probably a few hours."

"Where are you going?"

"That's my business, Mum." He wasn't about to open the way to any interference from her this time. "You can always reach me on my mobile telephone if you're worried about anything."

"All right, dear," she quickly backtracked, offering an appeasing smile. "Enjoy yourself."

He nodded. "I'll be off now. Goodnight."

"You, too."

A very good night, he hoped, patting his trouser pocket to check that the packet of condoms he'd bought on the way home was still there. A pity he hadn't had one handy in his office this morning. The temptation to forget protection had been almost irresistible with Katie so obviously willing to go with him, but…nothing was worth the risk of getting a woman pregnant when she didn't want to be. He couldn't face the fight against a convenient abortion again.

And certainly Katie wasn't planning on having a baby in any near future. She was totally committed to building up her specialised taxi service. He might even use it for Susannah on her play-school mornings, though the day-care nanny he employed handled those trips. Still, it was an option he'd keep in mind if the nanny called in sick. Why not put some business Katie's way? Her bid to be free of her father's power deserved respect.

Rupert Beaumont could hardly scorn him now, Carver thought, lifting his car keys from the hook in the kitchen—keys to the Volvo wagon the nanny used for transporting Susannah and his mother, plus keys to the Audi Quattro he drove himself. He might not have as much buying power as Katie's father, but he had more than enough to acquire whatever he wanted.

Like this big house with its large grounds in Hunters Hill, and setting up a specially equipped apartment in it for his mother, employing a nanny, a housekeeper, a gardener, giving his family every material comfort and convenience. Carver felt a deep satisfaction in all he had achieved as he walked through to the garage and settled himself in the powerful Audi sports car.

He switched on the engine, activated the remote control device, and caressed the driving wheel as he waited for the garage door to lift. It wasn't far from Hunters Hill to North Sydney where Katie Beaumont lived, but he'd stop along the way and pick up a bottle of fine champagne to celebrate her new business venture. He could well afford a nice touch, to soften the rawness of what he wanted with her.

Money couldn't buy everything. The wild and wonderful love he'd once felt for Katie Beaumont was irretrievable, yet because of his current position, she was still there for the taking.

And take her he would, whenever it was mutually desirable.

Katie had been in and out of several outfits, the vain impulse to look her best for Carver warring with the suspicion he wouldn't care what she wore and probably would prefer her in nothing at all. But she couldn't bring herself to be quite so blatant about what would undoubtedly happen tonight. On the other hand, she didn't want to appear off-putting, either, not in any sense.

Did Carver want only a sexual affair with her, or did he nurse a hope—a wish—for something deeper to develop between them?

What signals should she give him?

In the end, she put her cherry red sweater back on. Without a bra. No point in making difficulties with undressing, she told herself. Having made *the choice*—as Carver worded the decision to pursue the desire they both felt—she was not about to backtrack on it.

Anyhow, he wouldn't read anything wrong in her wearing the same sweater she'd worn this morning. It might even reassure him that nothing had changed since then. But the black suit was too formal for now and stockings were as much a nuisance for getting off as a bra, so she chose a pair of black slacks and settled on looking casual and…accessible.

She'd dithered over buying wine and beer but wasn't sure either was a good idea since Carver would have to drive home. Besides, she didn't have a lot of money to splash around. Coffee was surely acceptable. And she had bought a pizza to heat up for supper if they got hungry. If they didn't, she could eat it tomorrow so it wouldn't be wasted.

As the minutes ticked towards nine o'clock, Katie grew more and more nervous. Her little bed-sit apartment was tidy; clean towels in the bathroom, clean linen on the bed, the heater on to keep the room warm. Never in her life had she prepared for such premeditated sex with a man, not even with Carver when they'd been so madly in love. It felt…well, not exactly wrong, since it *was* Carver she was waiting for…but not quite right, either.

It would be better when he arrived, she kept assuring herself. It would feel natural then, more…more spontaneous. It was just a long time to wait…until nine o'clock. Sighing to ease the tightness in her chest, she forced herself to sit down and try to relax, though being comfortable was beyond her. Propped on the kitchen stool, poised to leap off it the moment

Carver arrived, she started wondering why he hadn't been able to come sooner.

Did he still live with his mother?

Katie shuddered at the thought. Lillian Dane had been so cuttingly cruel, accusing her of being a spoilt little rich bitch, obsessively blind to anything except what she wanted. At the time, Katie had been too confused and distressed to fight the bitter criticism. And there had been some truth in it, enough to make it even more of a slap in the face.

No truth in it now, she thought, ironically aware of the reversal in their lives. Though she could always go back to her father and…no, she had come too far from all that to ever go back. No going back to what she'd once shared with Carver, either. There was only going forward.

The doorbell rang.

Her heart leapt.

He was here!

Her feet hit the floor and she was off the stool, almost giddy with rocketing anticipation. She barely stopped herself from running to the door and flinging it open…as she had always done in the past, welcoming Carver with uninhibited joy. But this was *now,* not *then,* and she swiftly cautioned herself not to rush *anything.*

Even so, when she opened the door, the sight of Carver took her breath away. The successful business image was totally obliterated. He was dressed all in black, and like the buccaneer at the masked ball, the dark and dangerous impact of him instantly evoked the same sizzling sense of strong male sexuality, ruthlessly intent on claiming her.

Somehow it was more potent with his unmasked eyes raking her from head to foot, desire blatantly simmering in them as he asked, "May I come in?" making the innocuous words mean far more than a request to enter a room.

Her insides were quivering, reacting to a magnetism that was impossible to reject or defend herself against. It was an act of will to step back, her nod giving him silent permission to move forward, which he did, standing right beside her as she shut the door after him and fumbled with the safety chain, finally sliding it into place, wildly wondering as she did so if there was more safety outside than inside.

It was a relief to find him smiling at her when she swung around. "I brought a bottle of champagne," he said, holding it out for her to see. "A celebratory drink seemed in order since you're setting out on a new course in life."

With him?

"It's a hard road, going into business for yourself," he added, deflating that wishful thought. "But very satisfying if you make it work."

"Yes," she agreed, her responding smile somewhat rueful as she glanced down and noticed the Veuve Cliqot label on the bottle, one of the best French champagnes. "Thanks, Carver. I'm afraid I haven't got the proper glasses for this..."

"Doesn't matter."

His gaze skimmed around her small living area, making her acutely aware of the change from the luxurious surroundings and amenities of her father's home, which Carver had to be noting although he made no comment, simply moving to place the bottle on the small counter that was the only serving space in her kitchenette.

The action prompted her to rise above the embarrassment of not being able to match his gift, and deal with it as gracefully as she could. "I do have a couple of wineglasses. If you'd like to do the honours with the cork..."

She flashed an inviting smile as she skirted him and hurried to the kitchen cupboard where the few glasses she owned were stored, mostly tumblers for water or juice. Wine was not part of her daily diet. In fact, the two cheap glass goblets had been left behind by the previous tenants and needed a wash before using. Accomplishing this as fast as possible in the small sink, Katie had them wiped dry and set down on the counter before she realised Carver had not started to deal with the champagne cork.

She glanced a sharp query at him. He was watching her, his gaze lowered to her breasts, seemingly studying their shape. Her nipples instantly tightened into prominence, and an ironic little smile curled his mouth as he refocused on her eyes.

"It wasn't your hair that gave you away, Katie."

The soft words confused her for a moment, until she recalled questioning him in his office about recognising her in Carmen.

"Quite a few women have hair like yours," he went on, the irony becoming more pronounced as he added, "It's something I always notice."

Every nerve in Katie's body tensed at this information. How many women? Had he been attracted to them, and had he acted on the attraction as he'd done with her at the ball? Had it been any different with her?

''But I must admit it did remind me of you,'' he conceded, stepping closer to her, close enough to rake his fingers through the soft tendrils that framed her face, tucking them behind her ears while his eyes burned into hers. ''I don't suppose anyone forgets their first love.''

The words poured balm over the emotional wound of being likened to others who had passed through his life. At least she was unique in his memory.

''Did the buccaneer remind you of me?'' he murmured, his head bending towards hers.

''Yes,'' she whispered, unable to find more volume. ''In lots of ways.''

His lips grazed around one earlobe, raising a shiver of sheer erotic pleasure. ''You're still wearing the same scent Carmen wore.''

''Oh!'' she breathed, instantly picking up on his cologne again…the trigger to her own wild coupling of Carver and the pirate king. Understanding blasted across her mind, followed by the niggle…how could anyone base sure recognition on a scent? But that thought disintegrated as Carver's voice washed over it.

''It wafted from you this morning and I remembered…'' His hands trailed slowly down her neck and over the taut peaks of her breasts, pausing to cup the soft mounds. ''…I remembered how Carmen's breasts looked and felt just like Katie's…everything about them…but I dismissed the uncanny similarity then. Like hair, I thought. Not unique to one woman. And I couldn't imagine it was you at that ball. To me you were a long way away.''

In time and distance, Katie silently finished for him, having felt exactly the same… *It couldn't be him!* Yet it had been him and he was here, and as his hands reached down and gathered up the soft knit of her sweater, lifting it, her whole body yearned to know him all over again, the intimate reality of him, not fantasy—Carver, the man. Carver…

His name seemed to pulse through her heart. She was only too happy to let him remove her sweater, didn't care that it left her half naked because she wanted his hands on her, wanted to feel everything he'd ever made her feel, and she looked for the heart of the Carver she'd loved in his eyes, but they were lowered, gazing raptly at what had been uncovered.

''It was these that gave you away, Katie,'' he murmured, slowly circling her aureoles with feather-light fingertips, making them prickle with pleasure in his touch. ''And learning you were here in Sydney. The same scent…''

He drew in a deep breath and lifted his gaze, instantly capturing hers with a glittering challenge that pierced the enthralment of intimate memories and evoked an electric awareness of here and now. He took off his leather jacket, tossing it back towards the door. The black shirt was just as quickly and carelessly discarded.

Katie didn't say a word, didn't make a move. There

was no denying she wanted his chest bared—to see, to touch, to feel—and excitement welled up in her as she watched it happen, the emergence of naked flesh and muscle, the strong masculinity that appealed so powerfully to the woman in her, the sprinkle of black wiry curls accentuating his maleness, the gleam of his skin. To her eyes he was beautiful, perfect, and she couldn't resist lifting her hands to press them across the expanse of his chest.

He caught them and carried them up to his shoulders, then grabbed her waist, controlling all movement towards him, bringing her close enough for the tips of her breasts to brush his skin, swaying her slightly from side to side to capture more of the feeling, savouring it, then intensifying the contact, her softness gradually compressing against the unyielding wall of muscle, a slow revelling in the sensation, a build up of heat, and Katie closed her eyes, focusing on the feeling of sinking into Carver, merging with him.

He had meant to go slowly, to enjoy every exquisite nuance of Katie's femininity, to indulge every desire she'd ever evoked in his fantasies over the years, to erase the frustration of not having her when he would have given his soul to have the need for her satisfied. So much to make up for…

Yet he found himself hauling her over to the bed he'd spotted, tearing the rest of their clothes off, barely remembering to snatch the packet of condoms out of his pocket. And there she lay, her legs already spread enticingly, so voluptuously seductive in her abandonment of any inhibitions, waiting for him, wanting him, her eyes swimming over his nakedness, absorbing his maleness, exulting in it, driving him to plunge inside her, to make her take all of him.

And somehow…feeling her welcome him unlocked a mad fever in his brain, and the name, Katie, accompanied every thrust, a wild rhythmic mantra—Katie…Katie…Katie…the sweet convulsive heat of her enveloping him, squeezing him, urging him to spill himself into her.

But it wasn't enough. There was so much more he wanted, needed…the long, long hunger of years seizing him, demanding satiation, compelling total immersion in the whole sensual experience of Katie Beaumont…the feel of every line and curve of her body, the taste of her, the scent of her, the intoxicating excitement of her mouth, her sex, the variation in sensations with having her on top of him, tucked together spoon-fashion, any and every position that appealed.

He didn't know how many condoms he reached for and used, glad there was always another one, no reason to stop. Her passion for more of him—her kisses and caresses and erotic teasing—was constantly exhilarating, and Carver was loath to bring this night of such intense pleasure to a close. But Katie Beaumont was not the be-all and end-all of his life and eventually the call of responsibility could not be ignored any longer.

He kissed her one last time, reluctantly lifting his mouth from hers to murmur, "It's time for me to leave, Katie." Then he heaved himself off the bed and started hunting for his clothes, knowing he had to resist any further temptation to stay with her.

"What time is it?" She sounded slightly stunned, bewildered by the somewhat abrupt separation.

"Midnight."

"We...we've hardly talked."

He slanted her a satisfied smile as he fastened his trousers. "I thought our communication was perfect."

Having slid his feet into the soft leather loafers he'd worn, he swiftly crossed the room to where he'd dropped his shirt and jacket near the door. He had his shirt on and was thrusting his arms into the sleeves of the jacket when Katie spoke again.

"Is *this*...all you want from me, Carver?"

He frowned over the emphasis she gave the words and the tone of voice she used...cold, not warm. Having shrugged on his jacket, he spun around to face her. She was lying on her side, her head propped up on one hand, her eyes half veiled by her long thick lashes, her expression tautly guarded, no longer exuding sensuality.

"No, it's not," he answered, unable to stop his gaze from skimming the lush curve of waist and hip and thigh. "I'll call you...set up another time for us..." He raised a challenging eyebrow. "...Unless this is all you want from me."

His confidence in their mutual desire was instantly affirmed.

"It's nowhere near all I want."

"Fine!" He smiled. "We'll meet again."

She didn't smile back. "Just remember I'm a person, too, Carver."

Was there a slight wobble of vulnerability in her voice? What *did* she want from him? "I do know that, Katie," he assured her quietly, thinking of how she was standing up for herself in spite of her father's opposition—a person in her own right.

"Then make me feel like one," she burst out, jerking herself up to a sitting position, her face flushing as she glared at him in angry pride. "Tell me why you must go now. Don't just pick me up and put me down."

Her fierce resentment stirred his. She'd run away, stayed away…all these years. Given their history, he didn't want to tell her anything about his family. She hadn't been there when it had mattered, when it would have meant…what he'd wanted it to mean. Too late now. Yet, if they were to keep on meeting, he would have to reveal his circumstances sooner or later, and like her, he hadn't had enough. Not nearly enough.

"I do have others to consider, Katie. My mother might need pain-killers to sleep…"

"You still live with your mother?" she cut in incredulously.

He felt his face tighten and hated her ignorance. "She had a stroke some years ago and is…disabled," he stated grimly. "Should I dump her in a nursing home?"

Shock and shame chased across her face. "I…I'm sorry, Carver."

"She's minding my daughter for me."

"Your…*daughter?*" More shock, almost strangling her voice.

From the marriage I wanted with you, but you weren't there, he thought bitterly. Out loud, he laid out the situation that circumscribed his free time, keeping his tone flat and matter-of-fact, not caring what Katie Beaumont thought about it.

"The pain-killers usually induce a deep sleep and my mother won't take them until I get home, in case she doesn't wake if there's some need to. Susannah is only three and sometimes has a disturbed night."

"Three..." she repeated distractedly.

"Yes. So...will you excuse me now?"

"I...I didn't know, Carver," she appealed.

He looked at her pleading face, the erotic tumble of wild black curls around it, the infinitely desirable body that had pleasured him so much tonight, and deliberately softened his voice, though a thread of irony crept through. "How could you? You've been away."

"You will call me?"

For a moment, her uncertainty stirred a vengeful streak, but what was the point of paybacks when he wanted what she could give him. "Yes. Soon," he asserted decisively. "Goodnight, Katie."

He turned to the door, removed the safety chain, and opened it, ready to exit.

"We...we didn't drink the champagne."

He glanced at the bottle, still on the counter where he'd set it down. Another time, he thought, and looked back at her, a whimsical little smile playing on his lips. "Yes we did. We drank it all night. The very best champagne there could be between us."

To him it was true. No bad memories taking the

fizz of pure pleasure away, no complicated demands being made on each other, just a man and a woman fulfilling a natural desire, revelling in the blissful taste of it, letting the sweet intoxication simply take over and bring all the physical joys of loving without any of the emotional burdens. There had been nothing bad about this. Nothing bad, nothing flat, nothing bitter.

''The very best,'' he repeated softly, nodding his satisfaction as he closed the door on a night he would always remember as *good.*

CHAPTER SEVEN

AFTER a hellishly restless night, Katie tried hard to focus her mind on all the things she had to achieve *today.* It was almost impossible to switch off the treadmill of thoughts Carver had left her with, but somehow it had to be done. The only sensible course was to keep pursuing the goals she'd set herself, goals that were attainable.

As she arrived at the entrance gate to the day-care centre, where handing in her notice had to be the first item on her agenda, Katie's determined purpose was waylaid by her old friend, Amanda Fairweather.

''Katie! Wait up!'' Amanda was hauling her four-year-old son, Nicholas, from his car seat in the back of the BMW she drove. ''I want to know how your interview with Robert Freeman went.''

Carver instantly dominated Katie's thoughts again—her meeting with him and all that had ensued from it. ''I didn't see Robert Freeman,'' she blurted out.

''What?'' Amanda looked stunned. She set Nicholas on his feet, closed the car door and herded him towards the gate, her expression swiftly changing to delighted surprise. ''You decided not to tie yourself up with it!''

''No. I am going ahead,'' Katie corrected her. ''I've got the money I need.''

Amanda's eyebrows rose. ''Your father came good with it?''

Katie shook her head as she opened the gate to let Nicholas through. ''I went to the investment company Max recommended.''

''But you said...''

''Robert Freeman was busy. One of the other partners took over the meeting.''

''And agreed to the deal?''

''Yes.''

''Who?''

Katie shrugged. ''Does it matter?''

''Max will want to know,'' Amanda insisted.

Realising that the favour Max had done her deserved some return of courtesy, Katie steeled herself to look squarely into her friend's inquisitive blue eyes and flatly state, ''It was Carver Dane, Amanda.''

''Carver...?'' A shocked gasp. ''You don't mean... not the Carver Dane you were...''

''The same.''

''How? Wasn't he supposed to be going for a medical degree? Working part-time as a landscape gardener?''

Katie gestured helpless ignorance. ''I don't know how he got to where he is.''

''Well, I'm certainly going to find out. Max will know.'' Avid interest lit her eyes. ''Wow! The guy your father beat up on shelled out the money. Do you think it could be personal?''

''Definitely not!''

Amanda's expression slid to salacious speculation. ''I remember him as a gorgeous hunk!''

"Who married someone else," Katie snapped, unwilling to confide the sexual outcome of the meeting, especially since it was far from clear if there could be any other outcome but a sexual one. "I've got to go, Amanda," she quickly added, nodding to her friend's little boy who'd skipped up the path ahead of her.

"Right! I'll see you this afternoon when I pick up Nick." She grinned gleefully as Katie moved onto the path, closing the gate behind her. "I'll talk to Max in the meantime. I'll bet there's more to this than meets the eye, Katie Beaumont."

With a cheerful wave she was off back to her car, leaving Katie with the unsettling certainty that no stone would remain unturned in Amanda's search for *interesting* information on Carver Dane. Whether this was good or bad, Katie had no idea. It might satisfy some of her own curiosity about Carver's move into finance, but it didn't help the personal side.

No doubt Amanda would discover he was a widower and seize on that fact for matchmaking possibilities. She wouldn't understand there were other barriers—like a handicapped mother who'd hated Katie and wouldn't welcome her into a home she shared with her son; and a three-year-old daughter who clearly had first claim on Carver's heart, the child of his marriage to another woman.

Katie's stomach clenched over that last thought. His wife might be dead but she lived on in the child she'd borne to Carver, a constant reminder of what Katie didn't have with him and a lifelong commitment that couldn't be ignored. Carver wasn't *free.*

He'd never be free. Not in the sense Katie would have liked him to be.

He was *morally* free to have sex with her.

Could she accept that limitation, knowing she would always crave more from him? Was more possible, given these circumstances?

Still churning over her dilemma, Katie entered the day-care centre and checked to see that Amanda's son had joined the group of little children already gathered in the playroom. Her gaze lingered on the two- to five-year-olds, happily settling themselves with books or toys until more organised activities began. Carver's pertinent question of yesterday—*You're not looking for marriage? Having children of your own?*—suddenly brought a surge of bitterness.

He'd been married.

He had a child…like one of these in front of her.

While she…

No! It was futile letting such thoughts and feelings eat at her like this! Taking a firm grip on herself, Katie swung away from the sight of the children and moved purposefully to the administration office.

Today she had to start the moves that would hopefully secure some future business. She was now committed to her specialised taxi service and making that work well was top priority. She'd told Carver so. In fact, it was probably that assurance which made him feel free to pursue a sexual connection with her. No strings attached.

Forget him, Katie told herself savagely.

Until he called again.

If he did.

* * *

Soon, Carver had said. Katie lay in bed on Sunday morning, telling herself she was a fool for even thinking about it. After all, it hadn't even been a week since he'd been here, and he'd probably made prior plans for this weekend. Though he could have called and simply spoken to her...

"How are you, Katie?

"I've been thinking of you.

"All your business plans going smoothly?

"When do you have a night free?"

She rolled over and buried her face in the pillow, wishing she could blot out her thoughts. Sunday was supposed to be a day of rest...from everything. As far as the organisation of her business was concerned, that was true. There was nothing productive she could do today. Except take calls and possible bookings from prospective clients who might have picked up the leaflets she'd left at various child-care centres. And that wouldn't keep her busy. Not busy enough to keep her miserable mind from wandering to Carver.

The telephone rang, jolting her out of the pillow and up on her elbows. It was almost nine o'clock, a reasonably civilised time to call on Sunday morning. It could be anyone. Yet her heart was catapulting around her chest as she reached for the receiver and the one name throbbing through her mind made it difficult to produce a crisp, business-like voice tone.

"Hello. Katie Beaumont..."

"Katie..." came the terse cut-in "...now don't you hang up on me."

Her father, commanding as usual. Her jaw tightened. She was not about to be intimidated, dominated, or spoken to as though she were some recalcitrant child. Just let him start down that track and…

''I'm sorry I blew up the last time you were here and I promise I won't do it again,'' he stated gruffly. ''You're my only child, Katie, and I'd like us to be friends. So…'' A deep breath.

''I'm not a child, Dad,'' Katie bit out, warning him he was on fragile ground.

''I know, I know,'' he swiftly assured her. ''I'll respect your independence. I just don't want this rift between us to go on. How about coming over here and having brunch with me this morning? Talk things over…''

Katie sighed over the appeal. ''I'm not going to fit into what you want for me, Dad, and I really don't feel like arguing with you.''

''No argument. I'll even consider investing in this scheme of yours,'' he offered handsomely.

''I don't need your help. I've managed to get the money from another source.''

Silence.

''So you can't pull that string, Dad,'' Katie interpreted bitterly.

''Now hold on there! I know I've made a lot of mistakes with you and I'll probably make more because I don't understand where you're coming from or where you want to go…''

''You could try *listening.*''

''Okay! I swear I'll listen. Try me out over brunch. Will you do that?''

''You won't like it,'' she said with certainty.

''Then I'll lump it.'' His tone changed to a soft

cajoling. ''Anything to get us together again, sweetheart.''

Katie closed her eyes and fought the sudden lump in her throat. She'd adored her father all throughout her childhood and teens, loving the way he always called her *his little sweetheart.* Yet his violent rejection of her love for Carver Dane had soured that pet name forever, giving it overtones of unhealthy possessiveness.

''All right. I'll come,'' she choked out, deciding she needed to clarify her relationship with her father, once and for all. She'd run from it for years, then turned her back on it when he wouldn't support her plans. Maybe it was time to reassess, get a more definitive perspective on where they both stood. ''Expect me about eleven.''

''Fine! It'll be like old times,'' he pressed warmly.

''No, it won't, Dad. It can never be like old times. Please accept that,'' she told him flatly and ended the call.

Two hours later his housekeeper ushered her into the conservatory which was her father's favourite room in the large old English manor-style home he'd bought to please her mother in the early years of their marriage. Never mind that the house overlooked Sydney Harbour on a prime piece of property in the prestigious suburb of Mosman. The architecture and furnishings inside were every bit as British as any house in London. All very establishment correct.

Like SCEGS, the private and very expensive girls' school Katie had attended.

Like everything her father had planned for her

life…until Carver had derailed the exclusive train to the social superiority of wealth and class.

''Katie…'' A warm, welcoming smile.

''Hi, Dad. Don't get up.''

He was sitting at the wrought-iron table which was strewn with the Sunday newspapers and she quickly stepped forward to drop a kiss on his cheek, avoiding the hug she didn't want to return. The sense of alienation went too deep to pretend uninhibited affection.

''You're looking good, Katie,'' he complimented, looking admiringly at her as she busied herself getting coffee, fruit and juice from a side table.

She flashed a smile at him. ''You, too.''

For a man in his early sixties, Rupert Beaumont, was both fit and handsome, his tanned skin somehow minimising his age, making his blue eyes more vivid and his wavy white hair quite strikingly attractive. He was broad-shouldered, barrel-chested, and if his muscular frame had turned the least bit flabby, it certainly wasn't noticeable in the casual grey and white tracksuit he wore.

''Great display of orchids this year,'' she commented.

The conservatory was lined with the exotic plants, many of them in bloom. Cultivating orchids was her father's hobby and he'd collected a huge variety of them. It was a safe, neutral topic of conversation and he seized on it, chatting away about his success with some newly developed specimens, pointing them out to her, beaming pleasure in her interest.

The housekeeper wheeled in a bain-marie containing a variety of hot breakfast foods; bacon, eggs, sausages, mushrooms, grilled tomato, hash browns, corn fritters.

They served themselves as appetite directed, and it wasn't until they were sitting back replete, sipping more coffee, that her father asked the first leading question, his eyes wary but sharp with speculation.

"So...whom did you interest in your children's taxi service?"

"I went to an investment company." She returned his gaze with steely pride. "It *is* a sound business idea, filling a need that isn't being met."

He grimaced. "It wasn't the idea I objected to. It was the hours you'll have to put into it."

"My choice," she reminded him.

"You're almost thirty, Katie," he said quietly. "Why have you written off marriage and having a family? You're a beautiful woman. It doesn't seem right to..."

"Remember Carver Dane, Dad?" she cut in fiercely. "The guy you thought was a sponger who wouldn't amount to anything on his own? The guy whose jaw you smashed when you found him making love to me?"

He frowned, dropping his gaze and fiddling with his coffee cup. "That was a long time ago, Katie. Surely..."

"I met him again last week. He's a partner in the investment company I went to."

He looked up, startled, perplexed.

The information Amanda had siphoned from her husband poured off Katie's tongue. "He has quite a record of seeing the potential of new businesses and making big money out of them. He started off with a landscape company called Weekend Blitz where a whole team of people come in and create a uniquely styled garden in one weekend. The owners of the property can have the pleasure of watching it happen in front of their eyes.''

Another deeper frown. ''I've heard of Weekend Blitz. Didn't know he was behind it.''

''He sold it off years ago and created other equally successful businesses. Sold them all off at huge profits to himself. And now he's a highly respected financier in the city.'' Her eyes derided her father's judgement of the man she'd loved. ''Not bad for a sponger who saw me as an easy ride to money.''

He shook his head, pained by the revelations she was tossing at him. ''All these years…you've never forgiven me, have you? And you've still got him in your heart.''

''Yes.'' Her mouth twisted. ''But I don't think I'm in his. It's just one of those bleak ironies of life that Carver Dane supplied me with the money you refused to lend.''

''Dammit, Katie!'' He thumped the table as he pushed back his chair and rose to his feet. ''I was only thinking of what was best for you,'' he gruffly excused as he began pacing around the conservatory, too agitated by the situation to remain still.

''You never asked *me* what was best for me, Dad. Not back then. Not now.''

It stopped him. He stood at the far end of the conservatory, his shoulders hunched, seemingly staring out at the view of the harbour. Again he shook his head. ''A man tries to protect his daughter.''

''I was nineteen. Not a child. And now I'm twenty-nine. Even less of a child. I want respect for my thoughts, my feelings, my judgements and my decisions, not protection.''

The vehemence with which she spoke echoed through the silence that followed, pleading for—demanding—a response that acknowledged her as an adult who had the right to make her own choices. Katie sat with her hands clenched with determination, not wanting to fight, simply waiting for the outcome of this last attempt to reach an understanding with her father.

He spun around, eyes sharp under beetling brows. ''Is he married?'' he shot at her.

''What?''

''Carver Dane. You met with him last week. Is he married?'' he asked more forcefully.

''No.''

''Then go after him, Katie. All the business success in the world won't fill the hole he left in your life. If there's never going to be any other man for you, go after him.''

It wasn't as simple as that, Katie kept thinking, long after her father had finished hammering out his advice. The odd thing was, she'd been so stunned by it at the time, she hadn't realised he was still doing what he'd always done…deciding what was best for her.

Though at least he had listened, and weighed what she'd said, which was something gained, Katie decided. And he wasn't about to criticise any relationship she did have with Carver, so maybe their estrangement could be bridged by more open communication and the desire to understand.

Which was precisely what she needed with Carver,

too...if he called...if he came to her again. If he didn't, could she brave her father's advice and go after him? Would there be any happiness in it if she did? Apart from the negative emotional baggage they both carried, there were still his mother and his daughter to contend with.

Tired of her own endless questions, Katie picked up the television guide to see if there were any decent Sunday movies on. She was just settling down to watch the end of the current affairs program, "60 Minutes," when the telephone rang. Having lowered the sound volume, she picked up the receiver and rattled out her name, not really feeling like conversation with anyone.

"It's Carver."

Her heart stopped.

"Are you free this evening, Katie?"

"Yes," rushed off her lips with the breath whooshing from her lungs.

"Okay if I come over?"

"Yes," she repeated, her need to see him obliterating any doubts about the wisdom of it.

"Be there soon."

Click!

Katie put the receiver down, her mind dizzy with anticipation. She didn't have to go after Carver Dane. He was coming to her. And she didn't care what happened.

She wanted him.

CHAPTER EIGHT

SHE wanted him.

Carver barely stopped himself from exceeding the speed limit on his way from Hunters Hill to North Sydney. The power of the Audi sports car could be contained. Not so the power of the desire coursing through his blood, hot, urgent, pulsing with the need to be satisfied, and inflamed by Katie's ready response to his call.

Yes…yes…

No quibbling, no time-bargaining, no game-playing. Just simple, straightforward honesty. Like the Katie of old, welcoming any time with him, whatever he could fit in around the various workloads he'd carried.

Though, of course, it wasn't the same as then. The romantic dreams were long gone. And Sunday night was usually a free night for most people. He'd counted on that. Still, she might have had second thoughts about carrying on an affair with him, revisiting an intimacy that had ended badly.

On the other hand, the sex last Tuesday night had been great. The memory of it had tantalised him ever since. He'd had nothing like it in the ten years she'd been gone. And maybe she hadn't, either. If that were the case, it put a high value on what they could give each other.

Sensational pleasure…

The anticipation of it zinged through him all the way to Katie's door. She opened it and his body instantly reacted at the sight of her wrapped in a red dressing gown, presumably with nothing underneath it. He stepped inside the small bed-sit apartment, hauled her into his embrace and swung her around so he could close the door and apply the safety chain, not missing a second of feeling her against him.

No greeting from Carver. Not a word spoken. Even as he secured the door behind them, his mouth took hers in a hot, hungry kiss, making words irrelevant. He wanted her, and the urgency of his wanting shot a wild exultation through Katie. It meant he'd been thinking of her, anticipating being with her again, and he couldn't wait any longer.

She could feel the hard roll of his erection, pressing for release, and the adrenaline rush of her power to excite him this much was a heady intoxicant. Her mind swirled with memories of how passionately needful they'd been for each other when they were in love. It was no different now…the same avid kissing, the compulsion to feel all there was to feel of each other, revelling in the sheer excitement of the silently promised intimacy.

Where did sexual attraction end and love begin? Wasn't it all mixed up together? Desire like this…was it really only physical? Or was the force of it driven by a host of things that lay unspoken between them?

Go after him…

Yes, she thought on a fierce wave of primitive aggression. This man was hers and nothing was going to come between them. Nothing!

Her hands attacked the buttons on his shirt. He threw off his jacket and no sooner had she succeeded in parting his shirt than he tore it off, as eager as she to get rid of barriers. He pulled her dressing gown apart as she unfastened his trousers. His hands were savouring her nakedness, sliding, clutching, possessing, warm, strong, exciting…but not as exciting to her as feeling his arousal, freeing it of clothes and grasping it, stroking it, savouring the throbbing tension of his need for her.

Go after him…

Kisses down the hot muscular wall of his chest, over his flat stomach and then she was taking him in her mouth, her hands freed to push his clothes lower, to revel in the hard strength of his thighs, to cup him as she teased with her tongue, flicking, swirling, loving him as she so fiercely wanted him to love her.

His fingers clenched in her hair. Need pounded through him, tightening every muscle. She could sense every atom of his body yearning. His back arched as he instinctively thrust forward, blindly responding.

"Katie…" The cry ripped from his throat.

Her name.

No one else ever, she thought wildly, drawing him into herself, intent on possessing his mind and heart as well as all his body would give up to her. Yet just when he seemed at the point of uncontrollable surrender, another raw cry burst from him.

''No...''

He wrenched her head back from him. His face was contorted with the anguish of denial as he reached down and pulled her upright. Even so, his eyes glittered with savage self-determination.

''This isn't how I want it.''

''What about how I want it, Carver?'' The words spat off her tongue, frustration firing the challenge.

''No one takes me,'' he bit out and whipped off his trousers, ready for the action he chose, standing apart from her with all the independent pride of a warrior without weakness, flouting his nakedness as though it were impervious armour.

''But it's okay for you to take me,'' she shot at him, lashing out at the power of mind that somehow diminished hers.

''Have you said no to anything I've done?'' The knowledge that she'd hadn't blazed in his eyes as he swooped, scooping her off her feet, cradling her across his chest as he strode the short distance to her bed. ''Say no, Katie, and I'll stop right now.''

Choice...

He'd laid that out from the beginning.

And, of course, she didn't say no. Cutting off her nose to spite her face was a totally self-defeating exercise. Besides which, she didn't want to say no, especially not when he laid her on the bed and set about kissing her, wreaking erotic havoc wherever his mouth moved, not when he paused to sheath himself in protection—though the action did trigger the same separating sense of Carver keeping himself to himself—and not when he took possession of her because she craved the feeling of him inside her, gloried in it, loving the deep rhythm of union that took them to the shattering bliss of climax.

Except the sweet warm sense of fusion wasn't there. The safe seal of a condom kept it from her, and even as Carver withdrew from their intimate linking and discarded the protective device, Katie found herself resenting it, even more resenting the control behind its use, though the more rational side of her mind argued he was only being sensible and taking care of her, as well. Though, as it happened, any form of contraception wasn't necessary tonight.

''You don't need to use those,'' she blurted out. ''Unless there's a health reason,'' she swiftly added, realising she didn't know his recent sexual history.

His mouth quirked. ''No social diseases?''

''Not on my side.''

''Nor mine.'' He stretched out beside her, seemingly relaxed as he propped his head up on one hand and softly raked the rioting curls back from her face, but his eyes scanned hers with sharp intensity. ''Are you telling me you're on the Pill, Katie?''

''No. Though I will get a prescription for next month.''

''Then there's a pregnancy risk.''

''I'm past my fertile time. My period's due in a day or two.''

''Maybe.''

She frowned at the hard cynicism that had flashed into his eyes. ''Do you think I'm lying to you?''

''No. But mistakes get made. I'd rather be safe than sorry.''

No one takes me.

The harsh words he'd spoken earlier zoomed back into Katie's mind, taking on darker shades of meaning. He had once taken a physical beating from her father and she had known then he hadn't fought back for her sake. But it hadn't won him anything in the end, not from her nor her father. Was that at the root of his resolve to hold himself apart, to only do what he felt he had control over, to never again allow anyone to *take* him on any level?

Or was there more grist to that mill?

''You used to trust me with this,'' she said quietly, searching his eyes for answers.

''It's not a question of trust. It's a matter of ensuring there are no slip-ups. After all, having a baby is not in your plan,'' he lightly mocked.

''I'll take responsibility for that, Carver. You don't have to.''

''And if you fail?''

''I'll take responsibility for that, too.''

His eyes narrowed and his voice lowered to a tone that had savage undercurrents. ''So what would you do, Katie? Sneak off and have an abortion without telling me? Come to me for help in getting rid of my child? Have you even stopped to think of the cost of failure?''

She stared at him, her heart pounding at the realisation there had to be answers behind the cuttingly derisive words. ''Has that happened to you, Carver?'' she asked, every nerve in her body tautly waiting on his response.

Bitter venom blazed for his eyes. ''Oh yes, I've

been there. It's not an issue I want to get into. Ever again. The woman has all the say, doesn't she? She can hold a man to ransom…if he wants his child. And the cost doesn't stop at mere money."

The instant leap in Katie's mind tumbled into speech. "Your daughter?"

It was terrible to want it to be so, but a part of her couldn't bear Carver to have loved his wife. It was much, much easier to accept an accidental pregnancy had led to the marriage. Which would also explain why it had happened so soon after his trip to England.

But it was obvious Carver wasn't about to reveal any more, a cold mask of pride closing off any other expression. "My daughter is strictly my business, Katie."

Warning bells clanged. She was on hostile ground and every instinct told her to retreat to what was currently personal between them. Compelled to touch, to bring his mind back to her, she reached up and ran a finger down his cheek to his chin, holding it there in deliberate challenge.

"You asked me two questions. Do I get to answer them or are you going to assume the worst anyway?"

It evoked a glimmer of interest and a quirky little smile. "By all means speak and enlighten me."

"Firstly, I have no intention of risking an accidental pregnancy."

"Given your commitment to the business you're starting, that would seem logical."

"Should biology somehow defeat normal nature and medical science," she drawled, mocking his distrust of her earlier claim of being safe from conception, "and I find myself unexpectedly pregnant, I would not seek an abortion."

He raised a sceptical eyebrow. "Believe me, a child changes everything, Katie. No part of your life remains unaffected."

"Whatever the consequences, I would have the child," she declared unequivocally. "My decision. My responsibility."

"And what about me…the father of the child?"

"How much of a father role you'd want to take on would be entirely up to you, Carver. I wouldn't ask anything, knowing it was a child you didn't want."

He shook his head. "This is all theoretical. The reality is something different. You haven't been through it, and better that you never be faced with it." He took the hand touching his chin and placed it on the other side of her head as he leaned over and grazed his mouth over her lips, murmuring, "Let's keep things simple, Katie, and have the pleasure barricaded against pain."

She didn't know—couldn't tell—if she'd made any opening in the brick wall he'd constructed around himself. He breathed warmth into her with his kisses, built it with his hands, fanned the heat of desire so skillfully and relentlessly, nothing else mattered but the intense waves of pleasure that ebbed and flowed on a tide of enthralling sensuality. She didn't care that he continued to use condoms. She would rather have him on his terms, than not at all.

Yet the issue of trust did linger in her mind, as did the question about his marriage, suppressed by layers of other feelings while the physical magic of their intimate togetherness lasted, but when Carver called an end to it—time for him to leave—and moved away from her to get dressed, those underlying niggles rose to the surface, demanding more attention.

She watched him getting ready to close the door on her again until next time. At least she was confident now there would be a next time, though little else had been achieved in this meeting. The only hint of new information she had was Carver's references to the realities of an unplanned pregnancy.

He hadn't actually linked those realities to his marriage and he'd snubbed her attempt to connect them to his daughter. It was true enough that in all the years they'd been apart, he might very well have been involved in such an experience, ending in an abortion and leaving an indelible impression about the wisdom of safe sex. It might not have anything whatsoever to do with his marriage, yet…

The need to know welled up in her.

Go after him…

But how?

He was shrugging on his leather jacket, his departure imminent. His face wore the expression of a closed book. Desperate to open up the hidden pages, Katie used the only lever she could think of.

''You know…when I called you from London after reading your letter…it was a big shock to find you married.''

His hands were on the jacket hem band, fitting the zipper together for fastening. His fingers momentarily stilled on the task. He sliced her a hard glittering look. ''Was it?'' Apparently dismissing any reply she could make, his focus returned to doing up his jacket, which he accomplished with swift efficiency.

The non-response left Katie floundering. Repeating the assertion seemed useless and the sense that she had alienated him rather than prying him open was very strong.

He regarded her with derisive eyes. ''Did you think time would stand still for you, Katie?''

''No.'' She shook her head, not comprehending the intent behind the question.

''My recollection is that it was some six months after I left the U.K. before you bothered to call and catch up with me.''

''You left your letter with my aunt,'' she reminded him.

''Yes. She told me you were expected back from your Mediterranean trip within a few weeks.''

''My aunt forgot about it, Carver. Before I got back to London she learnt a dear friend of hers was dying of cancer and between the distress of that news and caring for her friend...'' She heaved a rueful sigh. ''Anyhow, the letter was mislaid and she didn't come across it until after her friend's funeral. I called you the day she gave it to me.''

His stillness this time was so prolonged, it was as though he'd been turned to stone. He was staring straight at her, not so much as a flicker of movement in his eyes, either, yet she was sure he wasn't seeing her. It was as though she didn't exist at all, his mind having travelled to another time and place.

The *nothingness* of it was chilling. Katie wanted to break into it, bring him back to her, but her mind seemed frozen, incapable of producing anything sensible. She waited, somehow afraid to move herself. She'd laid out the truth. It was up to Carver to make something of it...if only he would.

A perceptible shudder ran through him, like a switch being thrown. The glazed eyes clicked into sharp focus. His face cracked into a sardonic little smile. ''Well, that's all water under the bridge, isn't it, Katie?'' he drawled.

It left her with nothing to say. Her mind screamed, *Why didn't you wait?* But what reason had she ever given him to put his life on hold for her? She hadn't put her life on hold for him, though he'd always been in her heart, the one—the only one—who'd ever captured it.

''Goodnight,'' he said curtly, and made a swift exit from the apartment, closing off any further chance of reaching him.

Katie heaved a sigh of defeat.

She still didn't know if he'd loved his wife or not. It was probably foolish to let it be so important to her. Yet most of the shock she'd felt at the time of that fateful phone call was centred on the fact that he'd found someone else...and she hadn't. Hadn't even come close.

However, a different picture emerged if an unplanned pregnancy had drawn him into marriage. She could understand that. It was much more acceptable. It made her feel less...discarded. And more positive about getting Carver back. Though how she was going to smash through the brick wall around him, she didn't know.

She buried her face in the pillow that still carried a hint of the cologne he used. The buccaneer's cologne. The masked man. But she would unmask him, given time. If it was the last thing she did, she'd uncover what beat in the heart of Carver Dane!

CHAPTER NINE

CARVER switched off the engine of the Audi. The action triggered the realisation he was home, parked in his own garage, without any recollection of the drive from North Sydney to Hunters Hill. He'd left Katie, got in his car, and now he was here.

The sense of having lost time had him glancing at his watch. It was only just past midnight, not much later than he'd planned. The shock of learning Katie had called him the very day she'd read his letter had totally spun him out. Automatic pilot had got him safely home. But there were still things to do, checking in with his mother…

His mother…

Carver's chest tightened as he climbed out of his car. But for her he would have stayed in England long enough to meet up with Katie when she returned from her trek through Greece and Turkey. Just a couple more weeks. No counting on a response to his letter. One look and he would have known if it was still there for them. And it would have been. No doubt left about that, given their current desire for each other.

A rage of frustration gripped him, lending an angry momentum to every step he took through the house to his mother's apartment. *But for her…*

She'd never liked Katie, always bad-mouthing her,

resenting the time he'd spent with her and the love he'd felt. What he'd wanted was irrelevant. Mother knew best, and any subversive force to her ambition for him had to be pushed away.

Even five years on, after he'd more than proved he could be successful following his own chosen course, she'd been grimly tight-lipped about his trip to England and his intention to bring Katie back with him if he could.

He'd forced her to accept he had a right to his own life, a right to love any woman of his choice, yet had she ever really accepted it in her heart? Had she made herself sick over it? What had brought on the life-threatening bout of pneumonia that had fetched him home from London?

His mother hadn't died.

The only death had been the death of a dream.

And now he knew the dream had been viable, back then…

He found his mother still in her custom-made armchair, disarmingly asleep, having dozed off reading a book which lay askew on her lap. Though she was only in her fifties, she looked old and worn and very vulnerable and the anger in his heart drained away.

He couldn't blame her for the mislaid letter. He couldn't blame Katie's aunt, either, for being too distressed about her friend's illness to remember something that would seem unimportant—a message from a man who'd played no part in her niece's life for years. Illness, particularly the illness of someone close and dear, played havoc with everything.

His mother certainly hadn't chosen to have the

stroke that had done so much damage to her physically, weakening her whole system so that it was vulnerable to any virus. He'd done his best to provide her with a safe environment, but inevitably there were trips to medical appointments, doctors' offices where other patients were gathered in waiting rooms. How could he blame her for getting pneumonia at the worst possible time for him?

He should be blaming himself...giving in to the black moment at that stupid party he'd gone to, telling himself to get Katie out of his mind once and for all. Then seeing Nina—Nina with a head of rioting black curls—being blindly drawn to her, using her...so wrong! It was *his* fault he was no longer free when Katie had finally called. Not his mother's.

Sighing to ease the ache of tension, Carver reached out and gently shook his mother awake. Her lashes flew up and the first moment of disorientation cleared into relieved recognition.

"You're home."

"Yes." He picked up her book, closed it, and set it on the table beside her chair. "Would you like me to help you up?"

"No, thanks, dear. I'll gather myself in a minute."

Her frailty suddenly smote his conscience. "Mum, if it's too much for you to mind Susannah when I'm out at night, please say so. I'll arrange for the nanny to come back and sit."

"No...no..." she cried anxiously, reaching out to grasp his hand and press it appealingly. "I need to feel needed sometimes, Carver. You do so much for me and Susannah's no trouble. She hardly ever wakes. Let me do this for you. For both of you."

He frowned. "You're sure it's not asking too much? You'd tell me if it is?"

"I promise I'd tell you. I would have woken if she'd called out. It was just a light doze. I wouldn't put Susannah at risk for the world. I love that child, Carver."

"I know you do, Mum." He smiled. "She loves her nanna, too."

She smiled back. "So there you are. Go off to bed, dear. You have work tomorrow."

"Yes, Mum," he said with ironic indulgence. He bent down and kissed her cheek. "Goodnight, and thanks for staying up."

"Goodnight, dear."

He left her and went down the hall to Susannah's bedroom. The door was slightly ajar and he slipped inside the room quietly, moving across to the bed where his daughter was tucked up, fast asleep. From all appearances, she hadn't moved since he had left earlier, the bedclothes unruffled, her head turned to the same side on the pillow. His mother was right. Susannah was a good sleeper, happy to go to bed when the day was over and rarely waking up through the night.

He leaned over to press a soft kiss on her cheek, breathing in the endearing young child smell of her and counting himself lucky to have her in his life. She had been unthinkingly conceived and had cost him dear in many ways, yet no way would he be without her now.

His fingers brushed lightly over her silky black curls and a heart-twisting thought savaged his mind. *She should have been Katie's. Not just his by another woman. Katie's, too.* Given a different set of circumstances, she might well have been, and Katie would have *wanted* the child, not fought him over giving birth to their baby, nor deserting it once it was born.

But that wasn't how it was.

The water under the bridge had flowed another way and it was impossible to go back and change it. Years on...it was Katie's choice now not to have children, to pour her time and energy into a business. Other people's children were an integral part of that business, but looking after them was not loving them.

He couldn't expect her to love Susannah...another woman's child. Not as he did—his own flesh-and-blood daughter—and he'd hate it if she didn't.

Yet...he wanted Katie Beaumont. He'd never really stopped wanting her. Even when she'd fled to England, he'd tried to understand her reasons for turning her back on the love he would have fought anyone for. He'd thought she'd come back when she was ready to face down her father's wrath...but she didn't. In actual fact, he didn't know what her response to his letter would have been if he hadn't married Nina.

Dreams...

At least his daughter wasn't a dream. And she would always be his, a lifelong love that nothing could ever break.

As for Katie...well, time would tell.

Sexual attraction was one thing, love quite another.

CHAPTER TEN

IT WAS ten days before he came again.

The longer span of time between visits had Katie swinging from bitter cynicism—did the mention of her period keep him away until he was sure he wouldn't be denied his sexual fix?—to emotional torment—had she made a bad mistake in bringing up the letter, somehow driving a wedge between them instead of opening up a bridge of understanding?

The problem was she didn't know what had been going on in Carver's life at the time and what effect her delayed response had had. Not good. That was obvious from his reaction to her explanation of what had happened. But how bad…it was impossible to know unless he told her, and he wasn't about to tell her. *Water under the bridge…*

It was a relief when he called again, wanting to be with her. She instantly agreed, needing the chance to sort out some of her miserable uncertainties. This time she *would* get answers and not be so quick to fall into bed with him, thinking that intimacy would soften the brick wall.

Go after him…

If sex was the only bargaining chip she had, then as much as she recoiled from the calculating nature of the tactic, it had to be withheld until Carver gave her some satisfaction on where he was coming from.

He knew what she'd been doing in the years they'd been apart. He'd read her references. Her life had run along a relatively clear path, while his had a number of murky areas that were endlessly tantalising.

She was fully dressed—determinedly armoured—when he arrived at her door, once again emanating the same strong male sexuality and triggering a host of weak flutters that instantly tested her resolve. Katie fiercely resisted the temptation to simply let him come in and take what he wanted—what she wanted. It wasn't enough!

"Hi!" she said firmly, hanging on to the door while gesturing him inside. "I've just made a pot of coffee. Come and sit down and I'll bring you a cup, if you like."

Her skin prickled as he scanned her body language. The simmering anticipation in his eyes winked out, replaced by a mocking wariness as he answered, "Thank you. I could probably do with a caffeine shot."

He walked past her without touching, and the rack on which Katie's nerves were screwed tight moved up another notch. She closed the door, at least keeping him momentarily in her company. Panic churned her stomach as she forced herself to walk back to the kitchenette and attend to the coffee, excruciatingly aware that he was making no move to sit down.

Having stepped into her living space, he simply stood watching her, and she could feel the acute concentration of his attention like a burning presence. Her hands were trembling so much, it was all she could do to pour the coffee into the cups she'd set out without slopping the liquid into the saucers.

''Milk and sugar?'' she asked.

''Just black,'' came the flat reply.

While she was adding sugar to her own cup, he stepped over to the kitchen counter and slid his along to the end of it and stood there, virtually blocking her exit from the kitchenette.

''So what's this about, Katie?'' he asked quietly. ''You've had a long, tiring day? You don't really want me here?''

''No...yes...'' She shook her head at her own confused replies and swung to face him, her eyes pleading for patience and some giving on his part. ''I want... I need...to talk with you, Carver. To clear up some things between us.''

Again the mocking wariness. ''Like what?''

Her inner anguish spilled out, too pressing to be held back by any fear of consequences. ''You wrote me that letter. You know what was in it. Yet you were married to someone else within six months. That's a bit inconsistent, isn't it?''

He shrugged. ''The silence from you seemed remarkably consistent with the silence you'd held for years. Like I no longer existed in your world, Katie.''

''So you just went out and found someone else.'' The bitterness lashed from her tongue before she could even begin to consider his point of view.

It evoked a sharp flash of derision. ''I wasn't looking for anyone. I would characterise my connection with Nina as a moment of madness. Hers to me, she told me bluntly, was an act of careless drunken lust.''

"Nina..." The name of the woman who'd answered her phone call, as *his wife.* "Why marry if you weren't in love?"

"Because she fell pregnant and there was a child to consider."

His daughter. So the mind-leap she'd made about an accidental pregnancy had been right! "But if the parents don't love each other...I've never thought that provides a good home for a child," she put to him, remembering how shattering the news of his marriage had been, resenting it even now. "I understand that..."

"You understand nothing," he cut in, glowering scorn at her reasoning. "Being pregnant and having a child didn't fit into Nina's lifestyle," he went on. "She was, by nature, a great opportunist, taking chances as they presented themselves. Finding herself pregnant, she came to me for money to pay for an abortion."

"But you...you didn't agree to it."

"I paid her to go through with the pregnancy and I married her so I would have legal claim to the child."

"You *paid* her to have the baby?"

"My daughter is *someone,* Katie," he grated out. "Someone who's an intrinsic part of me. Would you have preferred me to pay Nina to get rid of her?"

Katie shook her head, realising the child was someone Carver could and did love, especially at a time when there'd been no response from her—no response to a love that might have been. Yet she couldn't help thinking if Nina had not told him she was pregnant…how differently the course of their lives would have run.

''Once Susannah was born, Nina left the baby to me and picked up her own freewheeling life, with considerable funds to do whatever she wanted,'' Carver explained, spelling out the *payment* he'd made.

''She just walked out…on everything?''

''A divorce and paternal custody were already agreed upon. As it happened, she died in a sky-diving accident before the required year of separation ran its course.''

The shocking list of facts left Katie appalled by the situation he had been through. ''She didn't mind leaving her baby to you?''

His mouth twisted. ''Nina didn't like being pregnant. The only feeling she expressed to me was relief that it was over.''

What a terrible marriage that must have been, Katie thought, both of them trapped by the life of a child that meant nothing to Nina, and was precious to Carver. ''So your daughter has never really had a mother,'' she mused sadly.

''She has me.''

The grim vehemence in his voice instantly drew her gaze up again and she flinched at the cold glittering indictment she read in his eyes. It was as though he was saying only his love could be counted on, and he would never let his daughter down, never turn his back on her, never leave her wanting in any capacity…as he'd been left wanting by Katie Beaumont.

''And she has my mother, her nanna, to give her plenty of love, as well,'' he added, driving home the point that his mother still lived under his roof. A tight pride hardened his face. ''Don't think of my daughter as a deprived child, Katie. She's not.''

''I'm sure she's...very special to you.''

Taking desperate refuge in sipping her coffee, Katie tried to get her thoughts in some semblance of purposeful order, but her mind kept whirling around the word, *love.* Carver hadn't loved his wife but he did love his daughter, a love that was supported, not destructively undermined by his mother.

''Why didn't you become a doctor, Carver?'' she blurted out.

''I lost interest in fulfilling my mother's ambition for me,'' he stated tersely, then picked up his own cup and drank its contents, grimacing as though the dregs were bitter as he set the cup down again.

Afraid this was a sign he was about to walk out and leave her, Katie plunged into explaining her question. ''I used to think of you, moving up through the years it takes to get a medical degree. And you'd talked about specialising in surgery...''

''I'm sorry I've disappointed you,'' he slid in sardonically, impatient with her memories, uncaring.

After all, how could such memories mean anything to him when she'd never contacted him to make them mean something? He straightened up, poised to move, and the cold rejection in his eyes told her he hated revealing all he had. It was none of her business. She hadn't been here.

Feeling hopelessly guilty and desperate to keep him

with her, Katie plunged into more speech. ''You haven't disappointed me, Carver. It was just that your mother was so adamant that I shouldn't stand in your way.''

At least that gave him pause for thought. Frowning, he objected to her claim. ''You never stood in my way, Katie.''

''Perhaps...'' She took a deep breath, frantically trying to select the right words, not wanting to offend. ''Perhaps, I got it all wrong...at the time.''

''If you had such an impression from anything my mother said...why didn't you ask *me* about it?''

When he was lying in hospital, having his broken jaw wired?

Her father hating Carver... His mother hating her...

She heaved a hopeless sigh, recognising belatedly from the harsh tone of his question that there could have been another answer back then...an answer she hadn't sought because it hadn't seemed possible. Having had her justification for fleeing to England swept out of the equation, all she could do was trot out the reality she had accepted.

''I just had it fixed in my mind that becoming a doctor—a surgeon—was important to you. And I used to think...one day when you had all those impressive qualifications attached to your name...'' Bleak irony twisted her attempt at a smile. ''...I'd come home and congratulate you on the achievement.''

''And check if there was anything left between us?'' he finished for her, the same irony reflected in his eyes.

''It was...a thought.''

A thought that reminded him of what they had been sharing since they'd met again. His gaze slowly raked her from head to toe and back again, making her whole body flush with the memory of the physical pleasure they'd taken in each other.

''So what do you think now, Katie?'' he softly challenged, moving towards her. ''Is it worth going on with, given the separate directions our lives have taken?''

''Do they have to stay separate?'' It was both a protest and an appeal.

He took the coffee cup she was still nursing out of her hands and set it on the kitchen counter. His eyes simmered with sexual promises as he slid his hands around her waist. ''I consider this link worth having. Don't you?''

''Yes,'' she whispered, unable to deny the need to feel him holding her.

''Then let's dismiss the past,'' he murmured, planting seductive little kisses around the face she automatically turned up to his. ''And move on from here.''

''To where?'' It was a cry from deep within her heart, a cry that the physical desire he stirred didn't answer. She wound her arms around his neck, driven to hold him as close to her as she could. ''To where, Carver?'' she repeated, desperately seeking some emotional reassurance.

''Who knows?'' His eyes blazed with a more immediate fire. ''Right now, all I want to know is this.''

His mouth covered hers and any further questions

were seared from her mind by a burst of explosive passion. It was all too easy to dismiss everything else, to let herself sink into the enthralling excitement of his aggressive desire for her. There were so many years behind her that had been empty of such intense physical feelings, and the sensations Carver aroused were so chaotically acute, there simply was no room for questioning where or what or how or when or why.

Yet when he kissed her breasts, she remembered what he'd said about them giving away her identity, and felt giddily proud they were unique, at least to him. In her mind, he had always been unique. Best of all, he hadn't loved another woman. She was still the only one. She had to show him, make him believe they were meant for each other, now and forever.

Consumed by her need for him, Katie was just as eager as he was to get rid of their clothes, to move to the bed, to embrace all they could share together with a fervour that knew no limitations. She loved his strong maleness, loved the tautness of his muscles, loved the whole sensation of his body moving against hers, naked and yearning for their ultimate union.

''Katie, did you go on the Pill?''

''Yes.''

He didn't hesitate, didn't question further, didn't reach for a condom, but went straight ahead, sheathing himself only with her, flesh around flesh. Her mind almost burst with happiness. He was giving up his protection, giving up the last barrier that kept him apart from her. So maybe the talking had been good…painful but good. He was letting it be as it had been between them when he'd trusted her love.

And it was wonderful, feeling him inside her like this, so hot and hard and *real,* moving them both to exquisite peaks of pleasure. It gave her an ecstatic sense of satisfaction when she felt him climax, the warm spill of him a deep inner caress of total intimacy, the sharing truly complete this time. As though he felt the sweet harmony of it, too, he kissed her with a loving tenderness that filled Katie's heart with hope.

When he held her close to him afterwards, idly caressing her and luxuriating in the sheer sensuality of being naked together, it was as though they had moved into a peaceful truce, with the angst of the past laid to rest and a future yet to be written. She no longer had the sense of a brick wall around him, sealing off any entry to his personal life. He felt… reachable.

She lay with her cheek over his heart, feeling the gentle rise and fall of his breathing, wondering if fortune favoured the brave. All those years ago, she hadn't been brave enough to fight for a love she'd convinced herself was doomed. She'd projected it into some vaguely possible future, letting it become more a dream than a reality. But she was more than ready to fight for it now.

''Carver?''

''Mmm?'' It was a drowsy sound of contentment. He was gently tracing the curve of her spine with his fingertips.

''Ten days was a long time without hearing from you.''

He sighed and moved his hand into her hair, weaving his fingers through the curls and tugging lightly as he answered, ''Don't try to tie me down, Katie. I do have other commitments. And this is new. It needs time.''

To Katie's mind, too much time had been lost already, but she didn't feel she had the right to be demanding. ''I didn't like feeling I might have lost you again.''

He gave a low, amused chuckle. ''You can take it for granted you haven't.'' Then his voice gathered a harder edge. ''I've never run away from anything, Katie. Whatever has to be faced, I face…upfront.''

Not like her. But she *was* facing issues between them now. The problem was in learning not to push too far too fast. And not be too selfish, either. Lillian Dane might not have been so wrong in calling her a spoilt rich bitch, expecting everything to be handed to her on a plate without earning it, or paying for it.

''I won't make promises, Katie,'' Carver went on in a softer tone, stroking her hair now, soothing. ''You have a business to run. I have a family to hold together. Let's just see what we can fit in.''

With that, Katie firmly told herself, she had to be content.

For now.

CHAPTER ELEVEN

KATIE found a parking place for her people-mover behind the Lane Cove public library and double-checked that her precious vehicle was locked before leaving it behind. Since it was expensively equipped with baby capsules, toddler car seats and boosters, she certainly didn't want to invite any thieving by being careless.

It was right on ten-thirty as she made her way up to the mall where there were open-air cafés under the leafy canopy of trees—a really pleasant venue on a hot sunny morning. She was looking forward to spending a half hour or so with Amanda, who'd taken to grumbling that Katie was always too busy to have any *fun.* Which, Katie had to admit, was mostly true these days.

She spotted her friend at a table, easy to do with her bright clothes and bright personality, topped by lovely blond hair and sparkling blue eyes. The moment Amanda saw her, she signalled a waiter and had him at the table before Katie even sat down. They both ordered cappuccinos.

The waiter departed.

Katie relaxed.

Amanda leaned forward, resting her forearms on the small table, her whole body expressing an excited eagerness to impart some news she couldn't wait to share.

"I've done it!" she declared, her eyes twinkling with triumph. "It's taken me a while, finagling the social links to ensure success, but I've done it!"

Katie shook her head, amused by the secretive glee emanating from her friend, but having no clue whatsoever to the achievement she was gloating over. Since it was clearly the key to Amanda's pressing invitation to join her for coffee once the heavily booked morning runs to child-care centres and schools were done, Katie obligingly fed her back the leading line.

"What have you done?"

The grin that spread across Amanda's face beamed conspiratorial delight. "I've got Carver Dane!"

Katie could feel all her nerves clenching. Her mind flashed to the previous night—two sizzling hours snatched with Carver midweek—and a tide of heat started whooshing up her neck.

Amanda laughed as she observed the revealing flush. "Now don't tell me you're not interested, Katie Beaumont. He's a widower, available, very very eligible, and there's no reason why love can't flourish the second time around."

Matchmaking!

Katie didn't know whether to laugh or cry. She took a deep breath to settle the wild hysteria that threatened to spill into a highly questionable response, and concentrated on finding out what Amanda was setting up for her.

"I think you'd better explain just how you've *got*

Carver Dane, Amanda,'' she said, striving for a non-committal tone.

''Well, I started off working through Robert Freeman...'' Her voice brimmed with enthusiasm for the chase as she detailed the step-by-step plan which had drawn Carver into her social net. ''Anyhow, he's accepted my invitation to bring himself and his daughter to the barbecue lunch Max and I are holding for some of our friends this coming Sunday,'' she finished with smug satisfaction.

''His daughter...'' Katie couldn't help picking up those words.

She and Carver had been lovers for three months, yet he had offered no invitation to meet his daughter, not even dropping a suggestion that he might favour introducing them to each other. Katie herself was in two minds about the child he loved so much, sometimes fiercely resenting her existence, other times seized by an avid curiosity to know what she was like.

''Now don't let a child by another woman get in the way,'' Amanda quickly advised. ''You're great with little children, Katie. With all your experience as a nanny, that can't possibly be a hurdle to you.'' Her eyes danced with sexual mischief. ''And he's still a gorgeous hunk! Well worth having!''

She was hardly missing out on *having* him, Katie thought with considerable irony. But meeting his daughter...would that move her closer to him? Or would it bring a divisive element into their relationship?

''Besides,'' Amanda went on reassuringly, ''there will be other children for her to play with. I've invited quite a few families. And my Nick will draw her into games. Meeting the child won't be awkward for you at all.''

''The master planner,'' Katie mocked, not at all sure if she should go along with Amanda's scheming. But it was tempting...meeting Carver's daughter in such casual circumstances.

Amanda preened. ''I certainly am. Quite brilliant when I put my mind to it. And don't think you can give me the slip, Katie. I know you're free on Sundays.''

Undeniably true. During the first month of building up the highly specialised taxi business, taking every booking she could manage, Katie had realised she was pushing herself too much—to a dangerous fatigue level—and she'd decided Sunday had to be a day of rest.

It was the least demanding day for her services because parents were generally home to drive their own children around. Apart from which, the safe and reliable transport she provided had proved very popular and profitable so she could afford to take a day off.

''I do have a standing invitation to brunch with my father,'' she remarked, not quite ready to commit herself.

Amanda waved a dismissive hand. ''Don't come the dutiful daughter bit with me, Katie.'' Her eyes narrowed meaningly. ''Your father interfered with the course of true love before and he should be grateful to me for trying to put it right. You are not to let him put a spoke in this wheel!''

He wouldn't. Katie knew that. In fact, he would be full of approval for Amanda's initiative.

''Apart from which,'' her friend ran on, ''after all the trouble I've gone to—a very lengthy and delicate campaign—I shall be mortally offended if you don't come and snag the guy as you should.''

''He might not want to be *snagged.*''

''Nonsense. He probably had a stiff dose of pride at that interview you had with him. But he gave you the money, didn't he?'' Amanda pressed eagerly.

''It was a sound business investment,'' Katie asserted, still hiding what had ensued from the interview on a very private and personal level. She didn't want to confide the truth. Amanda could never resist passing on a juicy piece of gossip and Katie was not about to risk testing her friend's ability to hold her tongue.

''He could have been prejudiced against you,'' Amanda argued. ''Giving you the money proves he's open-minded. That's a plus to start with. And a nice relaxed lunch on Sunday will give his pride time to unbend. You'll see,'' came the confident prediction.

The waiter brought their coffees and there was a pause in the conversation as they paid for them and stirred in sugar to their taste. Katie tried to envisage a nice relaxed lunch with Carver and his daughter, but could only see problems with it. Amanda, however, was determined on pursuing this course, jumping in again with more persuasion.

''I bet he won't be able to leave you alone. No one forgets their first love, Katie. A little fanning of the embers…?'' Her eyebrows arched a challenge. ''Why not give it a try?''

The embers didn't need fanning. She and Carver had a significant blaze already going. The problem was its restriction to a very fine line between them. Would it help broaden the line if she met his daughter and managed to establish a positive rapport with the child?

Go after him…

Nothing ventured, nothing gained, Katie argued to herself.

''All right. I'll come.'' She eyed her friend warningly. ''Just don't get too cute with either of us, Amanda.''

''Who, me? The very soul of subtlety?''

''And if it goes wrong, don't try to stop any exits.''

''I shall facilitate them with tact and grace,'' she declared airily, then grinned from ear to ear. ''Sunday. Twelve noon. Out on the patio by the swimming pool. Bring your sexiest bikini.''

Sunday came, bright and sunny, a perfect summer day although it was only mid-November. Katie was in a nervous flutter all morning, telling herself again and again this meeting with Carver's daughter was surely harmless, yet unable to stop worrying over Carver's reaction once he realised Amanda had deliberately engineered their coming together. Impossible for him not to, once he was aware his hostess was an old school friend of Katie's, and Amanda was bound to let that pertinent piece of information drop.

In a way, it was a test of where she stood with him. But did she want to know the results?

No point in hiding her head in the sand, Katie decided. Either Carver was going to let her into his family life or he wasn't, and what happened today should be a clear indication of future direction with him.

It would also be a test of her feelings about his daughter.

Not that she worried any more about the little girl being a reflection of the woman Carver had married. Nina was completely out of the picture now in any emotional sense. However, Katie's experience had taught her not every child was easy to love. Some would test the patience of a saint. So it was probably good to get an idea of what she faced with Susannah Dane, should Carver decide he would like a relationship between them to develop.

She didn't take a bikini with her. Fanning embers was not what today was about. She wore a pair of deep fuschia-pink jeans with a fitted white blouse embroidered with tiny fuschias. It was a feminine outfit without being in-your-face sexy. It felt right for meeting a child.

The ten-minute drive to the Fairweathers' home in Lane Cove was a smooth run, although possible problems started multiplying in Katie's mind, filling her with so much trepidation there was no pleasure at all in arriving. Quite a few cars were parked in the street outside Amanda's house, which seemed to suggest she was late, but a check of her watch assured her she was not.

Was Carver already here?

His Audi sports car certainly wasn't, but he probably used some other vehicle when taking his daughter out.

Gathering up her frayed courage, Katie forced her legs to carry her to Amanda's front door and she rang the doorbell to make her arrival final. No running away from this confrontation. Stand and fight for what you want, she fiercely told herself.

The door opened.

Amanda, in white slacks and a multicoloured striped top, clapped her hands in excited anticipation—let the fun begin! Katie ruefully interpreted—then grabbed her and hauled her into the house, winding her arm firmly around Katie's to ensure captivity.

"They're here!" she declared, her eyes dancing with gleeful satisfaction. "And you'll be gobsmacked when you see his daughter!"

"Why?"

"You'll see."

"Is there something wrong with her?" Katie pressed anxiously, wanting to be prepared.

"Not at all." Amanda grinned her delight. "In fact, she's absolutely perfect!"

"Then what are you going on about? And how come everyone's here before me? I'm not late."

"I invited those with children earlier. Gives them more playtime before lunch. Then hopefully they tire themselves out and go to sleep in the afternoon, giving the adults more play time," came the wise explanation.

Katie frowned. "Am I the only one late?" she asked, hating the thought of making *an entrance.*

"Only by half an hour. Perfectly reasonable." Then with a mischievous twinkle in her eyes, she added, "I wanted Carver settled in and comfortable before hitting him with you. He can't make an excuse to leave if he's comfortable, can he? Especially if his daughter is obviously having fun. And she is. The moment she saw Nick's little yellow Jeep, it was love at first sight. Hasn't stopped playing with it.''

They reached the kitchen where Max was unloading a tray of iceblocks into a pitcher of fruit juice. He looked up and gave Katie a welcoming smile. ''Hi! Looking good, Katie! And Amanda tells me your taxi business is thriving.''

''Yes. Thanks, Max.''

He really was a lovely man, not exactly handsome but with the kind of looks you warmed to because he was so nice. He was shorter than average height, his greying brown hair was receding at the temples, he was carrying too much weight, but he had friendly blue eyes, an infectious smile and a charm of manner that always put people at ease.

''You can catch up with Katie later,'' Amanda swiftly advised her husband. ''We've got more important business right now.''

He rolled his eyes and mockingly sang, ''*Come tiptoe, through the tulips…*''

It paused Amanda at the door, causing her to cast a warning. ''Now you just stop that, Max. This is serious.''

He broke off into a resigned sigh. ''I know, darling heart. Three months of relentless scheming. Do try to give her a pay-off, Katie, or my life won't be worth living.''

''*C'est la vie,* Max,'' she said, grimacing her sympathy, grateful to him for the light moment which had eased her tension a little.

''Too true,'' he answered, nodding his head sagely.

''I am acting for the best,'' Amanda declared emphatically and hauled Katie outside to the patio which provided a splendid outdoor family entertainment area.

Part of it had a louvred roof to protect the barbecue and several tables from inopportune rain. Other sections were shaded by vine-covered pergolas. There was a large open play area for the children, and beyond that a fenced swimming pool, where Nick and a couple of other young boys were dive-bombing big floating plastic toys.

Several children were playing in and around a brightly coloured cubbyhouse which had a ladder leading up to one window and a slippery dip coming down from another, but a quick, cursory glance didn't identify any one of them as definitely Carver's daughter.

''Now where is he?'' Amanda muttered, checking the various couples who were seated around tables, enjoying cool drinks and nibbles. Most of them Katie recognised from the masked ball where the masks had come off after midnight. Some remembered her and smiled, raising their hands in greeting.

''There, by the barbecue!''

Katie looked where Amanda directed. Three men stood by the cooking grill, idly watching sausages sizzle as they drank beer and chatted to each other. Carver, his powerful physique clothed in dark blue jeans and a royal blue sports shirt looked, as always, stunningly male, his handsome face expressing interest in the conversation.

There was a burst of amused laughter between the men, then Carver's gaze roved past Katie towards the cubbyhouse. Her pulse leapt as her presence registered and he did a double take. His whole body stiffened with the shock of seeing her. For several moments, he stared, consternation drawing his brows together. Then something else caught his attention and his head jerked towards…

A little yellow Jeep being propelled into view from behind the cubbyhouse.

In the driver's seat was a little girl wearing a pretty pink hat printed with yellow flowers. The Jeep had no pedals. It was pushed forward by little feet in pink sandals. Clearly the child had got the hang of making the wheels take her where she wanted to go and she headed straight towards Carver with a very proficient scooting motion. She stopped the Jeep in front of him, opened the door and stepped out, looking very cute in a pink singlet and a pink skirt printed with yellow flowers—a perfect match for the hat.

Carver's gaze was now fixed on the child. He set his glass of beer down on the serving bench beside the barbecue grill as the little girl yanked her hat off and handed it up to him.

"I don't want to wear this, Daddy," she said very clearly.

He took it and bent down to scoop the child up in his arms.

It was Katie staring now…staring at a mass of black spiral curls, shorter than her own, but exactly the kind of hair she'd had as a child. With a weird sense of déjà-vu, she watched Carver settle the little girl against his shoulder. She had photos of herself with her father, posed just like that, the curls spilling around her face like an uncontrollable mop.

Katie's heart turned over.

This child could be her!

Or her daughter!

Then she remembered Carver saying that her hair wasn't unique…only her breasts. Other women had hair like hers. And since she hadn't given birth to this child and Carver's hair was not curly, then the birth mother…Nina…Nina who had been only too ready to hand when Katie hadn't responded to his letter…Nina with the same hair!

She felt sick.

''There's someone I want you to meet, Susannah,'' she heard Carver say, the words ringing hollowly in her ears.

He started walking towards Katie and the child turned her head, looking directly at her…definitely Carver's child; big dark brown eyes, straight neat nose, lips that were emphatically delineated though in a softer, more feminine mould. Katie knew she should acknowledge Carver but she couldn't tear her gaze from his daughter…with the hair like her own.

''Got to speak to those boys in the pool,'' Amanda said, unlinking herself from Katie and shooting off, obviously deciding this meeting could go ahead without her.

She was right to leave.

A spate of bright banter would have been intolerable.

Katie stood like a stone statue, unable to muster even a semblance of social geniality. Carver came to a halt directly in front of her, the child in his arms eyeing Katie with an expression of fascinated curiosity, probably wondering why the strange woman was staring at her as though she saw a ghost.

"Hello, Katie."

Carver's greeting forced her gaze up. His eyes burned into hers with a defiant pride that rang a host of alarm bells. She would lose him if she didn't respond with some positive warmth. The test she'd anticipated—so mistakenly—was here and now and if she failed it, there'd never be another chance.

"This is...a surprise," she desperately excused herself, somehow managing to construct a rueful little smile.

"Yes. Quite a surprise," he agreed. "This is my daughter, Susannah."

Katie flashed a brighter smile at the child. "Hello, Susannah."

"Hello," came the shy reply. "This is my daddy."

"I know."

And the knowledge hurt...hurt more than Katie had ever imagined it would...because she could have been this child's mother...and would have been if only her path and Carver's had crossed at the right time.

CHAPTER TWELVE

"JUICE or wine, Katie?" Max called out, emerging from the kitchen with the freshly filled pitcher of fruit juice and holding it aloft.

Grateful for the distraction, she quickly answered, "Juice for me, thanks Max."

"Coming right up." He turned to a serving table where clean glasses and plastic tumblers were set out and started pouring. "What about you, Susannah? Are you thirsty? All that driving around in the Jeep is hot work."

"Yes. Hot work," she repeated, nodding agreement.

"Need a refill on the beer, Carver?"

"No, I'm fine."

He brought over a glass for Katie and a tumbler for Susannah, smiling at all three of them. "Robert told me it was you who gave the green light to Katie's taxi service, Carver, and Amanda tells me she's been a slave to it ever since she started up."

"I did warn her it would be very demanding," Carver answered easily.

"I don't mind being busy," Katie put in, trying desperately to get her shattered mind to focus on carrying off this meeting with some grace.

"Well, it's a good day to put your feet up and laze away a few hours. Come and sit down." He herded them towards an unoccupied table under one of the pergolas. ''Maybe you should check up on how your investment's doing, Carver,'' he ran on. ''Katie's probably bursting to brag about how successful her idea has been.''

''I'm glad to hear it,'' Carver said obligingly.

''Good! Take a chair. I'll go and fetch your beer from the barbecue.''

Having been deftly paired by their hosts, even given the prompt to a ready conversation, Katie and Carver settled at the table assigned to them, obliging guests who followed the leads handed out to them. Except Carver knew all about the progress of her business and Katie was hopelessly fixated on his daughter.

He set the child on her feet and turned her towards the barbecue. ''Better go and get the Jeep, Susannah. Drive it over here so you can show Katie how well you can do it.''

She put the tumbler on the table, flashed Katie a big-eyed look, clearly wanting her interest, then ran off to follow her father's suggestion. Katie watched the curls bobbing, her mind too much of a mess to even think of saying anything.

''It seems our hostess fancies a bit of matchmaking,'' Carver dryly remarked.

''Yes.'' Her cheeks bloomed with hot embarrassment. She couldn't bring herself to look at him. She gabbled a jerky explanation of the situation. ''Amanda and I are old friends. I was on her table at the masked ball. She was trying to pair me off there.''

''Ah!'' A pause. ''Does she know I was the buccaneer at the ball?''

''I don't think so. I haven't told her.''

Silence. Katie imagined speculation was rife in Carver's mind. She felt driven to say, ''Amanda means well, arranging this opportunity for us to get together socially. She has no idea we're lovers.''

But not lovers at the right time, she thought on a wave of bleak misery, her gaze fastened on the daughter who wasn't hers. Susannah manually turned the Jeep around, then seated herself behind the driving wheel with an air of taking proper control. She smiled at Katie, a bright eager plea to be watched, and as Katie automatically smiled back, an assurance of full attention, she pushed off with her feet, steering the toy vehicle across the playing area to the cubbyhouse.

There she alighted, reached into one of the window seats inside the cubby, lifted out a red plastic cylinder, loaded it into the back compartment of the Jeep, then resumed driving the rest of the way to the table where Katie sat with her father. Out she popped again, grabbed the cylinder and carried it over to Katie. She picked out a plastic letter and offered it to her.

''This is an A,'' she announced proudly.

Katie took it, pretending to examine it. ''So it is. An A,'' she repeated in pleased affirmation.

''And it's red.''

Katie nodded agreement. ''Yes, it's red.''

''That's 'cause A is for apple and apples are red.''

''That's true. How clever you are to know that.''

Susannah beamed delight and produced another letter. ''This is a Y, and it's yellow, 'cause Y is for yellow.''

Katie accepted it with an air of surprise. ''Do you know all the letters of the alphabet, Susannah?''

She nodded. ''Daddy taught me.''

Daddy... Katie took a quick breath to counter the pain in her heart. ''It's very good that you can remember them. Do you want to show me another?''

''Yes.''

The cylinder was being gradually emptied when Max interrupted the game. ''Come on, all you kids! The sausages are cooked. Time to eat!''

''Out of the pool, you boys,'' Amanda instantly commanded, opening the safety gate for them to exit. ''You can bring your towels with you to dry off.''

Her four-year-old son was first through the gate and was instructed by his mother, ''You can go and collect Susannah and help her get some lunch, Nick.''

''Okay!'' He spotted the three of them and his face lit up. ''Hi, Katie! Did you see me diving?''

''Big splash!'' she replied with a smile.

He laughed and turned back to his companions. ''Hey, guys! Katie's here!''

His loud announcement spotlighted her to several of the children whom she regularly transported to play centres, instantly drawing them to where she sat. They all clamoured for her attention, wanting to tell her what they'd been doing.

''One at a time,'' she instructed, ''and let's go and have some sausages.'' She stood up, holding out her hand to Susannah. ''Do you want to come with us?''

She nodded, eagerly grasping the offered hand, and they all set off to the barbecue.

Behind them Amanda stepped in to attend to

Carver, saying, "Katie's like the pied piper of Hamelin. Children will follow her anywhere."

His reply was lost in the lively chatter being aimed at her. Not that it mattered. Amanda was being rather heavy-handed in driving home the obvious. It was true that most children took to her. Mostly it was about accepting them on their level and giving approval, paying attention to them, projecting an interest that made them feel like people worth knowing.

As a nanny, she'd found a lot of adults—and parents—couldn't be bothered. It was like—when they grow up they might be worth listening to. And, of course, time was a factor. Caring for little children took up a great deal of time and no one seemed to have enough of it these days.

Carver obviously didn't fall into that category. The child holding her hand was very much cared for. *Daddy taught me.* Katie imagined he gave his daughter all the time he had between his work and when she was finally bedded down at night. It wasn't until Susannah was asleep that he ever came to Katie's apartment.

This child—who could have been hers—came first in Carver's life. As she should. But seeing them together made Katie feel even more sidelined. They were a unit while she…well, she was obviously good for sex but it was now painfully apparent she was not needed for anything else.

She helped Susannah get her lunch—two sausages with tomato sauce, some potato salad, a bread roll, all on an unbreakable plastic plate—then directed her back to her father.

The little girl hesitated, big eyes appealing. "You come, too?"

"When I've finished helping the other children," Katie excused, needing time to paste a social demeanour over the pain. "You go on now," she added persuasively. "Your daddy will cut up the sausages for you."

She trotted off, assured Katie would follow eventually, a very biddable child, and completely innocent of doing any wrong against her, Katie savagely reminded herself. Susannah had not asked to be born and she had every right to be loved by her father. *Every right!*

"You don't have to help, Katie," Amanda muttered in her ear. "I'll fix up the kids." She gave her a nudge. "Go on back to Carver."

"I don't want to," she stated flatly.

Amanda frowned at her. "Why not?"

"Just let me have some space, Amanda." She flashed her a fierce warning. "Stop pushing. I'll work it out my own way."

Inevitably all the children were served with as much lunch as they wanted, and short of snubbing Carver and his daughter altogether, which would be hopelessly wrong in the context of forging any kind of future with either of them, Katie had no choice but to join them again and try to make something positive out of this day. She put a scoop of strawberry ice-cream into a plastic bowl for Susannah and took it across to the table where they were seated.

"Do you have room in your tummy for this?" she asked the little girl, setting the bowl down in front of her.

An eager nod and a big smile as Katie sat down with them.

''Say thank you, Susannah,'' Carver gently instructed.

''Thank you,'' she repeated shyly.

Max promptly descended on them with two wineglasses and flourishing a bottle of chardonnay. ''A reward for your labours, Katie,'' he declared, pouring her a glass. ''Carver?''

''Yes. Thanks, Max.''

Alcohol couldn't smooth this path, Katie thought sardonically, wondering if Amanda had worded up her husband on tensions to be eased.

''Steaks are sizzling now. Won't be long before we eat,'' he cheerfully informed them before heading off to look after his other guests.

Susannah was digging into the ice-cream.

''Don't feel awkward, Katie,'' Carver quietly advised. ''I don't mind our meeting like this.''

She looked him straight in the eye and couldn't stop herself from saying, ''But it wasn't on your agenda, was it, Carver? In fact, you could have invited me to accompany you here if you'd wanted to. You know I have Sundays free.''

''Which you usually spend with your father,'' he countered, his eyes cooling.

Her father, who had subjected him to irrational and brutal violence when they were last face to face. And no apology had ever been extended.

''I've told him about our…our coming together again. I'm not hiding you from him,'' Katie blurted out, wanting to clear the air on that score.

He looked surprised. ''You've told him?''

''Yes.''

His brows creased into a V as he considered what this might mean—like their affair was not quite as private as he had believed, as he probably wanted it. The urge to press him on that point was suddenly compelling.

''My father no longer has any objection to a relationship between us,'' she stated, watching to see what that piece of news stirred.

Carver's mouth curled cynically. ''He no longer has any grounds for the accusations he once made.''

''No, he doesn't,'' she agreed, flushing at his response and defensively asking, ''What about your mother? Have you told her about me?''

His eyes glittered a challenge. ''What is there to tell, Katie?''

''That I'm part of your life again.''

''How much a part?'' He gestured to the guests around them. ''These people are obviously more your friends than mine. They would have been happy for you to bring someone. Just as they're happy to see you with me now. So why didn't *you* invite *me* to accompany you here today?''

The implication was that he still wasn't good enough for her, which was so terribly wrong—it had always been wrong!—Katie was instantly stung into attacking *his* motives.

''Because you hadn't made any attempt to make me a part of your family, Carver.'' She nodded to his daughter who was still thankfully occupied with her ice-cream. ''And right now I feel your hand has been forced beyond where you wanted it to go.''

''That works both ways, Katie.''

What did he mean? Did he imagine she was content with the occasional sex on the side? That she didn't want the commitment of a relationship that would demand more from her than just going to bed with him when it was convenient to both of them?

''I don't mind your being here, Carver,'' she said quickly, disturbed by the impression his comment had evoked.

Again his mouth curled. ''You're not exactly demonstrating pleasure in my company.''

''I wasn't sure how welcome I was.''

''Do you want to be welcome…'' His gaze flicked to Susannah and moved back to hers with a sharper intensity. ''…to my family?''

''Yes,'' Katie stated unequivocally, defying the emotional turmoil stirred by his daughter and the prospect of meeting his mother again.

''Will you invite me to meet your father?''

''Yes,'' she answered without hesitation. ''Any time you like.''

For several long, nerve-racking moments his eyes studied the belligerent determination in hers. Katie was not about to back down. She'd thrown the ball well and truly into his court now. It was up to him to answer.

''I hope you realise what these decisions mean, Katie,'' he said with slow deliberation. ''Other lives get touched by them, not just yours and mine.''

He was prevaricating, probably wanting them to stay private lovers, but the closed doors had been opened today and Katie didn't want to be locked back into that restricted space.

''You face those decisions, too, Carver,'' she pointedly retorted, resolved on assessing how much she was worth to him.

Yet when his answer finally came, what it told her was something else entirely, something that rolled back the years and silenced any further argument.

''I just hope you're sure, Katie. Very, very sure... *this time.*'

It was in his eyes...the memory of how she had run away when the going got tough. She had claimed to love him then, but what was love worth if it didn't stand fast, for better or for worse? Neither of them had declared *love* this time around. It was an empty word unless it was surrounded by proof of it.

She would show him, Katie fiercely resolved. She would set up a meeting with her father. Regardless of how his mother reacted to her, she would somehow win Lillian Danc over. As for his daughter...

''I'm finished,'' Susannah declared, catching Katie's eye on her and putting her spoon into the emptied bowl with elaborate care.

Katie smiled. ''I think you must really like strawberry ice-cream.''

The little girl nodded. ''Strawberries, too. Daddy buys them for me.'' She looked at her father. ''They're good for me, aren't they, Daddy?''

His smile bestowed both love and approval. ''Yes, they are.''

Amanda swept in and picked up the bowl. ''Had enough or would you like some more, Susannah?''

''Enough, thank you.''

''Good!'' A bright hostess smile was directed at Katie and Carver. ''Now that the children have eaten, we're going to join some tables together to make one big party for the adults. Will you give us a hand with them, Carver?''

''Of course.''

Which neatly broke up their twosome in case it was not as harmonious as Amanda had hoped. Katie definitely had to give her friend credit for tact and grace. As soon as the tables were rearranged to her satisfaction, she ensured that Katie and Carver were seated with other people on either side, as well as across from them so conversation could be turned wherever they chose. Clearly this was to diffuse any one-on-one tension.

They were served with a veritable barbecue feast; big platters of steaks, sausages and fried onions, baked potatoes split and heaped with sour cream and chives, a variety of popular salads, foccacio bread, warm and crusty from the oven. It should have been wonderfully appetising but Katie found it difficult to do justice to it.

Despite the ready distraction of interesting chat, witty remarks, and clever jokes, with Carver demonstrating he more than held his own in this company, her mind kept fretting over his lack of trust in her staying power, and the more she thought about it, the more unfair that judgement seemed.

It was a long time ago...what had happened when she was nineteen, only one year out of school and still living with her father who'd been the dominant influence in her young life. She was ten years older now, with obvious proof she was of an independent mind, making big decisions for herself and having the strength of purpose to go through with them.

Increasing her inner angst was the endearing yet

tormenting presence of his daughter. All during lunch Susannah kept popping up beside her chair to show her something, choosing to bask more in Katie's attention than in her father's. It hurt. It hurt more all the time, because Carver had committed himself to this child, and because of her, considered committing himself to Katie a risk he was wary of taking.

A sweets course was served. Platters of cheese accompanied coffee. The party at the table broke up somewhat as some parents attended to their children's needs. Susannah was obviously tired, climbing up on Carver's lap and resting her head on his chest—father and daughter.

But she didn't close her eyes. She gazed fixedly at Katie, not saying anything, seemingly content just to see her seated right next to them. There were lulls in the general conversation now, with people moving around more. In one such lull, they were left to themselves and Katie simply couldn't summon the will to break the silence with inconsequential chat. Mentally and emotionally she'd been stretched too far today.

She sat, gazing blindly at the swimming pool until she felt a tug on her sleeve. It was a child's hand, wanting to draw her attention. Until she turned to look, she didn't realise it was Susannah's. The little girl had stirred from her resting position, leaning over from Carver's lap, clearly wanting to quiz Katie on something. There was a hesitant shyness in her big eyes, yet an imploring look behind the uncertainty.

Katie managed one more encouraging smile.

It worked.

The little girl rushed into speech.

"Are you my mummy?"

The soft question was asked so innocently, so appealingly, it pierced Katie's heart with devastating force. Her eyes filled with tears and an impassable lump lodged in her throat.

''Susannah...'' Carver's voice was gruff. ''I told you your mummy had gone to heaven.''

She turned her face up to his. ''But you said she had hair like mine, Daddy. And I heard you say to Katie...'' She frowned, trying to make sense of it. ''...about coming into our family this time.''

Katie pushed back her chair and stood up. She couldn't bear this, couldn't bear to hear how Carver would explain it away. She swallowed hard. Impossible to stop the gush of tears but she managed to speak.

''I'll leave you to sort it out, Carver...with your daughter.''

He was a blur. Everything was a blur as she fled, too helplessly distressed to stay at the party or even stop to excuse herself to Amanda or Max.

It wasn't until she was almost back at North Sydney that it occurred to her she was running away again, but it was too late to turn back. Probably too late for everything.

Too early...too late...

It summed up the whole story of her love for Carver Dane.

CHAPTER THIRTEEN

CARVER'S gaze darted to the dashboard clock as he backed the Audi out of his garage, hand clutching the lever, ready to change gears the moment he was on the street. Almost half past five—over two hours since Katie had left the barbecue party in tears.

He savagely wished he'd been free to pursue her much earlier, but he couldn't just dump Susannah, nor subject her to the burning issues between him and Katie when she was the focus of them. No, he'd had to deal with her first. He could only hope he wasn't too late to fix things with Katie now.

He swung the car in the right direction and pressed the accelerator, telling himself to control the urge to speed, though he couldn't help feeling control was his enemy. It was eating up time, like the control it had taken to explain to his daughter about Nina and Katie, to make excuses to the Fairweathers for Katie's abrupt departure, to extricate himself from their well-meaning clutches.

Then having to call Susannah's off-duty nanny, pleading an emergency and getting her to come and stay the night, brushing off his mother's shock at his announcement that Katie Beaumont needed him and he was going to her…it had all taken time which his instincts were warning he could ill afford.

He drove as fast as the legal limit would allow,

knowing if he was stopped for speeding, it would delay him further. And there'd been too many delays already. More critical ones than a traffic policeman would cause.

A thousand times he'd thought of introducing Katie to his daughter. If only he'd done it, this crisis would have been avoided. And he had no excuses. Not now. The truth was he'd fed himself doubts about the wisdom of letting any attachment form on Susannah's side.

After all, Katie had claimed her top priority was getting her business running successfully. Proving her idea was worthwhile to her father had seemed second on the list. Besides which, it had seemed eminently clear that getting married and having children were not on her agenda. It had been all too easy to argue what possible good could come from introducing the child he'd had with another woman.

Wrong! Wrong, wrong, wrong!

Today…so many things she'd said today strongly indicated she had wanted more involvement with him all along, that her relationship with him had been more important to her than anything else.

The pain on her face…the tears in her eyes…

His hands clenched around the steering wheel as he cursed his blindness in settling for what had seemed readily available instead of reaching for more. She'd *wanted* more. And he hadn't even offered it, let alone given it.

The only thing going right for him at the present moment was the traffic lights—all green so far. If he got a red light from Katie, he had no one to blame but himself.

Pride…that had played its part, too. Her father's social prejudice against him had tainted his thoughts about Katie's view of him—fine to take as a lover on the side as long as he didn't assume a prominent position in her life.

Given what she'd said today, that couldn't be true.

And if he was totally honest with himself, there'd been pride behind his vacillation over introducing Susannah to Katie. It was so obvious Nina had shared a superficial resemblance—the hair!—even a three-year-old child had made the link, thinking Katie might really be her mother. He hadn't wanted to lay himself open so far, revealing such an *obsession* with her.

Damnable pride!

For all he knew, it could have been pride that had made Katie dismiss a desire for marriage and children. At their meeting in his office, she could not possibly have foreseen any relationship developing with him. It had been nothing but business being discussed then.

But there'd been no pride in the eyes that had filled with tears this afternoon…tears that had welled because she was not the mother of his daughter. She had missed out, and was still missing out…would always miss out because he hadn't waited for her.

Had that silent, grief-stricken accusation been behind her tears or had his own sense of guilt read it into her pain? All he truly knew was the depth of pain had been very real and he had caused it. Not

Susannah. She was a complete innocent in all of this. *He* had driven away the only woman he'd ever wanted and somehow he had to win her back.

He glanced at the dashboard clock again as he turned into her street. Eight minutes. Record time. He probably had exceeded the speed limit on the way. No matter. He was safely here.

Determination pounded through him as he parked the car, alighting quickly and heading for her apartment door at a swift stride. *It's not too late,* he fiercely told himself. *I won't let it be too late!*

His thumb depressed the doorbell button for several seconds, the urgency he felt driving him to an emphatic summons. He rocked impatiently on his heels when the door remained closed longer than seemed reasonable. A pang of uncertainty hit him. What if she hadn't come home? He had assumed she would.

He backtracked to the foyer of the apartment block to scan the street outside. His tension eased slightly when he spotted the vehicle she called her people-mover, parked in a side lane. She had to be home, possibly too distressed to open up to anyone.

Intensely disturbed by this thought, Carver returned to her door and pressed the bell again, hoping that persistence might pay off. It didn't. Not only was there no response, but he couldn't hear any sound of occupation, either. The silence started to worry him. Badly.

He thumped on the door with his fist with no more success than he'd had with the doorbell. Wild thoughts jangled through his mind. ''Katie!'' he shouted, banging harder. It occurred to him that she wouldn't be expecting *him* to come by at this hour. He never had before.

"Katie, it's me, Carver!" he yelled, thumping with both fists. "If you don't open up, I'm going to smash this door down!"

The threat was driven by the fear of not getting the chance to fix things between them and he kept bashing at the door until he heard the metallic click of the deadlock being operated. His chest was heaving and he struggled for some purposeful composure as the door opened…to the short span of the safety chain.

There was no face peering out at him. All he saw was a sliver of empty space inside her apartment. Sheer instinct jammed his foot in the small opening, protecting what little territory he'd won until he could think of how else to achieve what he needed to do.

"What do you want, Carver?"

Dull, flat words, half muffled by the door. She was standing behind it, out of any possible line of vision, obviously avoiding eye contact with him.

He took a deep breath, the memory of her tears vivid in his mind, the need to soothe her pain pumping through his heart. "We have to talk, Katie. Let me in."

All his senses were acutely alert now, aware that this was a battleground and he was fighting for his life with Katie Beaumont. His ears picked up the soft shudder of a sigh.

"I don't feel like talking, Carver. And I don't feel like anything else with you, either. You've had a wasted trip."

He would not accept defeat, yet he could not force

her to accept his presence. Persuasion was the only course he had. Yet the words that came expressed the sudden desolation he felt rather than reaching for some possible soft spot that could be tapped in his favour.

"Is it *all* wasted, Katie?"

Heart-squeezing silence.

Stupid, stupid question, Carver railed at himself, accentuating negatives instead of something positive. But what was positive? On the whole, he had come here to have sex with her and she certainly didn't want that now.

"If you don't feel like talking, that's fine," he said in a softer, hopefully soothing voice. "If you'll just listen… Please? I know I've kept too much back. I'd like to put things right between us, Katie."

"Right for what, Carver?" came the weary question. "I won't be your hidden mistress anymore."

Hidden mistress? He mentally recoiled from the demeaning image…yet wasn't that how he'd treated her?

"You can talk until you're blue in the face and it won't change my mind," she went on, her voice carrying a bitter strength. "And if you think touching me will win you anything…"

"No!" he cut in, anguished by her certainty that he'd only ever wanted sex with her and he was intent on continuing down that path. "I just want to explain to you… Susannah…my mother…all the things you brought up today. I'm sorry I've made you think as you do, Katie. It was wrong…and I want to turn that around."

"Wrong?" she echoed, and he didn't know if it was disbelief, derision, or simple uncertainty wavering through her voice.

"I think I've been wrong about a lot of things," he plunged on. "I need you to tell me, Katie. Set me straight."

Another tense silence.

"Then let it be just talking, Carver," she warned, her tone harshly decisive.

"Yes," he swiftly agreed, removing his foot from the gap it had seized.

She closed the door to release the safety chain, then opened it again, allowing him entry. And that was all it was—a permission, not an invitation. She had retreated from the door before he realised he was to push it open himself. By the time he stepped inside and closed it behind him, she was right across the other side of her living room, her back rigidly turned to him.

He stood still, watching her sit on the edge of the bed where they had shared so many physical pleasures. She was still wearing the clothes she had worn to the barbecue, just as he was. No thought of changing. Thoughts too focused inwards. She wrapped her arms around her midriff, hugging herself to herself, then lifted her head and glared defiance at him.

It sure as hell was not an invitation to join her on the bed!

Carver made no movement whatsoever. The burning question was—how to reach across the distance that now lay between them? It bristled with dangerous pitfalls and any step might mean death to what he wanted. Very slowly he gestured an open-handed appeal, then spoke what was true to him.

''I never thought of you as my hidden mistress, Katie. To me it was like having a little world of our own, where nothing else intruded. Where nothing could harm it. There was...just us.''

Her mouth curled. ''A private love-nest.''

''Yes.''

''For the purpose of pursuing strictly sexual desires,'' she mocked. ''I might as well have been a whore except you didn't have to pay anything.''

''On the same basis, I could have considered myself your gigolo,'' he retorted, stung by her interpretation of what they'd shared.

Her mouth thinned. Her lashes lowered. The negative jerk of her head expressed disgust at his lack of understanding. Carver instantly realised his mistake. This was not about scoring points off each other. It was about correcting what was wrong.

''I'm sorry. I guess I wanted to believe it was mutually satisfying.''

She said nothing. Her gaze remained lowered. Splotches of colour bloomed on her cheeks. He sensed she was hating being reminded of how *sexual* their relationship had been and quickly changed tack to the far more important issue.

''Susannah liked you very much.''

Again her mouth curled. ''It's my one talent...an affinity with children. I've based my business on it.''

Business!

No, he was not going to let that cloud his vision

now! It was a red herring to the critical issue of his daughter.

"How did you feel about her, Katie?" he asked softly, not wanting to cause more distress, yet needing some hint as to whether she could bear a close involvement with Susannah.

She bit her lips. Her thick lashes hid her eyes. Carver suspected tears might be hovering again and cursed his lack of positive action on this front.

"I know it was a shock, seeing her without any warning," he said on a rueful sigh. "If the meeting had been planned, I would have prepared you for…the likeness. Prepared both you and Susannah. She would have known you weren't her mother."

Still, she didn't look up or speak. Her hands clutched her arms more tightly. Hugging in the pain?

What could he do? What could he say to take it away? There was only the truth to hold out to her.

"I wish you were, Katie. In fact, how Susannah was conceived… I went to a party and through an alcoholic glaze, Nina looked like you. It was like… like a substitution…through a dark dream. That's how it happened and I can't take it back. But there's not a day goes past that I don't look at my daughter and think of you, wishing the situation had been different."

She raised tear-washed eyes. "Do you, Carver? Do you really?"

Her torment ripped away the last shreds of pride. "Yes. I've always wished it."

"Then why?" Her anguished cry left no doubt

about how she felt. ''Why have you kept her from me all this time?''

He took a deep breath, fighting the urge to charge over to the bed, sweep her up in his arms and hold her tight, giving all the physical comfort he could impart. Such an action was too open to misinterpetration to follow it through. The touching had to be done with words. Yet he didn't have them. Only a welter of feelings that had swirled and tugged like a treacherous undertow, most of them unexamined.

''Lots of reasons,'' he muttered, trying to find the sense of what he'd felt. ''Hangovers from the past. A misconception of what you wanted.'' It was all he could offer and he shook his head over the paucity of the explanation. ''None of it is relevant anymore, Katie.''

She sighed and looked bleakly at him. ''So what is relevant, Carver?''

He had that answer ready. It had been building to a certainty from the moment she had cared enough to overcome her shock and be kind to Susannah.

''Whether we can get it together so it can be right for us this time,'' he said purposefully. ''All of it right. As far as it's humanly possible.''

''And what does that entail for you?'' she asked, the bleak expression still holding sway as she wryly added, ''You haven't even told your mother...''

''Yes, I have. She knows I'm here with you. And she is well aware of how important it is to me...to keep you in my life.''

Surprise lent a spark of life to her face. ''You told her?''

"Yes."

"How did she react?"

"It doesn't matter how she reacts. It doesn't change anything for me where you're concerned." He paused, frowning over her fixation on his mother. "It never did, Katie. Not the first time around and certainly not now."

A startled wonderment accompanied the slight shake of her head. There were definitely hangovers from the past on her side, as well, Carver decided. However, only action was going to resolve them now.

"Would you accept an invitation to my home for lunch next Sunday?" he said impulsively.

"Lunch? You mean…with your mother and daughter?"

"Yes. Unless you'd prefer…some other arrangement."

She looked uncertain.

"My mother has a self-contained apartment within the house. She won't mind if…"

"No. No, I *want* to meet her," she said with an air of grim decision.

He sensed it was a big hurdle for her and it was a measure of her wanting their relationship to continue that she was prepared to face it. At last he was winning some ground here. Even if it was only a testing ground.

"So you'll come?" he pressed.

Her brow creased anxiously as she considered the invitation. "Did I upset Susannah this afternoon? Is she worried that I…"

"No. She understands that she was wrong and

thinks you'd be just as good as her real mother anyway.''

Tears blurred her eyes again. ''She's a lovely child, Carver. A credit to you…the way you've brought her up,'' she said jerkily.

''She would like to see you again, Katie. Do you mind…too much?''

Slowly she shook her head, then managed a rueful little smile. ''Life happens. We just have to accept it and make the best of what we're dealt, don't we?''

''You managed admirably today. And I thank you for it.''

She sat there, looking at him as though she was not quite sure how much to believe of this turnaround of attitude and direction. The fragility of the lifeline he'd hung out made him acutely aware of how vulnerable she was in her hope for something better between them.

And she was hoping.

He had achieved that much.

Carver again fought the urge to grab her up and make wild tempestuous love until she was thoroughly convinced nothing could ever separate them again. The problem was, he doubted she would be convinced, not by physical means. Best to get her away from the temptation of that bed.

''Why don't we go for a walk, Katie?'' he suggested. ''It's a pleasant evening for a stroll and there's a whole row of pavement cafés and restaurants along Miller Street. We could stop somewhere to eat when we feel hungry.''

She looked stunned. "You're...asking me to go out with you?"

Carver gritted his teeth as the phrase—*hidden mistress*—hit home with a vengeance. What had he done to her in his own blind selfish desire to hold her to himself?

"Would you like to? I noticed you didn't eat much at the Fairweathers' lunch party."

"No. I..." She jumped up from the bed, looking flustered, one hand lifting to her hair. "I'll need to tidy up a bit."

"Take your time. I'm happy to wait."

She hesitated, her gaze directly meeting his. "Thank you. I would like a walk."

He smiled his pleasure in her agreement and won a tentative smile back. Then she was heading for the bathroom and Carver was heaving a huge sigh of relief. There was serious damage to be undone before they could move forward, but at least he had reached her.

He glanced at the bed. No more, he vowed. Not until he'd given Katie a true sense of her worth to him.

He opened the door and stepped out to the corridor that bisected the block of apartments, making his intentions absolutely clear. No lingering in her apartment. No hiding anything. He was taking her wherever she wanted to go, giving her whatever she fancied, telling her whatever she wanted to know. This was *her* night.

When she joined him a few minutes later, her face was shiny from having been washed, her mouth was shiny from a fresh application of lipstick, and her eyes were shiny…but not with tears. He read hope in them and the tension tearing at his guts eased.

She locked the door behind them, put her key in the shoulder-bag she'd collected for the outing, and turned to him with an air of knowing she was taking a risk but not knowing what else to do.

He held out his hand to her.

She looked at it, then slowly, almost shyly, slid her own hand into its keeping.

Trust, Carver thought, begins with this.

CHAPTER FOURTEEN

ANOTHER Sunday...and this one loaded with as much hope and fear as the last, Katie thought, dithering over what to wear for the critical meeting with Lillian Dane.

It was all very well for Carver to say his mother's reaction didn't matter. Katie did not find it so easy to shrug off the weight of disapproval she had always felt coming from the older woman. Not just felt, either. There had been words spoken that were etched in her memory.

Admittedly that had all been ten years ago, and circumstances had changed, so she shouldn't be stressing out about it, yet Lillian Danc's attitude towards her had cut so deeply, influencing actions that had altered the course of her life, Katie could never forget that. She wasn't even sure she could forgive it. But she *would* try to let bygones be bygones if Carver's mother demonstrated a true willingness to accept her as a fixture in her son's life.

Approval was probably asking too much.

Nevertheless, the need for it swayed Katie into deciding on a modest little dress. The simple A-line shift was black but printed with colourful little flowers—red, pink, violet, yellow and white—making it bright and summery. The mix of colours made it practical for wearing around children, who were apt to have grubby hands at times. It certainly couldn't be called a flashy or sexy or stylishly *rich.* The little girls she regularly transported had said it was pretty.

Maybe Susannah would think it pretty, too.

She stepped into the dress and zipped it up, smiling over Carver's assurance that his daughter was looking forward with great excitement to seeing her again today. All the negative feelings she'd had about the child were gone. As Carver had said, he couldn't take back what had happened, but his wishing his daughter was hers…that made such a huge difference. She didn't feel…*cut out*…anymore.

Not on any level.

Which still amazed her.

Everything was so different.

Having slid her feet into the pink sandals she'd bought to go with her fuschia jeans and checked that they looked all right with the dress, she headed for the bathroom to put on make-up and tidy her hair, proceeding to perform these tasks automatically as the events of the past week kept teasing her mind.

No sex.

She could hardly believe it.

Twice Carver had taken her out to dinner—last Sunday evening and again on Thursday night. Nothing really fancy. She didn't have time for dress-ups during the week. But it had been so nice strolling out together, choosing a place to eat, sharing a casual meal and a bottle of wine…just like any normal couple who enjoyed each other's company.

Best of all, Carver had opened up about areas of his life he'd kept from her before. She hadn't known his initial move into the landscaping business had been triggered by the urgent need for money—fast and big money—to meet the costs of his mother's rehabilitation from a paralysing stroke, the equipment and medical care she needed if there was to be any chance of recovery.

It had happened just a few weeks after Katie had gone to England. In just a few seconds everything had changed. His mother could no longer work. Without her wage coming in, he had to bear the whole financial burden of keeping a home for her to come back to, as well as assuming the responsibility for her recovery. The circumstances were such that even considering pursuing a medical degree was unrealistic.

Working hard, helping his mother, and never any word from the girl he had loved, the girl who'd run away when everything had turned too difficult for her to handle—Katie marvelled that he had ever come to England to look her up. Then no response to his letter…

She understood so much more now, even why he'd kept all this from her. In a way, she hadn't deserved his confidence. And there was pain attached to almost every connection with her. Perhaps that was why he had sought only pleasure with her…a need to balance the scales.

The question he'd asked through her door last week—*Is it all wasted?*—had echoed what she had felt in her heart.

Carver didn't want to let it go any more than she did, and he was trying very hard to make a new start with her, opening the doors into his life for her to enter if she wanted to, offering her the choice, not assuming anything or taking anything for granted.

She was still coming to terms with the sense of freedom it gave her with him. It was so good to feel there weren't any barriers between them. Except those in her own mind. It was now up to her to try hard, too. Today, with his mother. The past had to be buried if they were really looking at a future together.

Satisfied that she had achieved a readily *acceptable* appearance for the critical eyes of Lillian Dane, Katie took a deep breath to settle her fluttering nerves and set about collecting the items she wanted to take with her. She put her lipstick and hairbrush in her shoulder-bag which she laid, ready to hand, on the kitchen counter, then dealt with the pretty bunch of spring flowers she had bought as a peace gift to Carver's mother.

The doorbell rang just as she finished tying a ribbon around the cone of tissue paper. Cradling the bouquet in one arm and slinging the strap of her bag over her shoulder, Katie told herself to approach this meeting with smiling confidence, knowing she had Carver's support. Which his mother had to know, as well. And it was ten years down the track. So it shouldn't go wrong.

Nevertheless, her heart was pitter-pattering as she opened the door. To her surprise, it wasn't only Carver who'd come to collect her. Susannah was holding his hand, looking absolutely adorable in a lime green top and a white bib and braces skirt outfit, printed with violets. Her big brown eyes sparkled excitement at Katie, who instantly forgot Lillian Dane in the pleasure of this child's pleasure in seeing her.

A bubble of inner delight instantly spread into a smile. "Hello, Susannah!"

A big smile back. "Hello, Katie."

"I wasn't expecting you to come for me, too."

"Daddy said I could."

"Waiting was beyond her," Carver said dryly. "Ready to go?"

"Yes."

Somehow Susannah's presence made everything easier. The car trip to Hunters Hill in a Volvo station wagon felt like a family affair with conversation flowing from the front seats to Susannah holding forth from her special seat in the back, a much more confident child in a familiar environment, with her father in obvious control of the situation. Carver's relaxed manner was infectious, and Katie found herself laughing along with him at Susannah's artless enthusiasm in engaging Katie's attention.

Several times she caught herself remembering the old days when laughter had been part and parcel of their relationship—having fun together. Laughter and love should go hand in hand, she thought, sharing joy. *This* was champagne, far more so than great sex, though glancing at Carver in his physique-hugging, cotton knit white shirt, and the blue jeans stretching around his powerful thighs, the physical desire he stirred was as strong as ever.

She shouldn't be thinking about it—especially when he was exercising restraint to prove she meant more than a convenient sexual pleasure to him. But it was difficult not to be aware of his attractive masculinity and all it promised on a physical level. He didn't have to keep holding back, she decided. It *was* different now. Though there was still the meeting with his mother ahead of her.

She loved Carver's home at first sight, a long sprawling redbrick house set on large landscaped grounds. It looked friendly, welcoming, not the least bit intimidating though she realised it represented a very solid financial investment. Carver drove straight into a garage big enough for three cars, and they used a connecting door to enter the house.

As he ushered Katie into a well-appointed kitchen, he urged his daughter forward. ''Run ahead, Susannah, and tell Nanna we're here.''

The little girl was only too eager to carry the news, which allowed them some private time together. Katie glanced at him, nervous now at not quite knowing what to expect.

He smiled, his eyes caressing her with warmth. ''You look beautiful, Katie. I just wanted to assure you my mother is more than ready to welcome you.''

''That's good to know,'' she said gratefully, though she couldn't help wondering if he had pressured his mother to accept what she was in no position to refuse. Clearly he had provided her with so much, what choice did Lillian Dane have?

''The flowers are a kind thought.''

''I hope she likes them.''

''I'm sure she'll appreciate the gesture.''

The kitchen opened onto a large casual dining area where the table was already set for lunch with many covered dishes suggesting everything was pre-prepared for easy service. Double glass doors gave access onto a wide verandah and Susannah's voice floated back to them from outside.

''Nanna, she's here! Katie's here!''

The answer was indistinct.

One of the doors had been left open and Carver waved her forward. Katie stepped out, her gaze catching a fine view of Sydney Harbour, then a wheelchair ramp leading from the verandah to the extensive lawn below it. The ramp was a jolting reminder that Lillian Dane was no longer the formidable figure memory conjured up, and as Katie turned to the sound of Susannah's bright chatter, she was shocked to see how *little* Carver's mother looked, little and white-haired and older than she could possibly be in years.

She was sitting in an electric wheelchair which was angled towards Susannah and slightly away from the table in front of her, a table strewn with Sunday newspapers. She held an indulgent smile for her granddaughter who was claiming her attention, but her eyes flicked nervously at Katie as Carver escorted her along the verandah.

Nervously!

''Look, Nanna! Katie brought you some pretty flowers. Just like on her dress,'' Susannah said admiringly.

''How lovely! Thank you,'' she said, accepting them graciously as Katie presented them.

''Mrs. Dane, how are you?''

''Fine! It's good to see you again, Katie.'' She gestured to one of the ordinary chairs at the table. ''Do sit down. Carver?'' She looked up at her son. ''Will you put these flowers in a vase for me? I'll take them to my living room later. They look so bright and cheerful.''

''Sure, Mum.''

She handed them to him. ''And I switched the coffee-maker on so it should be ready by now.'' An anxious flash at Katie who was settling on the chair indicated. ''Carver said you liked coffee.''

''Yes, I do. Thank you.''

''Bring it out, dear,'' she instructed her son. ''And Susannah, will you fetch the plate of cookies from the kitchen counter?''

''Yes, Nanna.''

Father and daughter went off together, leaving the two women together. Katie sat warily silent, sure that Lillian Dane had just manipulated a situation she wanted. The moment she felt it was safe to speak without being overheard, the older woman leaned forward, her dark eyes determined on the course she had decided upon, but seemingly fearful of it, as well.

''I know you couldn't have told Carver what I did. What I said to you all those years ago,'' she started, clearly searching for answers to end the torment in her mind.

''No, I haven't,'' Katie said quietly, stunned to find Lillian Dane frightened of *her* influence over Carver's feelings.

''Will you?'' she pressed, resolved on knowing Katie's intentions.

''No. That's behind us, Mrs. Dane.''

She shook her head. ''The past is always with us.

I know it's my fault. My fault that Carver's been unhappy all these years.'' Guilt threaded her words, yet there was pride and purpose, too, as she added, ''He's been so good to me. The best possible son. I want him to be happy. He deserves to be.''

Katie couldn't think of anything to say. As always, Lillian Dane thought only of what she wanted for her son. It seemed some strange irony that she now saw Katie as a possible source of happiness for him. But then, hadn't her father accepted the same thing—that Carver might be the man who could make her happy?

A claw-like hand reached out and clutched Katie's arm. It stunned her even further to see tears film Lillian Dane's eyes. Yet when she spoke her voice was strong, with the kind of strength that had always driven this woman to do what she had to do to achieve what she wanted.

''I know you wouldn't want me here, Katie Beaumont. How could you?'' The thin fingers dug deeper. ''I promise you I'll go. Being a handicapped person, I'm given a good pension. I can get myself into an assisted-care place...''

''Please, I have no wish to put your out of your home. What kind of person do you think I am?'' Katie cried, appalled by what was being suggested. ''Besides, nothing has been decided between Carver and me.''

''But it will come up. I know it will. And you won't want to live with me under the same roof.''

''Perhaps it's you who won't want to live with me,'' Katie flashed back, the memory of this woman's scathing diatribe slicing through her wish to make peace.

''Don't you understand?'' It was an urgent plea. ''I don't want to be a factor in stopping what Carver wants with you. Nor will I get in the way. God knows I've learnt my lesson about interfering in what I shouldn't.'' Her eyes looked feverish with determination. ''I can't take back what I did, but I can clear the way this time. That would be some reparation.''

''Truly, there's no need for this,'' Katie asserted, thinking there had to be some better way of resolving this conflict.

''*Listen* to me!'' It was a desperate command. ''Back then…it felt as though you were taking him away from me. I was jealous…cruel…wanting to get rid of you so I could have my son to myself again. I remember it all, so don't pretend it's not in your mind, too.''

She darted a look along the verandah, afraid she was running out of time. Katie held her tongue, realising Lillian Dane had to unburden herself of the torment she must have been going through since Carver had told her Katie Beaumont was in his life again.

Her gaze fastened once more on Katie's, anxious to make the situation clear. ''I won't stay and be a bone of contention between you and Carver. All I ask is you don't tell him what I did. I couldn't bear it if…'' The strength of her resolution gave way to a burst of emotional agitation. ''…if he didn't visit me now and then. With Susannah…''

''You have my solemn promise I won't tell him,

Mrs. Dane,'' Katie stated emphatically, intent on removing that source of fear.

''You promise...''

''Yes. He will never know from me.''

She sagged back into her wheelchair, her hand sliding from Katie's arm. Her eyes were still not at peace. ''He has a good heart, Carver.''

''I know.''

''And Susannah...she's the sweetest child.''

''Yes, she is.''

''Can you be happy with them?''

''I am happy with them, Mrs. Dane.''

She folded her hands in her lap and heaved a deep sigh, looking both relieved and drained. ''Take this as my apology, Katie Beaumont...that I'm ready and willing to leave my son and grand-daughter to you.''

Katie took a deep breath and stated her own position. ''I don't want that apology, Mrs. Dane. What you've been planning is as divisive as anything you've done in the past.''

She looked startled, as though she hadn't seen it that way.

Katie ploughed on. ''Once again you're making me out as the spoiled rich bitch who thinks only of herself.''

A negative jerk of her head which only riled Katie further. She wasn't going to let Carver's mother have her way this time. She was going to fight the prejudice and wear it down if it was the last thing she did!

''Do you imagine Susannah will thank me for losing the Nanna who has cared for her since she was born?''

''She'll have you,'' came the flash of blind reasoning.

''And Carver had you when you succeeded in getting rid of me. Did *you* make up for the loss of that love, Mrs. Dane?''

She stared at Katie, a painful confusion of guilt in her eyes.

''Perhaps you want Carver to think that I now want to be rid of you. Another contest between us, Mrs. Dane? Is that the twisted motive behind this offered sacrifice of your home here?''

''No.'' Her shock was genuine. ''I swear it's not!''

''Then make the effort to live *with* me,'' Katie bored in, determined to shake this woman into seeing the real truth. ''Try getting to know me, instead of treating me as a hostile force. Running away doesn't resolve anything. That was the lesson I learnt, Mrs. Dane. Ten years in the wilderness...''

''I'm sorry. I'm sorry I did that...to both of you.''

''Then stay and help to make it better,'' Katie argued with a ferocity of feeling she couldn't temper in the face of the entrenched view Carver's mother had of her. ''What good can it do...making this grand gesture of leaving? Why don't you work at being friends with me? For Carver's sake. For Susannah's sake. Am I so abhorrent to you that you can't stand the thought of even trying for a truce between us?''

''You want...a truce?'' The idea seemed alien to everything she had thought about this meeting.

''Why not? Don't we both care about the same people? Isn't that a bond we can share?''

Carver's and Susannah's voices drifted out from the house, indicating they were on their way back.

"Think about it, Mrs. Dane," Katie urged. "If you're really sorry for what you did, try making it better. For all of us."

CHAPTER FIFTEEN

KATIE had just completed the last booked trip for the morning when her car phone rang, which probably meant a job she didn't want right now. Every day this week she'd been planning to get to the Formal Hire shop at Chatswood, needing something to wear to the FX Ball, but she'd been picking up so much casual business, here it was, Thursday, and time was getting short with the ball happening tomorrow night.

In two minds about accepting any extra work today, Katie activated the receiver, and was instantly relieved to hear a familiar voice.

"Katie, it's your father. Are you finished for the morning?"

"Yes, Dad."

"Then come and have lunch with me."

She frowned, wondering if it could be fitted in. With the last two Sundays having been taken up with very personal business, she hadn't seen her father for almost three weeks. "Where are you?" she asked, thinking of distances to be covered.

"Where are *you?*" came the immediate retort.

"I'm at St. Leonards, heading towards Chatswood. I need to a hire a ball gown for..."

"*Hire?* You mean...get some second-hand dress? You're going to a ball with Carver Dane in a second-hand dress?"

Katie sighed at his outraged pride. "No one will know, Dad."

"Katie, just you turn around right now and head into the city," he commanded autocratically. "You can park under the Opera House. I'll pay the parking fee."

"Dad, that's right out of my way," Katie protested. "I don't have a great deal of time."

"If Carver Dane could make time to have lunch with me yesterday, my daughter can certainly make time today," he declared.

"Carver? You've met Carver?"

"I'll wait for you at the oyster bar on the quay. Fine morning for oysters."

"Dad…"

He was gone. And trying to call him back was bound to be futile. She knew he wouldn't respond. He'd put in the hook to get his own way and the bait was too intriguing for Katie to resist. The ball gown could wait. Knowing what had transpired between her father and Carver couldn't.

It both stunned and alarmed her that her father had chosen to contact Carver at this somewhat delicate turning point in their relationship, probably deciding *he knew best,* as usual, and a push from him would get his daughter what she wanted.

Katie gritted her teeth in frustration at his arrogance. Didn't he realise that interference—especially from him—would be unwelcome? Had he suddenly decided that offering an apology—a very, very late apology—might help? If so, how had Carver responded to it?

With her heart fluttering in agitation and her mind whirling with wild speculation, Katie took the road which would lead her across the Harbour Bridge to Benelong Point. It was a waste of time, wishing her father had left well enough alone. It was done now. But she couldn't help worrying about the effect of his intrusion.

She really didn't need this complication. It had been difficult enough last Sunday, moving into a truce situation with Carver's mother. Lillian Dane's pre-determined decisions might have been well-meant, but hardly helpful. Potentially destructive would be a better description. Katie hoped she had set the older woman straight on that score.

Certainly, after their altercation on the verandah, Carver's mother had made the effort to treat her as a welcome guest, though it was impossible to tell if that was more to please her son and grand-daughter than to actually extend the hand of friendship to a woman she'd previously planned on avoiding as far as possible.

Carver had been pleased with the meeting, believing it had established a bridge from the past to a future where rejection was not in the cards. Katie had not cast any doubt on this belief. She hoped he was right. The burning question now was if any hopeful bridge had been established between him and her father?

Since it was almost midday, the traffic was flowing fairly easily and Katie made it to the car park under the Opera House in good time. She hot-footed it to the oyster bar where she found her father settled at one of the open-air tables with a commanding view of Circular Quay. A plate of empty oyster shells implied his appetite was not the least bit diminished by the prospect of confessing his interference in *her* relationship with Carver. Katie hoped that was a good sign.

''Ah, there you are!'' he said complacently, smiling as she took the chair waiting for her.

''What did you say to Carver?'' she burst out, intent on pinning him down.

''First things first.'' He signalled a hovering waiter and received instant attention. ''A dozen Kilpatrick oysters for my daughter and another dozen natural for me. And some of that crusty bread. Better bring two cappuccinos, as well. My daughter's in a hurry.''

Katie barely contained her impatience. The moment the waiter, who'd undoubtedly been liberally tipped already, moved away she went on the attack again. ''How could you, Dad?''

''How could I what?'' he answered, infuriatingly effecting a sublimely innocent air.

''Stick your nose in,'' she fired at him.

His eyebrows arched. ''You would have preferred me to refuse Carver's invitation to lunch with him?''

''Carver's?''

''*He* called *me,* Katie. I didn't think you'd want me to snub him.''

''No, of course not,'' she said weakly, the wind completely taken out of her sails. ''What did he want with you?''

''Oh, I guess you could call it touching base,'' came the somewhat ironic reply. ''Some diplomatic easing around what happened in the past. My equally diplomatic apology was accepted. In fact, it was quite a masterly exercise in diplomacy all around.''

''No fighting?''

''Katie...'' he chided. ''...I promised you I wouldn't put a foot wrong this time around.''

She heaved a sigh to relieve the tightness in her chest.

''Your Carver was clearly prepared to fight with words,'' her father went on, ''but given no opposition from me, we reached an understanding very quickly and had quite a pleasant lunch together.''

''No sparring at all?''

''Merely a little deft manoeuvring until positions were made clear.'' His eyes twinkled amusement. ''We parted on terms of mutual respect so you have nothing to worry about.''

''Mutual respect,'' she repeated, wondering why Carver had taken this initiative. He could have waited until she set up a meeting. On the other hand, maybe a man-to-man talk was better for sweeping problems out of the way, and more easily accomplished without her being present.

''He's turned into a very impressive young man,'' her father commented.

''He was always impressive.''

''Well, I'll not be arguing with you. Just rest assured that your old dad does want to see you happy, Katie. If Carver Dane is your choice, he's my choice.''

She eyed him uncertainly. ''Did you really like him this time, Dad?''

He nodded. "If I were doing the choosing for you, he'd definitely be a prime candidate."

She relaxed into a smile, recognising the accolade as genuine.

"Now tell me about this ball you need a dress for."

"Carver's asked me to partner him to the FX Ball. It's all financial markets people, a networking evening for him."

"When is it?"

"Tomorrow night. It's being held at Sheraton on the Park."

"Uh-huh."

The waiter returned with their lunch order. Now that her stomach was unknotted, Katie attacked her oysters with great appetite, mopping up the Kilpatrick sauce with the crusty bread.

"That *was* good!" she declared, sitting back replete and smiling her satisfaction. "Thanks, Dad."

"My pleasure. And it would give me even greater pleasure if you let me buy you a ball gown."

She eyed him wryly. "Please don't start trying to run my life again. Just because..."

"Now, Katie, you haven't let me buy you anything for a long time," he broke in, frowning his frustration. "A father's entitled to give his daughter a few fripperies."

"A ball gown isn't a frippery."

He waved a dismissive hand, and she knew the cost was irrelevant to him. He wouldn't even blink at tossing away a few thousand dollars on a dress that might only be worn once. Was she clinging too hard to her independence? Her father had put in a huge effort to reduce their estrangement. Maybe it was time to go his way…at least a little.

''You can't partner Carver at a ball like that in a hired gown,'' he insisted, leaning forward to lay down his law. ''He'll be out to impress people and… dammit, Katie! You're my daughter! He'll be introducing you to all these top-level people in the finance world—Katie Beaumont—and I will not have you dressed in second-hand clothing.''

Pride!

Well, there was no escaping the fact she was her father's daughter, and if it made him happy…a dress was only a dress.

''I admit I should have backed your business when you asked me to,'' he rolled on, gathering steam. ''I admit I've made a lot of mistakes where you're concerned. But, Katie…''

''All right, Dad.''

It caught him off-stride. ''All right what?''

She grinned at him. ''You can buy me a ball gown. As long as we do it quickly because I've got to get back to work.''

His face lit with triumphant pleasure. Action stations instantly came into play. ''Waiter! Waiter! The bill?'' A finger stabbed at Katie. ''Get that coffee drunk right now. We're going shopping, my girl, and *you* are going to *slay* Carver Dane tomorrow night!''

CHAPTER SIXTEEN

IT WAS a fabulous dress—a Versace design that fitted her like a second skin. Fashioned from Shantung silk, a shimmering scarlet shot through with gold, the strapless bodice hugged her curves, and the slimline front view of the skirt accentuated the rest of her femininity and highlighted the lustrous fall of a graceful train at the back. It hadn't cost a million dollars, but Katie felt like a million dollars in it.

A gold bracelet had a special clip to which she could attach the train when dancing, and long dangly gold earrings were the perfect accompaniment to the dress. Katie had fastened her hair back from her face to show off the earrings, and the tumble of black curls behind her ears made a great frame for them.

When the doorbell rang, announcing Carver's arrival, her eyes were sparkling with the pleasure of knowing she couldn't look better. Her father was right about some things. She did want Carver to feel proud of her as his partner tonight, in front of his peers in the business world. Such a *public* outing was another step up in their relationship, and this dress certainly gave her the confidence to carry it off successfully.

She was smiling over her father's words—*You're going to slay Carver Dane*—as she opened the door, but seeing Carver, so strikingly handsome in a formal dinner suit, she forgot all about her own appearance.

She loved this man, and her desire for him squeezed her heart, caught the breath in her throat, and shot a tremulous feeling through her entire body.

For several seconds they simply stared at each other, the hunger of years burning slowly to a crescendo of need that pulsed with the sense that at last, *this* was the time, *this* was the moment when everything could be right.

Carver took a deep breath. His dark eyes glittered with an intensity of feeling that pierced Katie's soul. This was how it had once been. This was how it was now. And she revelled in the moment of magic that had leapt the terrible gap of missed chances and brought to life this elated certainty that nothing more could go wrong. Ever!

''You make me feel…very privileged…to be your escort tonight, Katie,'' Carver murmured.

She took a deep breath and a bubble of sheer joy broke into a smile. ''You're the only escort I've ever wanted, Carver.''

Her impulsive response seemed to evoke a shadow of pain in his eyes before he smiled back and held out his arm. ''Shall we go?''

''Yes,'' she answered eagerly, telling herself she must have imagined the slight darkening of his pleasure.

Once he tucked her arm around his to take her out to his car, everything seemed perfect again. He saw her settled into the passenger seat of the Audi roadster, carefully tucking in the train of her dress before closing the door. The hood of the sports car was up tonight, and Katie was grateful for the forethought. It saved her hair from being tossed into an unruly mass of curls by the wind.

She watched Carver settle into the driver's seat beside her and close his door, sealing them into an intimate little world of their own. We're on our way, she thought, as he leaned forward to insert the car key into the ignition. On our way together. Really together.

Carver gripped the car key, telling himself to switch on the engine, get going, move on. Katie wouldn't want to revisit the pain of the past. She'd put it behind her. What she'd said to his mother proved that beyond a doubt—wanting it set aside, forgotten and forgiven. And she was here with him, her whole body language poignantly telegraphing this was *right* for her.

Which made it all the more impossible to wipe out the injustice he'd done her in his mind—an injustice that had influenced his attitude towards her, inflicting more hurt. He couldn't turn the key. He had to *put it right* first. This journey tonight had to start with a clean slate.

He sat back, reaching over to take her hand in his before he spoke, needing a physical link to lighten the burden on his heart. Katie was startled by the action, her eyes filling with questions at the delay in their departure. Carver secured his grip on her hand by interlacing their fingers, then faced her with what he now knew.

"I've always believed you didn't love me as much as I loved you, Katie. For you to cut and run as you did..."

She sucked in a quick breath, clearly feeling attacked.

''But it wasn't like that,'' he quickly asserted. ''I know you left me because of all my mother said to you at the hospital when the doctors were working on my broken jaw. Her virulence, coming on top of your father's violence...you thought it was best for me if you took yourself out of my life.''

''Yes,'' she whispered. ''I didn't want you hurt because of me, Carver. And your mother...''

''She told me, Katie.''

''When?'' she asked, clearly perplexed.

''A few days ago.''

''Since...Sunday.''

''Yes. All these years I didn't know. From the time you left I thought...I imagined you...finding other *more suitable* men...''

''No,'' she cried, squeezing his hand in agitation.

Realising he'd used a bitter tone, Carver tried to correct it. ''I couldn't blame you if you had, after being treated like that by my mother. I'm trying to explain... I lost faith in your feeling for me, so when we met this time, I wouldn't let you close to me.''

''But you have, Carver,'' she said, her relief palpable.

''I wish you'd told me, Katie. I wasn't fair to you.''

''She *is* your mother. You wouldn't have wanted to believe me.''

It was a truth he couldn't deny. Even from his mother's own mouth, the admissions of her malicious venom had appalled him...how she'd seized the most opportune time to make Katie feel like the lowest of the low, flaying her with vicious names, accusing her of selfishly ruining his life, blaming her for crimes that hadn't even been committed.

"They were lies, Katie. Lies about your effect on me and my studies. Lies about me wanting to drop out because of you. And she hated you because she saw you as being of a privileged class—a silver spoon in your mouth—while she had had it tough all her life, working hard to give me the chances she'd never had. To her, being a doctor represented success on every level and she saw you as getting in the way."

"Perhaps I was," came the sober comment.

"No. I would have worked my butt off at anything to secure a good future for us. My mother simply couldn't bear you being the focus of my life instead of her."

"I think my father felt the same way."

"Possessive parents," he grimly agreed. "But mine was far more destructive. The scathing way she cut you down..."

"I don't want it recalled now, Carver," she pleaded.

"I'm sorry. I just..." He caught himself back. The horror of it was new to him, but she'd lived with it all these years and risen above it. "It's incredibly generous to let it all slide as you have," he said with deep sincerity. "In fact, it was the generous way you dealt with my mother last Sunday that shamed her into confessing the part she'd played in driving you away."

"Part of it was my father, too, Carver. For me, it was shock on top of shock."

''I understand. It all makes sense to me now. And I'm sorry I ever thought harshly about the decision you made.''

''Your mother asked me not to tell.''

''So she said. I think that promise finally forced her to be fair to you, Katie.'' He rubbed his thumb over her skin, wishing he could dig under it. ''Can you forgive me for doubting your feelings?''

''You had reason to, Carver,'' she said softly. ''I should have talked to you.'' Her eyes shone with eloquent emotion. ''But I promise…this is true. You are—you've always been—the only man I've ever loved.''

''And you the only woman I've ever loved,'' he returned, intensely grateful for her response to him and seizing the moment to press what he most wanted. ''I told your father so on Wednesday.''

She looked dazed. ''He didn't tell me that.''

''I wanted him to know I intended to marry you…if you'd have me.''

''Marry?'' It was a bare whisper, as though she couldn't quite bring herself to believe it, but she wanted to. Her eyes glistened with the inner vision of a dream coming true.

Carver reached into his pocket and brought out the velvet jeweler's box he'd planned to open some time tonight…when it felt right. The sense of rightness was coursing through him so strongly, waiting another second was beyond him. He flicked the top up as he held the box out to her.

''They say diamonds are forever. Will you marry me, Katie?''

She stared down at the ring—a solitaire diamond set on a simple gold band. Then she looked up and there was no mistaking the love swimming in her eyes. "Yes, I will. I will marry you, Carver. And it will be forever."

He had to kiss her. He yearned to make love to her, but that had to wait until later. It was a kiss that filled him with the sweetest satisfaction he'd ever known.

"My fiancée, Katie Beaumont."

Every time Carver said those words, introducing her to the people he knew at the ball, Katie felt as though she would burst with happiness. It was difficult not to keep glancing at the magnificent diamond ring on her finger—the ring that proclaimed to everyone that she and Carver were engaged to be married—the ring that promised this really was forever, symbolising a love that had lasted the test of time and always would, despite anything the future might throw at them.

It gradually dawned on Katie that her father had guessed what Carver intended tonight. That was why he'd been so insistent on buying a special dress—to make the night even more special. A gift of love, she thought, not pride, and made a strong mental note to give her father a big thank-you hug.

Lillian Dane's confession to Carver was a gift of love, too—a setting straight, putting doubts to rest. Katie silently vowed to view her much more kindly in future.

Her father...his mother...both of them had made amends as best they could.

''Katie?''

Amanda's voice?

She turned to see her old school friend on Max's arm, both of them paused on their walk down the ballroom, their faces expressing uncertainty in her identity.

''It *is* you!'' Amanda cried in delighted surprise. ''Why didn't you tell me you'd be here? And how!'' She rolled her eyes down the Versace gown and up again. ''You look fabulous!''

''Yes, doesn't she?'' Carver warmly agreed, swinging them both around for a more formal greeting. ''Good evening, Amanda…Max.''

''Carver!'' Amanda's eyes almost popped out.

''Good to see both of you,'' Max rolled out smoothly.

''Good to see you, too,'' Katie replied, her inner joy sparkling through an extra-wide smile as she held out her left hand. ''Look, Amanda!''

''I don't believe it! A rock!'' she squealed, then looked goggle-eyed at Carver.

He grinned at her. ''Katie said yes.''

''You got to a proposal in less than two weeks?'' she said incredulously.

''Oh, I'd say it was about ten years overdue,'' Carver drawled good-humouredly.

Amanda heaved a sigh of triumphant satisfaction. ''I just knew it was simply a matter of getting the two of you together.'' She hugged her husband's arm. ''We did it, Max.''

The band started playing an introduction to a

bracket of dance numbers. Carver turned to Katie, his eyes dancing with wicked mischief.

"Shall we dance, Carmen?"

She laughed and gathered up her train, clicking the end of it onto her bracelet. "Where you lead, I shall follow," she responded flirtatiously.

"What do you mean...Carmen?" Amanda demanded, eyeing them suspiciously.

Carver slid his arm around Katie's waist, ready to swing her out to the centre of the ballroom. He grinned at Amanda and raised his other hand in a salute to her. "The masked buccaneer thanks you for bringing us together."

"The masked buccaneer?" Amanda gaped as enlightenment dawned. *"The pirate king!"*

Definitely *her king,* Katie thought, as they moved across the dance floor, in tune with the music and beautifully, wonderfully, in total tune with each other. The desire which had been ignited so strongly at the masked ball, simmered between them, their bodies once again revelling in touch and feeling, loving the tease of sensual contact, exulting in the certainty that the most exquisite satisfaction was theirs for the taking.

"This dance will never be over, Katie," Carver whispered in her ear.

"No more walking alone," she sighed contentedly.

He pulled her closer so they moved as one.

Not too early...not too late.

This time was right.

Emma
DARCY
AUSTRALIA
IN BED WITH A BACHELOR

Emma
DARCY
AUSTRALIA
IN BED WITH A KING

Emma
DARCY
AUSTRALIA
IN BED WITH THE PLAYBOY

Emma
DARCY
AUSTRALIA
IN BED WITH THE BOSS

Emma
DARCY
AUSTRALIA
IN BED WITH HER GROOM

Emma
DARCY
AUSTRALIA